BUSHWHACKED

BUSHWHACKED

THE JOHN BISHOP
SHOTGUN SAGA

C. COURTNEY
JOYNER

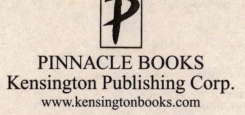

PINNACLE BOOKS
Kensington Publishing Corp.
www.kensingtonbooks.com

CONTENTS

SHOTGUN

"You damn well know, I'll do it."

"Major" Beaudine's spit-shined boot was flush against John Bishop's right arm, pinning it down, while he turned the blade in the moonlight to heighten the threat.

Beaudine said, "So, your choice?"

Bishop managed, "You're thinking I know something I don't. I swear, I've told you everything. You got no reason to touch my family."

Beaudine gripped the handle of the long cleaver, saying, "A liar always boils my blood."

Bishop was on the edge of consciousness, trying to take in the faces of the other men holding him to the frozen ground. They were dirty fragments: mustaches dropping into beards, fresh burns, and one curtained eye. Their names were nothing but jumbled noise, while the screams of Bishop's wife and son cut through everything to reach him. Their voices didn't even sound like them anymore, though they were just a few feet away. Bishop cried out, twisting his head to see, as Deadeye and another man gripped him by his ears and jaw.

"Them ears'll come right off!"

Deadeye asked, "Why are you tryin' to look, anyways?"

Beaudine let Bishop know, "They're breathing. I see her little bosom moving in and out, but it's not honorable for you to make your wife and boy pay for your being contrary. Do you understand the penalties, what it means to incur my wrath?"

Exactly fifteen minutes before, Amaryllis Bishop had joined hands with her husband and son for a Methodist grace. John always gently rubbed her fingers with his thumb while his wife asked for blessing, and she flashed her blue eyes in a way that was supposed to be annoyance, but was something else.

Their son giggled as he reached for a piece of chicken before the plate was offered. Mama issued a smiling warning. "I know somebody's birthday is in three days, but it may not come at all, if—"

Amaryllis's voice was cut off when the front door was kicked off its hinges.

"Major" Beaudine and his men exploded into the house, tossing the dinner table, splintering a bookshelf, and slapping the youngest to the floor. Bishop sprang at the "Major," but heavy fists from behind pounded him down, and Beaudine's heel cracked his ribs with little effort.

Beaudine warned one of the others not to do more. "Show restraint, gentlemen. Our friend is essential to our mission."

He knelt next to Bishop, measuring his words. "I am aware of the gold you and your brother liberated, one half of a million dollars. Don't deny it. The letters he wrote you from prison, finalizing your confidential plans? I wrote them. You know your brother could neither read nor write, and so he trusted me to set down his thoughts. Devlin and I were cellmates, until the morning he was hung. He took me into his deep confidence, which I honor. You have all that money, John, and you need to share. Your brother is departed, but I am here. Death's arrived, and I want paying."

"I'm swearing, I don't know a damn thing about any gold. There's nothing between me and my brother. Never was."

"No, that's not the answer."

"Where's my wife?"

"You must think clearly now, about the gold. Nothing else matters at this moment, I promise you."

The man with the trimmed mustache and salvaged grey Confederate tunic, who spoke as if he were reading holy scripture, pressed his knee deep into Bishop's back. Bones cracked. Beaudine asked again about the stolen gold.

"If anything happens to my son . . ."

Beaudine pressed his knee again and Bishop couldn't move, his thoughts slipping away with his bleeding.

Beaudine said, "There's a Foster Brothers cleaver with a polished blade on a thirty-one-inch handle resting across my saddle. It's a thing of beauty, but you do not want me to fetch it."

Beaudine put the last of his weight on Bishop's spine, dropping his voice. "You need to concern yourself with gold. Try again."

The outlaws waited for the answer, and Amaryllis swung a pork-fry pan from the Crawford stove, spattering hot grease across the face of one of them, sending him screaming into the cold. Time stopped for a few heartbeats as Amaryllis Bishop scooped up her son, his arms around her neck and their tears mixing on their cheeks, as she whispered a kiss to him.

That's when the first shot was fired.

CHAPTER ONE
Nothing Dies Like a Man

Huckie's Saloon, with its caving roof and sides, was a whipped dog cringing in front of the Colorado Mountains, ready to snap. It was the only place John Bishop saw with any signs of life, and he angled his horse toward it.

He was navigating a tough trail winding out of the steeper foothills that led to what was passing for some kind of a town. Bishop's bay horse was cautious with her footing. The snow on the trail wasn't deep, but a layer of ice beneath the white cracked under each footfall, throwing off her steps. Bishop patted her neck to tell her she was doing well as she managed a narrow cut between some tall pines.

There was another rider following, about half a mile back, but Bishop didn't even turn to see, his mind and eyes locked straight ahead, the reins steady in his left hand to keep the bay sure. She responded.

The frozen white was blowing just enough that he had to squint to read the battered sign that declared Huckie's. A pack mule snorted out front, and a mutt scratched at the front door, until someone let it in.

There was loud, drunken talk followed by laughter. Bishop figured there had to be at least five in the place, including a cackling woman.

Bishop clenched the reins. His memories from months ago, the ones that beat hell out of him every other minute, had brought him to this place, but now he had to put feelings away. He was going to do this, and had to be clear about it. No backing down.

Chester Pardee liked Huckie's. The drinks and the one woman were so watered and worn that even he seemed like a big shot in the place. He took another swallow of no-name whiskey and tried to fan his cards, but they were too ear-bent to separate. Pardee then studied each of them, pausing for a sip, making a show of what a fine hand he was holding.

Chaney, who had killed someone someplace, was getting tired of the put-on. "You ain't droppin' anything on the table, Chester."

"I like to think my bets through."

"Nobody's got that much time. Play or fold."

Pardee adjusted his fingerless gloves, and reached into his pocket for the last bit of paper he had. He'd gotten the coat from a dead man, and it was stained with his fortune, but the money was his own, and he placed an old Union twenty on the torn felt like he was presenting a king's crown.

Chaney said, "The bill's got blood on it."

"What doesn't? I know'd every one of ya and your dirty habits. I say can't none of ya match it."

Chaney nodded. "Things are temporarily lean, but I have twenty-three in silver, and this banker's watch you've always admired. You're being raised, Chester."

Pardee reached into his jacket, and took out a letter that had been roughly folded into five sections, the words smudged by whiskey rings. Too many reads had frayed the paper, but Chester Pardee waved it at Chaney like a red veronica in front of a Brahma bull.

Pardee said, "You know what this is?"

Chaney didn't change his expression. "You jaw about it enough."

"Right, it's a goddamn treasure map. I'll throw ten percent—no, one percent—into the pot. One percent. One."

Chaney said, "You might as well say you wipe yourself with it."

"You won't take that much of a chance, Chaney? You ain't a gambler at all."

Chaney looked up from his cards.

The Colorado snow eased as Bishop rode to the hitch rail. He threw his weight to one side, angling his right arm from its special sling on the saddle, almost turning in the stirrup, before dropping to the ground. Here, the snow was slush under his boots, as he listened again to the voices escaping from Huckie's. Bishop rolled his shoulders and said something like a prayer before walking the last steps to the batwings that were banging against the front door.

The glass in the front door had a little split, and for some reason, Bishop almost knocked. Instead, he opened it with his left hand and let the door swing free inside, the glass breaking in half to announce him.

Pardee turned in his chair to see Bishop standing in the doorway. One of the others at the table belched, "You're gonna have to pay for that."

Bishop kept his head down with his arms straight at his side, his black duster a size and some too big, hanging scarecrow loose, but it gave him the freedom of movement he needed. The first time he saw himself, he thought he looked like a specter from Poe. Bishop cleared his throat, but didn't speak.

Huckie's was all whispers and mutterings; guesses

about Bishop passed from the drinkers who sat at the old silver exchange counter that now served as the bar, to the laughing whore on the straw bed tucked away in a corner, with the pull curtain above it. Bishop had their attention, until he raised his eyes. The whispering stopped, and then started again, punctuated with loud snickering.

Bishop's face was softly round, and not protected at all by his blond beard—the kind of face that made men like these laugh among themselves before trying something.

"Chester Pardee."

Pardee paid no mind. He slipped the letter back into his jacket, and said to Chaney, "You can't kill me for tryin'."

Chaney said, "Find somebody to stake you, or fold."

Bishop hadn't moved; he tried again. "Chester Pardee."

Pardee said, "It's freezin' in here."

"That's all you have to say?"

"We've got a game, jackass."

Bishop took a single step closer to the table. "Then you don't know me?"

Chaney said, "You lost, Chester."

Pardee said, "Hold up! You say you know me? Stake me to this pot. I got the cards, amigo."

"You really don't remember?"

Chaney said to Pardee, "I called, that's it."

Chaney laid out two pairs of faces, while Pardee tossed a weak five-high straight on the table. Chaney gave Pardee a smirk with some pity.

Pardee faced Bishop with, "Whatever the hell you're on about, it didn't mean nothin'! You just cost me!"

"Slaughtering a man's family doesn't mean anything?"

"What man?"

The first blast ripped through Pardee's shoulder and

sent him spinning out of his chair, spurs catching the edge of the table, sending the whiskey, cash, and five-high flying. Pardee twisted on the bowed floor, screaming out for Jesus, but Jesus didn't make a move. Nobody did.

The whore burst into tears because she'd never seen a shooting up close before; everyone else rubbernecked for a look, not exactly sure what had just happened.

Bishop stood over Pardee, gun smoke drifting from the end of his sleeve where his right hand should have been, but wasn't. Instead, the two barrels of a Greener shotgun poked from the ragged cuff, which had been singed by the blast. Burning threads danced from the cuff to the floor.

The double barrels were in place of Bishop's right arm, attached somehow at the elbow, and held waist-high steady. He shifted his weight from one leg to the other, keeping the weapon dead-centered on Pardee's chest.

Pardee was still crying out for Jesus as he struggled to stand, red spreading across his jacket. He tried drawing his Colt with fingers that wouldn't work. "You ain't given me a sloppy Chinaman's chance!"

"What kind of chance did you give my wife and son?"

"Jesus Lord."

"I've still got the second barrel."

"Can't you just let me out, Bishop?"

"So you know me now."

"What happened wasn't my doin', I swear. That's not why I was there."

"I can barely see where my wife threw the grease from that hot skillet."

"Please, let me ride out and you'll never hear my name again."

"Beaudine."

Pardee said, "If I live another twenty years, it won't matter. I'm already dead."

Bishop had to shift his weight again, but, with effort,

he kept his voice calm and the shotgun aimed at Pardee's chest, "You wanted to know about gold I didn't have. Well, now I want to know something. I'm counting."

"Beaudine's crazy, and I fell in with his gang. That's all it was: us tryin' to eat. Nothin' personal."

"I'm only going to five."

Pardee stammered through tears, giving up a cross-roads where Bishop could look for Beaudine, and kill him, if that's what he intended. Pardee even gave his permission.

Bishop said, "You know what retribution is?"

"It means I'm done."

"If you can get off the floor, I'll let you try."

Pardee didn't move. Bishop said, "I'm not a murderer."

"You're a blessed man, Doc. Better than I'll ever be."

Pardee dropped his words as he grabbed Bishop's left hand, and yanked him forward, slashing him with a rifleman's knife he had strapped to his boot. The blade sliced deep, from earlobe to the corner of Bishop's mouth.

Pardee whooped, "How you like that—?!"

Bishop heaved backwards and brought up his right arm in a single motion. Buckshot 'n' fire erupted from the sleeve a second time, rag-dolling Pardee into a stack of empty beer kegs. Wood and bone shattered together, then settled into silence. Pardee's eyes stayed wide and his grip on his pistol never relaxed.

Everybody froze for a moment, and then the talk started, along with nervous laughter. One old boy said something about a "nice killin'" and spit a stream of tobacco juice that spattered a brown halo around Pardee's head.

Bishop waited for someone to try something, but no one bothered. The mutt in the corner wagged his tail and barked his approval. Chaney, the card player, scooped the poker pot into his hat as Bishop took careful steps to the shattered door.

Chaney said, "You blew both barrels."

Bishop jerked his arm, and the shotgun breeched inside the duster, the sleeve tenting the open barrel. Bishop reached inside the sleeve, coming out with two spent shells and dropped them on the floor. He grabbed two fresh from his jacket, and reloaded, before bringing his arm upward in a motion that snapped the barrel shut.

This took moments, with everyone watching, their eyes wide and "goddamns" whispered. Bishop aimed the rig directly at Chaney's gut. Chaney showed his palms. "Hey, nobody gave a shit about Chester, except you."

"You going to bury him?"

Chaney shrugged while winding his watch.

"The railroad's probably put up a price."

Chaney said, "Knowing Chester, they're offering the lowest bounty in history."

Outside, the midnight wind stung Bishop as he checked the cinch on his bay, but his one hand was shaking, and his chest pounded. A lot had led up to this, and in a few moments it was over. Well, Pardee was over, but there were still the others. At least now Bishop knew he could go through with it; he had to keep that in his mind, the knowing, no doubts at all. He had to.

His face was sticky with the wash of blood from his sliced cheek, and as Bishop calmed, he started to feel the pain. The batwings creaked, and a few drinkers poked their heads over the doors. The whore moved to Bishop, holding out a lace handkerchief. "It's clean."

Bishop wrapped the handkerchief around his face to soak the bleeding. He felt the girl behind him tying it off and caught her heavy perfume. Bishop thanked her and she nodded before wiping her wet eyes on her sleeve.

The others hung back on Huckie's porch, watching as Bishop hefted himself onto his saddle, again throwing himself wide and keeping the shotgun clear of any tangle. He played it slow for them, settling against the leather, and sliding his double-barreled right arm into the canvas sling.

The bay was ready to run, but Bishop kept the reins tight around his only knuckles, holding her back.

Old Spitter hollered, "Hey! You busted some good bottles killin' that piece of sheep dip! Plus the door, and a couple of chairs!"

Bishop took fifty from his vest and tossed it. "You're going to tell folks about this, right, friend?"

Spitter gum-grinned. "I'll be talkin' about tonight for the next five years, five months, or five days. Dependin' on how much time I got left."

"God only knows, and I'm obliged to you both."

Bishop brought his horse around slow for that last look, and then heeled her. The bay took off toward the blue-black silhouettes of the rising hills, and the high Colorados beyond.

Spitter whistled with gums and two fingers, but Dr. John Bishop didn't hear it. His horse was running strong into the winter night, knowing where to go, even if his mind was taking him someplace else beyond the hurt— maybe back to his wedding day, or the birth of his son.

Behind him, a rider was charging hard to catch up, a Cheyenne war club in their hand.

CHAPTER TWO
The Fox

White Fox kept her body low and tight against the painted stallion. They moved as one, racing down the trail, the snow kicking up around them like bursts of brake steam. She grabbed the horse's mane, fingers tangled in wiry brown, and gently pulled. The painted slowed as the path through the trees widened into an easier slope that led to the "town" just below. It was a mule squat for drifters who still had hopes for the played-out silver strike at Cherry Creek—stop for a drink or an ash hauling, and ride on.

But this was where Bishop had to go, so White Fox had to follow.

She pulled up to watch Bishop's silhouette pause outside Huckie's, say something with a roll of his shoulders, and then go in. White Fox dropped from the painted, and walked him around the burned skeleton of an old barn to a water trough thick with ice. She broke the icy surface with a kick and tossed away the pieces.

The painted inspected the trough with his nose, then drank.

While he watered, she scraped packed snow from his hooves with a six-inch blade. She had the feeling everything in this place was dying or dead. Two loud voices from Huckie's stopped her.

White Fox stepped into the moonlight, craning her neck toward Huckie's to hear. A voice she didn't know was yelling about Jesus. Two shotgun blasts followed; that low rumble mixed with those louder cracks that ring in the air and ears.

The painted lurched as the blasts smashed against the hills. White Fox said, "*Nâhtötse,*" close to the stallion's ear, calming him, before swinging herself on his back, and circling around the far side of the barn. She saw Bishop on his bay, talking to the Spitter on the porch. White Fox dug in, and the painted broke into a run, while Bishop rode off without looking back.

The Spitter whistled loud after Bishop, before looking up to see White Fox charging toward him. It was either an image from some kind of holy book or his best damn whiskey dream ever: the beautiful Cheyenne woman, onyx hair spreading behind her, riding out of the night just to take the old man away. White Fox pulled a war club she'd tethered to her belt and held it high.

Spitter closed his eyes and smiled, thinking, *This is a hell of a way to go, and why not?*

White Fox rode close, swinging the club into the skull of the drunk standing next to the Spitter, creasing his head. The drunk fell forward, the revolver in his hand hot-blasting the muddy snow instead of John Bishop's back, where he had been aiming.

Spitter grabbed the pistol for a trophy, and White Fox threw him a stony nod while the painted galloped toward Bishop. Bishop turned at the sound of the shot, just as White Fox rode up next to him, still holding the war club. They rode side by side for a moment, the legs of the painted and the bay falling into sync.

White Fox said, "*Hetómem.*"

Bishop spoke through the bloody handkerchief, "He remembered me."

White Fox pointed to the nearest mountains with the club, and broke ahead. Bishop heeled the bay.

The cave was a huge, yawning smile beneath a jagged slope of blue rock, sheeted by snow and protected by daggers of ice formed by the water flowing from up-mountain. Bishop followed the barely-there trail for more than a mile, guided by a small fire White Fox had left burning inside the cave's mouth, its drifting heat melting hanging icicles. Bishop felt comforted by the distant, flickering orange, even as a raw burning raced across his face and down his right half-arm.

The painted was tied to a Rocky Mountain birch, eating fresh snow, when Bishop reached the cave. White Fox stood just inside, waiting to see if he could get down from the bay by himself. He did, a scream jamming the back of his throat. Fresh blood specked Bishop's sleeve and the shotgun barrels. She took a step toward him that he stopped with a raised hand. He nodded that he could beat it, allowing himself a moment to let the throbbing from his arm and face ease with deep, cold breathing. It didn't.

White Fox slipped herself under his shoulder and helped him to the fire. "Bi-shop."

Bishop smiled at the way she said his name, breaking it gently in two, as if each syllable had a spiritual meaning. She eased him onto a blanket on the cave floor, where he stretched out, propping himself on his right elbow, the shotgun rig resting on his knees.

White Fox pulled off the blood-flecked duster and folded it carefully, before putting more wood on the fire, sparking the flames. She then opened one of the redware jars she'd arranged around the cave, along with bedrolls, a cook pan, a coffeepot, a lot of ammunition, and a small leather satchel that had Bishop's initials stamped on it in gold.

Bishop said, "You're nesting—Jesus!"

He cried out raw as she peeled the pink handkerchief from the drying blood caking his cheek. White Fox tossed the rag, and dabbed the wound with a soft cloth she'd wetted with melted snow. It was cool, and felt good against the damage.

Bishop said, "Stitches. You know how."

White Fox ran her fingers along the inside of the jar, gathering yellow salve. She smeared the mixture on the wound, then cut a piece of yucca in half, opened it flat, and pressed it against Bishop's face.

She took Bishop's left hand to hold the plant in place and he said, "This won't be enough. *Ma'heo'o Ôhvó'komaestse.*"

Bishop got the words out, but White Fox didn't hear them. Her jaw was set, which meant that she would take care of him in her own way; she didn't need white medicine.

She unbuttoned his shirt, and he automatically leaned forward so she could pull the right sleeve free, gathering the rest around the shotgun rig, then slipping it off. The shirt caught on the hammers, and White Fox yanked it.

Bishop swore in Cheyenne, and White Fox gave the back of his head a gentle slap before allowing him a swallow of mescal.

Bare-chested, he leaned to one side, his back toward her, so she could unhook the canvas strap that was tight across his shoulders and connected to the two triggers of the Greener twelve gauge. The strap dug into him, leaving marks like the bite of a whip, and was connected to a looped piece of fabric that ran down his right arm and anchored to the triggers, so that the action of bringing the shotgun up to waist level would pull on the strap, firing either or both barrels.

The bleeding started around the leather cup that was fit to Bishop's right arm just below the elbow joint. It was a standard prosthetic that rebel and union boys now wore as a battle prize, but had been modified to allow the short stock of the Greener to fit where a metal hook would replace the patient's hand. The stock was secured in the cup with small metal bands that joined the shotgun and prosthetic together as one.

White Fox loosened the ties that held the cup tight to Bishop's arm, and pulled the entire rig away, revealing a bleeding stump. More mescal from the heel of the bottle, and Bishop's head lolled back, his hand still holding the yucca against his cheek as she checked the arm for fresh wounds.

He said, "Nothing's opened up?"

She examined the corrupted skin and muscle that was a knot around the bone, and saw that none of the crude surgical scars lacing it together had ruptured. The blood was smeared from small wounds around the elbow, where the amputation point met the healthy rest of the arm. White Fox swabbed away the streaks of wet red.

Bishop said, "It's not setting right, rubbing raw. I know you don't understand everything, but you did a fine job. I'm the doc, but you're the surgeon."

White Fox dressed the wound with salve and wrapped it, saying, "I still am, Bi-shop."

"Not always, not always."

White Fox allowed the corners of her mouth to turn up, as she settled Bishop down on the blanket. A last bit of mescal and he closed his eyes at her touch treating his wounds.

"Where's my medical bag?"

"Close."

Bishop barely opened his eyes to see the small, black

leather bag, age-cracked, with Lt. Bishop embossed in flaked gold on one side. It was Bishop's field kit, blood-stained and heavy with instruments. White Fox had arranged it among the other supplies, but knowing that piece of himself hadn't been lost eased Bishop, and he closed his eyes again.

Bishop said, "You take care of me."

White Fox rested the shotgun rig between the medical bag and the stacks of ammunition, all the time watching Bishop as he drifted, his words folding into each other.

"When your husband stabbed you, I sewed you up. And when he broke your arm? You were a good patient."

White Fox treated the slice on Bishop's face with the last of the yucca pulp. His eyes were heavy with sleep coming, but his thoughts were fighting the peace.

"Pardee had never seen anything like me. Nobody had."

Bishop lifted what remained of his right arm to reach out to White Fox, but he couldn't. She touched the side of his face, lightly tapping the pulp onto the wound so it would dry in place.

Bishop said, "I've watched a lot of men die, but I never killed one. Not even in the conflict."

White Fox lay next to Bishop, pulling a blanket over them both, keeping one hand on his chest.

Bishop said, "It felt different than I thought it would."

White Fox understood but didn't react; she just lay next to Bishop, feeling the still-excited, rapid beat of his heart and quietly murmuring his name until his body eased, and he fell, peacefully, asleep.

CHAPTER THREE
Deadeye

"Death ain't much of a threat."

The Spitter pounded his glass on the counter of the old exchange station for another pour, while Lem "Deadeye" Wright tried to cut through his jabber. "I got no interest in killin' ya, old man."

"You're the ugliest son of a bitch I've ever seen. You tellin' me you never killed nobody?"

"No, I just ain't interested in you. Yet."

Wright rubbed his white-curtained eye, and took in the rest of Huckie's with an exasperated breath. The saloon was now empty, save for the whore, a deaf miner, and the fat-neck behind the bar. Fat-neck poured the drink that separated night from morning, pocketed his cash, said nothing, and wandered off.

The Spitter said, "He took it in the guts right there."

The poker table had been righted, and the whore was sharing Pardee's chair with the miner, letting his grubby hands absently roam while she dozed. Wright moved to the spread of dried blood on the floor in front of them, then looked to the shattered door, figuring the distance between Pardee and the stranger who had killed him. He could still smell the shotgun's smoke.

Wright said, "I've seen some things, but nothin' like what you're talking about."

Spitter was getting the last of the shot glass as Wright scraped the red-black stain with his toe. Spitter asked, "Want me to tell it again?"

It was damn late, and Wright's patience was running thin, his sightless eye aching him, but he had his task. Wright said, "Just about the fellow with the shotgun. I got the rest."

"He was younger than you, and a damn sight better lookin'."

Wright let it pass. "You said he knew Pardee?"

"Called him by name."

"And the shotgun was under his coat?"

The whore yawned awake and said, "More like it was a part of him."

"So you rode with that sheep dip, he was a friend of yours? Or some kind of kin?"

Wright let the Spitter fix on his dead eye, and then, "That why you thought I'd kill ya? To revenge Pardee?"

Spitter puffed out his boney chest as far as it would go, coughed, and then said, "It's happened before. I've done it, and I'm ready for your worst."

"Stand down. Pardee was no friend, no kin. But we were supposed to meet up. Where'd you put him?"

Lying with the empty whiskey crates next to Huckie's outhouse seemed as good a place as any for Chester Pardee, who was supported by mounds of packed snow under his head and back, with a small rise beneath his knees to keep his body straight for burying. Ice locked his hands on his chest as if he were praying, while a comforter of new snow covered him, hiding his open wounds and their stains. Someone had grabbed his boots, and his toes were turning from blue to black to match his lips. His eyes were frozen-open blanks.

Spitter said, "At least he'll keep. We don't got no undertaker here."

Wright's teeth were chattering as he tried to pull apart Pardee's fingers, but they wouldn't give. He said, "You could use one. He don't look natural with his hands like that."

"If you're worried about it, leave me twenty and I'll make sure they burn off a piece of ground, warm it up for diggin', so he can be planted. If you don't, he could be here 'til the spring thaw."

"I ain't worried."

"So what now?"

Lem Wright squinted his good eye and blew a hole in the Spitter's chest, sending him spinning, and spraying Pardee with fresh red. The sound brought the whore to Huckie's back window, but this was her second killing in less than a day, and she hadn't been the one who had taken the bullet, so it didn't matter to her. Not in this place, not this morning.

Wright stood in the blowing snow, with two dead men, as small traces of morning broke apart the night sky. A few minutes, and there was enough light for him to see to go into Pardee's pockets.

The coat was stiff with blood and ice, but Wright found the letter, and held it close to his good eye with just enough new sun behind him to read it.

Except the page was blank.

Wright turned it over, and then he heard Chaney behind him. "You're pretty quick with that Colt, but I'm dead-center on your head."

Chaney was on his horse, new snow spotting his bowler as he aimed down at Wright. Wright took a few steps back, gun holstered, before turning around.

Chaney said, "There's been a lot of blood spilled, my friend."

Lem was calm. "You want some more? I'll accommodate you. You've got a good chance at a dead shot aiming down from that saddle, but all I have to do is take a half-step to the left, and I can put one in your throat before you'll know what happened."

Chaney lowered his gun, just a bit. "You don't have to do that. We can bargain; seems to me there's more than enough gold to go around."

Wright shook his head. "Christ on a busted crutch, you got the letter."

"I'm one of the few in this dog pile who could read it."

"It's a crock."

"Not according to Pardee. He was a hell of a chatterbox when he was at the poker table, so it's a good thing he was cut down, or everybody in the territory would know."

"We got no money, and all Pardee got was a belly full of twelve gauge."

Chaney touched his false tooth with his thumb, as he always did when considering a situation. "Except this Major Beaudine wants to see you about something, and the man with the shotgun wants you dead. When folks get this worked up, it's always about money."

"And you're cuttin' yourself in?"

Chaney found some of his gambler's bravado and said, "Let's call it taking over Pardee's share. Besides, I'm thinking you need somebody to watch your back."

Wright said, "Or shoot me in it?"

"We'll see how it goes."

Wright half-smiled at the thought of killing Chaney right then. He walked around Huckie's and got on his horse, pulling up his collar against a sharp lash of wind from the mountains.

In less than a moment, Lem had pulled his gun and

fired, blasting apart the buckle of Chaney's gun belt. Chaney scrambled to grab hold of his holster, steady his gun, and fire back. He managed to do nothing.

Lem still had his Colt out, and said, "Just so you know how things really are. But I might find some use for you if you want to tag along."

Lem turned his horse around, and started for the miles of white that lay between them and Cheyenne. His back was a perfect target, but he never flinched.

After a few minutes, Chaney fell in alongside, his gun belt slung over his saddle, but the pistol within reach. Lem said nothing to him, and neither of them looked back at the dead men lying together in the blood-pink snow, waiting for someone to give a damn.

CHAPTER FOUR
The Major

Major Beaudine called the young woman by her Christian name, even though she claimed it was something else.

Beaudine said, "Being truly coy is an attractive and vanishing art, Miss Nellie, but you don't have to be that way with me. Certainly not now."

Knowing better, she didn't protest. She would listen, call him "Major," hand him his cooled julep, keep the pipe filled, and then listen more. Sometimes he would pause to emphasize a phrase, looking for a reaction. If she reacted correctly, then he would chuckle because they'd shared a moment. She always tried to react correctly, because she didn't know what would happen if she did not.

Beaudine heard her call him "a man of power."

They would lie together, and he allowed her questions, even when they touched on painful memories. He'd answer them as well as he could, even helping her take notes so she'd have them for her newspaper articles.

Beaudine knew she'd try to be impartial, but lying

next to him, her body tangled close, her questions whispered, the best she would be able to tell her editor was that her impression of Major Beaudine was "tainted. In a sweet way."

Beaudine spoke without looking at her. "People don't understand how two such as ourselves could ever be brought together."

"Unlikely, but not unheard of."

"You're a woman of fine character."

"Not all would agree."

"Because you're consorting with the enemy?"

"You're teasing this Pennsylvania girl."

"Victory was yours."

Beaudine heard her quiet laugh as she pressed herself against him and said the words, "The more I know about who you are, the more I'm fascinated."

"I don't want to be another object of curiosity for the unwashed."

"What you tell me in confidence remains so; what you want the world to hear, I'm honored to help you."

Her hands stayed on his shoulders, massaging them, while her breath kissed behind his ear. "Tell me."

Beaudine shut his eyes and said, "I've been torn by conflict; seen too many men die, too much blood. It changes you forever, from what you were."

"What were you before?"

"I recall mopping the floor in a house of ill repute. Can you even dream such a thing? A sensitive lad forced to associate with that kind of society, then becoming a decorated officer, commanding troops in the field? It amazes me still."

Without being asked, she handed Beaudine his bourbon and branch and let him sip. "You've done yourself proud."

"You have to send men to their death. It's a Godlike burden, but I feel I wore it well. Every man in my command snapped to his feet when I approached. Once a young private whose weapon misfired, his eye destroyed, stood to salute me. His head wrapped in bandages, but he had to show that kind of respect. He's with me still."

"You have a quality that your men respond to."

"Only the best. I won't abide a liar or ne'er-do-well. The orders I give come from heart and experience, which is why I expect them to be obeyed. It's for their own good, but I've met the defiant, and taught them this lesson."

"I can't imagine anyone defying you."

"One did. Only one."

Her voice was like distant music to him. "You can tell me if it will lighten your heart."

Beaudine allowed himself another cool sip. "It was a man who had committed a crime and had never been brought to justice. I'd been entrusted to see that he paid for his wrongdoing, but he defied me. Wouldn't acknowledge the wrong, and put his family in harm's way. Disgusting."

"What did you do?"

"I took a part of him. It was important that he bleed, hover near death, so he could reflect on his circumstances, and how he brought it all on himself."

Beaudine said that the first shots fired were like thunder claps in the dining room, and had to be shouted over to restore order. His men obeyed commands, dragging John Bishop and his family outside, and waited in the snow for his next instruction. It filled his chest, that power. He remembered stepping on a crystal flute that had fallen to the floor, he could still feel it under his feet, and thought what good taste Mrs. Bishop obviously had.

Beaudine had complimented her, even as she was dying, "I don't know if she heard me, but if I had been in that home for another purpose, we would have had a lovely talk, I'm sure."

"What was your purpose that night?"

Beaudine said nothing about the liberated gold bars,

but only spoke of the weight of punishment, the cleaver in his hand, and the force greater than himself that had brought it down on John Bishop more than once, separating him from his right arm.

Beaudine said, "I admit I let loose the beast."

"Did this Bishop die?"

"He met his god that night, yes."

Widow Kate pounded on the door with bear-size fists until it swung open. She came in, coughing back dust-thick air and trying to clear her painted eyes, "Beaudine, you've been doing a damn poor job of clock watchin'. Find your pants."

Beaudine was sitting on the edge of the cot, its knotted-rope center giving way, his eyes fixed on the pages of the Sears catalog that papered the slat walls and ceiling of the room. Ads for lady's corsets and iceboxes for a fair price surrounded him, their edges curling yellow. There were no windows in this place, just an opening for a stovepipe, and the only light came from a small oil lamp that smoked acrid brown.

Beaudine said, "I've asked that you refer to me by my officer's status."

Kate snorted. "I'm not playing games with you. This place is a trash pile."

A bourbon bottle, neck snapped off, lay empty by his feet, which were laced with blood from stepping on the broken glass. Behind him, a redhead of some age was curled into a corner, her stained nightshirt bunched around her. She didn't utter a sound through her frozen smile.

Beaudine said to Kate, "Madame, do you think I owe you an apology?"

"Forty more dollars. At least."

"Speaking of money in front of a lady like Miss Bly is a true insult. You've interrupted us. Miss Bly and I were having an interview for an Eastern newspaper. She's come a very long way to talk to me, and she deserves my full attention."

"Nellie Bly again, huh?"

The redhead sucked her thumb, while playing with her curls with her other hand. Her eyes were vacant spaces in her wide-white face, and she giggled when Kate asked her if she was hurt.

Widow Kate said, "Whatever he did, you didn't feel it. How much laudanum did you soak?"

The redhead came back with a blank grin.

Beaudine said, "If you leave us now, you won't incur my wrath. We have important work yet to do."

"Where the hell do you think you are?"

"The sanitarium at Milledgeville. And again, please show respect for my rank."

Widow Kate held back a slap and said, "You're in the attic of my house, *Major*! With one of my public girls. You got that?"

There was a moment of thought, and then Beaudine met her glare, saying, "This hospital, and the way you treat a decorated Confederate officer, is a disgrace, and Miss Bly is here to expose these conditions. When her articles appear, there will be a clean sweeping, including you, Madame."

"At least you got that right."

Widow Kate put one of her giant hands on the redhead's face, gently wiping her nose with her thumb. "Look at me, honey. Anything happen that I should charge extra for?"

The redhead settled for a moment with her thoughts. "No. He just talked like a genteel man—and I didn't say nothin' at all. He'd ask a question, and then answer it his own self. Carried on like he was two people."

Her words slurred together, but she made a point of saying "genteel," and was proud of the choice, before slumping back into the corner of her own world.

"So just the forty." Kate turned to Beaudine. "You're crazier than a shit-house rat. How'd they ever let you out of anywhere?"

Beaudine covered his face with his palms. "You're pressing me to an edge. Madame, you do not want to incur my wrath."

Widow Kate grabbed Beaudine's uniform jacket from a hanging peg. "That goes both ways. Downstairs. You know what happens when you owe the house."

"When my release is secured, my men will be coming for me."

"We'll wait downstairs for them, and if they bring cash, they're as welcome as spring."

Widow Kate held up the grey tunic, seeing that it was pieces of two or three Confederate uniforms of different rank sewn together. The brass buttons across the front were mismatched, and the epaulets looked to be an afterthought. Blood spatter stained one side.

Widow Kate said, "Honey, you need someone who knows what they're doing to take of this. You want to appear your best, don't you?"

Beaudine looked at Kate with calm eyes, "That's part of my battle dress. Every spot of blood is a badge of honor."

Kate took a Bowie knife from the inside pocket before handing back the tunic. She said, "I'll put this in the office with your guns, and they'll stay safe, until you get right with the house."

"You're putting me in jeopardy, Madame. How am I to properly defend Miss Bly and myself?"

Kate took Beaudine's hand, her palm smothering his. "Against what, Major? Against what?"

Beaudine said, "The traitorous enemies who're plotting against us."

* * *

The trickle of water from the morning-melted snow laced along the bites of the cave roof, before finding a place just above John Bishop's head, where it rained into his mouth. Bishop leaned back, took a drink, and then stepped away from the cave wall, all the time holding his right half-arm in front of him as an exercise.

Two pieces of heavy scrap iron were laced together with a leather thong, where White Fox had tied them to his arm, just below the elbow joint. The pieces dangled free, clanking together with every move. Bishop strained. The leather gutted tight, as he lifted the weights with the small section of arm that Beaudine had allowed he could keep.

Bishop straightened his elbow, fighting the iron as if he were leveling the shotgun. "You counting?"

White Fox gave her answer with her deep, black eyes: she was.

Bishop lifted again, drawing his arm as close as he could to his shoulder. He lowered it slowly, stopping waist-high and holding. He stole another drink from the ceiling.

White Fox said, "Too much water."

"Who's the doctor, huh?"

She settled cross-legged between the ammunition and medical supplies, wiping the dried blood from inside the leather cup that held the shotgun rig. She soaped the cup, kneading it with her fingers, before folding a small piece of tanned deerskin around the edges. She put her hand inside the rig, gauging its comfort, while keeping a watch on Bishop. Always keeping watch.

Sweat beaded his face, as he held out the scrap iron, his body shaking. Finally, he exploded, "God almighty!"

Bishop and the iron banged to the cave floor. White Fox moved to him, untying the leather thong with a quick pull, releasing the weights.

White Fox smiled and said, *"Koké'ahe."*

Bishop leaned back, catching the stream from above, "I thought my arm was going to come off, 'least what I have left."

"Beaudine is with you."

"Always."

"*O'osó.*"

"I'm not wrong. The bastard's the reason we're here." Bishop smiled. "Amaryllis'd be so angry that I cussed."

Bishop took a small mirror from his field kit and examined the deep slice on his face, which was now purple with healing. He said, "He cut everything I had to pieces."

White Fox stood, opening her blouse to reveal a scar that snaked from the edge of her rib cage to just above the curve of her right hip. The raised tissue was ten inches long and a quarter of an inch wide, with the jagged pattern of sutures now flesh-permanent. She ran her fingers over the area, which was still dead to the touch.

Bishop said, "I did a sloppy job there."

"You saved me."

"But that's the reminder of your husband and that night. You can't forget."

"*Tóxetanó?*"

"You haven't taught me that one."

"Good memory—what makes you sing. Bad memories are a fog."

Bishop shook his head. "You act like you don't understand," he said, then held out his right while White Fox fitted the shotgun rig onto him.

"I killed a man last night and I'm ready to go after a hell of a lot more. A year ago such a thing would have been unthinkable. Everything's changed."

"Not changed, changing."

With the deerskin lining, the cup fit snugly over Bishop's arm, cradling it instead of rubbing it raw. He leaned forward without being asked, as White Fox fastened the straps across his shoulders before tightening the slack of the line to the shotgun triggers. The rig felt good this time.

White Fox said, "You're not clear. Not yet."

Bishop would have started his old argument, but stopped when White Fox pressed her hand against the back of his neck, just two fingers squeezing, as a signal. He turned as she tilted her head in the direction of the cave entrance, listening.

The wind outside was a low whistle, but someone's words were carried on it, and then lost. They sounded close, though. Bishop thought he heard the nickering of several horses; White Fox was sure.

She leapt to her bedroll, lifted the blanket, and grabbed her short bow and beaded quiver, which she slung over her shoulder. She moved along the cave wall, staying on the balls of her feet as she worked her way to a small outcropping of rock by the entrance. The quiver was tight with arrows as she pulled one, fitted it to the bow, and drew back, waiting.

She threw Bishop a nod; the look told him there was no more time for doubt.

Bishop understood. "Maybe I should forget about Beaudine, my brother, all of it." He spoke loudly enough for his voice to echo through the cave, and to cover the sound of his dropping two shells into the Greener, locking the double barrel.

Bishop stood, bringing the weapon up. "That is the best way to find peace."

He moved his shoulders, adjusting the strap to tighten the slack on the line to the two triggers. He started for the cave entrance, then planted his feet, with the rig waist-high. Whoever was outside was sure to see him.

White Fox approved with a blink of her eyes, keeping her bow and breathing tight.

There was more low speaking from outside, and a few heartbeats. Bow and triggers were ready, when a ragtag soldier charged the cave entrance, brandishing a torch in one hand and a Navy Six in the other.

Ragtag screamed, "Welcome to Hell!"

White Fox let go, and the arrow tore through Ragtag's jawbone, shredding his cheek. His scream choked into a gurgle.

CHAPTER FIVE
Dead Man

Just ten minutes earlier, and Captain Creed brought his tall chestnut around to face the men riding with him. He threw an arm toward the cave. "Bishop's hole up with that dog-eater. I can smell 'em. Earn your pay."

Ragtag, in Union blues, grabbed Creed's reins to lead him to a small slope, just to the side of where the cave split the mountain face. Creed kicked at Ragtag from his stirrup, keeping his voice low. "*Their* horses!"

Ragtag quick-stepped to the tree where the painted and the bay were tied, while Creed's other men cleared the snow in four small areas about ten feet from the cave entrance. They worked in joined silence, their leathered faces covered by rough wool scarves and with collars turned up. Ragtag led the painted and bay away, the horses nickering.

It was a bright, clear morning with no warmth to be felt, just bitter cold, even as the sun threw diamonds off the snow and ice. This was the kind of February that had strangled everything on Creed's place, with no hope of resurrection in the spring. But Creed didn't blame the weather or the Almighty for his plight; he blamed the man in the mountain.

Creed eased back on the cantle of his hand-tooled saddle, taking off his amber-lens glasses to rub his sightless eyes and saying to no one, "I know this country just by its feel."

One of the men, with a Colt double-action pistol tucked in a belt loop, moved to Creed quietly. "We got her the way you wanted."

Creed responded, "You better."

The man with the Colt whistled a bluebird's song, and two others cut a bulging canvas sack from the back of a horse, and hauled it over. They slit the sack as they would a hog's belly, then pulled out a scorched red, white, and blue flag of the Tennessee Volunteers.

The burned tatters were held with respect, even as others were yanked from the canvas one after another: shredded sections of the Stars and Bars; the Georgia "Cummins White Cross," with its field of red now torn in half; bloody shreds that had once been infantry banners.

Creed said, "Whatever you've got, bring it here."

Colt unfurled a dark blue flag that had been punched with bullet holes, and held it up to Creed, who ran his fingers across the large white star in its center.

"Bonnie Blue."

"You don't have to do this, sir. We can cut some branches."

Creed said, "Burn them."

His men heaped the battle colors and banners onto the cleared areas of frozen ground. Jugs of kerosene were tossed from a pack mule, and the fuel was poured over the piles of torn cloth. The air bent with the smell of the kerosene, and the men fought their hacks. A boy choked and spit. The last bit of fuel was dribbled onto the old flags, but the men said nothing as they looked to Creed for his reaction. Colt almost spoke, but held back.

Creed adjusted his glasses, pushing them up on a

nose that had been deformed by frostbite, and finally said, "At your ready." Colt lit a torch, then passed the flame to the others as they checked their weapons. A fat gut with a plaid kerchief, who'd always crowed that he was Creed's cousin, pumped a shell into the chamber of a Winchester and took position to the side of the others. Ragtag almost danced in place, ready for Creed to give the signal.

Creed waited, his blind eyes fixed on a memory, and then he ran his hand across his grey beard, lightly tugging on his chin.

That was it. A torch was put to the fuel, the flames sputtering in the chill before catching and racing along the kerosene trail to each pile of flags. They burst into flames.

Fat Gut, his stomach sucked in, shouldered his rifle while the rest of Creed's men stood as a firing squad, pistols aimed at the cave.

Creed said, "Bring him to me."

Ragtag threw his head back with a wild howl, before charging the cave, a Navy Six in one hand and a torch in the other, screaming, "Welcome to Hell!"

Ragtag's cry was cut dead short. Then, the echo of him from the cave died, and there was no sound from anywhere except for the sizzling of the kerosene pools.

Creed backed his tall horse a few steps, which was the cue for his men to move away from the flames, but to keep their guns aimed beyond them, into the cave's mouth. Fat Gut let out his breath and then dropped to one knee, his Winchester steady on some shadowed movement.

Creed called out, "Dr. John Bishop, this is Captain Dupont Creed! Don't come out? You're going to roast alive! I don't give a rat's ass about the squaw. She can cook."

* * *

Inside the cave, the growing flames kept John Bishop and White Fox low against the outcropping of rock that offered protection. Ragtag had hold of Bishop's ankle and tried to speak without a jaw. His words were sloppy nothing, as he swallowed hot smoke and the blood that wasn't pooling around him.

White Fox readied her second arrow.

Ragtag's fingers opened slowly around Bishop's ankle. Bishop reached down for him as if to help; it was a doctor's instinct to give aid, even as Ragtag tried to aim his Navy Six at Bishop's face, but couldn't.

White Fox said, "*Nâhtötse.*"

Bishop knew the meaning and pulled back his feelings. Ragtag made a final sound with his tongue and his eyes stilled, as Bishop stepped over him and braced himself against a small rock shelf. He extended his right-arm rig toward the growing flames blocking the cave entrance.

The heat hard-slapped Bishop, but he found his first target behind the moving curtain of fire: It was the man with the double-action Colt, his dark shirt outlining him against the hot orange-white.

Bishop took aim, bringing his shoulders together to tighten the slack on the trigger line. It was a natural movement now, and the rig was feeling right to him. He glanced back at White Fox, who lowered her bow barely a quarter inch. Smoke from the burning flags sanded her eyes, but she would not blink.

Creed shouted, "John Bishop! It's been twelve years, and you know goddamn well—"

Bishop pulled the trigger-line with his shoulders, blasting through the fire to the man with the Colt and knocking him back onto a mound of snow, where he lay holding his pouring stomach.

Creed's men opened up.

The bullets screamed into the cave, sparking off the

walls, spitting rock and ice with each hit. Their echo brought each ricochet back twenty times, piercing the ears.

A slug tore by White Fox's face as she released her arrow steady, hitting one of Creed's men in the throat, sending him spinning into a fire pile. The kerosene-soaked flags pasted themselves to his flesh, instantly swallowing his head and shoulders in flames, killing his cries for help.

Bishop swung the rig to the other side of the cave opening and fired again, blowing apart the shoulder of a crouching hired gun before White Fox's arrow punctured his eye. Hired Gun flopped onto Fat Gut, who threw him aside, and racked off four rounds from his Winchester.

Fat Gut's voice was a banshee's scream, and louder than the shots he fired. A flaming arrow whipped into his leg just above the knee, opening a red geyser. His scream became a sob.

Creed shouted, "You're gonna taste hell now or later, Bishop! Your choice!"

The layer of thickening smoke tied Bishop and White Fox to the cave floor, wet with blood and melting ice, even as she let fly another arrow at Creed's men, splitting the flames.

In response, muzzle flashes could be seen through the heat and choking grey. Again, the slugs careened from stone wall to jagged ceiling, and back again. Bits of lead splintered into White Fox's back and creased Bishop's thigh. Neither cried out.

Bishop stayed on his back, cooling the shotgun barrels with a handful of snow, before breaching them. The smoke from the fires was heavier now, churning the air in the cave from grey to black, as Bishop fumbled for his twelve-gauge shells. He reloaded, his tears stinging him, then snapped the rig shut, his chest heaving. He fired both barrels toward the cave's mouth.

There was no specific target, nothing Bishop could

see. Someone cried out. Bishop's eyes were lost to their whites as his throat seized, strangled by the heavy smoke.

White Fox scrambled to him, turning Bishop on his back and opening his mouth with her fingers, when the lasso dropped around her neck from behind, and was pulled tight.

White Fox spit, "*Mé'anéka'eškóne!*"

A yank on the rope silenced her.

CHAPTER SIX
Blood and Trust

Chaney could feel Lem Wright watching him from his spot a few paces behind him. They'd been riding all night, guided by a bright winter moon, and Lem had slowed his horse, letting Chaney get farther ahead but keeping steady behind him, like he was planning an ambush. Instead, Lem did nothing; even if he wasn't going to make a move, Chaney hated his watching.

He'd tied his gun belt together with a small piece of rope, so at least his holster was back on his hip, but it kept slipping and this compromise to his draw edged his nerves. Chaney pushed on, trying not to ponder it, but he was the one who was supposed to have the winning hand, holding all the cards. Somewhere he'd lost his advantage.

Dawn broke in streaks of orange as the horses angled down the small, snowy grade to the road that led directly to the Overland Trail. Chaney looked over his shoulder to see Lem dozing in the saddle, his curtained eye locked open as he slept. The reins were slack in Lem's hands, but his chestnut mare followed Chaney without prodding, while the eye did its job watching. Always watching.

The eye looked back at Chaney from behind its white film, darting on its own as Lem started to snore. Chaney turned away with a shudder, wishing he had a decent bottle to kill the queasy feeling. He swore like he was praying, getting up his nerve to try something, but brought his thoughts back to Major Beaudine's letter and its life-changing promise.

Chaney thought, *Hell, I know where to go; I don't need that ugly son of a bitch at all.*

Suddenly, Lem was riding beside him and yawning. "You could've shot me and left me in a drift. One good snow and they wouldn't find me for three months."

"That's not what was in my mind."

"Sure it was, but you couldn't tell if I was sleeping. I can't see out of this damn thing, but it does have its uses."

"You were snoring."

"And you still didn't make a move."

Lem's statement was just a fact, said in a flat way that hit Chaney in his guts. He was losing his bluff. Chaney brushed the snow from the rim of his bowler, and said, "I thought we were trying a partnership."

"Oh, building trust so the other fella doesn't know he's being suckered."

Chaney said, "I know you ain't no sucker, Mr. Wright. You made that mighty clear."

"Glad to hear it. So who'd you sucker to get that fine Denver saddle?"

Chaney straightened. "Barbed wire salesman from Jackson Hole. It never ceases to amaze me what folks will chance when they're sure they have a winning hand."

Lem shook the ice around in his canteen, considering something, before taking a drink to wake up. "And they never know you're beating them until it's too late?"

"That's how I eat."

"Not lately. I know broke when I see it."

Chaney said, "Like most of the country. So why'd you come to that dog pile? To team up with Pardee, or kill him?"

"I hadn't decided."

"I was gonna blow his guts out, take his stake."

"But the man with the shotgun got there first."

Chaney tried a push, asking, "The man you know?"

Lem said, "He was just a fella Beaudine told us about."

"Holding a chest full of Army gold?"

"You read the letter, you talked to Chester."

Chaney said, "I surely did."

Lem's voice dropped. "Then what the hell you asking me for?"

"To see if Pardee was bluffing; he'd always try to bullshit his way out of a hand. So he was telling the truth about the gold."

Lem gave Chaney a dose of his eye, "None of us will know a damn thing until we get to Cheyenne; that's the point, ain't it?"

Chaney flicked his tooth with this thumb, figuring the best way for the conversation to go. "There's a pot on the table? I'll try for it, but I know the odds of catching a bullet instead. Like I said, you made that real clear."

This was good enough for Lem, who handed Chaney his canteen. The ice-cold metal numbed Chaney's fingertips, but the water tasted good and clean going down. Chaney knew enough not to drink too much, or else he'd cramp up. He handed the canteen back to Lem, in case that was his plan.

Chaney said, "Tell me about Beaudine."

Lem didn't respond, so Chaney tried, "Did you meet in the war? That what happened to your eye?"

"My eye was lost during a conflict. I'll let Beaudine tell ya the rest, if he's of a mind."

"Pardee said you all came together at the territorial prison on the Wyoming border. That nobody in Beaudine's Raiders ever did no military service, 'cause you were all locked up."

Lem pulled his horse to a near stop, and Chaney knew he'd overplayed his hand. "You ask questions you think you know the answers to; that's clever, but not too smart."

"You said Pardee was full of shit, but maybe not this time."

"I know what I said."

Lem put a period at the end of his statement, allowing that they'd ride in silence for a while. Lem kept his hand on his pistol the next few miles, forcing Chaney to do the same. Chaney's fingers ached, and he jumped every time Lem made the slightest move, which is just what Deadeye wanted.

The road widened, and their horses stepped around the ruts left behind by a thousand wagons meeting the Overland. Ghosts of schooner canvas, bits of wagon tongues, and shattered wheels lay frozen in the blue-black ditch that ran beside the road these last miles into Wyoming. The pieces reminded Chaney of grave markers.

The two continued riding without speaking, although Chaney kept clearing his throat. Lem offered no more water.

After an hour, Lem noticed his first Wyoming cottonwood, standing bare against the grey sky, and said, "That man with the shotgun?"

Chaney coughed, and said, "What about him?"

"At Huckie's, he let you go. But now you're with me, so next time, he's going to cut you in half, which'll give me a chance. Thanks, partner."

Chaney mumbled something. He'd bought into this game and now was wishing he was out of it. He should be someplace like Kansas City, holding a middling hand, bluffing his way to a small pot to cover his hotel and drinks. That was what he knew, what he liked. Not these stakes.

But there was still the chance at the treasure—more damn money than he'd ever know. Who could give that up?

Chaney couldn't help himself, and glanced over his shoulder to see who might be riding up from behind, maybe with a shotgun sling on their saddle. Lem couldn't help himself, and laughed like hell.

CHAPTER SEVEN
Brothers in Blood

White Fox twisted, angling her back to the flames as she was dragged through the burning kerosene pool, the rawhide lasso biting her throat. She tucked her muscular legs in, bending at the knee, and then sprung forward with all of her strength, pushing herself closer to the two cowboys who were pulling her, forcing their line to slack.

She could hear Creed's voice above the shouts and cries of his men. "You've done well! Tend the wounded, then take a moment to enjoy victory."

The rawhide loosened, and White Fox clawed, pulling it over her head as Creed's men bulldogged her around the waist before tossing her into a small, slushy snow bank away from the cave's mouth.

"You ain't goin' no place, *nésé'kêhá'e!*"

White Fox's neck whipped against the frozen ground as she rolled into the snow, keeping her face away from Creed's men. Her long black hair shielded her movement as she turned her head just enough to see everything in that moment when the shooting finally stops—pools of fire and blood, hired killers lying wounded, and others dead.

She wasn't yet twenty-five, and couldn't count how many like these she'd left bleeding.

Creed brought his horse a few steps closer to the cave's mouth; smoke poured from it like a grey scream. His men kicked snow onto the still-burning flag piles while, feet away, another died with his buckshot-ripped stomach pouring through his fingers. Nobody gave their dead amigo a glance, even as they stepped over him.

Creed used his saddle as a pulpit, calling out to his flock, "You've earned your pay and my respect, but remember why we're here!"

Someone said, "Long as we get ours."

Creed adjusted his glasses and said to anyone close, "Did the dog-eater survive?"

The one with the lariat said, "Squirrelly as hell and took some of yours with her. Turn your head, you can spit in her face."

"That won't be necessary."

White Fox raised her eyes, meeting Lariat, who thought he was clever misusing "bitch" in Cheyenne. Wobbly on his feet, he was coiling the rawhide, red spreading from the wound he'd gotten above the knee. His hands were shaking, and his smell stung her nose.

Creed said, "Where's the prisoner? Where's Dr. John Bishop?"

Lariat said, "Close."

Lariat smiled toothlessly, cocking his head toward Bishop, who was lying in the snow beneath the Rocky Mountain birch where the painted and the bay had been tied.

White Fox saw that Bishop's right arm was almost behind his head, with the double-barrels of the rig leveled naturally at his temple, so that if he moved his shoulders hardly an inch, the triggers would be pulled.

But he wasn't moving, at all.

White Fox couldn't help whispering, "Bi-shop."

As if in response, Fat Gut bellowed, White Fox's arrow still protruding from his leg. He grabbed his Winchester and aimed it at her, pumping off an empty chamber, and then bellowed some more, because she refused to react.

Instead, White Fox kept her eyes on Bishop, waiting for him to stir, or speak. There was nothing. For a moment, she felt relief that the rig wouldn't go off accidentally, and then fear that Bishop was still as death. Her hands stayed around her neck, massaging the feeling back into it, but ready to grab the next lariat they tried to slip over her or a knife from the boot of one of the *mé'anéka'éškónes*, if he got close enough. She counted how many of Creed's "bastard sons" were left, and figured which ones to kill to get to Bishop and a horse.

Lariat checked the pockets of the dead for cash, pried guns from their hands, and inspected their boots, yanking off two pair that caught his fancy. He kicked at Bishop's boots, waiting for White Fox's reaction before throwing his head back in a Georgia howl.

That's when Bishop's left hand moved, barely making a fist. Barely.

White Fox saw his fingers closing, and drew herself in, muscles tightening. She thought Bishop had murmured something, his lips just parting, forming a word. She couldn't hear him, but watched for another sign of life, while slipping both arms out of her buckskin jacket without notice. She sat up, arms out of the sleeves, palms flat against the ground, ready to spring.

Creed called, "Where's the boy?"

The youngest of the bunch, all straw-white hair sprouting over a wide face, ran from the cave and dumped Bishop's field medic kit, blanket, and some ammo onto the wet ground in front of Creed.

Smoke from the fire smeared him, and he coughed, "Right in front of you, sir."

"Ragtag?"

"They really killed him, sir. I never seen worse."

"What did you find?"

"There weren't no gold, but I think I got the valuables you wanted."

Creed looked down from his mount, sensing the boy's expression. "You're a good man, follow orders. You understand this is about a lot more than money."

Lariat yelled, "What about this fancy gun rig?"

Creed said, "Bring it to me."

White Fox watched Lariat draw a blade and crouch next to Bishop. Blood soaked his pant leg and the knife wasn't steady as Lariat cut through the straps holding the shotgun in place. White Fox bit her lip as the trigger lines caught on the knife before being sliced. First one, and then the other; Lariat hadn't checked the breach and didn't know what the hell he was fooling with. He yanked Bishop forward roughly, his head lolling, before pulling the rig away from his half-arm.

Bishop flopped back onto the ground, as Lariat struggled to his feet, pockets bulging with the other guns he'd stolen, holding his shotgun trophy in the air.

Lariat was weaving when he crowed, "Bastard won't be usin' this again!"

The buckshot wound was bleeding Lariat dry, and he managed a few steps before his leg gave way, dropping him dead. The shotgun fired, blasting the rotting top of a tree stump. Creed's men ducked.

White Fox sprang from the snow bank in a burst of ice 'n' white, as she leapt for Bishop's leather medical bag. Her moves were whip-fast, her body a blur, as she grabbed the bag, swinging it wide to smash one of Creed's men in the temple with its hard corner. Dazed, he stumbled backwards, even as she took two gigantic strides toward Bishop. Pure grace and speed.

Creed shouted, "Tell me what's happening!"

White Fox jumped over Lariat, grabbing one of the stray pistols around him. She turned about, and dropped to one knee, leveling the Colt on Creed.

The boy said, "Sir, she's set to kill you."

One of the men said, "Ride like hell, Cap'n. We'll punch ten holes in the bitch before she gets off a shot."

"I might be blind, but I know our dead belong to her. Nobody makes a move, unless you want to join them."

Creed let his words echo for a moment, before calling out to White Fox, "You think you're going to get out of this? You're not. Savvy?"

White Fox stood, her skirt torn almost to the waist, the gun perfectly leveled from her naked hip. Blood and melted snow had pasted the shreds of her blouse to her body, outlining her flat belly and the curve of her breasts.

Creed's men traded snickers and made gestures, shrugging off how many of their own she and Bishop had just killed.

White Fox let the fools be fools. "Bi-shop is mine."

Creed said, "You're both my prisoners. I know you understand."

White Fox took two steps to the side and one of the men fired. The shot ripped the mud at her feet, but she only turned and knelt by Bishop, dumping his medical bag. One of Bishop's eyes opened.

Creed said, "Is she hit?"

The boy said to Creed, "No sir, didn't even flinch. She's doin' somethin' to the prisoner, like a doctor would."

Creed wiped the grit from his eyes. "I wonder if she'll leave him blind."

Creed heard one of his men cock a hammer. "The next man that shoots without my order'll be executed! We came for prisoners, not corpses."

The device White Fox placed on Bishop's face was made of yellow celluloid shaped like the breast of a rooster, and it fit snugly over his mouth and nose, sealing them. The mask was attached by rubber tubing to a small brass and wooden cube, with a music-box-style cranking mechanism on its side. She attached a small leather bellows to a nozzle on the side of the cube, and cranked the handle, expanding the bellows and pumping air through the cube and into the mask.

Bishop's eyes struggled, the lids sticky with soot, as his lungs heaved, and he spit charcoal-streaked phlegm into the mask. She reversed the crank, drawing the fluid out of the mask, then pressed the bellows to force air in.

One of Creed's men said, "That's a long way 'round just to kill somebody."

Creed said, "You're a fool."

More brackish fluid erupted from Bishop's mouth as White Fox worked the small machine, until Bishop's lungs swelled with new air and released. White Fox tore the mask away, and pushed hard on his chest, forcing out the pockets of smoke still trapped inside him.

The boy said, "I've never seen no miracle before."

Creed kept his head locked toward Bishop and White Fox as if he could see them, and said, "This is no miracle, boy."

Blood sprinkled Bishop's chin as his chest racked. White Fox pulled him forward, and wrapped her arms around him and clamped them together in a fist in the center of his back. She yanked her arms inward, forcing more smoke from his lungs.

Bishop gulped for air, struggling for breath, his lungs burning.

White Fox called, "Water!"

Fat Gut screamed out, "They almost killed me, Cousin! Why the hell you helpin' 'em?!"

Creed said, "Because we're not finished."

Creed handed the canteen from his saddle to the boy. "Give him all he wants."

"Yes, sir."

The boy tried a salute, his hand tangling in his stalks, before taking the canteen. He hitched up his tattered pants and stepped around two bodies, trying not to look at the faces with mouths and eyes locked open. He stopped a few feet away from White Fox, before looking around at Creed's men, their guns aimed right at him. A couple of them were smiling.

The only sound was the hack ripping from Bishop's chest.

Creed said, "Give him the water!"

White Fox snatched the canteen from his hands. "Hold him."

The boy slipped an arm around Bishop, propping him up. "I swallowed some smoke in the cave myself. It's god-awful."

Bishop drank, coughed, drank some more. He looked to White Fox, managing, "*Eametanéné.*"

CHAPTER EIGHT
Coffin Man

Resurrection, Wyoming, was the kind of place that Chaney loved and Lem Wright hated. It was a new border town, being built from the mud up. For Chaney, that meant rail workers and teamsters who could be stupid-drunk with their pay, and ladies who had set themselves up to take as much as they could.

Fresh-cut lumber, glass, and wet paint were everywhere you looked, and the air was full of the noise of saws, men, and working animals. To Chaney, it was music: the sound of cash being made.

But for Lem Wright, Resurrection was something blank, with no tradition or history. The kind of place "that might be something someday," but wasn't yet, and likely he wouldn't live to see it. New places reminded him of his own mortality.

So it was all right that Lem and Chaney guided their horses past the freshly painted porch of a feed store, to Gutterson's Funeral Parlor. The name was scrolled on the front window, with a discreet crucifix and Jewish star tiny in the corner of the glass.

Lem tied his horse and went for a close look at the symbols. "Wonder who buries the Chinamen?"

The window, backed by purple drapery, bloated Lem's face, but was kind to his wandering eye.

Three old women in mourning black stepped from Gutterson's, and Lem moved aside, taking off his hat in elaborate fashion, and half-bowing his head. One of the women was crying, with the other two at her elbow, offering comfort.

The crying woman stared at Lem's face long enough to get out some words. "My Edward was injured in the war, too. Thank you for your brave sacrifice."

"You're welcome, ma'am."

She began sobbing again, guided off by the other two. Chaney watched all this, flicking his tooth with his thumb, thinking what he could do with a widow's bank account, when Lem's voice snapped him back. "Ready to take care of some business?"

Chaney joined Lem by the front door. "Haven't said a damn word in four hours. I got distracted."

"I've been deciding if we should stop or not."

Chaney slipped his hand inside his jacket, an obvious move for a weapon, before asking, "Why this place?"

"So you can meet another one of your partners."

Lem opened the door to the funeral parlor, gesturing for Chaney to proceed. Chaney held back, keeping his hand out of sight, ready to draw. Their words were steam in the air.

The pretense meant nothing to Lem. "Your gun belt's comin' apart, partner. Better take care of that."

"In case I haven't told you, thanks for your brave sacrifice."

Lem stored his response for later. Chaney kicked the snow from his boots before going in.

The sun sliced the dark of Gutterson's in long slivers, landing against a small wooden pew, a rude coffin set up on a pair of saw horses, and paper flowers knitted into a wreath. What Chaney could make out in the rest of the room was unfinished: bare walls waiting for paint, against which there were two new rugs neatly rolled, floor planking, and some nail kegs. Ten raw coffin lids were stacked against the opposite wall, with prices scrawled on each. The prices had been crossed out several times, replaced by higher ones.

Lem said, "Howard! Show your worthless ass!"

The response was a dog barking up the street. Lem started for a small door at the back of the parlor, with Chaney following. Chaney regarded the empty pews and coffin, and Lem said, "That's what you have to look forward to." He continued into the backroom, adding, "Me too."

The back room was less finished than the rest of the place, with tools, scrap wood, and several bodies lying in rows on the dirt floor. The bodies were wrapped in heavy cloth, with lengths of rope securing the necks, arms, and feet like so much packed meat.

There was a slapped-together box in the middle of the floor, with a man laid out inside, his huge arms folded on his chest. His mouth was smothered by a drooping mustache that laced into muttonchops along his jowls, covering most of his pitted face.

Lem Wright looked into the box, which was just slightly smaller than a piano crate, then turned to Chaney. "You know a dead man can still break wind?"

The man in the coffin sat up. "You want me to show ya?"

"I think you already did. Jesus, Howard."

Howard said, "Those boys are just going a little ripe. Get me the hell out of here."

"You could stuff a family in that thing."

"All of them, or maybe just me."

Howard held out his tree-trunk arms, as Lem shouldered him from the crate. Lem bellowed in pain as Howard's weight almost pushed him to the floor. Howard swung his legs over the side, with Chaney steadying it as best he could. The wood buckled.

"Jesus is crying, hurry up!"

A couple of bent nails tore into Chaney's hand, prompting Howard to say, "I ain't much of a carpenter."

Lem said, "Then what the hell are you doing here?"

"There's so many killin's, with all the crews comin' in. The coolies and the Micks and the Jews all want a piece of each other. Old man Gutterson can't keep up, so he hired me on."

Chaney regarded Howard's work, sucking the blood from his thumb and forefinger. "A gunny'd be nicer."

"Pulled up the floor for the boards, got a stack of bags for when we run out. One more team of railroad men, and we're good for at least five shootings. That's money, man. I gotta finish this one and two more before tomorrow."

"What about those fellas?"

Howard nodded toward the five on the floor. "Teamsters got ambushed outside of town. Nobody's claimed 'em, so we'll dump in the same hole. I'll give ya each ten if you help me dig it."

Lem said, "Sounds like you're doing all right."

Howard held up a pair of iron pliers and a small chisel. "Between their teeth fillin's and whatever Gutterson misses in their pockets, yeah, I'm stayin' out of jail."

Lem said, "Better that than dead."

Chaney said, "Especially if you're handling the funeral."

"It's probably a toss-up."

Lem looked at Howard and said, "We're going to see Beaudine."

"Why tell me? I don't got to do nothing with that crazy son of a bitch. Ever."

"Howard, Chester Pardee got himself killed."

"That's no surprise. Good riddance."

"By John Bishop."

The chisel hit the floor, and Howard knelt to pick it up. Lem was right beside him. "Bishop survived, and he tracked Pardee down and shot him."

Chaney said, "He ain't lying."

Howard crossed himself, then pulled a crooked, square-head nail from the side of the coffin crate, tearing through the wood planking like it was paper. He spit.

Chaney said, "I was with Pardee, read Beaudine's letter."

"That letter meant squat then, and means double-squat now."

Chaney said, "It might mean a hell of a lot of money, if it's true."

Howard looked up from the coffin, leveling on Chaney. "But it ain't. You don't know shit about this, mister."

Lem said, "Don't get riled. He's riding in with me."

"I don't like guys who flap their gums. You two do what you want, I got men to bury."

"Who's gonna bury you?"

"I ain't too worried."

"About dying?"

Howard said, "We make our choices in this life, and I'm at peace with whatever happens. I brought it on myself."

Lem smiled, "That's straight from the prison preacher."

"Go to hell."

Chaney said, "I'd rather die rich than poor. But you've got guts to face what Bishop's carrying—a double-barreled shotgun, like it's growing right out of him. If I've ever seen the Angel of Death, it's him."

Howard said, "Then you ain't seen shit," before bringing the hammer down on the square head, missing, and pounding into the coffin's side, splitting the green pine in half. He hollered from his guts, grabbed two pieces of the crate and hurled them across the room with amazing force. The wood broke apart, crashing into the pile of corpses and tearing open their burlap shrouds.

Chaney took a step back, and Lem reached up to put hands on Howard's huge shoulders. "This is the time to think, right? Hear me, Howard? Calm down and listen to what we're sayin'. We need you. If John Bishop's coming, let's take care of it together, and not have him pick us off when we're not looking. Doesn't that make sense?"

Howard looked to Lem. "You scared, Deadeye?"

Lem said, "No, but I hate unfinished business. Beaudine got us into this."

Howard nodded. "Uh-huh. The Raiders. Just a gang of thieves."

"Yeah, shitty ones. Thieves and fools."

Chaney said, "Maybe Beaudine was right about all that gold."

Howard moved on Chaney. "You keep talkin' like an expert 'cause you read a letter? I was there when it was written so don't tell me shit! If Bishop's alive, then he's coming for us for what we done. And we deserve it."

Lem got Howard to sit down before Chaney said, "Or maybe he's out to protect what's his. You boys could have been right all along."

Howard barked, "There's no gold, no payroll, no cash."

Lem said, "Either way, we've got to finish this. You want to stay here, building coffins, waiting for death to come through that door? Or ride to Cheyenne, maybe cut it off? If nothing else, you really wouldn't like a chance to drop Beaudine?"

Howard said, "I'm trying to keep peace in my heart, and you're tempting me."

"Maybe you could finally break the Major in half with your bare hands? You'd like that, Howard, I know you would."

Howard spit again, kicked away the remains of the

box, moving to the pile of bodies. He regarded the corpses for a moment, and then looked to the heavens for a sign, a message. The dog down the street started barking again.

Howard said, "The end's comin' no matter what I do. Might as well enjoy it, I guess. First, help me bury these fellas."

Chaney said, "They're dead. What difference does it make what happens to them now?"

Howard threw one of the corpses over his shoulder. "That's what I've been sayin' to *you*, jackass."

CHAPTER NINE
Eyes of the Dead

Creed sat command-high on his chestnut horse, doing a blind man's inspection of the shotgun rig, pulling the trigger line, and testing the straps that secured it. He shucked the spent shells, holding the gun next to his ear, snapping it shut, listening for rattles. There were none. He measured the stock with his palms, then ran his thumbs over the end of the barrel for sharp edges or sloppy job where it was sawed off. He gave his silent approval of the gunsmith.

Creed held the rig out in front of him, sensing its weight. "Just move your arm and it fires?"

Bishop's words were a strain, even as White Fox spread cinnamon oil on his lips with her index finger so he could speak. "My shoulders."

"Do all the work yourself?"

"There was a smith, followed my design."

"Damn clever, but that's you, Dr. Bishop."

Creed hung the rig on the saddle horn, while dropping from his tall horse. The chestnut sensed Creed's every move before he made it and adjusted, patiently helping his blind master.

Creed scratched behind the horse's ears, "Where's the boy?"

"Here, sir."

The straw-haired boy led him around the dead, the smoky kerosene pools, and the bloody snow, to the little clump of trees where Bishop was lying. White Fox, next to him, rose up on her knees, but her hands were always on Bishop's chest, protecting him.

One of Creed's men shouted, "She's startin' somethin'!"

Bishop said, "No, she's not. And you men don't either."

Creed was standing over Bishop now, and the doctor's gaze locked on to Creed's amber glasses. Creed cocked his head, sensing the moment, and nodded to Bishop in formal recognition. Spread out a few feet behind, Creed's men casually waited to shoot, guns resting on hips but with hammers back.

Creed said, "Let me see that thing she was after."

Bishop said, "Your men need to stand down."

"Apparently, you didn't leave many."

"I see a lot of guns."

Creed ordered, "Holster weapons!"

Some of the men obeyed. The one bleeding from the head didn't and Bishop said, "There's still one."

"And always will be. You fought a good fight, but you're my prisoners, Doctor. Maybe you better explain to her just what that means."

White Fox said, "I know."

"Then toss away that pistol you had aimed at me."

She threw the gun, with Creed listening for it to land in a bank of snow with a pillowed thud.

Creed said, "I'm entitled to inspect all spoils, even if I can only see them with my hands. Your latest invention, Doctor, the one that saved your life."

"She saved my life."

Creed laughed, "Bullshit. Go ahead, boy."

The boy reached down for the breathing device lying next to White Fox, then stopped. Her eyes cut him.

He swallowed. "Ma'am."

Bishop asked, "What's your name, son?"

"Hector Price, sir."

White Fox kept her other hand hidden in the field kit, clamped around a scalpel. Bishop squeezed her arm, and she let the knife go.

Bishop said, "It's all right. *Otséeme.*"

She smiled to herself at being called "brave" and handed the device to Hector, who held it out so Creed could turn the small box over and over, fingers tracing its edges. He fit the mask onto his own face, drawing deep.

Bishop said, "Turn the crank."

Hector turned the crank, as Creed continued with the mask; then the captain took it off, saying, "I feel my blood pumping."

Bishop said, "Pure oxygen. The crank draws the air into the device which filters it through a cell filled with purified water, and the bellows pumps it out through the mask."

"How'd you come to this?"

"Remember the fire at Lynchburg? Our men choking to death, and there wasn't a damn thing I could do about it."

"So, you're still a soldier."

"Still a doctor."

"And you carry your weapons with you."

"You never know when you'll need them, Captain."

"You were an officer, and proud to display your rank on your field kit. Maybe I can't see, but my vision's clear."

Coming up out of some bloody slush, Fat Gut screamed, "What about the bitch with the arrows? She killed near half of us! And me!"

"You survived." Creed handed White Fox the breather. "Be grateful for that."

Bishop said, "I remember you saying that before, after a skirmish on the other side of the Shenandoah."

"Because we have history."

Bishop looked at all the guns ready for him, and the men behind them. "I might even recognize some of these faces, under the scars."

"Scars you left them after our battles. These men have stayed loyal, all these years. Unlike you."

"Revenge?" Bishop let the word hang in the air before asking, "How long have you been tracking me?"

Creed said, "Not long after you struck out on your own. You're wanted for killing the gunsmith who made your rig. He was married to the squaw? That's reward money, and who better to collect? Obviously, I can't read signs the way I used to, but you weren't hard to find. Not if you keep using that rig."

"And when are you going to kill us?"

Creed took off his glasses, to wipe them with a handkerchief from his pocket. His eyelids were heavily corrupted with raised tissue, and the eyes themselves seemed solid black, but were actually blood-flecked purple. Blinking was a slow impossibility.

Creed faced Bishop's voice and said, "No one has more cause than I do."

Bishop said, "But you're holding back."

"You know me, Doctor. You know there's a strategy."

"Hell, yes."

Creed let his words go flat. "I have some planning to do yet."

"You're still riding Pride. He's about the finest animal I've ever seen."

Creed said, "Of course, I haven't seen him in years, but Pride's the one thing I value from my days in command."

White Fox helped Bishop sit up against the tree, and

he gestured toward the smoldering piles of cloth with the right hand that wasn't there. "Those fires to smoke us out, they're old flags. You took that Bonnie Blue when we fought those guerillas out of Baton Rouge."

Creed stood at attention. "Damn right. I captured them, so they're mine to keep or burn. I can't see them anymore, so they're nothing but shitty rags."

"No, they have meaning. Every battle you won, and every man you lost. I know your feelings about them."

Creed dropped to one knee. "Tell me, Doctor, that you're not using a bedside manner with me. Who do you think you're talking to? The only thing that's keeping you and the dog-eater alive is I haven't given the final order. You've got a lot of tricks in that bag of yours—you have my eyes?"

Bishop said, "I did my best."

Creed pulled himself to his feet on Hector's arm. "You know how I lost my sight? What a fine field medic Dr. Bishop was? He was with the Virginia Volunteers. He saved hundreds of lives, but not my eyes. That was beyond him."

Bishop hacked, his throat still burning, even as White Fox let him drink from a water bag. It went down cool, but there was still a taste of gunpowder and fire in his mouth and nose. That hot-metal taste brought the sound of screams and a battery of cannons back to Bishop's ears.

John Bishop looked at the dead men sprawled around the entrance to the cave, the light afternoon snow beginning to shroud them. But it wasn't the memory of their screams he was hearing.

It was the screams of Captain Creed, as he worked to remove the Howitzer shrapnel from around his eyes. Bishop slit his lids, and dabbed away each sliver of torn metal. It took hours, because Creed would stop him, and insist he help one of the other wounded, even as he cupped his hands over his eyes, to hold back their bloody wash.

Bishop said, "The Battle of Buffington Island. You wouldn't let me put you under."

"I was in command."

"You were out of your mind with pain."

Creed said, "The pain was hellish for sure, but, Doctor, I was never out of my mind."

White Fox helped Bishop to his feet, and he said to Creed, "It was the infection that took your sight. You'd just been sutured; you never should have crossed that river."

"My men needed me. I didn't matter that I was wounded; it mattered that I lead."

"That river was filled with bodies, disease. You slipped, and your bandages got soaked. Nothing was going to save your eyes after that."

"You know the last thing I saw?"

"You're going to tell me."

"The bandages pained me, and I tore them off while I was in the bloody water. There was a body of a little girl who'd been shot in the throat, just moving with the river. I don't know who killed her or why, but when I went under, her face was right in front of me and I looked into her dead eyes. Then mine were gone, forever."

"Then how am I to blame for what happened?"

Creed kept his hand on Hector's shoulder as he faced Bishop and said, "Because I choose to."

The gun with the head wound yelled, "What happens now? Firing squad? They took out half of us, they got it comin'!"

Creed said, "I think I'd enjoy that, but it doesn't serve the purpose. Doctor, tend the wounds of my men. The boy and your squaw can help. Then we march."

"Where?"

"A blind man can't do much in the world. My ranch

was lost, and my pension wouldn't keep a dog fat. So now, I do what I have to do. Just as you are."

Bishop stood, picking up his field kit with his one hand. "And what do you think I'm doing?"

"Going after Beaudine and his gang of egg-sucking gutter trash."

Bishop regarded Creed for a beat, the mention of Beaudine's name pulling him up short. Creed said, "I told you we've been tracking you for a while. You must remember I credit myself with knowing my enemies. I know all about it."

Bishop said, "Is this your get-back for your blindness? Deny me *my* revenge for my wife and son?"

"The world will be a better place without Beaudine's gang. Hell, every one of them deserves to be shot, hung, and shot again."

"So what's your strategy, Captain? What are my orders?"

Creed said, "You have wounded to attend to, Dr. Bishop."

"I need that device."

Creed threw it to Hector. "He means the breathing gizmo, not the shotgun. That rig's mine."

CHAPTER TEN
Dead Letter

"Brother John,

"My guess is that when you read this, I will be gone. We will have had a little talk, settle our scores, and considered what might have been if I'd taken a different road. I know you feel superior to your older brother, and probably with good reason. I have many thoughts to express, and since I never learned to read or write properly, my cellmate is setting all of this down for me, using the best language in his capability.

"You were barely in long pants when I left Virginia, and Ma and Pa had long before decided you were the favorite. You were smart, took to school, and looked like our father. I hated school and don't resemble either of our parents, and those differences have been between us ever since.

"I was in jail for robbery when you were getting out of school. That was not my first time locked up, but the first time you were able to visit me, which I appreciated. When you were studying medicine, I was on the other side of the law in the wild country, and was then in jail again for the manslaughter of a miscreant. You did not visit me then, but I understood that mama refused to give you her permission, so I hold no grudges.

"With the war came your commission and my own difficulties; I killed my fair share, but was not in official uniform, and so I am now to be hung. That uniform makes all the difference doesn't it? As do the rules, which you have always respected, except that one time.

"That one time is why I now regard you as My Brother John.

"Since my death is now a thing of yesterday, it is my desire that you should keep all of the Army gold that we hijacked together from the troop train coming from Richmond. I don't know why you threw in with me on this, but I am glad that you did, brother. This fortune has always been our secret, and since you were the only one to know its final location, it was also our trust. Despite the end of conflict, the government will never stop looking for that money, and I know you have the strength to keep it safely hidden. I thank you and respect you that you did not spend it, as I knew you would not, but now all of it is yours to do with what you will.

"One half of a million dollars is a great deal of money, John, and I am facing the hangman with at least the good feeling that after a life of doing wrong, I helped a good man provide a special life for his wife and son.

"I look forward to the day when we are joined again on the Streets of Glory.

"Your older brother, Devlin Bishop."

Widow Kate read the last paragraphs aloud a second time, then leaned back in her overstuffed velvet chair, her fat fingers locked together in pause. She wiped away a small mustache of sweat before speaking.

Kate said, "That's what you've been chasing all these years, Beaudine?"

"Pilfering that letter from my jacket was a foolish mistake. I remind you, again, of my rank and the consequences of disrespect."

"Oh, no disrespect intended, but you should be glad I read it. You owe me quite a sum, and this gives me some hope of being paid."

"Madame, you'll get yours."

Beaudine sat opposite the large, dark oak desk that hid half of Kate's massive body, adjusting himself on a stack of fine silk cushions that had been sewn to the seat and back of a finely carved rocking chair. Like the desk, the chair was highlighted with streaks of lamé, while the rest of Kate's bordello office was all silk wallpaper, carved ivory dragons, and Chinese vases on thin pedestals. Heavy drapes killed the sun, and the oil lamps around the room burned low.

Kate removed the glass flute from the small lamp on her desk, turning the flame down to a blue burn as she said, "The chance at half of a million dollars in one fell swoop is a hell of a thing, if it's there. I've had my chances to grab quick fortunes, but let them pass. I prefer to amass my fortunes a few dollars at a time. That way, I know it's real."

Beaudine leaned suddenly forward. "Now you don't think it's real? Dev Bishop was my cellmate."

Kate smiled, shaking her head. "I know you wrote the letter, Major. It has your exaggerated flair."

"You compliment and offend at the same time."

"One of my many talents."

Kate took a jade pipe from her top desk drawer, and held the bowl over the lamp's flame. Her concentration was total, her thick fingers now delicate instruments, as she felt the pipe's temperature before opening a small ivory pillbox and removing a pea-sized dollop of opium to drop into the pre-heated bowl.

"My third husband was a sea captain who introduced

me to the ways of the dynasties. I learned a lot from the Chinese, not the least of which was how to run this place. They know their business."

After a few moments, the green-yellow started to smoke, and Kate took a long draw on the pipe before leaning back in her chair and allowing the feeling to wash through her.

Kate judged Beaudine's dark expression and said, "The girls have no idea I allow myself this. If they did, they'd assume I condoned use for the non-injured, not understanding the discipline it takes to control your consumption. Fighting the tiger keeps me strong. Do you understand, Major?"

"As a matter of fact, I do, given some of my extreme hospital experiences"—Beaudine's voice was drifting— "and the soldiers I know prefer opiates to whiskey. Miss Nellie Bly, who I had an interview with earlier, will be writing extensively about the problem for *The Pittsburgh Dispatch.*"

Kate said, "That wasn't Nellie Bly, Major. Remember where you are."

"I do—I do—but you interrupted us, while we were discussing dire issues. Some of which concerned you directly, Madame. That wasn't appreciated."

"There was no interruption, no Nellie Bly. Just one of my whores and, a crazy man." Kate added after drawing on the pipe, "Maybe not all his fault."

Beaudine studied his boots, the ragged edge of his sewn-together tunic. He cleared the air with a wave of his hand. "I get lost sometimes, Madame, but I always find my way back. Always."

Kate said, "That's why I allow you to bed here."

Beaudine bowed his head. "I know, truly, that I never had the chance to talk to Miss Bly, and tell her of the terrible conditions in the hospitals where I was a guest. But I should have, really. That would have been valuable."

"I agree."

"Hospitals and prisons, that's been my life. Did I say anything to that girl? Do anything unseemly?"

Kate put another match to the pipe. "You were a gentleman in your session, and if you said anything to Thelma, she'd forget the next minute. She's a sloppy girl. Swills laudanum like it was fresh cider and thinks I don't know it. Doesn't have the character to indulge and still keep her wits about her. Not like me."

Beaudine nodded to Kate and said, "Some are born to lead."

"And some are born to stay on their backs."

Laughter ripped Kate, flesh jiggling, before she drew deep on the pipe and closed her eyes as the feeling kissed through her. Her eyes were still closed when she said, "That gold shipment is real, not a flight of fancy, or something for you and Nellie Bly?"

"Real as death."

"Why don't you have it yet?"

"The good doctor John Bishop wouldn't cooperate."

"Did you kill him?"

Beaudine's voice lowered. "He was—destroyed."

"That doesn't say it, and you didn't get the money."

"There's tracking to be done. My men will be joining me, and we'll set off on our mission. That's the last question, Madame. I've already given one interview today, and your tone is grating."

The Colt Lightning was in Kate's hand instantly, her flabby arms steadying the gun directly at Beaudine's head by resting on a large dragon carved from a solid piece of jade.

Beaudine said, "Threatening an officer is a very serious offense."

"Living in that head of yours must be a hell of a thing. I'd hesitate killing you, but I'll shoot. Or, you can come upstairs with me for a moment."

Beaudine stood. "I understand. Opiates have poisoned your reasoning."

"No, they just keep my aim relaxed. Afterwards, I wouldn't mind having a little late supper, since you're spending the night."

Kate moved around the desk as Beaudine stood. He didn't put his hands up, but kept his eyes on the Colt pistol following him. "Are you really that worried I won't be paying your whore her piddling amount?"

Kate said, "This is the problem, Beaudine. You can't follow the path of a conversation: we're talking about something bigger than what you owe. Understand? Come on. Let's see if you can make it upstairs without straying."

Kate opened her office door. "Major."

Voices, mild groans, and laughter from the other bedrooms drifted about the hallway in a mix as Widow Kate and Beaudine made their way to the small set of curved steps that led to the attic bedroom. She kept the Lightning close to his spine, and he buttoned his tunic and flattened his lapels before going up.

Kate said, "Your session was fine, and I trust you'll pay what you owe. It's what happened afterward that's a problem."

The cramped attic room was the same as Beaudine had left it, except the redheaded girl was lying on the bed, night clothes shredded, her head cocked at an impossible angle with deep purple bruises smothering half of her face and the sides of her neck. Kate stood behind Beaudine, close enough to see a shimmer of sweat on the back of his neck, but there was no other visible reaction, even as she gently prodded him with the barrel of the gun, poking his ribs. He ducked under the doorframe to enter, then took a few steps to the bed.

Kate said, "You claimed you forgot something and had to come back up. Remember?"

"No, I do not."

"But that's what you told me, Major. Then the girls and I heard the screams, and found this."

Beaudine bent down, brushing his fingers across

Thelma's strawberry curls. His mouth went slack, as he leaned just an inch from her face and blackening lips, before looking back at Kate. "It's the one I knew as Nellie."

"You can call her any name you want, it don't make no difference to the law."

Beaudine swallowed his words. "You're trying to hood-wink me, Madame. It's not appreciated."

"But we all heard it. Thelma screamed at you, dis-obeyed orders, and you set her straight. Now the Marshal likes to stay over when he's riding through the territory; would you like him to know about this and the treasure, or should we keep today's interview between us?"

Beaudine stepped away from the corpse, his fists clenched. "Is this supposed to frighten me?"

"No, but your loss of freedom might. Your gold quest will be a damn sight tougher if you're in a jail cell, wait-ing for the hangman."

"I've been there, and now I'm here."

Kate met Beaudine's hard look. "Don't act like I haven't taken everything into account. I'm not one of the dog-tail felons you ride with. I'm talking real business— are you up to it?"

Beaudine slumped against the doorjamb, his shoul-ders and arms sagging with all that he was carrying. He looked to Kate, rubbed his temples. "My mind's swim-ming, and that's a dangerous thing."

Kate said, "I've got just the cure for that downstairs."

"You have me at a disadvantage now, Madame, but to-morrow won't be the same. All this betrayal will come into focus, boiling my blood. I'll be hell-fired for sure."

Kate eased Beaudine out of the room, pulling the door shut behind them, "We'll see."

The coffee had cooked down to acid-brown when Lem poured himself a cup. Howard pulled a new shoe from the coals of the campfire, and Chaney struggled with his horse's left hind leg until Howard shoved him aside, straddled the shank, and nailed the shoe into place.

Lem tipped his coffee. "Tubal-Cain from the Book of Genesis, the first blacksmith! I bet you could give him a run for his money, Howard!"

Chaney said, "You got the strength for it."

Howard gave the horse a pat. "Takes more than that. You have to know your animal, which you don't. If he'd walked one more mile on that shoe, he'd be lamed for sure."

Chaney offered, "Then I'm obliged."

Lem said, "See? It's a good thing you're here."

Howard looked to Chaney. "Yeah, so why are *you* here?"

Lem countered, "Come on, we talked that through. It never hurts to have an extra gun."

Howard said, "Or target—what you got painted on your back?"

Lem finished the coffee. "It's all going to depend on Beaudine, and if we want to carry on."

Chaney said, "I thought that was Bishop's call. He raised the stakes by coming for your bunch."

"That's true, and if I had more than forty dollars to my name, I'd say the hell with Beaudine, the hell with Bishop, the hell with it all."

"But now you're thinking about the chance of that gold."

"I'm thinkin' about death, and the money. And wondering which we're going to find first. Just wondering."

Howard drank some coffee, then spit it into the fire and said, "You're not all in, Lem?"

"Hell, yes, I am. But I'm feelin' better now that there's three of us."

Howard said, "And the law."

Chaney looked to Lem, who was grinning. "What do you mean?"

"He means this." Howard took a bent deputy's badge from his pocket, and pinned it on his torn vest, directly over his heart.

Lem snorted a laugh. "He got it when he was leg-breakin' agitators for the railroad, just to keep things nice and legal."

Howard said to Chaney, "See, I'm not just some big, dumb, son of a bitch. I'm the law."

CHAPTER ELEVEN
Into the Storm

"You gotta be shittin' me!"

Hector was propping Fat Gut by his shoulders as Bishop pulled the chrome instrument from his med kit. Gut winced when he saw the thing: it was tong-shaped, with a metal clamp mounted between curved scissor blades that opened wide enough to fit around the top of Fat Gut's leg, while the clamp extended to grab hold of the arrow shaft that protruded eight inches out of the calf. The snow was falling heavier now, sticking to the open wound.

Bishop said, "This instrument's designed for removing bullets, but it's adaptable. Unfortunately, I only have this left hand, and can't perform the procedure myself."

Fat Gut "what the hell" squinted, and then Bishop added, "It won't work without two hands."

Fat Gut yelped, "Then who in tarnation's gonna do it? And I don't get no painkiller or nothin'? I know you got powders!"

"Your ambush broke everything we had. Maybe one of your buddies has a bottle in his saddle?"

One of the hired guns wiped his nose and said, "Creed don't allow nothing. Thinks it keeps us sharp. Bullshit."

Creed called out, "Where's the boy? Where's Hector?"

Hector made some noise, his nose buried in Fat Gut's shoulders, propping him up for surgery, as Bishop tightened the metal clamp around the arrow. His moves were left-hand clumsy, but the instrument locked into place. Hector strained against Gut's rolling weight, "I'm here, sir!"

"Front and center."

Bishop countered, "I need him, Creed, if you want your wounded tended. I'd bet you still have that bottle."

Creed took a bottle of Evan Williams pre-conflict bourbon, wrapped in oilcloth, from his saddlebag. The hired guns spit and grumbled, as White Fox stood directly in front of Creed, fixed on his amber glasses as they were being dotted with fresh snow. "*Eó'ó'éne vo' éstanéhotame.* Do you know its meaning?"

Creed sniffed the air, then handed her the bottle. "Dr. Bishop wanted this. For medicinal use only."

Bishop took stripped bandages, antiseptic, and scalpels from his bag; suddenly he was a field medic again, prepping, but with only his left hand. White Fox sat next to him, holding the bottle just out of Fat Gut's reach, as she waited for Bishop to give the nod.

Fat Gut said, "That bottle's for me!"

Creed said, "That's not coffin varnish, it's fine sipping whiskey, with a history."

"You claim that about everything, 'cuz."

Dr. Bishop checked the clamp, the tongs on the instrument, the leg's torn muscle and flesh. Fat Gut grabbed for the bourbon again, but got nothing. White Fox fought her smile.

Fat Gut let it out again, "Come on! I'm dyin!"

Bishop said, "Well, you were trying to kill me."

Fat Gut snorted like White Fox wasn't there. "Just her.

We had orders to take you, but you ain't the one who shot me."

Creed said, "Doctor, I expect you to do your duty."

Fat Gut wiped his mouth and said, "There's your orders, Doc," before nodding toward White Fox. "I've left 'em dead and wishin' they was dead. Had some fun, too. But not this time, huh? Not with you?"

White Fox looked to Bishop, her eyes solid, black pools with blood red around the iris, a circle of fire. This only happened in moments of rage, just before exploding. Just before.

Bishop watched the moment pass, White Fox never looking away from him. Then he said to Fat Gut, "You're damn lucky."

"Quit stallin'! Fix me up!"

Creed said, "Conduct yourself properly, or I'll order the doctor to let your leg rot."

Bishop said, "Give me a Winchester shell."

"Spent. More in my pocket. Can't move my arm."

"Boy?"

Hector reached into Gut's pocket, pulling out two cartridges. White Fox took the bullets, pulled away the brass and emptied the black powder around the shaft of the arrow, just below the clamp. The arrowhead wasn't barbed, but it had sliced beneath a muscle and had to be cut free from the tissues before removal. Fat Gut grabbed the bottle of bourbon like he was wringing a chicken's neck.

"Drink. Your captain got that bottle from Ulysses S. Grant."

Hector gulped air. "Is that a true fact?"

Fat Gut took three long pulls, wiping the rest from the scraggle of his beard. "He's told me a hundred times."

Bishop said, "That's a true fact. Creed knows Grant."

One of the guns fashioned a cigarette, lit it. Bishop

looked up just as he flicked the match away. "Got another light?"

"Sorry."

"Then come over here."

Creed said, "Whatever needs doing."

The gun sauntered over, a Morgan-James long-sighted rifle slung on his back. He stood by Fat Gut, snickered, and blew smoke into the light-falling snow.

Bishop looked up at the gun. "What do they call you?"

"My given name's Epiphany. My Christian name's Fuller."

Bishop said, "Mr. Fuller, when I tell you, put the cigarette to the powder on his leg. It's going to pain."

Fuller said, "I never cottoned to this son of a bitch anyway."

Fat Gut screamed with spittle, "I ain't lettin' that darkie do nothing to me!"

White Fox grasped the tongs, Bishop positioned the scalpel and said, "Now!"

It all happened at once. Fuller put his cigarette to the black powder, flaming it around the wound, as Bishop cut the arrowhead free. White Fox threw her weight against the clamp, forcing it to pull the arrow from Fat Gut's leg in a single motion. Blood was a fountain, spraying her, before the powder burned over the wound, sealing it.

There was a meat-sizzling, even as snow cooled the wound, and Bishop swabbed it with iodine. Hector grunted as Fat Gut slumped back, unconscious.

Fuller pulled Hector from under Gut's massive weight. "Come on, tadpole, before he crushes you."

Fat Gut's head hit the ground, his mouth sagging.

Bishop said, "He'll be out for a while."

Creed said, "Take care of these other men, then we'll get him on his feet. We're moving before the sun sets."

"The snow's going to get worse."

"Then you and the dog-eater better work as fast as you can, because you've got a long walk."

The gun known as Fuller rolled the last of his makings and popped it in his pocket before untying Bishop's bay and White Fox's painted stallion. No matter how he moved, his sniper's rifle stayed perfectly slung across his broad shoulders.

The snow was a straight curtain now, still light, but not melting when it reached the ground. The kerosene pools and bloody slush around the mouth of the cave were again pristine white, and the dead were in a neat row beside the tree line. Lariat was face down, to hide his twisted expression.

Fuller led the two horses to where Creed was now sitting atop his chestnut, away from the few men who were still being bandaged by White Fox, as Bishop guided her. The doctor inspected every dressing, and Creed listened for his approval.

Fuller said, "They're almost done. I've got the horses. The snow makes it look like nothing's happened here. It's all brand new again."

"What about the boy?"

"Helping your doc friend."

Creed said, "That's a prisoner."

Fuller reached into Creed's saddlebag, found a match to go with his last cigarette. He struck it against Creed's stirrup. "He's gold to me, Creed."

"You're forgetting yourself, Fuller."

"I ain't forgetting nothing. I've been with you since Richmond, and I always appreciated that you saw my blue uniform, instead of my black skin. You were always blind to that, now you're blind for real."

"But still in command, here."

"You're not an officer anymore. We're just trash the army threw away, the ones who should've been killed,

but weren't. We're the walking dead, and now we got a
shot at real money? This ain't about loyalty, Captain—
it's about leaving my kids something. Without my uniform, I'm just another runaway slave with a gun, so this
better work out."

The acknowledgment of rank pleased Creed. "You'll
always be a soldier; a fine sniper with a good eye. Maybe
I can't see it, but I know your skills. Conduct yourself
with discretion, and you'll be rewarded."

"I can keep my mouth shut, but one way t'other, I'm
getting mine."

Creed finally said, "We all will."

The colorless sky and white earth met somewhere,
forming an empty void, barely broken by the distant
sketch of a mountain or the dot of trees, all obscured by
blowing snow. A hanging fog turned any landmarks into
grey-blue ghosts, as Creed's prisoners trudged through
the building cold.

Behind them, they left hoof prints in furrows of snow
that were being filled in from the sky, while ahead there
was only blinding white.

Bishop and White Fox led the group, the bay and the
painted stepping high out of the snow and coming down
through a frozen crust, almost to the knee. White Fox's
hands were tied at the wrist behind her back, while
Bishop's left was knotted to his saddle horn.

Creed and Fuller rode side by side, the painted and
the bay tethered to Fuller's horse so Bishop and White
Fox couldn't break away. Fuller's Morgan-James hung in
a scabbard by his leg.

The rest of Creed's men followed in line, some band-
aged, their weapons casual on their laps, ready to shoot
Bishop or White Fox, or anyone, between the shoulders.
Hector was the last rider, sharing his horse with Fat Gut.
Gut was still dazed from the surgery and heaving into

the frosty air. Even when he waved in the saddle, he held onto his Winchester like it was precious treasure.

Everyone kept their faces low, the horses angling slightly to the side, against the beating wind as they trudged. Bishop pulled up, and the other riders stopped behind him, the animals bobbing their heads, snorting. Hot breath hung in the air.

Bishop called out, "Why are we setting the pace? We'll freeze before we get anywhere."

Creed said, "When I want us to move faster, we will."

"Then where the hell are we going?"

"You're heading in the right direction, Doctor. That's all you need to know."

"You can tell?"

"I can tell."

Bishop said, "Then how about this: are we wanted dead or alive?"

"There's a price to be paid. Now move."

Bishop looked to White Fox, who kept her gaze straight ahead, seeing something beyond the yawning white. Snow hung on her eyelashes and lips, and she didn't meet Bishop's face when he asked if she was all right. She just gently heeled her painted, starting the trek again. Bishop did the same.

The group followed in line, with the hired guns muttering. Fuller looked back from his saddle and said, "You boys want to see some shares, I'd keep my opinions quieter than that."

One of the guns said, "The house slave never has to worry about nothin'."

Fuller cocked the Morgan-James, the metallic click of the hammer hidden by the howling wind, and was drawing it from its scabbard when Creed said, "Rise above it."

Fuller regarded the blind man who'd heard the weapon, and said, "You've been grinding about the doc for years."

"But I waited, and now is the time. Be patient, and

you'll have your time, too. Should I make that an order, Fuller?"

Fuller glanced over his shoulder at the seven men behind him—bloodied, bandaged, with guns instead of sense. The ones Bishop and White Fox hadn't killed. He'd ridden with some of them for years, knew who they were inside, and usually let their talk pass right over. But now he was going to have to share money with this bunch, maybe a lot. He threw them a strained grin that one of Creed's men returned, full-tooth. Easy target.

Fuller's eyes narrowed, even as his grip relaxed on the Henry, letting it slide back into its place. "No need."

Bishop said, "Sounds like trouble in the ranks."

Creed didn't raise his voice. "It's handled."

"Like the time we crossed into the Ohio Valley? You'd been pushing the men for days, they could barely stand, and that's when the attack came. We lost a lot that day."

"You lost a lot."

"Most were passed saving, Creed. And none died by my hand."

"You mean the one you have left?"

Bishop said, "We've both seen miracles on the battle-field, but there sure weren't any that day."

"I don't need your voice of conscience. I learned a long time ago that doctors aren't gods."

"Neither are officers."

Creed let the words settle before he said, "Even a blind man could hit a target as close as you are to me."

"Wouldn't that lessen our value? Or is it 'dead or alive'?"

Creed chose his words. "I haven't decided."

Creed felt Fuller's hand on his shoulder for a bit of reassurance, and said nothing. They all rode on for a few minutes, the snow cutting harder, before Bishop said, "In case nobody's told you, the sun's going down."

CHAPTER TWELVE
Reunion

The three-story house, with the lattice protecting each floor, looked as if it had been plucked from a tony street in St. Louis and dropped in the middle of nowhere. Years of weather and living in the hard country had left their mark on this beauty, but she still stood tall, the lamps in each window welcoming strangers as they approached.

A soiled dove, with tight, blond curls pulled the Navajo blanket closer to her shoulders as she watched the three riders tie their horses to the hitch rail in front of Widow Kate's. The night was damn cold, with her unmentionables sticking to her skin, but at this moment she liked it better on the porch than being curled up in her warm bed, with nowhere to run.

She seemed to Lem Wright to still be of schooling age when she asked, "Is you the law or customers?"

Howard said, "The law."

Soiled Dove dropped a pinch of snuff behind her lower lip, sticking it out while she thought, then said, "Good. There's been too much trouble tonight."

Chaney took out his small-handled Colt, and Howard sniffed, "Borrow that from your granny?"

Howard pushed around the horses and opened his coat so the Dove could see his deputy's badge pinned over his huge belly, "Look at me, little girl. What the hell's the problem?"

She blinked twice at Howard. "That crazy man killed Miss Kate. I had to get out."

"What crazy man?"

"The one who never pi-roots, just talks. He was a general or somethin.'"

"What room's he in?"

"He was in Miss Kate's office, but I dunno now."

Lem smiled at the girl. "You forgot your shoes. Your toes'll freeze off."

The Dove moved the snuff with her tongue, wiggling her grubby feet. "I guess I wasn't thinkin'."

Lem Wright tucked the blanket around the Dove's feet, then held open the large door with the stained-glass Chinese symbol for "love" in its center, keeping his gun hand ready over his Remington New Model.

Lem's deadeye fixed on Howard and Chaney. "Time for the reunion."

They went inside, while the Dove rubbed her toes and started a song she didn't know all the words to. Lem drew his pistol, and was careful not to let the door slam behind him.

The blood pooling around Widow Kate soaked the Persian rug, casting it purple where she was lying. Her body was balled together next to her comfortable chair, hands clamped against the side where the blade had slit deep. Kate's eyes were closed, and there was no reaction when Beaudine nudged her with his boot. A few of the line girls peered silently from the office doorway, while the only one saying anything was doing it in shrill Chinese.

Beaudine was unfazed as he wiped the blood from

the ivory letter opener before slipping it in his pocket; the staring eyes, the Chinese accusations, weren't reaching him at all. He moved quickly, snatching up carved jade and cast-gold trinkets, then stuffing his coat until it bulged. He gave Kate's pipe a deep sniff, tasting the opium residue in the back of his throat, before noticing Howard, Lem, and Chaney standing just feet away.

Beaudine waited for a sign of respect from his men until Howard offered, "Still crazy as a shit-house rat?"

Beaudine said, "I hear you build coffins for heathens," as he opened the drawers of the large desk, dumping out letters, paperwork, ledgers, and more onto the floor.

The Chinese girl started yelling again, and Howard thumbed his badge at her face. "Get upstairs. I might even see you later."

The Chinese girl dry-spit, "Yeah, without paying," but the line girls all backed their way up the front stairs as Beaudine kept rifling, smashing an abacus against the floor, then tearing through the bottom of a drawer, bloodying his knuckles.

Beaudine's face was washed with sweat, his words strained, "That cow has cash hidden somewhere, and she's not keeping any secrets. Not now."

Lem Wright said, "Nobody ever gives it up easy, do they?"

"Always a joke, Deadeye."

Beaudine grabbed a box decorated in filigree and topped with a two-headed dragon with ruby eyes. The ornate heads were locked in battle, and when he pressed down on one of them, the lid sprung open, revealing another stash of opium. Beaudine dumped the pure on the desk, then pocketed the box.

Lem said, "Is that why we're here? Robbing a whore-house?"

"You're here for gold, the letter." Beaudine nudged Kate again with his toe. "Kate tried to include herself in our plans, and had to be dealt with. The cleaver's tied to my saddle, and she's damn lucky I didn't want to brave the cold to get it. Is that Betsy?"

Howard had his Remington New Model out, the hammer back. "You remember."

"She doesn't look like you've taken very good care of her, or yourselves."

"She still shoots."

Beaudine ripped aside the drapes, revealing bare walls. "But can you?"

"You dragged me into somethin' 'cause we shared a cell one time, and I'm still not one dollar richer, but my soul's poorer."

"Not much I can do for your soul, but you're closer to that Bishop gold now than you know."

"By walking into another killing?"

"I was defending what's ours."

Lem said, "We've been through a hell of a lot, but we made it. You've got one minute to tell us what this is, and then I ride out—clean."

Beaudine studied him. "You giving me an order, Deadeye?"

Lem's gun was leveled. "A choice."

Howard kept the Remington New on Beaudine's chest, the grin on his face spreading. "I know I ain't that bright, but I'd say you got less than a minute, by that clock on the wall?"

"Or Betsy screams?"

"Oh, I'll bust your back first. Then, when you're screamin', I'll let Betsy do her job."

Beaudine stepped around the desk. "Bishop survived his punishment."

Lem said, "I know. He cut down Chester, 'cause he was after you. I missed him by a couple of hours."

"I'd say that was fortunate for you both." Beaudine looked beyond the guns to Chaney. "I didn't recruit you."

Lem said, "He was with Chester and figures to take

his place. Probably be of more use, if this ain't another bullshit run."

"Bishop still has the gold he stole with his brother, and we can get it."

Howard said, "Jesus save me, I wanna bust you in half."

Beaudine continued, "An officer of my acquaintance will be taking Bishop prisoner, and will deliver him. To us."

"Here?" Lem's voice raised.

"A two-day ride into the hills to the old Goodwill strike. We'll need supplies, and some extra guns. Kate should've ponied cash, but she gave us plenty to barter with."

Lem said, "You still haven't said exactly what we're walking into. I like to know what to carry, what to load."

Beaudine gave his words mannerly import. "You were always thorough, Deadeye. My co-officer, Captain Creed, thinks he has a right to an equal share for delivering Bishop, but we'll disabuse him of that notion."

"Bull—!"

The rest of the word was the scream of Howard's giant fist crashing into the top of Kate's desk, splitting the wood nearly in half. He raised Betsy like a club to smash across Beaudine's head, but instead took a deep breath they all could hear, and turned the gun around in his palm, aiming it again at the major.

Howard's hand and voice were shaking, his chest heaving, "I made a promise I wouldn't swear or kill no more, but you're pushin' me with this; this part of a million dollars, that ain't real!"

Beaudine said, "Howard, I know what it is to be out of control, but I'm about myself right now, and you need to be the same. This money is real. You know that."

"What makes it more real now than that night with the doc and his family?"

Beaudine looked straight down the barrel of Howard's gun to his flicking eyes. "All of these people who want a piece, like Madame Kate on the floor. Doesn't that tell you? I wrote that letter for Dev Bishop, believing every word. Men facing death tend to be truthful."

"John Bishop wasn't."

Beaudine corrected Lem with a scolding. "Bishop refused to cooperate. There's a difference. After that night, I never stopped looking. You scattered, but I stayed with it, and every time I turn around, there's someone new who wants a share, because they knew that gold was someplace. And the doctor's the key to the moneybox."

Lem said, "He didn't give it up before, and now he's got nothing to lose, so why would he tell?"

"Because there's only one thing he cares about now— us. He'll bargain."

Lem smiled. "The gold for the chance to wipe us out." He put his hand on Howard's arm, lowering his gun. "This Creed will deliver?"

"He will, but won't be alone."

"This half a million is gonna have a lot of blood on it."

Beaudine pocketed one last jade trinket. "What half a million doesn't?"

Chaney finally said, "Maybe everyone here, if Bishop uses that double-barrel rig. I've seen it, you haven't."

Beaudine looked down on Chaney. "You're new to me, and not impressive at all."

Lem cut him off, "He'll be more use than Chester was. At least he's seen Bishop, the way he is now."

Chaney said, "So did Chester Pardee."

Beaudine straightened his collar. "Then it's up to you to be properly prepared. You want some kind of a share of this? You're going to earn it." He walked out of Kate's office tall and straight, ready for a parade.

On the front porch, Soiled Dove was rubbing her feet with both hands, as Howard and Chaney swung onto their horses. Lem took a torch from a barrel by the front door, watching Dove as he lit it.

Dove's lower lip protruded, more snuff filling it. "That's a courtesy for the boys who ride in at night. The good customers."

Lem got onto his horse with the torch. "I'll come back, and promise to spend a fortune."

Howard punched the air with a giant fist, and said, "I'm back-slidin'. Five minutes with Beaudine, and I don't have a Christian feeling left. There's lumber 'round back. I could make that dead woman a coffin. It won't take long."

Lem said, "You're wanting to do it is enough to keep your soul safe."

Chaney said, "I figured we'd be given a map or something, not drafted into another war."

Lem turned his eye on Chaney. "Another? I didn't know you served. Thank you for your sacrifice."

Lem snickered at his own joke, making Chaney feel like a fool, again. Chaney let his fingers dance on the Colt he'd just re-holstered, playing with the idea of ending this game right now.

Lem had been watching Chaney's hand. "Stakes getting too high?"

That's when Soiled Dove piped up. "So, you all arrest that crazy man?"

Lem said, "He's coming with us."

"The regular sheriff's away 'til tomorrow sometime, and he's gonna be awful touched up about this. He makes a lot of money from Miss Kate."

Howard said, "You tell the sheriff that we got the killer, and he don't need to bother with nothin'."

"Somebody'll have to step up, take Kate's place," Lem said.

Soiled Dove wrinkled her nose at him. "Maybe me?"

"Maybe. Go on inside, and get warm for real."

Soiled Dove got up, and padded inside as Beaudine rode around the far side of the porch, sporting an officer's hat that had been stripped of its braiding, and his many-grey tunic, newly sewn together. Even made of bits and pieces, Beaudine was again impressive, with the long cleaver tied behind his saddle, the blade wrapped in butcher's paper.

Beaudine said, "How're you fixed?"

Howard was still holding Betsy. "Belly wash and jerky."

"That's going to change."

"Words."

Beaudine looked to Howard. "We've had our wait, but now the Bishop gold is ours for the taking. Are you loyal or not?"

"To you?"

"To the mission. If you have to light out"—Beaudine pulled the cleaver from behind his saddle, and hefted it with both hands—"I'll hold no ill feelings."

Lem said, "What if we turn our guns on you?"

Chaney sat up alert, his hand on the Colt, but again, he was holding back. Waiting. He looked to Lem's frozen eye, to Howard and his clenched fists, and finally to Beaudine.

Everyone seemed ready to pull when Beaudine spoke, his eyes fixed on something none of them could see. "Delivering death is our mission. It's your choice who we deliver it to: each other, or the bastards who're denying us a better life."

Beaudine urged his horse, breaking away from the three. "I know where I'm heading."

Howard, Chaney, and Lem turned their mounts around, guns back in their holsters, or tucked into belts. Lem held the torch for all of them, showing the way.

Howard said, "Shit-house rat crazy."

Deadeye Lem Wright added, "And we're gonna follow."

Chaney said, "For now."

CHAPTER THIRTEEN
The Heart of the Enemy

"Sir, I'm getting our dinner. I can't be sitting around doin' nothing. Uh, with your permission."

Hector stood at attention before Creed, pointing to a distant gathering of trees that were being swallowed by the long shadows of the setting sun.

After a moment, it dawned on Hector that his pointing was useless and he dropped his arm. "Them rabbits went right for the woods. I can still see their tracks. Must've been five or six. I can get 'em and we'll be eating for the rest of the trek, sir."

Captain Creed said, "Take one of the men with you, and be back in an hour. You can tell time?"

"Yes, sir."

The pocket watch that Creed took from his jacket was a fine, ornate piece, presented to him by his men for his leadership skills. He held it in front of the boy by its gold chain. Hector swallowed air before gently putting it in his palm. "Thank you, sir."

"I expect my watch and you back in an hour, with or without dinner."

The hour bled forty minutes, and White Fox had built a fire to burn low and steady. The fire was obeying, shielded from the wind by a small wall of snow that she'd iced from a canteen, making it solid. Bishop and Creed were beside the flames, as she stood by, waiting for Hector to return from the woods with an armful of rabbits.

Bishop said, "Hector's a good boy."

"Yes. He volunteers for every duty he can. Now he comes up with his own."

"My son was a lot younger, but there's a resemblance of spirit."

"All boys look the same. That's why we give them uniforms."

"They weren't the same to me, Creed."

"Keep telling yourself that. You seem to need it."

Just beyond the fire, the horses and Creed's other six men were dark shapes, outlined by the orange flicker. The six stretched out, assuming positions that favored their bandaged wounds. Their talk was all worn-out sneers.

Fuller took hold of Creed's horse, pulling the bottle of sipping bourbon from the saddlebag, where it was tucked next to the shotgun rig. Little of the bourbon was gone.

Fuller said, "Captain, you think—?"

"Each man gets one swallow to keep out the chill."

"I'll make sure."

Fuller walked to where the guns were stretched out, and handed off the bottle to Fat Gut, who guzzled deep. Fuller snatched it back, wiped the top, and passed it on to the next.

Fat Gut leaned against his Winchester like a crutch, bourbon wetting his chin. "You're really pushin' it with me, boy."

Fuller said, "No, I ain't," before letting the next one drink and throwing Fat Gut some more words. "I outranked you during the conflict, so I figure I still do. Wanna try? I'll even help you stand up."

Fat Gut rubbed his leg wound, shrugging. "It's too damn cold. Lucky for you."

Bishop watched Fuller pass the bourbon among the hired guns before saying to Creed, "Your bottle's getting some real use. Grant'd be proud."

Creed's voice was in the back of his throat. "I expected better of you than cheap jokes. We're bundled around a campfire, not sitting back in front of a fireplace. Men who served are supposed to have a better fate."

"Who claimed that?"

"It's not policy. It's what you hope for: that sacrifice will be rewarded."

"Like the money you're going to get for us?"

Creed said nothing, just let the flames bounce across the dark amber of his glasses, outlining the edges. Finally, Bishop said, "There's a bounty on me, and I never robbed a bank or a train."

"You killed a man."

"That you said needed killing. You agreed with me."

"I still do, but that don't change what's going to happen."

Bishop felt the piece of arm that remained through his sleeve. "So how the hell do you know about Beaudine?"

Creed took warmth from the fire. "Because he tried to join my regiment. The man'd worn the grey, claimed he had a change of heart. But then we found out he was wanted for strangling some strumpet, arrested right after he'd signed his papers. Not even Southern-born, but claimed he was a plantation owner—with acres of cotton and a hundred slaves—who felt the need to serve. He never served anywhere, except in prison or the crazy house."

Bishop let Creed's words sink in before he said, "You

told me something, Creed, but it's not enough. It's just a hell of a coincidence."

"One of God's jokes—the war connects us all."

"More than the war. I want Beaudine dead."

"I know the feeling."

"You lost your eyes, I lost my family."

"And your limb."

"I don't care about that."

"I wouldn't give it no never mind if I found the replacement you did."

Bishop paused, and then, "You've known me a hell of a long time. You're really thinking you can play with me like this?"

"I'm in command, and you're a prisoner."

The back of Bishop's left hand smashed into Creed's jaw, sending his glasses flying into the fire. Bishop grabbed Creed's blue lapel. "You're talking in circles! Tell me what the hell your intentions are!"

Creed smiled, his scarred-over eyes meeting Bishop's. "Only give the enemy enough information to confuse."

The barrel of Fuller's rifle was sudden, and steady, over Creed's shoulder, pointing right in the center of Bishop's forehead.

One of the guns shouted out, "Problem, Creed?"

Fuller said, "No problem, go back to your bourbon." Then, to Bishop, "Know why I like the Morgan-James, Doc? It's lighter than a Sharps, and balances easy. I still have to load every shot, but that just means I can't waste any. So you let go of the captain, and fetch his glasses."

White Fox stood perfectly in place, letting the wind blow through her hair and the fringing on her jacket, while casting her eyes to Bishop, then Creed, and the rifle Fuller had leveled. She nudged Bishop with her foot and said, "*Ována'xaeotse.*"

Bishop released the lapel, but stayed fixed on Creed's face, which showed no movement, no feeling. He then grabbed the glasses from the low-burning fire, the flames snapping at the metal frames, before cooling them off in the snow. Bishop pressed the glasses into Creed's palm. "Not even scratched."

Fuller didn't lower the rifle even a quarter inch.

Creed inspected the lenses with his fingertips before slipping them on. "The Dr. John Bishop I knew would never strike a man in anger."

Bishop took a breath. "He's dead."

Creed said, "Then maybe we should bury him."

"Or each other."

Fuller kept aiming even as Bishop held up his empty right sleeve. "See? Nothing. My temper got the best of me. It won't again."

"But you're smarter than any man here, Doc. That means you can't be trusted."

White Fox looked to Fuller and again said, "*Ována'x-aeotse.*"

Bishop said, "That means 'calm down.'"

Fuller held for a few more heartbeats, then rested his rifle on his shoulder. "I know what it means. My mama was half-Cheyenne. Didn't look like her, though."

White Fox unclenched her fists, returning her gaze to the distant trees, which were now sharp black jags against the white, separating the moving snowdrifts from the starless night. The moon fought to break through the heavier clouds, to throw a shred of light on the miles of blanket below, but couldn't.

Creed said, "What about the boy? Do you see him?"

Fuller said, "Not yet."

"It's been exactly one hour."

"I don't have no watch, sir."

"Don't need it; I know what an hour feels like."

Creed wiped his eyes under his glasses. "He shouldn't have gone."

"Hector's chasing rabbits and he ain't alone. You sent that one with the busted head with him, the loudmouth who always cheats at Monte."

"I know all that. Someone needs to find them both."

"You want me to stand guard on these two, or start a search party?"

Fuller half grinned at Bishop, while Creed said, "We've got enough guns for the prisoners. Are they sober?"

"Sober enough."

"I'm ordering someone to go into those woods and find Hector!"

Fuller nodded, about to assure Creed he'd bring Hector back safe, when White Fox bolted. In a single motion, she sprang beyond the firelight, landed in the snow, and then started running for the tree line. Fuller whipped his rifle to his shoulder, pressing his eye against the long sight that was nearly the length of the barrel.

White Fox darted in one direction, breaking into another, then off again. Animal-fast, but she was shadow-boxed by the snow, her back and shoulders coming into brief focus in Fuller's sight. His trigger finger tightened.

A shout ripped from Bishop as he blocked Fuller, grabbing the barrel with his left hand even as pistol shots popped from the other hired guns. Fuller hard-swung the rifle, catching Bishop in the shoulder, knocking him back, onto the fire.

White Fox dove into the trees.

Creed barked, "Sniper, what do you have?"

Fuller focused his sight on the movement he could barely make out along the deep shadows of the woods; it was something dark moving through something darker. Fuller wiped snow from the front of the scope with his thumb, and then pressed his eye to the piece, aiming down. "I'm seeing some shadows, but can make out her head. Your call, Captain."

Bishop said to Creed and Fuller, "Fox can see in the dark. She's not escaping—she's going to find your boy!"

"We're losing the shot!"

Creed finally said, "Don't take it."

Fuller lowered the rifle. "She's gone."

"I recall seeing you pray, Bishop. So you better get to it, begging God to make sure that dog-eater comes back with Hector. Because I am thirsty to have you shot."

Bishop said, "But you have to deliver us alive."

Creed almost smiled. "A dying man still counts as alive, and that gives me a lot of leeway."

The dark was enormous and far reaching, growing out of the ground and towering into the surrounding night, where it met more darkness. Thick, mountainous clouds churned high in the Colorado sky, and let no light escape from the stars or the moon.

Hector sat at the base of one of the huge shapes, straddling the roots that twisted from its trunk into the snow, blowing warmth into his palms. At this hour, the woods weren't trees, just blackened giants, with a hundred huge arms, and standing so close to each other, they formed an enormous wall to the outside. The path between the trees was scraping-narrow, with each tangled access looking like the next and the next. Moving twenty feet in any direction only confused him more, and so he sat, with three dead rabbits and a man's corpse beside him.

Hector blew again into his cupped hands, feeling his own warm breathing against his palms and his face. Even the gloves his mama knit for him weren't helping. He began rubbing the cold-tingle out of his arms when he heard something: that almost-squeak of a foot pressing into the snow. Hector turned; the movement could be right in front of him or a hundred feet away, but all he could make out was the shadowed dark.

To Hector, it sounded like a critter, or a person, or another kind of critter. He tried to pull his pistol from his jacket, but the steel felt colder than ice, and the sight got caught on his pocket. He yanked the pistol, a piece of his jacket hanging from the barrel, but with nothing to aim at. Nothing. There was another footfall, that odd sound coming closer. Hector stumbled forward, pulling his leg away from the corpse folded beside him, and brought the pistol up, whipping it from dark shape to dark shape, wanting to shoot. At anyone, or any thing.

"Hector, put down that gun."

Hector gripped the pistol with both hands to steady it as he aimed blindly at the trees. Then he heard, "I'll take you to camp."

White Fox stood before the boy, holding out her hands. Hector blinked, thinking she was another trick of the shadows. "But you can't talk."

White Fox eased the pistol from him, lowered the hammer, and then slipped the pistol behind her belt. She waited until the weapon was secure, with Hector watching, before saying, "You mean I'm only able to speak my Cheyenne? No. I understand. Everything. I hate it, but use your tongue when I choose it."

"But why now?"

"You don't speak Cheyenne. And you're afraid."

"No, no, I ain't." Then Hector nodded with chattering teeth. "Jed died. Right where he's laying."

White Fox bent next to Jed's body, which was twisted in an impossible position, his legs tangled in the tree's knotted roots and his head half buried in the snow, a white frosting building on his face.

Hector said, "We got them rabbits and started back. He tripped and that was it. Said he was dizzy, that his head still hurt from when you hit him."

"*Onéstôhóné.*"

"I don't know what that means."

"He was a fool."

"Uh, yes, ma'am."

White Fox struck a match on her leathers, the tiny flame showing the cut between the snow-heavy pines.

Hector said, "I didn't see that. We kept goin' in circles. I was afraid I was gonna end up like Jed."

"I know these woods now."

"But ain't you still our prisoner?"

"Yes."

"You could leave me here."

"You belong at the camp, at the fire. *Néhe'éohtsé'tov.*"

White Fox turned for the tree-break. Hector grabbed the rabbits. "Ma'am, I surely hope you asked me to come with you," he said and followed her, sidestepping the snow-and-pinecone-covered branches that had walled him in.

Fox's movements were quick-sure, weaving around the trees without disturbing them at all while Hector was slapped by the branches as he tried to keep up, icy snow always in his eyes. Every twenty steps or so, he'd reach out to brush Fox's back, assuring himself she was still in front of him. She'd glance over her shoulder and tell him, in her own English, to hold the rabbits high so not to be torn by nettles. Hector did as he was told.

Hector said, "I-I got these right off, like I said. But then we lost the sun, and Jed tripped up. Nobody can see in this dark."

"Me."

"Except you, ma'am."

CHAPTER FOURTEEN
Snow Blind

More than an hour had passed, and the image Fuller saw through the long sight was hazy with cold fog: silhouettes coming out of the shadows of the pines, becoming clearer and clearer with each step, as they moved onto the expanse of snow between the trees and Creed's camp. Fuller lowered his sniper's rifle when he recognized White Fox, with Hector stumbling behind, keeping the rabbits over his head. Bishop stood.

Fuller gulped his laugh. "Tarnation."

Hector broke from White Fox, churning the snow as he ran toward the fire, waving his three trophies. He called to Creed. The captain grabbed Bishop's shoulder and pulled himself up, facing Hector's voice before opening his arms like a father welcoming a son back home. Creed then stiff-backed, froze his arms at his side, and killed the rush of feeling.

Creed's guard was barely down, but it didn't escape Bishop. "Hector's a good boy, like my son would have been. And Fox made sure he wasn't lost to you."

"That tripe won't work. Your debt'll be paid."

Hector offered Creed a flustered salute. "Reporting back, sir. Uh, mission accomplished."

Creed said, "Not well. I blame Jed for this foolishness."

"We lost Jed."

"Report?"

"Uh, he tripped, busted his head again. He'd been sneakin' from a bottle you didn't know about, sir. He was pretty drunk."

"No more missions, boy. No more losses. Where's the damn dog-eater?"

Hector coughed up his words. "Begging your pardon, sir, but she found me. I know I did wrong for the company, but she didn't. And she talked regular English."

"She's standing with you, Bishop?"

Bishop absently raised his right arm, as if the shotgun were there, to fire both barrels into the blind man. His anger heating, he chose his words carefully: "White Fox is right here with *me*, Creed. And you owe her thanks."

"Sniper Fuller?"

Fuller eyed White Fox as she laced her fingers around Bishop's left hand, then said, "Hell, yes. The prisoners are accounted for, sir."

That's when Fat Gut screamed from the other side of the fire, "My leg's killin' me, cuz! You've gotta do something!"

Creed said, "Either cure him or kill him. He's been a weight on us too long."

Bishop said, "You giving me an order, Creed?"

"And you both better obey it."

"Want your man treated? I'll need my kit."

"On my Pride."

Fuller stepped around Creed's tall horse, and opened one of the hand-scrolled saddlebags that draped Pride's haunches. He took out the shotgun rig, slung it over his shoulder, while finding the medical bag.

Fuller kept his back to Bishop, making sure he got a good look, teasing him with the rig. The shotgun was less than two feet from Bishop, and he raised his half a right arm as if to reach for the weapon, but Fuller was having his fun. White Fox gently squeezed Bishop's shoulder.

"Sorry, Doc, but that special rig ain't what you asked for." Fuller laughed, then produced the field kit, giving it to White Fox in a deliberate motion. "It's a good thing you came back. The doc needs you." She tucked it under her arm.

Fuller noted the LT. BISHOP in gold across the leather. "I am surrounded by officers." Fuller admired the shotgun before putting it back behind Creed's saddle. "That gun's a hell of a thing. It's a part of you, ain't it?"

Bishop let the words settle. "When I need it to be."

Fuller grinned, but there was nothing friendly there.

White Fox walked by the painted, stroking him along his withers as she moved to the group of hired guns crouched by their own, small fire. The painted snorted, bobbing his head in recognition. White Fox looked to Bishop, who was right behind her. Their eyes met, passing a message he understood.

The guns were snickering something, but it was too low to hear. Bishop stood in front of them, waiting for one of them to jaw something else. Nothing came, so he said, "One-armed man and a woman, and we cleaned your clocks pretty good."

One of them, sporting a fancy blue kerchief, threw out, "But it didn't change nothing. You're here. The squaw had her chance, and she comes back. How mule-ass stupid is that?"

Fat Gut yelled, "Oh, you're a great one, Doc! Shoot us, then dig the bullets out! My leg ain't nothin' but a lick and a promise, you son of a bitch!"

Bishop and White Fox settled by Fat Gut, who was sprawled on a filthy blanket, his wounded leg stretched out with a bandage newly pink from leaking. Gut was cradling the Winchester, its stock muddy from where he'd been using the rifle as a crutch, sinking it into the wet ground.

"Lose the rifle."

Fat Gut wrapped his paw around the trigger guard. "That ain't happening."

Bishop said, "You have to be able to sit up so I can do this properly. You can't with that thing on your chest."

Gut looked around at the others: two were ready to shoot, casual as hell, and Blue Kerchief wasn't tamping down his hatred for Bishop at all. It read on his face, and Gut liked that, so he let Fox take the rifle. She placed it near the med bag.

Fat Gut said, "Needs more than one hand to shoot it anyways."

That's when the knives came out.

In the light of Creed's fire, Fuller drew his Bowie dagger from the beaded sheath on his belt, while thirty feet away, White Fox handed Bishop a surgical blade. Fuller "ringed" the largest of the rabbits, slicing a notch through the fur just above its feet, separating the skin from the leg muscles. As he did this, Bishop laid the surgeon's blade across Fat Gut's bandages.

Gut sniffed, "You and your squaw gonna operate again? I didn't say nothing about that."

"The wound has to be checked, and I need her hands."

"Her hands and those nice titties. I like them hangers. How about sharing a little? That'd make me feel a hell of a lot better than what you're doin'."

White Fox didn't allow herself a reaction to Fat Gut's mouth. She couldn't. Instead, she held his leg steady as Bishop cut through the last of the bandages, exposing the wound.

"She might just finish what she started. She's taken scalps," Bishop said as he tossed the bandages into a stained pile. "Got a little infection. I'll clean it, but it'll burn."

Fat Gut turned his head away, snorting. "Just hurry the hell up. Do it."

"Never argue with a patient."

By the fire, Fuller tossed Hector the rabbit. "Peel him," he said before casting his eye back on White Fox, as she wiped a surgeon's blade, laid it aside, and handed Bishop another.

Sometime, when Fuller wasn't watching, Fox had tied her hair tight behind her with a leather thong.

A feeling nudged Fuller: it was the bristling he felt when there was an enemy sniper close by, but couldn't be seen. During the war's last days, he'd climbed a tree to take position, and there had been a Reb, perched on a branch and hidden by leaves, loading a Sharps long-range rifle. He'd gotten him with the same Bowie he was using on Hector's rabbits. The Reb hadn't made a sound.

Now, that bristling was back, and White Fox was the reason. Fuller was ready for her move, prepared to shoulder his weapon. He said to Hector, "She talks English?"

"Better than me."

Creed barked, "Fuller, you can't skin a jack faster than that? Boy, stop the jabber and get the meat on the fire!"

Hector said, "Yes, sir!" as he peeled the fur down the big one's legs to its belly, where it gathered in folds. Sniper Fuller ringed the next jack, cutting quickly, and a little deep, before grabbing the last one, its blood sticky between his fingers.

White Fox tore a shirt into clean strips, and Fuller whipped around at the sound. The bandages, scalpels, and Winchester were set out between her and Bishop, who was daubing Fat Gut's wound.

Creed barked, "Doctor, finish up your business!"

White Fox regarded the blind man shouting orders before saying, "*Exanomóhtá?*"

"Yes."

Fat Gut winced. "What the hell's that?"

Bishop looked up from the arrow wound. "She asked, am I prepared?"

The scalpel was a flash from White Fox's hand into Blue Kerchief's throat, the blood-jet around the blade instant as Blue fell back, firing his pistol wild into the sky.

Bishop grabbed the Winchester in front of him, pumped it with his left hand, and blasted the next hired gun who was reaching. The slug sent him spiraling off his feet, his pistol not clearing his holster. He hit the ground red, calling for his ma.

Fox grabbed the scalpels, then busted Fat Gut's lower teeth with her heel, cracking his jaw sideways.

It all took less than a minute.

Fuller turned, swinging his rifle around on its strap, bringing the sight to his eye, just as Fox leapt on the back of her painted. Fuller thumbed the hammer. Easy kill shot.

Chaos exploded.

The painted reared wild, his head whipping from side-to-side, with Fox hanging on, turning the animal on Fuller. The horse's huge legs smashed Fuller square in the chest like two pistons, tossing the sniper clean off his feet, hard into Creed and Hector, shattering ribs, and Creed's dark glasses.

Screams and gunfire polluted the air.

One of Creed's men used Fat Gut for cover, blasting at Bishop and White Fox from behind Gut's huge belly, scorching his shirt. Gut screamed himself raw, as Bishop fired a single shot from the hip, missing Gut and hitting Creed's man between the eyes.

Bishop was in motion, didn't look twice at the dead.

He cooled the barrel of the Winchester in the snow, before using it to snag the handle of his kit on its sight.

Gut's broken-teeth-screams never stopped as Bishop charged to Fox and the horses, the kit dangling from the rifle.

The painted chopped air with his legs, while Fox swung him around, kicking wild. Her weapon. A Creed man opened up with a revolver, and the painted bucked at him, shattering his arm to nothing. He went down shooting and screaming.

Captain Creed shouted blind: "The prisoners! Report! Goddamn you!"

Bishop yanked at Pride's saddlebags, grabbing for the shotgun rig. A slug ripped past his ear.

Fuller struggled to his feet, reaching his rifle.

White Fox called above it all, "*Asêsta'xêstse!*"

Bishop leapt onto Creed's Pride, just as White Fox and the painted bolted. Both animals ran for the open snow, the prisoners tight on their backs.

Creed's voice strained, "Shoot them, goddamn it!"

Hector had his pistol raised, both hands shaking. "I— I can't shoot her!"

"I sure as hell can!"

Fuller's words stretched into a howl as he brought up his rifle, pressing against one of his busted ribs. He steadied on his target, and fired. The hammer dropped, and the ball ripped from the Morgan-James in a spit of flame. Fuller's jaw clenched at the recoil, fighting the pain of the weapon slamming back into him.

The targets kept moving.

Captain Creed stood, hands deep in his pockets, listening for a scream. What he heard was the sniper's shot echo and die, above the cries of his own men.

A river and half a mountain away, on a trail that was little more than a finger poking through a frozen hillside, Lem and Chaney ate the last bit of their beans and jerky supper, while Howard shuffled a poker deck with massive fingers. Beaudine watched, drinking thick coffee.

Chaney said, "Look at the top card."

Howard turned over the four of clubs. "Shit."

"That's your card?"

"How'd you do that?"

Chaney took back the deck. "I can do it as many times as I want. That's my business."

Howard lunged, grabbing Chaney by the lapels. "You're cheatin' me!"

Lem eased the giant back. "How can he be cheating you when there's no money bet? You didn't lose nothing!"

Howard settled back, wiping the sweat from his face.

Beaudine threw the last bit of coffee into the fire. "When you go into battle, you better bring more than card tricks."

"I got more." Chaney spit out a chunk of hard gristle, and then drank deep from his canteen. Deadeye Lem laughed without making a sound.

Howard said, "I guess this ain't your style, is it?"

Chaney coughed. "I've done my time on the trail, but we're supposed to be eating better than this. Isn't that what you said?"

Beaudine took the long cleaver and a small wooden box from behind his saddle, and sat by the fire. He looked at Chaney as he opened the box, removing a Carborundum sharpening stone, and began running it against the cleaver blade. The sound of the stone against metal seemed to be Beaudine's answer.

Lem said, "You can't ask questions like that, gambler. You have to have faith, like the next card you draw is the one that gives you the winning hand. Only you can't cheat."

Howard snorted. "Winning hand. That's almost funny."

Beaudine didn't stop sharpening. "The troops are always impatient before the attack."

Chaney said, "We're not a troop. I've never been in any army, and they say you haven't neither."

Beaudine kept sharpening. "We were all denied that glory, but we won't be denied this. Chaney, if you're not a coward—"

"Coward has nothing to do with it."

"If you're not a coward, when we find that Bishop gold, you'll eat like a king for the rest of your life, however long it lasts."

"We got the extra rifles, ammo, and dynamite from that dry goods store." Chaney looked to Howard, who was tightening the cinch that held the crates of dynamite on a small pack mule. Two rifles were bound in cloth, and fit tight between the cases.

Chaney wiped his mouth. "But you didn't let us take any extra food."

Beaudine gave his response some pause. "You mean more whiskey, and that cake. A captain, a brother in arms, advises that a fighting unit runs best when it runs lean. I agree. You have a full belly and a purpose. *That* is doing better than most."

Lem raised his one good eye, tickled that Chaney had gotten caught up in Beaudine's obscure logic. He took a drink of Clinch Mountain whiskey and offered some to Howard, who shook his head. Lem had a little bit more, before: "When this Creed delivers Bishop, I don't know who the hell you think you're getting. The doc isn't the same man he was that night."

Chaney, under his breath: "No bullshit."

Beaudine held the cleaver out, inspecting the edge by the firelight. "You failed in your mission before, so I pray none of *you* are the same." Then he laid the cleaver by his side. "I know I'm not."

CHAPTER FIFTEEN
Bloody Dawn

They were running like hell.

White Fox leaned into the painted, her belly almost flat against his back, her face aligned perfectly to the side of his neck, holding on tight as they cut through the first row of pines and frost-bare shrubs that bordered the deeper woods. With her ear pressed to him, White Fox could hear the pounding strength of the painted's heart and lungs.

If White Fox glanced over her shoulder to check Bishop behind her on Creed's Pride, a low-hanging branch would smash her clean. So Fox kept down, the trees barely brushing over her, not catching her hair, and she sensed that Bishop was riding fine.

Bishop was handling Creed's horse well, keeping him near the painted, but with enough room to judge where Fox was leading next. The reins were knotted around his left hand as he kept the Winchester tucked under his right half-arm, barrel-down into the stirrup, so as not to catch a passing limb.

Every slight motion Fox made, Bishop did the same,

as she guided them through the woods, along the narrow trail she'd broken to find Hector. It was pure instinct, her knowing the cuts, slopes, and the icy bends, all in darkness.

They pushed their rides, gaining speed, dodging trees, their hooves just missing roots and tangles. The crack of distant gunfire split the air, and White Fox deliberately slowed, angling her ride too close to the base of a huge Colorado oak. The painted's legs half-skidded in the snow, and she fought a fall from his back, but Fox was still in control and the horse did as she wanted, before breaking into a hard run.

Creed's Pride stayed tight behind the painted, its legs more sure, keeping Bishop steady as they rode deeper into the dense black of the woods, leaving behind a mess of tracks for their pursuers to find.

At the camp, Fuller swung his pinto around as one of Creed's hired men fired more shots into the solid black of the woods.

"What the hell are you shooting at?" Fuller asked as he checked the ammunition in his jacket pocket. "They're running, and you're wasting shells! Grab some fire!"

The taller hired gun pulled a burning branch from the campfire, then mounted up. The other, shorter gun opened Blue Kerchief's fine jacket, liberating the pearl-handled Colt that was still holstered on his hip. Kerchief's blood smeared Short Gun's hands as he stuck the weapon in his waistband before grabbing the reins of Bishop's horse. The bay bucked as soon as Short Gun hit the saddle, not wanting him. The horse snapped twice more, then seemed to calm.

Short Gun howled, "The doc's got a hell of a ride! I want this one after we've dealt him his justice!"

"They're prisoners, and they need capturing! That's the order!" Creed shouted.

Fuller touched his arm for his attention, saying, "I'll shoot to wound."

"I heard you miss once already."

Fuller let the officious criticism go, turned to Hector. "Boy, you ride with the captain, take him along the tree line. Try and find your way over the hill. We'll meet on the other side of the woods come sun-up, *with the prisoners.* And watch yourself, there's nothing darker than Colorado midnight."

Hector saluted Fuller as Fat Gut tried to stand and talk through his busted, bloody teeth. "Wha' da thell am I supothed to do? D'at bitch got my Thinchester!"

Creed buried his anger under his words. "They took my Pride! One drop of that animal's blood is worth more than all of you put together."

Fuller gave a quick, "It's all cash to me, Captain!" and rode out, followed by the hired guns. The taller one rode with the torch, its flame showing the tracks of the escape running through the deep snow to the trees.

Fat Gut limped to a horse, but couldn't raise his leg to mount. "Boy, yuze got da' thelp me."

Creed turned to Fat Gut to blind-stare him down: "You've been a burden your whole life, and now you're worse than useless. If I didn't need every pair of eyes I'd tell the boy to blow a hole in you and be done with it."

No one moved.

"Get your horses! Move!" Creed's shout carried across the open snow, dying as jumbled noise just as Fuller rode to the edge of the tree line. He signaled for the gun with the torch to throw a light on the broken spot between the pines where White Fox and Bishop had run their horses.

Fuller made a slashing gesture across his throat for silence. He waved for Torch to stay close before they rode through the break. The only sound was of the horses cracking the snow's icy crust or snapping twigs, as they followed the tracks left behind by the prisoners. Fuller picked up the pace when he had a bead.

Short Gun kept Bishop's bay horse a few paces back,

as he ducked beneath branches and swatted pinecones away from his face. The swat sounded like the slap of a gun being pulled from its leather.

Fuller whipped around in his saddle, his Bowie ready to throw.

Short Gun rocked back in his saddle. "Goddamn, boy!"

"One or t'other, your mouth is gonna get you killed." Fuller replaced the knife. Short Gun nodded, clamping his hands over his mouth to show he wouldn't make another sound.

Fuller gaffed the pinto, breaking into a run. Torch followed, with Short Gun hanging back, until Bishop's bay horse galloped ahead on its own, as if it were searching out its rightful master.

Down the trail a mile, the woods were thickening into a maze, and White Fox held on to the painted's neck, slowing him. The shimmer of icicles on the trees was the only light that Fox could use as she turned painted toward a grouping of tall scrubs, marking where she'd found Hector.

Right behind her, Creed's Pride was running close. Bishop pulled back, breaking Pride's full-out run, stopping where Jed's twisted body was still lying. The horse stood in that spot, as if at attention.

The night's snowfall had tried to shroud Jed, while above him jags of ice fell from the high branches, bashing his face as if he'd been in an after-death brawl. For that moment, the hot breathing of the horses, and the crack of the icicles dropping was all that could be heard.

White Fox stepped over the corpse. "When I looked for the boy, I found the way out. Around the trees."

Bishop said, "The eye of the cat: *Ka'eeséhotame*?"

Fox allowed herself a half smile. "The gun."

They pulled the rig from Creed's saddlebags, a pocket of snow pelting them from the tall trees. Bishop shed his coat and shirt, and Fox fit his half-arm snugly into the prosthetic cup, then tightened the straps across his shoulders until they bit his skin. Bishop tied off the trigger line, with just enough slack to bring the double-barreled chest high. The gun was breeched, with only one shell loaded.

White Fox slipped Bishop's shirt and coat over the gun rig, her hand touching his chest to feel the steady beat of his heart. She nodded.

Bishop buttoned up with his left. "I didn't see their faces this time. At all. Just the eyes, so I could tell when they were about to make their move."

"Good."

Bishop then reached into the saddlebag for the twelve-gauge shells, but found nothing.

The posse was at the edge of the woods, where Fox's trail wasn't so distinct. Fuller halted the pinto to read the mess of horse tracks in the snow in front of them: nothing but mud and slush, sloppy in all directions. Torch stood in his stirrups, trying to make heads or tails: "I can't tell a damn thing. Maybe they doubled back."

Fuller said, "No, they're ahead of us, looking for a way out," and he kept moving, the others following.

Beyond the posse's view, Creed's Pride stood by Jed's body, lifting his legs in place, as Fox searched the rest of the saddle for shells. Reaching far into one of the leather pockets, she found a linen handkerchief tied neatly around a small object. The handkerchief was clean, with initials l.r.c. sewn into one corner. She loosened the knot, revealing a Union Army Medal of Honor awarded to Captain Dupont Creed tucked between the linen folds.

White Fox held the medal out in her palm.

Bishop said, "I was there when they gave it to him,"

before snapping shut the shotgun's breech, the left barrel loaded.

Fox dropped the medal back into the pocket. "No ammunition."

She stepped from Creed's Pride as splinters of orange flame spread across the surface of the icicles around her; bits of color reflected against the black pines.

White Fox and Bishop turned to see the torch, burning tiny-orange in the distance, but coming steadily closer to them. Bishop tossed her Fat Gut's Winchester. She checked it, pumped a round into the chamber, all the time watching the progress of the three-man posse.

Fox said, "I know places for us."

Fuller, Torch, and Short Gun reined in where the muddy trail was divided by the massive Colorado oak, its knotted branches blocking their way like giant arms. Horse tracks circled the base of the tree, and then seemed to lead off onto both of the trails behind it, going in separate directions.

Fuller recognized the Cheyenne trick, smiled, looked to his men: "They're not supposed to be together. These woods are too deep, they haven't had time to clear 'em." Then to Short Gun, "Follow that side south, we'll take t'other."

"But I won't be seeing nothing."

"You'll see us, and so can they. I got the doc's ammo, and that bitch can't hide in the dark if she's shooting."

The Torch and Short Gun exchanged looks about the black sniper, then split off.

Short Gun rode easily under the tree limb, and followed the left cut into the dark. Fuller and Torch ducked below the branches to get around the oak on their side. Fuller signaled for Torch to keep the flame high, as they veered right, keeping to the trail White Fox had used.

Deeper in the woods, Fox grabbed the reins of both horses, and led them down past a thick barrier of trees, holding the Winchester tight to her side. She tied the painted and Creed's Pride to a scrub pine, then crouched behind a large, ice-coated tree trunk that had been snapped in half by some forgotten storm. She braced the rifle and narrowed on her target.

Fox made no sound.

Fuller and the Torch seemed to be a few hundred yards or so down the trail, but riding closer. The flame of the torch danced off the Winchester's sight, as Fox narrowed her aim.

Following the trail, Fuller said to Torch, "Make yourself a good target."

"You don't give me orders, boy."

"You want to answer to Captain Creed?"

The Torch didn't say another word.

Bishop ran low, holding the rig to his chest, before rolling down a sloping grade, and coming up behind a spreading blue fir, its branches a perfect cover. He lowered the rig, keeping his elbow crooked so he was aiming from the waist, while watching the posse move toward White Fox's position.

White Fox held Fat Gut's Winchester steady against the tree trunk, her eye on the torch's flame as it vanished behind the silhouette of a tree, and appeared again moments later, bringing Fuller closer.

Then, the flame held steady. The riders had stopped, letting Fox make out the shapes of Fuller and one other man: just highlights, and the glint off their rifles. Two rifles. Fox tightened her trigger finger on the Winchester, counting the seconds.

Bishop watched from his position, and flexed his shoulders, drawing the shotgun's trigger line in tight.

Bishop knew the posse should be bigger than just two. Fox's trick had split them up, but where were the rest?

Bishop held his breath, waiting for the sound of a horse and rider coming down the small cut, to where he was hidden.

Waiting.

Fuller stepped down from his horse, and walked ahead, his footsteps breaking the snow. Torch was about to dismount, but Fuller hissed, "Stay there! Hold that thing higher!"

Torch did as ordered, telling Fuller to go to hell.

That's when the slug from the Winchester blew a hole clean through his chest, knocking him out of his saddle. The Torch, and the fire he was carrying, hit the ground, dead.

The fire sizzled to nothing in the snow, leaving darkness.

Fuller dove to the ground, Torch's chest wound a bloody geyser, soaking him. He wiped the blood from his eyes and took aim through his long sight, ready for the next shot.

Fox cracked off another round.

The flashes from the Winchester were spears of light that tore the dark, giving her away. Fuller eyed the flash, and zeroed in on the shadowed shape in the distance, half hidden by a fallen tree. He fired, yellow flame erupting from the Morgan-James, followed by a low thunder that pounded the ears.

The woman's scream that came next was a sudden burst of pain.

Bishop tore from his cover. "*Ma'êhóóhe!*"

There was no answer. Bishop waited, heart pounding. His eyes narrowed, watching Fuller's silhouette in the action of reloading, bringing the rifle to his shoulder and aiming where White Fox was hidden.

Bishop's heart was against his ribs.

The sniper drew his breath first, then tightened his

finger against the trigger. That's when the Winchester cut the dark again with a second shot that hard-spun Fuller to the ground.

Before Bishop could move, there was a pistol in his side from behind, and a nasal voice with a thick accent from the hills: "Doc, you're done. Your squaw and the slave killed each other, so now it's just us. Come on, I'm takin' you prisoner. Hell, I'll even let you walk alongside your own horse. I got it tied up yonder. Can't ask for more than that."

Bishop turned, the left barrel of the rig protruding from his sleeve and snug against Short Gun's stomach. Short looked to Bishop and said, "But, you doctored me up one time. Saved my life."

The blast blew out Short Gun's side, and he stumbled back against the blue fir, shooting near Bishop, into the ground, at the air, before collapsing. Bishop stood over him, watching his life soak into the muddy snow.

Short laughed, then blood-choked, "She's still dead. Settling up for that bitch wanting my hair. At least, we did that."

Dawn didn't come easy. The heavy clouds of night refused to break apart with the sun, draping everything in dull grey. It was the kind of light that cast no shadows, but you could feel sticking to your skin.

Hector guided his horse, with Creed riding tandem, down a small grade near an orchard that had been beaten by the snow: rows of apple trees stood dead in the blowing drifts.

Creed kept his hands on Hector's shoulders, making sure he had enough pull on the reins. "He was bred from the same stock as President Grant's own Cincinnati. Grant had Cincinnati all through the conflict, and never allowed anyone else on his back. I did the same. No one ever rode, fed, or watered Creed's Pride but me."

Creed rode on for a few moments. "Until now."

Hector said, "Pride won't do for anyone else the way he does for you, sir. You'll get him back."

"I can't see him anymore, but he's still the finest-looking animal there is. That I know."

"Yes, sir. All sixteen hands."

"That's right. Sixteen."

Hector stopped at the edge of the orchard, the thick woods breaking into distant pieces a few acres away, where the trees surrendered to this stretch of flat land. Hector shielded his eyes against the dull white to see any other riders.

Fat Gut galloped from behind, almost colliding with Creed and Hector, before pulling his swayback to a stop. Keeping his hand over his broken mouth, he chose words he thought he could pronounce. "I can't thee— make out—no one."

Creed said, "You in the right place, boy?"

Hector nodded, even though Creed couldn't see it. "Yes, sir. I think so."

"Either you are or you're not."

"No, sir, the other side of the woods. Yes, I'm sure."

Creed put a hand on Hector's arm. "Fuller said he'd meet us with my Pride. And the prisoners. You understand what that all means, boy."

"I do, sir. He'll be here."

Fat Gut spit pink, and tried again. "Did th-u—ever tell about de damn thorse?"

Creed said, "He knows."

"Ain't d'at your'n Pride?"

"What is it? Boy?"

Hector couldn't answer Creed right away; he was taken by the sight of Pride, running hard from the edge of the woods, the deep snow erupting around his every footfall. Glistening black against the acres and acres of white that met the grey sky.

The rider on his back had the reins clenched in his left hand, the right sleeve of his jacket pinned back.

"It's Pride, sir! And Bishop's on him!"

The bullet fired from the woods ripped through the rider's neck, sending him off the saddle, his foot catching the stirrup, his dead weight finally slowing Pride down. The horse dragged the body to the orchard, cutting a red furrow through the white.

Creed shouted for his horse, as Hector galloped to the orchard. Fat Gut hung back, as he saw Fuller following Pride's tracks out of the woods, his rifle across his chest, and his jacket a soak of dried blood.

Fuller actually nodded to Fat Gut as he rode to where Hector was helping Creed down from the saddle.

Creed said, "Pride?"

Fuller got off his horse with, "I never shot a horse I didn't mean to. He's fine. And I guess I am, too."

"The prisoners, do you have them? Bishop! Answer me!"

Fuller turned the body over with his foot. The slug had torn through Jed's neck, taking the bottom part of his face with it. Perfect sniping. After swearing under his breath, he had to admit, "No, sir. Just the wrong dead man."

"Report!"

Hector said, "That's Jed. I'd swore he busted his neck."

Fuller slipped his rifle bandolier over his head, and handed the weapon to Hector. "He did. Bishop used him as a decoy so they could escape through the woods. Almost worked, too."

Creed started through the snow, his hands palms out, reaching. "You failed."

"They outmaneuvered us, sir."

"But you're reporting that the prisoners are gone."

"Again, I said almost. The two idgits bought the farm, but I got the woman. Heard her scream after I shot. I took a bullet, and passed out. Not more than five minutes.

I came around, and saw your horse running through the trees, with Doc Bishop on him."

"Not Bishop."

Fuller opened his coat, and pulled at his shirt that was caked with blood that spread from a flesh wound just above his hip. White Fox's shot had passed clean through, and the cold had stopped the wound from opening further while freezing a curled snake of blood around his waist.

Fuller got the words out—"No, sir. That's my report"—before finding the ground. Hector took the rifle as Fuller lay down, eyes closed, the snow offering him comfort.

Creed spoke, with Fuller blind-feet away from the tip of his boots. "My Pride, with the wrong man on him? The only thing that's saving you right now is that horse."

Creed turned on his heel and started with purpose in the opposite direction, one hand sweeping the air in front of him.

"Captain?"

"Quiet!"

Creed kept walking a few steps, then stopped to listen. "Stay away from me, boy! No help! Mouths shut."

Creed heard a snort, and started for it. "So you followed the decoy? Damn foolish." Creed's hands found his horse, and a feeling of relief ran through him as he climbed onto Pride's back.

Humiliation spotted Fuller's words as Hector helped him to his feet. "I lost a hell of a lot of blood, but it got your Pride back. Sir."

"Not all of it, sniper."

CHAPTER SIXTEEN
The Price of Flesh

The stream was a slash of freezing black through a gentle slope of white-frosted hills, the running water showing up its stony bottom like a magnifying glass. Miles away from the thick woods that had hidden them, surrounded by emptiness, anyone who might be riding after Bishop and White Fox would be an easy target in the morning light.

Bishop crouched, refilling the breathing device with fresh water. Fat Gut's Winchester was within reach.

Bishop dipped the mechanical box into an icy shallow, then attached it to the rubber tubing that was hanging free from the mask covering White Fox's mouth. She was on the ground, lying next to the saddlebag they'd lifted from Creed's horse, with Bishop's medical instruments spilling from it.

The bay and the painted stood by, nosing the cold ground.

Fox rolled onto her back, her head lolling, while she tried to catch her breath. The air caught in her throat in sharp little stabs, as if she'd swallowed broken glass. Blood dotted the snow around her right ankle.

She tugged on the strap holding the mask in place, but Bishop pulled her hand away, attaching the rubber tubing, "I know you hate it, but don't move. Just be still and breathe. That's all you have to do, *háo'omóhtahe*."

Fox dropped her hand.

Bishop cranked the device, drawing the oxygen from the fresh water into the mask. The small leather bellows expanded, then contracted, forcing the air into Fox's lungs. Fox coughed, her body jerking forward, but she drew deep breaths through the spasms, and then laid back, her air flowing naturally.

He kept a steady motion, turning the handle, watching Fox's cheeks flush and her breathing relax. He said, "You saved me with this instrument, nurse. It's only right that I do it for you."

White Fox unhooked the strap that held the mask into place. "Not a nurse."

Bishop put the mask in his med bag. "Sorry, warrior."

"*Ho'toveotse.*"

"You're not weak."

"You carry the box because I'm too weak to breathe. *Ho'toveotse.*" White Fox spit the last word, as if she was cursing her own name.

"No, I've told you, it's called asthma. We don't know the cause, but your lungs close up. *He'poná*? Is that right?"

"*He'poná.* In the chest."

Bishop balanced the small box on his leg, and wrapped the tubing around it with his left hand. "I built this contraption for soldiers in the field, but carry it in case we need it. And we did. We. Not just you." He put that into his field kit also, and then put all of his gear into a saddlebag pocket. The bay was steady as Bishop buckled everything down tight.

Fox shook her head. "It shames me."

"You were strong enough to get us out of the woods, to take a bullet from Fuller."

White Fox rubbed her blood-wet ankle. "That was nothing."

"You got our horses back."

The bay lifted his head, snorting his comment, as Bishop pulled a piece of linen from the medical bag. "This should work. You prepped it." He wrapped the ankle wound. He tied it off. "Just a crease. I heard you scream. I didn't know what happened."

Fox retied the bandage. "Trying to get the sniper to stand. And I did. You were afraid for me."

"So, you're not weak."

When Fox stood, the painted came to her immediately. She swung onto his back without help. "You want Beaudine?"

The question seemed like a challenge to Bishop, but he looked into her eyes for a reason. Without her saying another word, she was giving him a way out, if he wanted it.

He understood and offered, "That's my cause."

"You got one man, and there will be many more."

"I'm ready. *Exanomóhtá.*"

Fox said, "Good. How do we ride?"

The bay pawed the cold ground, waiting, as Bishop tucked the saddlebag into place. "Pardee told me where Beaudine was going to meet his men."

"You trust this?"

Bishop mounted, slipping the shotgun rig into the specially made sling that hung alongside the saddle's leather fender. It felt good. "He was afraid of dying, and too small a man to try a lie."

"*Ho'toveotse?*"

"*Ho'toveotse.*"

Fox managed a rare smile. "You talk good. Now."

The grey light of morning died, as large snowflakes

drifted from the dark clouds that had rolled in over the mountains. The wind picked up, carrying distant thunder with it.

Bishop gently urged his bay, and the horse moved with trust and speed. White Fox was instantly, and naturally, next to him. They rode together in understood silence and with purpose, following the stream down a sloping hill, to the snowy valley beyond.

The dynamite was packed tight, the new, smaller sticks making perfect bundles of three for Howard to lay out on the ground. He pointed to the logo of the Nobel Dynamite Company on the lid of the crate. "This is their new stuff. It's got that nitro-glycer-een."

"What?"

Howard turned to Chaney. "Think I didn't know words like that?"

"I feel safer that you do."

"Maybe you better stop making me feel like a fool."

Beaudine stepped between them. "You're the best at what you do, or you wouldn't be riding with me." Then, to Chaney: "Better prove you can earn your share, boy."

Chaney said, "Yes, sir. Major."

Howard snorted his anger as he continued with the dynamite, setting the bundles next to each other on a blanket. His thick fingers played lightly across the explosives like they were piano keys, as he put them in perfectly even rows.

Chaney grabbed a coil of fuse, bringing his knife to meet it. Beaudine stopped him. "You don't cut 'til he knows where he's going to plant."

Howard was watching and burst, ripping the empty dynamite crate apart, and hurling the pieces toward one of the buildings, breaking some already broken glass. His chest was heaving, lips drawn over his black gums as he faced Chaney and shouted, "You got that boy? You have to do what I say!"

Chaney stayed still, his hand close to his Colt, and managed a half smile. "I know any one of you could kill me at any time. I know."

Howard said, "Damn right," anger rattling his words. Then he scrubbed his face with a pile of dirty snow, letting the cold feeling wrap his head, before shaking like a wet dog, bits of frost flying from his beard.

Beaudine said, "All right? Found your way back to us?"

Howard spit. "Look around. Half the damn mountain could come down on top of us. It's already blasted to hell."

"That's your professional opinion?"

Howard nodded. "Pro-fessional."

"Good. Creed's got a lot of men we have to bury." Beaudine turned to Lem. "Deadeye, dig in. And find the right place for this one."

Lem Wright nodded to Beaudine before tying his horse to a half an upright piling that stuck out of a massive gravel pile as if it were growing there. The upright was like the other broken pieces of wooden construction that had been left behind by the Goodwill Mining Company, as a sign hitched to a rusty chain so declared.

This nothing.

What was left of Goodwill was a deep pit, a scar blasted into the side of a small mountain. Along the edge of the pit, supported by tar-soaked rail ties, was a narrow, roofless shack that led to the shaft of the silver mine. Twists of steel that had been tracks into the shaft for the mule-drawn carts, curved out of the mine's mouth as fossilized tentacles, another useless reminder of a dead end.

Below the mine entrance, piles of jagged-black slag were pushed up against a few small buildings, their windows shattered and doors busted down by the weight of the mine's waste.

Behind an outhouse, rows of wooden markers made

up a weed-choked graveyard for the miners who hadn't made their fortune. The markers, all without names, were bent crooked by the icy winds that tore through the small canyon and were trapped there to beat the final remains of Goodwill silver into nothing.

Everyone in this part of Colorado knew Goodwill had been a false strike, and they'd cleared out as fast as they'd arrived, when the silver rush took the companies to Leadville. The few who'd stayed behind had ended up shooting each other, or freezing to death.

Lem said, "Major, if I can get on top of the old shaft, I'll pick off Creed's last riders as they come in. Howard sets off the dynamite, takes out some more, and the canyon's sealed. Then we'll clean up the ones who're left. I'll put Chaney in one of the outbuildings."

"He's with us on your say-so."

"He's with us because he smells the gold you've been touting. He's been having second thoughts, but if the gold's really close, he'll pull a trigger. I've seen it."

"So you trust him?"

"Not for one minute."

"Then if he's sacrificed, it's no loss. But we have to make sure to take all of Creed's men, so Bishop'll be ours. Alone."

Lem turned on his heel, his eyes fixed on the rim of the section of mountain that had been blown away. "We'll be trapped in here, too. Who picked this place?"

"Captain Creed."

"Perfect for a massacre."

Beaudine stood with his arms folded, staring at the entrance to the old mine, at something or someone that nobody else could see. Gone.

The body of the Döbereiner's lamp was jade, with a golden snake circling the base and opening its mouth where the small flame was lit. Soiled Dove held the head of the dragon pipe at an angle, catching the fire in the bowl so that the opium glowed, and then handed it to Widow Kate as the smoke began to curl.

Widow Kate drew the grey in slowly before John Bishop held out his left to inspect the ornate pipe. White Fox stood by, enjoying the waft of smoke as Bishop held it under his nose, nodding approval.

"This should keep the pain away."

Kate exhaled, "Then you should prescribe a little for yourself. Fine grade, direct from China, and Lord knows you could use it. Push me closer."

Soiled Dove, her hair now spit-curled and wearing a freshly laundered primrose, pushed the wicker wheel-chair, with Kate overflowing, around the desk to where Bishop and White Fox stood.

Kate said, "We don't need nothing between us."

"Including secrets?"

"That depends on your attitude, Doctor. Lock the door."

Bishop nodded courteously to Widow Kate, the bloodstained coat draped over his shoulders shifting as he moved to the door, and threw the bolt. He kept the rig against his chest, the double barrel tucked into his shirt like a broken arm in a sling.

Bishop said, "No one in, or out."

"Privacy's important in matters like this, so we can feel free to speak our minds, come to an understanding. Like this beautiful—is it Cheyenne, and maybe something else? She could be thinking anything."

Fox, barely covered by her rawhide jacket, her legs and hips bare through torn leathers, met Kate's stare, but not her smile.

"Honey, if you ever decide to go into business, I pray it's for me and not against me, because I'd be broke in a week." Fox didn't even blink. "You may hate the thought, but the fact is my customers would love to sample something like you. And we could charge 'em a fortune. I'd even make a special deal as long as you could stand it. That's real money."

Fox kept her face locked, but Soiled Dove frowned at the offer. Kate swatted Dove's hand, saying to Bishop, "She understands every word, right?"

"You can bank on it."

"No offense meant, honey, but you don't get anywhere without asking. I can't stand, so you sit. This meeting's eye-to-eye." Bishop settled on a small loveseat, sinking into the satin cushion. Fox held for a purposeful moment, before sitting beside him. Soiled Dove gave them each a snifter, then gifted Bishop's glass with a splash of Napoleon brandy.

Kate said, "To fight back that freezing cold."

White Fox covered the top of her glass with her palm. Dove looked to Kate, who shook her head.

"My comforts bring me enjoyment, and make my convalescence a little more bearable." Kate swatted Dove's hand again and was wheeled a little closer. "Doctor, we've got quite a bit in common."

Bishop sipped. "Beaudine."

"Look here."

The bandage was a large patch, wrapped in linen that went completely around Kate's middle, and was tied in the center of the acre of skin that was her back. Folds of flesh bulged beneath the cloth, straining the cotton that covered the wound, shifting the bandage from its place. Kate snickered as she held open her blouse for Bishop to see, her flesh rolling with her.

"It'd take more than some letter opener to get through all that. I played possum and let him do his crazy-ass business."

Bishop leaned forward to examine her. "Who attended you?"

"A sawbones who likes to have his fanny spanked. Did a nice job, so I gave him two free nights. He'll be back."

"Soon, I hope. Keep it clean. What sent Beaudine over?"

Kate snapped her fingers for her dragon. "Because I told him I wanted a percentage of your gold, Dr. Bishop. The major would tell anyone who'd listen all about it, and you. You're his favorite subject of conversation when he gets going."

Kate held the pipe to her mouth as Soiled Dove lit it. "And since you got yourself that fancy rig, well, you're a famous man. One of my old girls works Huckie's, and the word's been spreading. You even made the paper."

"And I'm sure they got the facts right."

"I'd say you're on the run now? Need some help?"

Bishop let Kate draw. "I don't have any gold. Nothing."

Kate coughed. "Well, there's something going on that you're a part of, but maybe you don't know it. This isn't just about avenging your family."

"It is for me. There's nothing else."

The pipe made a slight hissing sound as Kate drew again. "Beaudine killed one of my girls. Had some kind of a fit, and wrung her neck, but that brain of his wouldn't let him recall it. I guess that's his blessing."

"Where'd they go?"

"Oh, now we're back to business."

"Where?"

"What's it worth?"

"Everything."

"You claim your gold's a myth. I can find that out for myself, and you can bet I will. But if you swear you'll kill Beaudine, then that satisfies our negotiation. For now."

"I've already sworn, but your information has to be real."

"Here at Widow Kate's, we always guarantee satisfaction."

Bishop lifted the shotgun away from his chest, and held it out for Kate. She smiled. "That's a hell of a thing.

No wonder there's talk." Then she looked to White Fox. "And how well does he use it?"

White Fox said, "Well."

"You're building a reputation, Doctor. That's good, makes the men you're after nervous." Kate took a sip of Napoleon, cooling her cough, and then: "Beaudine and three others rode for the Goodwill silver mine north of here, and they're damn excited at the prospect of seeing you."

"Oh, we're expected, just not alone."

"You changed their plans without their knowing? Good. Ready to change them some more?" Kate winced at some sudden pain, and Soiled Dove had the dragon at her lips. Kate eased, her words washing out of her mouth. "You and I, we beat death."

"Nobody beats it."

"There's a reason we're both still here, and it's bigger than that fever-brained son of a bitch. Let me ask, how many died in the War Between the States? Half the country?"

"There are a lot of graves."

"Everywhere. You know, I've had blue and grey take off their boots, lie with my girls. The uniform didn't mean a thing; they were just men and boys, looking for comfort."

"And I doctored a lot of them, and their insides are all the same. That was ten years ago. What's your point?"

Kate leaned forward in her wheelchair, focusing. "That these same men who're shooting at each other are working together on the Colorado Central, or working the mines, or building new towns. And so are their kids, all pushing west. That's a lot of customers and a lot of money going into my purse. That means girls and houses, maybe a hundred, and run 'em all from right here. Or maybe a palace in San Francisco."

"Big plans."

"Everybody has them. What about you, Doctor?"

"I'm thinking about right now."

"It's eating you up. I can see it. Well, I like the future, and I'm not having some crazy toss all I want to do on the fire. Neither of us needs a wild card in the deck."

Kate wheeled her chair around, her hand slipping before she took herself the few feet to a tapestry that covered one wall of her office in ornate red and gold.

"Kill Beaudine, and we'll both move on. How're you fixed?"

Bishop breached the rig, showing Kate the empty barrels.

Kate nodded. Soiled Dove pulled a sash cord that gathered the tapestry up from the floor, revealing a case built into the wall, stocked with pistols of all kinds, short and long rifles, knives, a few swords, and ammunition.

"He missed all this." Kate fished a key from between her breasts, and opened the cases' intricately carved glass doors. "All left by customers, mostly in trade. Some clothes too. You're riding into an ambush, so take all you need. And honey, there's even a little something for you."

Kate removed a long bow, hanging on a hook with a quiver of arrows, from the case. "I've heard tell you're damn good. A cavalry lieutenant wanted an extra fifteen minutes with Delia, and used up his pay. It's not from a Cheyenne, if that makes it easier. Maybe it doesn't."

White Fox took the bow and pulled it taut, testing it for strength. It held tight. Kate shook her head. "If you ever think you want to go a different way, come see me. You'll be my star attraction."

Kate looked to Bishop. "You hardly touched your brandy, Doctor. You've got hell's own ride ahead of you, and not many pleasures along the way. Right?"

Bishop threw back the rest of the Napoleon in one swallow, and smiled.

CHAPTER SEVENTEEN
Condemned

The insulator shattered as the handle of Fuller's Bowie struck it from the side, the pieces of glass carried away with the blowing snow, exposing the hot telegraph line. Fuller steadied himself on the top of the far-leaning pole, looking as if it was about to snap in half against the iron railhead that was next to it.

The pole shifted in the wind, and Fuller hung on, legs straining, as Hector tossed him a coil of thin wire that was attached to a Morse sending key and receiver on the ground below. Fuller closed his eyes against the freeze, while securing the wire to a bare contact on the pole's crossbar. His hands moved fast; then his fingers numbed.

The brass key spark-jumped. Hector called out, "We got it!"

Fuller shimmied down, dropping the last few feet as Hector settled on an old crosstie, and began tapping a message on the portable field telegraph that fit in his lap.

Fuller pressed his side to ease a jolt of pain and called out to Fat Gut, "You couldn't have done this?"

"I don't climbth!"

Creed and Gut sat their horses, taking shelter behind the sections of oak and rusting tracks stacked at this end of the Colorado Central narrow gauge line. On a siding, an open passenger car, riddled with bullet holes, filled with snow.

Fat Gut said, "I t'ain't never theen tracks this smaw."

Fuller threw Gut a look as he wiped the blade of his knife. "It's the steam engine line that goes through the mountains to the mines. And this here's the only bit of telegraph line for a hundred miles."

Creed said, "A real man knows his own country."

"I knew all thath, too'd! I figgered thit!"

"I don't want to hear your mush! You getting anything, boy?"

Hector grinned back at Creed. "Yes, sir. What's your message?"

Creed ran his hands down Pride's neck, patting him as he considered his words. "No other way to say it. We failed. Tell them the prisoners escaped, and I will recapture, as ordered."

Hector tapped the message on the brass key, then turned to Creed to say, "Anything else, sir?"

Creed cocked his head for a moment, listening through the wind for the quick Morse tones in response, but none came.

"They're not answering."

Hector leaned into the receiver, almost pressing his ear against it. "No, sir. They're not."

"But it went through?"

"Yes. Yes, sir. And I sent it exactly the way you said it, them words. I didn't want to mess up nothing again."

"If you followed orders, you did fine. Let's move."

Fuller yanked on the telegraph wires, but they stayed fast. He tapped Hector on the shoulder. "Give me a boost."

Fat Gut laughed, "That's what yourth good at now, thniper! Monkey climbin'!"

Hector knelt by the pole. Fuller didn't take his boost. Instead, he walked to his horse and pulled the Morgan-James from its scabbard, being careful with the long sight. Fat Gut wiped his nose on his sleeve as Fuller faced him, while fitting a cap on the rifle's metal nipple and then thumbing the hammer to half-lock position.

The sniper smiled. "You don't be fretting, my real skills'll come back."

Gut swallowed air right before Fuller turned sharply and fired at the train car two hundred yards down the narrow track, blowing a hole clean through the first O of COLORADO CENTRAL.

Hector whistled his admiration.

Fuller turned to Gut. "Start climbing."

Miles away, in a stone room cramped with lockers of weapons and ammunition, a telegraph operator was hunched over a Patrick and Bunnell set, listening to the code it was receiving. Somewhere, water was dripping. He wrote by the flicker of a candle, and when the metallic tapping stopped, he took Captain Creed's message and the candle with him, leaving the room in darkness.

"You all watch where I'm pointing at. I don't want to say this twice."

"Or Betsy'll bite?"

Chaney wasn't looking at Howard when he let the words slip, his head down, and hands deep in his pockets. They were all standing in the center of the Goodwill Mining Company making their battle plan, but Chaney was sick of the big man, and only looked up seconds before Howard charged at him, eyes wild-wide and giant fists tight.

Howard had taken a wild swing when the long-blade cleaver cut the air between him and Chaney before splitting the ice-hard ground at their feet. The handle wobbled as the blade sunk in.

"I could've taken off your foot, cut right through your boot." Beaudine stepped in front of Howard, grabbing the cleaver and turning to Chaney. "Or your ear."

He pulled the blade from the snow, and ran a finger tip lightly across it. "The edge should never touch the ground. You got this, Deadeye?"

Lem Wright's Colt in his right hand was a few inches from Chaney's temple, while the Smith & Wesson in his left was aimed directly at Howard's broad stomach. "Oh, I got them both."

Beaudine wiped down the blade. "This personal hash isn't why we're here. It's the mission you have to remember."

"What about his flannel mouth?"

Beaudine stepped close to Howard, holding the long cleaver with both hands like a medieval executioner. "That's all it is. He's playing you like you're in a poker game, keeping you riled, so you'll be a fool. That's right, isn't it Chaney?"

Lem brushed Chaney's neck with the barrel of the pistol. Chaney nodded, and let go of the Apache brass-knuckle pistol he had in his right front pocket. He pulled his hand out, and raised them both in mock surrender. "Right, right. Just playing."

"And why did you do this, boy? Cause this commotion?"

Chaney felt Lem's pistol brush his neck again. "Sorry. You've been handing me shit, and I got a bad habit of pushing back. Bad habit."

Lem said, "You've got to be real careful about that."

Chaney agreed with a nod, and then Beaudine said to the big man, "You a fool, Howard?"

"No, I ain't."

"Because I don't need fools in my squad."

"I said I ain't."

Howard kept his fists tight and eyes on the gambler. Beaudine's voice never rose: "Then think about everything that preacher taught you at Rawlins. You said his words changed you. Got rid of your ill temper. You left the penitentiary a different man, a man who thinks a thing through."

Howard said, "I was, damn it. I am."

"I haven't seen it."

"That's because you're making me forget it all, going right out of my head."

Beaudine kept his voice level. "I know that confusion, but it'll pass. You're stronger than it is."

"I set the dynamite, and I shouldn't have done it." Howard's voice was frustrated shout. "This wasn't going to be my life no more! The gates of heaven were gonna open for me, and you're sending me down another road! Making me an outlaw again!"

"No, you're what you should be: a soldier in my army, and you got a mission." Beaudine kept turning the blade. "Treasure in gold. Just keep saying that, like a prayer, over and over. Treasure in gold." Then the cleaver was down at his side. "And you'll remember who you are. Not a paid-off deputy or a coffin builder making sixty cents a day, but a man with a mission. A soldier."

"No. Not a soldier."

"A powder man."

"With a damn short fuse?"

That did it. Howard cracked, maybe half a smile at Lem's bad joke, called him a one-eyed son of a bitch, and shook off some of his anger. Some. Everyone took a breath, and Lem flashed Chaney a look, reminding him how close he'd come to being beaten to death.

Beaudine stepped back from between his two men, wiping the smear of blood from the blade with his thumb. "You're calm now?"

Howard nodded. "Let's get to it."

"Hold. Boy?"

Beaudine turned and smashed Chaney's jaw with the long-handle, dropping him into the snow, his mouth spurting blood.

Beaudine took some deep breaths, his head jerking from side to side to order his thoughts: "Now, I don't want no more damn foolishness! We've got a hell of a battle in front of us. There's a plan here. A plan and you need to follow it, to follow me! Brothers in arms, understand? I want to hear you say it!"

Lem helped Chaney to his feet, and they all said, "Brothers in arms."

There were nods all around. Howard didn't look at Chaney as he started again. "We've got charges under the snow every twenty feet by my foot, so you best make it thirty. See how I got them in a circle? Them fuses are wrapped to stay dry, but you can see 'em. Each fuse sets off two bundles. The ones in them old sheds are bundled in threes, with short fuses, so light and run. That's what you wanted, right?"

Beaudine nodded. "There can't be a single place for anyone to hide."

Howard spit. "We set all this off, there won't be nothing left. The sticks on this other side of the pit are just sittin' under the snow, so you have to set them off with another stick, I saved ten, toss one, it'll set off them buried ones. But you got to hit it." Then, to Chaney: "No half-assed shots, no second chances."

Lem said, "That's enought to blow a hole straight through to Hell."

"I'm just doing what I'm told. That's what's going to get the gold, right?"

Beaudine was fixed on the mine shaft and its cross braces. "What about that?"

"You got two sticks on them four-by-fours."

"Just so long as my head's out of the way."

Beaudine turned to Lem as soon as he spoke. "That depends on where you're going to be, don't it?"

Lem pointed to the first small shack, one wall caved in. "Chaney'll be there. That's a good view of the trail in, and he'll be close if they open up. I'll be on top of the slag with a rifle, pick a few off, start some confusion before the first explosion."

"But you don't touch Bishop."

Lem spit, "I know Bishop's the money! But you don't know how many Creed's got with him. You said we could be facing an army. Well, let's get as many as we can, as fast as we can."

Chaney flicked his gold tooth with his finger, then said, "Yeah, even up the odds. Maybe."

Lem said, "Even if Bishop takes a slug, he can still tell us what we want to know. You got that all figured out, this time?"

Beaudine nodded, then smiled. "Two things we pay big money for: act out desires, and act out hates. I surely do."

Howard pissed in the snow. "Sounds like horseshit to me."

"This horseshit's going to make you the richest dynamiter in the country, so you better learn it like the gospel. He's got that girl?"

Chaney nodded, Beaudine continued: "After we wipe out Creed's misfits, you think Dr. Bishop won't strike a deal?" Beaudine chopped the air with the cleaver and grinned to himself. "To save her head, and get a chance at me? Hell yes, he will."

Lem said, "I've only seen Bishop twice in my life. The second time was in his house, and the first time I was in my cell, right after I'd had the living shit kicked out of me. Remember Smythe?"

Howard snorted. "Wanted to kill that bastard every day."

"He damn near killed me. Probably would have if Dr.

Bishop hadn't forced him to put me in the prison hospital. Remember? He was standing at your cell, saying something to Dev, and you hung back. Dev gave him a letter, then he was walking out and saw me lying on my bunk, and said I needed to go to the hospital."

Beaudine turned from Lem. "You're saying you owe him?"

"Nope. Just getting our history straight."

White Fox jammed the knife through the side of the sleeve, cutting the cloth along its seam, then pulling it back to the shoulder. Bishop watched her while laying out the pistols and ammunition he'd gotten from Widow Kate's weapons cache. She cut the sleeve off at the elbow, tossed the rag into the small fire that warmed their campsite, before threading a needle to sew up the torn edges. The flames ate the cloth.

She sat on a blanket, the coat in her lap, and looked up to see Bishop looking, but not recognizing her. "Beaudine?"

Bishop loaded a Smith & Wesson .44. "You know the last time I saw his face?"

"I asked if you wanted this. You said yes."

"And I say it again. There's no doubt. *Tóséé'e.*"

Bishop emphasized the final *e*, so Fox knew he was sure. She shrugged. "Then do your work."

Fox leaned closer to the fire, catching the light as she hemmed the jagged edge of the sleeve so the hammers of the shotgun wouldn't catch when Bishop raised his arm for a kill. The coat was special-made for an ammunition drummer who had secret pockets sewn into the lining for bullet samples, and he would never have left it behind except he had been shot by a drunken cowboy who'd thought one of Kate's China dolls was his personal property.

The drummer had been carried home naked with three holes in his chest, and his coat had gone into the closet, until Bishop and White Fox exchanged their bloody rags for what Kate had stashed. The widow opium-slurred, "It's purr-fect for your purr-poses."

Fox tugged on the tight denims she'd chosen, bringing them down to her hips so she could sit cross-legged, before drawing a last stitch on the coat sleeve, and biting through the heavy thread. She looked to Bishop, who was struggling to load the same pearl-handled Colt that Short Gun had tried to kill him with the day before.

Someone said, "Beaudine."

It was a distant echo in Bishop's mind, thick with a cigar smoker's hack and a Swedish accent. The name repeated itself, and Warden Allard became more and more anchored in memory: the voice, the cigar between his teeth, the wide mustache, and the wider belly that struggled not to burst the top button of his pinstriped trousers.

"Condemned men do get privileges for their last week. I insist on that. Good food, good drink."

Allard tried to stick out his sunken chest with pride at the declaration, even as he cigar-hacked again in his struggle to get out of his chair. John Bishop slipped his hands under Allard's arms, lifting the warden to his feet. "Your brother was given a chance to have a private cell these final days, but he refused. Wanted to stay with this crazy Beaudine."

"My brother can't write, sir. I think this prisoner's been his voice."

"He was being punished for an infraction, not his first."

"I'm sure."

"He chose to stay in the punishment cells with the other prisoners, rather than be moved." Allard spit his words out around his cigar. "Whatever the reason, I want it declared on record that I've offered him all possible comforts before his final day. And he's refused everything."

"It's on the record."

"With the family?"

"I'm all that's left, so yes."

"Then, you shall see him."

Allard took up almost half the width of the narrow stone hallway that connected his office to the cellblocks. Bishop walked alongside him, medical bag in hand, sometimes turning sideways to make room for the warden, as they maneuvered the corners. He listened dutifully, and the cigar never left Allard's mouth: "I've been given charge of the worst types this side of the Mississippi, and I do my best by them. That's not an easy task, if you think of what they've done."

"I'm sure it isn't."

Allard agreed with Bishop's agreement. "Every letter a prisoner mails, I read first. What your brother claims about his time here is slop for hogs."

Bishop nodded. "He's been a liar his whole life."

"But you're going to see for yourself? Fine. I am within the law, always. You treat all your patients the same, Doctor?"

"I try to."

"A killer comes to you with a bullet in his stomach, and you treat him the same as an old woman dying from consumption? I don't think so, because what you do is between you and your conscience. But here, the law dictates that I see every man the same way."

"Since one of them's my brother, what way is that?"

They had reached the end of the hallway and stood before a large door made of riveted steel plates, with a drop bar braced across it. The stone floor was spatter-stained, rust mixing with blood.

Allard pulled wet tobacco from the end of his tongue. "These are the cells. Smythe."

A guard, his skin and hair the same apple color, stepped from an anteroom jangling a set of keys. He lifted the cross-brace, then unlocked the door. The tumblers cried of old metal as Smythe grunted them open. He was shiny with the brown sweat of last night's whiskey, and wiped his face with a stained handkerchief he kept balled in one of his enormous hands. He looked to Allard, then to Bishop. "Well?"

"Take the good doctor to Devlin Bishop's cell, then escort him safely off the premises. And answer any questions he might have about our policies, my policies."

Bishop said, "What has you worried? I'm not here for an inspection."

"You're here for family, but you will talk about your experience, I'm sure. We don't have statehood yet, but this institution operates within the letter of territorial law. I insist on that."

"You've made that clear, Warden."

Allard said, "Letter of the law," again, pushing each word for emphasis, then added, "No favorites, no compromises. And that includes your brother's execution."

Allard extended his hand, and Bishop started to shake it.

"Your medical bag."

"I have no intention of cheating the hangman. Believe me."

"For your own protection, Doctor. These are desperate men—why tempt them? You'll get it on your way out."

Bishop handed over the bag, then stepped around Smythe into the shadowed corridor that led to the cellblock. The guard snickered at the formality, before pulling the huge steel door closed behind them.

The only light coming into the corridor was from the end that opened into the prison's common area. A heavy chain strung along the wall guided the way. Bishop regarded Smythe's near-blue knuckles that had been skinned almost to the bone. "Must have been a hell of a fight."

"Haven't met me match yet."

"Looks like a few knuckles are broken."

"After ten years on the job, I don't feel nothing."

A din of shouted curses, laughter, and crying rose as they got closer to the common. Incoherent, hysterical screaming hit Bishop between the eyes.

Smythe plugged his ears with thick fingers. "He sounds happy, don't he?"

Grinning, the guard fell back a step, letting Bishop into the common area first. This was the heart of the prison: a large structure that seemed chiseled from a single piece of rock, with curved, arena-like walls that supported a high, domed ceiling. There were no windows, and there was only a single stovepipe for ventilation.

The pitched screaming came from one of the community cells that were on all sides of the ground level: six prisoners together, with a piss bucket and a straw mattress for comfort. The air was choked by noise, stench, and the smoke from the torches mounted on the walls.

The middle of the commons was taken up by rude tables for meals, and a pair of whipping posts, while guards with Winchesters took position around the area like the points on a compass, kerchiefs shielding their faces.

Bishop said to no one, "The letter of the law. God almighty."

"Don't be getting yourself in a twist, Doc. It stinks worse than it is. Ain't nobody been on them posts since the war, and most of this bunch drew short stretches. Get caught with something that ain't yours, settle here for six months, and you'll never steal again."

"I sure as hell wouldn't."

"Hell's the word all right, but they eat pretty good. The circuit judge favors our example right well."

The scream ripped again, then became a laugh, then a sob. Bishop edged toward the catwalk that led to the cells, but Smythe's busted hand was instantly on his shoulder. "Bastard's all yelled out."

"Sounds possible, but he might need medical attention."

"But you don't have your little black bag. Want to see that brother of yours or not?"

Smythe took a step closer. Bishop said, "Where is he?"

"That way."

On the other side of the whipping posts, a bone-thin guard hooked one end of the crow bar through the metal ring on a trap door, and pulled, straining like hell and swearing through his kerchief. Smythe lent an arm. The door lifted up from the stone floor, revealing a set of iron stairs that descended into pitch-dark.

Bishop looked down into the opening. The skinny guard said, "Want your brother?"

The din around them was now the roar of prisoners banging tin plates and cups on their cage doors, slopped with a thousand obscenities in ten languages. Some chanted, "Smytheee!"

An old guard with a Spencer rifle fired a shot into the ceiling, a blast of thunder that stun-silenced them.

Then, in the last cell, Chester Pardee hurled his piss through the bars, trying for Smythe. "You're goin' to the Tombs, give my regards to Major Beaudine! Hope he guts ya like a deer, you son of a bitch!"

Pardee's gift didn't come close enough to splash. Bishop started down the stairs, with Smythe right behind, and the trap door closed above their heads, leaving them in total darkness. Smythe lit a small candle, a yellow flicker barely showing Bishop the way down the broken, wet stairs, and the squealing swarm of rats darting from the shadows.

The guard nudged Bishop down. "Rats. That's all what's down here."

"I thought it was prisoners who're being punished."

"Ain't that what I said?"

Devlin Bishop leaned back against the cell wall, almost totally lost in the complete dark that swallowed it. Even though he was just feet away in the same cell, all Dev could see of Beaudine was the shape of a man, sitting on the floor, with something resting on his knees. Not that Dev cared. He knew what his cellmate looked like, and more importantly, what he was worth.

Beaudine hunched over the student's tablet using the nub of a pencil to write on cream laid stationery. "We're truly suffering without a pen."

Dev half-smiled. "We're suffering anyway," he said and then, quietly: "And me, for not much longer."

"I meant this letter is your will and testament, Dev. It should have permanence."

"I don't get a real funeral. So if that can be read when I'm gone, it's enough."

"No need to fret, it'll be read."

"Just what I said?"

Beaudine continued writing. "Exactly your words."

Dev traced the edges of his mustache with his fingers, neatening its edges. "Maybe you could write something out for the hangman. Make sure things go just right."

"I don't think you've got much choice in that."

Dev shut his eyes for just a moment. "Just thinking out loud," he said, and then he snapped his eyes open at the sound of footsteps coming toward the cell, accompanied by the ghost of a yellow light.

One of the prisoners yelled from another cell, "Is that chow comin'?"

Dev Bishop sat up, wiping the stink of the Tomb from his eyes, as he focused on the man now standing by his cell door. Dev answered back, "It ain't chow! I'll be damned if it ain't my baby brother."

John Bishop stood near the bars, but not too close, with Smythe holding the candle just over his shoulder. Beaudine was on the edge of the tiny circle of candle-light.

"It's a fine thing to see you at last."

Dev took the five steps to the door. "You should introduce yourself, Major. It's been so long, my brother may think you're me."

"I recognize you, Dev."

"Don't see how. I never favored Ma or Pa, except her temper. And we sure don't look alike, but you haven't changed. Even as a kid, polished and respectable. But I guess brothers always know each other." Dev gestured toward Beaudine, who kept on writing. "The invitation to come was the major's. He's the reason you're here, Johnny. He puts down my thoughts better than I ever could."

"I'm here because of you. No offense, sir."

Beaudine didn't look up. "None offered, none taken."

"I'd want to see you, whether you wrote or not."

Smythe yawned. "And when are you bein' hung, boy-o?"

Dev paused as if he was figuring his answer. "Four days."

"Good. I've got duty that Wednesday. Wouldn't want to miss it."

Bishop said, "Can I talk to my brother?"

"I ain't stopping you."

Dev extended his hand through the narrow opening between the bars. "I wish we could have met at the Metropolitan House instead, but fate stepped in. They call this part of the prison the Tomb, 'cause it feels like you're buried. Gets you used to the idea."

Smythe low-whistled a little tune. "Better to be dead-alive, than dead-dead. And you're gonna find out the difference, boy-o."

Bishop shook his brother's hand. "Warden said you had a chance to get out, and wouldn't take it."

Someone in the dark snorted a laugh. Dev said, "I have business to tend to, and the major's been my—"

Beaudine threw in, "Representative. You wouldn't assume it, but during my time in the army, I became a top-level assistant to a number of generals and I've put those learned skills to use. Even here."

Bishop said, "I appreciate your writing letters for my brother."

"He's finishing one now. Something to remember me by."

"Dev, we haven't seen each other since before Mama and Pa died. I'm glad I'm here, but don't know what I can do to help. Tell me."

"That's your Christian side coming up. There's nothin'. You're the only family I've got, and I figured we should be together one last time before Wednesday morning." Dev took a step back, calling out to the Tomb, "My baby brother, the doctor! Who got the chances I never did! I know you've got a fine, fine life, with a wife, son, folks who respect you. You ever tell anybody about *your* brother, the outlaw? I'd bet Union money you don't."

"It never really comes up."

"Oh, I'm sure, I'm sure. Nobody wants a doc with mud on his boots, or blood on his family name."

"I don't think that way."

"My own fault. I'm the law-breaker, and you're the one everyone ass-kisses."

Smythe said, "This here candle's almost burned down."

Bishop turned away from the cell. "It's all right, I think my visit's done. Good luck, Dev."

Dev laughed. "You can't go yet. This is a special treat for us. They only bring candles when we eat. The rest of the time, we're in the dark."

Beaudine handed Dev the finished letter. "And I have learned to write that way, with a decent hand."

Dev folded the letter into neat threes, before holding it out to his brother. "I hope this will clear things up between us. I shouldn't have shot my mouth off, because I'm proud of what you've become."

Bishop slipped the letter into his coat. "Forget it. But, I haven't done anything, and I wish I had."

"I'm talking about our partnership, brother."

Beaudine stood, his eyes narrowed on Bishop's puzzled reaction: "We've never been partners, Dev. . . ."

"You don't have to say more, Johnny. Just know that I'm grateful. For everything you did, and helped with. And after Wednesday, I'll be eternally grateful."

The rest of the Tomb busted into laughter fits, filling the tiny space. Dev Bishop dropped back on his iron bunk. "I'll see you on the other side, brother! Now get out of here so that mule's ass can fetch us our dinner!"

Smythe roared, "You want me to put somethin' special in it?"

Bishop gave Dev a puzzled nod. "God have mercy, Dev," he said and started away. He stopped, using the last bit of yellow light to peer into the next cell. Lem Wright's body was twisted on the filth-thick floor, almost folded over, lying on his side. His face was a mush of purple folds, with dried blood outlining his mouth, nose, and ears. His cellmate, a massive, dark shape taking up most of the cage, snored in the corner.

"What the hell happened to this man?"

Smythe's breath was corpse-fresh. "Your visit's done!"

"Get him out of here, or he'll die. And I'll bring a murder charge!"

Dev said, "Better listen up, screw. My baby brother takes his doctoring very, very seriously."

Smythe placed his heel on Bishop's foot, shifting his

enormous weight. Something cracked. "The thing about the Tomb is, you can get forgotten down here."

Bishop didn't flinch. "That could be true for you as well. The best thing to do is help that man, and I'll have no reason to say anything to the warden, or the territorial authorities."

The keys rattled in Smythe's hands. "I don't give two shits about family. No more visitors!"

Smythe yanked the cell door open, and Bishop helped Lem to his feet, throwing his arm over his shoulder. Lem tried to speak, but nothing happened, his head dropping to his chest. Bishop made his way back to the trapdoor stairs, dragging Lem with him. Smythe kept his pistol on them both.

The candle flickered, before finally burning down to nothing, leaving the Tomb in pitch. One of the prisoners started to scream.

Lem's weight seemed to double as Bishop took each step, his arms under his shoulders for support, hefting him up the stairs inches at a time. Bishop grunted, asked for help. Smythe offered his gun on their backs.

There was a quiet laugh, but Bishop couldn't tell who it was, because the rats were scurrying again, squeals and toenails against the wet stone.

Beaudine called out from his cell, "It's been a sure pleasure to finally make your acquaintance, Dr. Bishop! Give my best to your wife and son!"

Bishop didn't answer as he struggled up another step.

A different voice in the dark, said, "Beaudine."

It was White Fox, pulling a heavy blanket around Bishop's shoulders, as he came back from somewhere lost in his sleep. "You don't need that dream."

He felt the warmth of the campfire, and opened his eyes to see weapons laid out, the saddlebags packed, the bay and the painted quietly grazing. Bishop started to sit up, but she stopped him. "You know what tomorrow brings. Clear your mind, build your strength."

She was right, and Bishop didn't fight the wave that was carrying him away. He heard her voice again, telling him what he needed. *"He'kotâhestôtse."*

Bishop whispered the word, as he knew it. "Peace."

CHAPTER EIGHTEEN
The Strength of My Enemies

Chaney was the first to hear the eight riders as they approached the mouth of the small canyon that shielded the Goodwill silver strike. They didn't speak, and their horses moved gingerly over the thin crust of ice that sheeted the ground during the night, but something bolted Chaney awake, and he was standing with his Colt 45 drawn when they pulled to a mutual stop.

The animals snorted, but the riders stayed silent.

The sun was struggling, and the sky was more the grey-blue of night, instead of red morning, which made making out the faces of the men near impossible. They were dull, broken shadows, with weapons resting across their laps.

One of them said, "It's too damn early to be dealin' with a fool."

Chaney didn't take a step. "I bet I can kill at least two of you before you take me."

The same rider said, "No need for that. We was told there was work here."

Chaney didn't flinch. "The mine's played out."

The other riders aimed their guns so all shots would pound into Chaney's chest in the same spot. "We didn't come here to dig no silver."

"Then what the hell are you doing here?"

Lem Wright stepped from behind the caved-in shack, a Winchester on his shoulder, and threw a smirk at Chaney. "Who'd you borrow your iron balls from, son?"

The riders gut-laughed as Lem shook their hands before turning to Chaney, who had holstered his gun. "These are the extra boys Beaudine said he needed." Lem shook hands with his old buddy in front. "Who passed you the word?"

Lem's buddy said, "Old Kirby. Had a wagonload of stolen dynamite, said you got some of it and could cut us in on something big."

"Did you leave him under the grass?"

"Nope. And didn't rob him neither, to thank him for the tip. He'll be easy to find if this don't work out."

Chaney barked, "Well, how are we knowing they're not the law?"

Lem turned and threw his dead eye at Chaney. "What?"

Howard and Beaudine were standing by the mine's old cross braces, Howard holding Betsy and Beaudine with a rifle aimed from the hip. He punched his words with the sound of the repeater being cocked. "The boy asked a question, and it was a good one."

Lem pointed to his friend. "I did a hard-labor stretch in Arkansas with this jaybird, and I damn well know he didn't go straight."

Lem's buddy flashed yellow 'n' green teeth. "I think I've killed three or four since I saw you last, Lem. And these boys, well, they ain't got nothing to lose."

"That's a meaningful endorsement." Beaudine let the

repeater drop. "Coffee's on the boil. I'll let you in on the plan of battle, and what's expected of each of you."

One of the new boys said, "We expect pay, brother."

"Not your brother, and there's money to be had."

The riders stepped down from their horses, chortling as they passed Chaney.

Beaudine said, "There will be a man with one arm, and a little Cheyenne girl with him."

Lem's buddy said, "What are we gonna do for the rest of the day?"

Chaney wasn't impressed. "This ain't going to be a hog killin'."

"Go boil your shirt."

Howard let go with a whistle-snort, then blew his nose on his sleeve. Lem handed Chaney a set of reins. "Don't get worked up again. These ponies have to get out of sight."

Chaney grabbed another mount when Lem prodded, "Now, where'd you say your new balls came from?"

Chaney flicked his gold tooth. "Guess I'm finally tasting the gold."

"And you're not keen on shares."

Chaney didn't add another word.

The trail White Fox and Bishop followed had been hard-beaten into the earth by the weight of wagons loaded with miners and silver, pulled through the rough by a convoy of steam tractors. The man and machine traffic that had travelled here, before the Goodwill was pronounced dead, had left deep scars the Rockies could never heal. A constant, bitter cold and whip-harsh wind, strangled any hope of plants reclaiming the place, and what trees there were had been cut and left to rot into grey nothing.

Snow dusted the blank morning sky.

"*Naévêháne.*"

White Fox nodded. "You're learning. Yes, it feels like death. And you?"

Bishop absently placed his left hand on the shotgun rig, his fingers sticking to the weapon's cold metal before answering. "We're riding into a massacre. This is how it should be."

"And death rides, with us."

"Creed used to say the same thing every time we went into battle. Win or lose, he was right."

The words settled. Bishop looked at her, waiting to see if Fox's eyes would meet his to offer reassurance of their survival, but they didn't. Fox wasn't going to give a false promise, and that was right fine with Bishop, who watched her ride a few paces ahead, saddle heavy with bow, arrows, and blades.

He kept the bay steady, his thoughts about what needed to be done for the memory of his wife and son; that was the bloody mission, though he knew well that Amaryllis would hate what he was doing. She had loved the doctor, not this assassin, and even though they both lived inside the same man, Amaryllis had never seen the latter. Only the good, only charity, found her eyes. That was her special gift.

Bishop almost slipped back to those memories, the light notes of her voice even when she was being strong; a joke that she always told wrong, but that he loved. He forced those thoughts down, killing them. He had to.

Bishop let the rig rest in its saddle sling, allowing him to relax his shoulder. His body was now serving the shotgun; the weapon had taken over, telling the healer what to do. And he wasn't fighting the change.

He and Fox rode farther, no words between them, before approaching the edge of the canyon that broke this side of the mountains in half. Fox eased the painted to a stop about twenty feet from the rough drop into the man-made opening, where she could see the bits of the braces and crumbling rooftops the Goodwill Company had built close to the edge.

Bishop took a brass field telescope from his coat as he light-footed to a place where he could spy the area below. Fox was suddenly next to him, pointing to the tiny figures huddled around the damaged buildings, their low voices garbled into a common echo. Bishop held one end of the scope between his teeth, pulled it to its length, and brought the glass to his eye. Fox leaned over his shoulder, twisting the focus ring so he could make out the face of the man standing apart from the others, making sweeping motions with his arms.

Through the lens, he watched as Beaudine gave orders to Chaney and other outlaws Bishop didn't recognize. Howard, holding bundles of dynamite, barked silent instructions, walking around the perimeter of the mining camp, before tying charges off on an old mine support. Howard adjusted the charge, and nudged Lem, who looked up, facing Bishop directly, his good eye maybe catching a glint of light off the scope. Bishop pulled back, snapping the telescope shut.

"He saw?"

"Not sure. They're not expecting us from here. They think we'll be coming from the canyon entrance, as Creed's prisoners. If they saw something, they don't know what it is."

"Too many. *Heómesto.*"

"Kate said it was a massacre. Creed thought he was getting paid, but they're going to slaughter him, and then Beaudine planned to do God knows what with us."

Fox's eyes met Bishop's this time. "There is no Creed."

Before Bishop could even agree, Fox put her hand up for silence, cocking her head toward a sound that was distant, but rising. The first shreds were low and vague; the echo of a thousand trees falling together, miles away.

Fox stood, turning toward an ice-scattered ridge that

had a small pass worn into it. Bishop turned also, with the sound growing louder from the ridge, like a constant beating of huge drums, and then, there was the stretch of moving red.

Men on horseback poured through the pass, nearly keeping shoulder to shoulder, their scarlet hoods and tunics forming a solid field of color that blew apart as they rode off in different directions. The thunder of running mounts pounded the air, becoming a roar as rider after rider followed, charging like a cavalry.

Bishop and White Fox leapt onto the bay and painted.

The Fire Riders circled wide, blocking the trail that led to the other side of the mountain. Others ran to flank the top of the canyon, drawing Prussian needle rifles from saddle scabbards and Colts from holsters. The guns were new, polished. Others swung knives, clubs, and axes. Strips of red cloth had been braided into their horses' tails and manes, so it looked as if flames were bursting from their bodies, while their heads had been painted silver-white, like bleached skulls.

Even in the light of morning, they were demonic.

Bishop and Fox pushed their horses fast along the broken rim of the drop-off, the rocky edge turning to gravel under their hoofs, as they angled toward a small grade leading to the canyon's mouth.

A patrol of Riders gave chase, shooting wild.

Their first shots were a miss, but another ricocheted off the barrel of the shotgun rig, sparking hot, nearly throwing Bishop from his saddle. Bishop swung the bay around and drew his Peacemaker, firing four times with his left and hitting two of the Riders chest-center. Red sprayed beyond their crimson tunics.

Fox kept parallel to Bishop, running close. She drew an arrow, then swung around on her horse's back, facing the Fire Rider closing in. She raised the bow, her muscled body compensating for the horse's every motion, absorbing its rhythm, making her aim rock-steady.

The Rider brought up a breach-loading Prussian rifle. She made her shot. It was clean, into the throat, pinning his hood to him. His scream was a muffled choke as he tumbled over his horse's neck, the arrow snapping in two, before he dead-rolled off the edge of the canyon wall, smashing onto the roof of a Goodwill mine shack below; shattered wood, glass, and bone.

The breach-loader never fired.

Beaudine stepped from a cut in the canyon wall, the repeater in one hand, long cleaver in the other. "Everybody hold!"

They all kept their positions, swearing.

Lem jabbed a thumb toward the Fire Rider corpse sprawled in front of them. "That ain't a Creed man! Look at him! What the hell do you call that getup? Beaudine!"

"It's what I said, what I told you." Beaudine rubbed his temple, as if pushing his thoughts together, before barking, "War!"

"With who? He's got an arrow in him, for God's sake!"

Lem's buddy perched low among the miner's graves, with two of his gang, one of them just a kid. He shook his head, lit a cigarette. "Them two sound worse than my wife and her sister. One dead ain't nothing. Let's do this, get paid, go home."

Beaudine stepped back. "You've got—you've got your orders! I'll tell you when to fire!"

Lem's buddy said, "Bullll-shit."

On the canyon rim, the Fire Riders called out commands, fragments of their voices echoing down to Beaudine's men. Lem shielded his eyes, to see the troop of red-clad demons staking the edge, targeting the mine area, weapons ready.

Lem said, "Sweet Mary, mother of us all," to no one, and stood beside the silver shaft's old cross braces, Peacemaker aimed, pockets filled with ammo, and a rifle beside him. He moved the rifle six inches closer, and said, "Seen that bunch? Still got your new balls?"

Chaney heard Lem and threw back "Hell's fire, yes," while pressed against a broken-in door of the collapsed mine shed, his Colt at his side and another tucked in his waistband. Howard was the closest to the canyon entrance, protected by a huge slag heap opposite the shed. He had Betsy out of her leather, but was damn ready to throw the dynamite stacked at his elbow.

Waiting. Ready.

Above the canyon, Fox and Bishop pounded the trail to the sloping grade that led to the Goodwill road and the mine. They were running, keeping a lead in front of the Fire Riders, but the Riders were closing. One broke ahead, pushing a tall stallion, getting close to Fox, his horse and her painted almost colliding.

The Rider fury-slashed with a cavalry saber. Fox dodged, but he cut, the blade slicing her shoulder, creating a bloody opening in her jacket and skin. She heel-kicked the Rider, cracking his knee. He howled through his red hood, twisting in agony. Fox pulled back on her painted, jerking the horse to slow his run, and getting out of the way of Bishop's aim.

Bishop's shot was now clear.

The Rider's eyes panicked wide as the shotgun rig swung toward him. Rider slashed again, the saber bouncing off of Bishop's saddle. One barrel of buckshot caught him solid in the side, tearing a good bit of him away. He hit the ground as a lifeless bag, his stallion still running.

The other Riders, in formation, reacted and charged faster.

Bishop and Fox broke hard down a small trail, the grade from the top of the canyon to the mine's entrance road only yards away. Fox glanced over her wounded

shoulder to see red demons taking positions with rifles
and pistols.

Bishop and Fox jumped a fallen log. The Riders leveled, shooting at them as a practiced one, a firing squad.
Their guns flamed, the joined sound thundering across
the flats, and bouncing against the canyon walls.

The log blew apart, but the targets kept moving.

A slug creased the side of Bishop's neck. He ignored
the burn, and angled the bay for the road. Fox got off an
arrow, tearing a lead Rider through the gut. He stayed his
horse, soaking red, while signaling the others to ride on.

A battle cry erupted from the Riders.

Fox called above them, *"Mâhenot!"*

At the mine, Chaney cleared his head of all but the
"gold reasons," before stepping away from the cover of
the shed, and shooting at the Fire Riders along the ridge
above, aiming at everything. And nothing.

Beaudine yelled, "I didn't give the command!"

Chaney emptied both pistols. "They're gonna wipe us
out!"

The Riders returned fire, blasting calibers of all types
from the backs of their running horses. Near impossible
to hit, as they swept the mine with bullets. The dead
buildings and dead ground ate the slugs, while Beaudine's men leapt from their cover, firing back at what
they could see. Quick shots, then ducking back.

Beaudine cracked his repeater until it was empty.

One of the new boys yelled to Lem, "Sweet Jesus on
Sunday, what did you get us into?" before a .44 slug blew
out his back, spinning him onto a slag heap. Smaller
slugs tore him up as he lay still.

The Fire Riders retreated from the canyon edge, reloaded, and started Hell again. Lem let it happen
around him, bullets chewing the wall of the building

where he was taking cover. He aimed carefully at them with his one eye, showing his hand, and killed three.

Smoke and sound thickened the air, as Bishop and Fox reached the road to the mine, their horses plowing gravel. A single Fire Rider stood as sentry, blocking the road in the opposite direction—an easy kill to get off the mountain, and ride away.

But that wasn't their mission.

The sentry moved to the middle of the road, but didn't advance, his horse pawing at the ground. He watched them, a new Smith & Wesson .38 hidden in the sleeve of his red tunic.

He saw Bishop breaching the shotgun rig, shuck the spent shells, and reload. He kept his hands tight on his gun, while Fox shouldered her bow and a sling of arrows, then took an ax from her belt and slipped her wrist through the leather thong on the end of its handle. Ready to throw.

Fire Riders were charging down hard from the top of the canyon, raising more dust and noise, but Fox and Bishop didn't bolt. Instead, they ignored their own wounds and shared a water bag with their horses. They did what they needed to do, never looking back at the Riders, or anything else.

The red-hooded sentry said, "You're damned to hell, Dr. Bishop," lifted his hood, and spit.

But they didn't hear or see him. Fox and Bishop only regarded each other for a moment, hands just brushing, before they urged the bay and the painted into full runs, galloping for the Goodwill Mine, and Beaudine.

Beaudine's hands were clamped around his skull, pain bursting through him. He murdered his own scream by locking his jaws tight, so nothing could escape. His back was shielded by the canyon wall, and he was in a good position, still ready to fight Creed's men, and take John Bishop as his prisoner. Still ready, but boiling inside his head. Boiling.

He dropped to one knee, water from his canteen washing over him. Cooling down, letting him find his thoughts. This wasn't the time to be lost, to be unsure. He drew a deep breath, neatened his hair as an officer should, before standing again. He stepped around a decaying mine support, noting the placement of his men: behind the old mining office and land shack to the right, and the slag heap on the left.

The pain behind his eyes eased, like a fever breaking.

He'd ordered the Goodwill ringed with explosives, and it was. He'd reunited his company, and even though there had been a burst of insubordination, his men were up to the skirmishes ahead. He knew that, and that calmed him. The pain continued to subside.

Beaudine knew he'd made a good plan, and could lead his men to victory, and allowed himself that satisfaction.

His mind was clearing. Calm before battle.

Beaudine saw Howard, his massive hand on Betsy, staring directly at him. Howard distinctly mouthed, *Loco*, with a twisted face and crossed eyes. Beaudine didn't flare. He steadied his rifle at Howard, and held the long cleaver like a battle ax, but the coffin maker was already looking away, shaking his head.

Beaudine reminded all, "We're doing this for gold!"

Howard gut-hollered, "Then where the hell is it?"

"You're forgetting yourself, soldier! I give the orders!"

Howard lit a cheap cigar, inhaled deeply. "I should've stayed where I was. Hell—"

Howard's words were shot dead by a .44 slug ripping the slag heap, pieces of rock flying jagged. He ducked, as more bullets struck around him. He rolled to one side, and Betsy exploded in his hand toward the red shapes riding along the canyon rim, her voice .44 thunder.

From his spot, Beaudine opened up with the repeater, laying fire on the enemy's position above, covering for his men. Beaudine got off as many rounds as his hands allowed, taking down two Riders, screaming, "You're outmanned! Come on down, and talk your surrender!"

He fell back just as the enemy returned maximum fire, blowing away huge chunks of the support braces. Beaudine kept low, fitting more ammo into the rifle, singing, "Roll out the drums of war, let's speak of things worth fighting for! Roll out the drums of war!"

The battle was erupting just as he'd always dreamed it.

Chaney kept close to the falling-in wall of the old shed, even as sniper shots blew out the window next to him. He fired back everything he had, tried to reload again, but the gun was too damn hot. More rounds pounded the Goodwill, ricochets screeching off rusty metal and powdering the rotting wood.

Two of the new boys were blasted from their place atop the four-by-four braces, and they fell without screams.

Lem's buddy cracked off rounds for cover, yelling from beside a grave, "They're going to bring out a damn Howitzer next!"

Chaney wiped dust and smoke from his eyes. "Beaudine said we'd have to take him!"

"From five men, not fifty!"

Lem Wright steady-aimed from the other side of the shed, firing twice and hitting two more of the Red Hoods, one in the face and another in the chest. Target practice. He lowered his gun, watched them fall back twitching, and their horses scatter along the top of the canyon. He refused to be rattled.

Lem cocked his own smile. "Dead or alive, we're in it now!"

CHAPTER NINETEEN
Taste of Hell

The sounds of the firefight surrounded John Bishop minutes before he passed through the split in the mountain that opened into Goodwill Canyon. It was a barrage he hadn't heard since the bloody fields of the war: all manner of gunfire, the shots crashing into each other, punched with the cries of men.

His reaction now was different from how it had been during the "conflicts." The shootings didn't matter, and the screams weren't reaching him. Bishop wasn't there to save anyone's life; his mission was his own. He lifted the rig from its saddle sling, keeping his arm extended, ready with double barrels as soon as Beaudine was in range.

Fox saw the dead look behind his eyes, and slowed the painted, giving Bishop the point, while covering his back. She knew he was riding alone, even if he wasn't. Her hand was tight around the throwing ax tethered to her wrist, and the bow was slung across her shoulder, rubbing her wound raw. Her breathing began to shallow, but she fought it. She had her mission, too, so pain had to wait.

Guns bellowed from the canyon, and Bishop raced to meet them, Fox riding close behind. He rode faster, determined, the rig hoisted like a battle standard.

At the Goodwill, Lem Wright watched the Red Hoods regroup after he'd shot two. He moved around the side of the old shed, where Chaney was pressing close to its shattered walls. An outlaw they hadn't even seen get shot was lying dead in the weeds, one of his boots blasted open.

Lem said, "Must've had his pistol pointed down at his foot when he took the bullet. That's a lesson."

Chaney could only nod.

Lem threw a smile to his buddy and the kid who'd taken cover in the miner's cemetery just beyond the shed's porch. They were hunkered by the graves, cracking off shots toward the canyon rim when it was clear. The kid was wiping away tears and sweat.

Lem called out, "Dead or alive, we're in it now!"

The kid froze, his gun hand shaking. Lem pushed it, as he brought up his Colt. "Boy, if you don't shoot, they'll shoot you. It's the way of the world."

Lem fired three times, delighting in his own marksmanship.

The kid shot toward the rim, forcing some Red Hoods back, but hitting nothing. You could almost hear the laughter, as they loaded up again, and the kid scrambled from the cemetery, toe-tripping over a marker.

Lem's buddy grabbed him by the arm. "I brought you in on this deal, your gun's mine!"

"You said it'd be a holdup! I did this when I was an infantry drummer, I ain't doing it again!"

"You're forgetting the gold."

"No, I ain't."

The kid blew a hole in his buddy's elbow, and made a panicked try for his horse. Running blind. That's when

White Fox saw him. She and Bishop were still a distance out. The Goodwill was in front of them, and the kid was dead set between the old mine buildings and the canyon wall, fear-struck, his feet refusing to move, with Red Hood gunfire pocking around him.

Lem's buddy fired the shot that mule-kicked the kid sideways. Somehow the kid couldn't believe he'd been hit. "I never been in no real gunfight before," he said as he collapsed, his own dead weight pinning him down.

Bishop and White Fox rode hell-bent into the canyon.

The Fire Riders watched it all from the rim, and opened up, their muzzle flashes streaks of heat lightning. Bullets cut the air like hard rain, as Fox and Bishop split, each running full-out on opposite sides of the Goodwill, trying for cover.

Another new boy shot at the Red Hoods from behind the old mining office, and got ventilated three times.

The kid struggled in the middle of the road: pushing himself off the frozen mud, trying to stand, his life pouring out. Not making it. Bishop rode to him, the bay rearing.

Bishop demanded "Beaudine!"

Above them, Red Hoods were refocusing their aim.

The kid tried to speak, his blood-slick hands a flag he was waving, but his voice had strangled to nothing. The kid pointed toward the mine entrance. Two shots from the rim dead-danced him a few feet, before letting him drop.

Enemy snipers had strafed Bishop before, and that instinct took him over. He gaffed his horse, breaking left, and then running right, to the old mine entrance.

The next shot hit the bay.

The horse screamed, bucking wild as a slug tore her rump. Bishop lurched from his saddle, landing hard on the rig, the double barrel bashing his ribs.

Chaney and Lem stepped from the cover of the old mine shack, crouching low, popping shots at the Red

Hoods above, then turning their guns on Bishop. Their buddy was holding his arm, gritting through the fire.

Chaney, the gambler, yelled, "And there's our goddamn gold!"

In a few simultaneous heartbeats: Fox's throwing ax hit Lem's leg above the knee, cutting muscle. He went down, trying to yank it free. Fox dropped from her horse, ran to Bishop, took the reins of both animals. Chaney followed her moves, thumb on the hammer of his Colt.

Bishop caught Chaney's action from the corner of his eye, got a sense of it, and protected her, shoulder-firing both barrels. The shotgun blew another hole in Chaney's hiding place, while he mostly dodged the blast. But it was a maneuver that worked, giving Fox time.

Bishop took cover in a small drainage ditch, slamming home two more shells.

Fox ran the horses toward a large stack of rail ties, bound with metal bands. The shots from above were random, targeting anything, chewing the ground around her. Fox kept the animals steady.

The bay snorted, as Fox worked to pull her down behind the barricade: getting her settled, on her knees, and then lying flat, so Fox could lie across her belly.

On the canyon rim, the Red Hoods opened ammo boxes, got set.

The bay was twisting, and Fox spoke, just letting the horse hear her voice. After some moments, there was no resistance as Fox pressed against her, the horse feeling the warmth of her body, calm in the chaos.

A new volley pounded every bit of the Goodwill, shooting the buildings and surrounding area to death: chewing the rail ties, ricochets screeching off the old iron, shattering already shattered glass.

The painted reacted to the gunfire, throwing his head back, biting at the air. Fox brought him down on his knees too, then to his side; finally, he did what she wanted. Straining, Fox kept both horses lying flat on the ground.

Bishop threw a shotgun blast at the old mine shed, turned and threw another at the slag heap where Howard was ducking low.

Lem screamed as he worked the throwing ax from his leg, pulling the blade free, red washing him. His buddy grabbed it, noting its feathers and markings, and yelled, "You're a coward, Bishop! Hidin' behind that Cheyenne bang-tail!"

Bishop lowered the empty rig, drew the Colt Peacemaker with his left, and shot Lem's buddy square in the chest. He turned, not returning fire, and staggered off the porch, and through the cemetery before crushing an old wooden cross that had Died Broke scrawled on it. The joke didn't escape him, and he death-laughed.

The Red Hoods, and the rim-fire, exploded again.

Bishop ran low across the field of battle, holding up the double barrels for protection, shots tearing at everything around him. He jumped behind the stacked rail ties as if tumbling into a shell hole. The bay reacted by sitting up, her muscles rolling, but didn't stand. Spasms racked her back flank.

The front of Fox's jacket was a wide smear of the bay's blood, but she calmed both animals as the shooting continued. She used her hands, voice, and body to keep them lying on their sides, out of the gun sights. Her touch was soothing and her quiet words somehow cut through the gunfire. The horses stayed down.

But Bishop's eyes were on the blasted-apart remains of the Goodwill and the scattered dead, as he tried to figure who was hiding where. "I couldn't find him, but Beaudine's here. He's got to be!"

"Then he is."

Bishop's voice was skidding. "Two of these men were there that night, I know it, as sure as anything."

"Oóoxo'eéstómáne."

The Cheyenne word for revenge had just been evenly spoken when more bullets tore into the rail ties, wood chips flying. Bishop and Fox kept the animals lying down. The horses didn't struggle.

The bay's head lolled, and Bishop said, "We can't lose these horses!" He pulled his medical kit from the saddlebag with his left hand, frantically going through it, finally dumping half of it. "Did you check the wound? Completely?"

"I was saving her."

"Not if she dies of blood poisoning! What about the slug?"

Bishop's words were sharp, impatient, as he cleaned the blood away from the bullet strike on the bay's rump. The wound was a crease in her flesh, the hair around it scorched.

Bishop absently touched the bullet trench on his own neck. "It's all right. There's no slug, no lead."

Bishop looked to Fox, took a breath. She nodded. He massaged the bay's neck, as he always had, before dabbing the wound with water and iodine. The horse half-kicked at his touch, straightening her leg and whinnying, but letting the doc finish. Trusting him.

Bishop dried the wound, then ran his left hand over the bay, patting her gently. White Fox watched him struggling to put the supplies back in the kit and snap it closed. She reached over and did it for him.

Fox said, *"Otahe."*

Bishop listened.

There followed a few moments of rumbled-echo gunfire, and then nothing. Not even the metallic cocking of weapons for the next barrage, or orders being barked.

Nothing.

No one spoke, or seemed to move. The shooting had actually stopped; the canyon was still. The steady wind disturbed pieces of broken glass and wood, jarring them to the ground, and then there was nothing. Again.

At the mining shed, Chaney stayed crouched, peeking his head around a corner to eye the movement along the top of the ridge. From what he could see, the Fire Riders had pulled back.

He stayed in place and checked his guns. Fully loaded.

A few of Beaudine's new boys emerged from their places behind the old shacks or piles of lumber, in bloody shock after the battle. One of them walked to the body of Lem's buddy, still sprawled in the miner's bone orchard, and kicked him over to make sure he was gone. Then he grabbed his wallet.

Behind the slag heap, Howard pressed himself against the rocky trash, holding his lit cigar half an inch from the fuse on a dynamite bundle. Listening. Waiting.

He got through half a prayer, but couldn't remember the rest. The smoke was tickling his nose, and he sneezed, giving himself away. Howard ducked for cover from the bullet rain he expected, but it never happened.

Bishop heard Lem Wright moaning in pain by the old shed, but there were no other voices. Not even whispers. He and Fox stayed low behind the stack of rail ties, their horses flat against the ground, starting to stir, snorting.

Bishop reloaded the shotgun rig, eased it shut, smothering the sound of the barrel locking with the palm of his left hand. Fox drew an arrow for her bow, and fitted it tight, but didn't draw back. Not yet.

They watched as Howard stood up from the cover of the slag heap, his fist around some dynamite, the cigar clenched in busted teeth. Betsy was holstered. He drew on the cigar, and sneezed again, his eyes watering at the awful smell. He was a huge target, but no one took a shot.

"See? You had no confidence, but I knew you were a good soldier. We shouldn't have revealed our positions all at once, but I suspect Dr. Bishop knows us by now."

The familiar voice spoke from behind the cross

braces that supported the collapsing entrance to the silver mine on the far side of the canyon. Bishop lifted the rig toward the voice, his body tensing as it continued: "I would say our common enemy has decided to let us settle our differences without them."

Beaudine stepped from his place between the large support timbers and the canyon wall, carrying his rifle and the long cleaver. He was over fifty yards away from where Bishop and White Fox had taken cover, and out of their range. They could only watch as he walked around the bodies of the Red Hoods and their horses, their blood mixing with the icy slush and mud, long gone.

He poked at each with the cleaver blade, as a triumphant warrior would use his broadsword. His tone was pure victory: "I brought this one down, and those other two, and more I suspect. But you all did your part, so earned your share. I'm proud of you, men."

Chaney barked, "Yeah, fine. When the hell do we get it?"

Beaudine took a few steps closer to Bishop and Fox, but kept his body angled, still at too far a distance for the shotgun's spread. Fox sat up on her knees, drawing her bow and aiming to shoot just over the top of their wooden protection, hitting Beaudine in the upper chest or throat.

He shielded himself with the cleaver blade, taunting. "That's up to Dr. Bishop, now that he's our prisoner."

Fox adjusted her shot, not taking her eyes off her target and reminding Bishop: "*He'kotóomoehá.*"

Calm in words, fierce in action.

Bishop then called out, "You made your deal with Captain Creed, not me."

"All that matters is you understand that you and your gold are now spoils of war."

Bishop squeezed Fox's shoulder, letting Beaudine's declaration bounce off the canyon walls and vanish before he stood up from behind the rail ties. The bay and the painted both got to their feet, flanking him.

Fox, and her aim, stayed low and fixed.

Bishop held the rig, taking in the damaged and dead of the Goodwill. Chaney, Howard, and Lem stayed on the ragged edge of their positions, holding weapons and the few new guns. Waiting to make a move, they stood bloody and tired.

Bishop measured his words. "Does this bunch understand that killing me gets you no gold?"

"They follow my orders."

"I'm barely holding back; a few of those dead are my doing, and I've left more behind." Bishop turned, pointing to Howard, Chaney, and Lem with the shotgun. "So, you might want to hear me out, Major."

Beaudine tossed an order, "You all stand at ease." Then he faced Bishop, "I appreciate the military courtesy."

"Did you forget that I used to be a doctor?"

Beaudine nodded. "No, I have not." Then he grandly pointed to the shotgun rig with the cleaver. "And that addition you've made for yourself is ample testament."

Bishop raised the shotgun level with Beaudine's stomach. "What I mean is, you think I don't recognize a man with a mental disorder?"

Chaney spit, "Jesus, another losing game."

Beaudine's words tumbled. "You're not in a position to be saying these things—things like this. Testing me is foolish. You, of all people, should know that! Howard, do you want your share? Ready to take it?"

Howard held up the dynamite bundle in one hand and the lit cigar in the other. "How many times you gonna ask?"

"That dynamite? Every shack. You're surrounded by it. Mr. Howard has made sure this entire place could be blown straight to Heaven." Beaudine turned the long cleaver in his palms, as he had that winter night. "We're all prepared to do what we need to do, so I'd think you'd stop flapjacking, and start cooperating!"

Bishop used his old bedside manner: "You need to stay calm, think, think of your officer's training. Get yourself clear." He adjusted his shoulders, tightening the line to the triggers. "Look around you. This didn't go as planned. These aren't Creed's men, so you tell me—vigilantes? Someone sent a damn army after you, Major."

Beaudine's voice jumped. "And we're victorious! We walked through the gates of hell for that gold, and it's ours! Are you saying you're not going to surrender it? Play that game again?"

"The gold's not here."

Chaney called out, "Then you take us to where you got it buried, or whatever. What's this stall for?"

"These aren't the only Red Hoods! They were riding down on us when we came into this canyon." Bishop yelled out to Lem, who had tied a belt above his knee to slow his bleeding, "You think this is over?"

Lem strained, "Going to help me, Doc?"

"Tell Beaudine what you think."

Lem threw it out, "We've got to get the hell out of here."

Beaudine shook his head, thoughts breaking. "No, no. We won this battle, and you're my prisoner, and you better damn well start acting like it!"

Bishop hit hard: "In truth, you're the prisoner. You believe I have this gold? If you don't follow my orders, you'll never see a bit of it."

Beaudine closed his eyes, sorting thoughts. Chaney stepped from behind the shed, arms outstretched. "What the hell do you want, then? This standoff isn't taking us no place."

"Beaudine, the bastard with the blind eye, and the big one. I don't know the rest of you, I don't care. Ride on."

Chaney said, "We're here for gold."

"We can talk about that, after I've settled my business."

Beaudine raised the cleaver, throwing away a laugh. "You are a man who refuses to accept his circumstances, and we will get that gold, one way or t'other."

White Fox stood, the bow drawn tight, the string slicing her fingers. A hint of sun highlighted the jagged edge of the arrowhead.

Bishop said, "The offer stands. The rest of you can ride out. Now. Maybe have a chance at that gold, but as long as this man's alive, you get nothing."

Lem quieted his moans, and Chaney was gun-ready. The last of the new boys looked to each other, not sure about their next move. One of them shifted on his feet, about to bolt.

Bishop didn't even blink, staying steady on Beaudine: "Just so we're clear: I came here to kill you. How many other enemies you have doesn't matter, because it's going to be *my* privilege to end your life."

Beaudine cleared his throat, and his mind: "Quite a declaration, Dr. Bishop. Not quite the Hippocratic oath, is it?"

Howard topped everyone: "What about our goddamn money! You're gonna come across this time!"

That's when the hammer dropped.

The black powder flamed on the Prussian needle rifle, sending the acorn-shaped bullet to find its target.

Time slowed on impact; the first shot hit one of the new boys in the neck, and traveled through to his partner standing next to him. The bodies were falling to the ground, pistols out of their leather and arms flailing, as all eyes turned toward the shots.

The Fire Riders, ripped into the canyon pass at full thunder on white-skulled horses. There were about twenty Red Hoods in the wave, attacking the Goodwill with rifles blazing.

White Fox let fly the first arrow, tearing into a Red Hood as he rode by shooting at Bishop with a pair of barking Colts. The arrow cut through the Hood's leg, his horse wailing back, as he fired. Bishop blasted him out of the saddle with a single barrel, turned around, and used the second on a Hood who was swinging an ax.

Bishop snapped the rig, loaded fresh shells, as the first stick of Howard's dynamite spun through the air over his head, fuse burning down. It landed between the Riders, the explosion erupting beneath Hoods and horses, catching them running, tossing them, slamming them down.

Fox whipped arrows in quick succession, hitting two more Red Hoods, as Bishop jumped over the barricade, and ran for Beaudine. Howard threw more dynamite, the explosion pushing Bishop to the ground, raining ice and bloody mud.

The Red Hoods rode in a wide circle around the small canyon, closing off the Goodwill, wiping out Beaudine's new men with rifle fire. They were knocked off their feet, sent spinning, landing dead.

Two of Beaudine's outlaws ran for White Fox, laying cover fire, diving for the barricade. Her war club shattered one in the temple, then she spun with a battle knife in her hand, opening the other one's throat. One tried to ask something before he dropped. She kicked both bodies against the rail ties, adding to her shield.

Bishop pulled himself up from the ground to see Beaudine through a veil of blowing smoke: slashing at the masked riders with the cleaver, laying open their chests or knees, whatever he could catch with the blade, as they rode down on him. His screams were louder than theirs, hysterical rage, as he battled his way past them.

One of the Red Hoods put a pistol to the back of Beaudine's head. Beaudine turned, with his blade, facing the gun. Another explosion tore the ground around them.

Howard lit one, then another, stick of dynamite, throwing each to opposite ends of the canyon. The blasts sent old lumber, hooded men, and horses scattering wild. Bishop rolled out of the way of two skull-headed stallions, their hooves just missing him.

Bishop stood and shot one Fire Rider off his horse, and he went down, firing back. He missed. Slugs from somewhere else finished the Rider off.

Lem Wright yelled to Bishop, "Think that came from one of us! Maybe you don't know who your enemies are, Doc!"

Bishop moved to Lem, still with one shell in the rig, and pointed directly at his head. "I know."

Lem cocked his dead eye. "If one of us just saved your bacon, then you'd be obliged. You see Beaudine?"

The smoke of the fires and dynamite blasts was blown aside by a whip-snap of cold wind, revealing hooded riders still tearing wild, guns roaring, a few men crawling before dying, but Major Beaudine was nowhere to be seen. There were just more casualties of battle, more bodies.

"He isn't hiding out here, if that's what you're thinking. You really want Beaudine or not?"

They both ducked Red Hood gunfire, before Chaney stopped it with five shots from behind the old shack. They heard a body crash.

Lem called out, "Good work, gambler!" Then, back to Bishop, "See? It just takes one, and you'll never get what you want."

"Where is he?"

Lem's pain was a whispered, "Help me, damn it."

Bishop was next to Lem, and used his left to unhook the belt around the damaged leg, with Lem watching through his good eye and gritted teeth. "That little Cheyenne can do some real cutting. I'd watch my back."

Bishop rewrapped the belt inches from the wound, and pulled it tight with his one arm, stopping the bleeding. "You had this in the wrong place, lost a lot of blood."

"Tell me I'm going to make it, at least to ride out of here."

Bishop didn't say a word; all around them was the sound of a new attack and retreat. Lem took a deep breath, and ran his hands over his leg, rubbing some feeling back into it. "Son of a bitch, that pains!"

"The nerves are getting blood again. You might pass out."

"But I be alive. We're in the middle of a battle, and you can't help being a doc. You want Beaudine? He had his escape all planned out, just in case. He's loco, but he knew."

"Help you, and let you go?"

"Then, I'm staying alive?"

"You need that leg sewn up right away, and my med kit's in my saddlebags."

"So I'll be fine? You haven't said it yet!"

By the canyon entrance, Howard puffed his cigar before lighting another bundle, and hurling it toward one of the buried charges. The ground blew apart, driving a posse of Fire Riders away from the old mine, their horses tossed off balance. The sound of the blast was trapped against the walls, and pounded back, over and over. One explosion became an echoed dozen.

Howard tossed the dynamite as grenades, every blast tearing through the Fire Riders.

A few Riders opened up on the slag heap, punching it with bullets. Howard shot back with Betsy, but stayed low after every trigger pull, their return fire slicing damn close. He drew deeply on the green cigar, eyes watering, before leaning close to the exposed end of the fuse to the dynamite bundles planted around the mine perimeter.

Howard sneezed out half his nose with the green smoke, then lit the fuse.

Lem Wright angled over in pain. "I can't sit a horse like this. You've got to do more."

"Where's Beaudine?"

Behind them, Chaney was belly-crawling from the old shack, stray slugs ripping around him.

Lem cried, "Think about that night! You know I didn't raise a hand to hurt your wife or son."

Bishop drew the trigger line tight. "Where?"

"This is worse than it was before!"

Bishop pressed the double-barrel rig against Lem's chest, boiling. "Where'd he escape to?"

"I'll show you, but—but you've got to fix me!"

Lem continued his begging, but Bishop wasn't hearing it. The outlaw's voice had been replaced by the screams of his wife and son. No words, just their sound, filling his head. Bishop felt his own blood pulsing, boiling through, as their painful cries grew louder and louder in his mind.

He leaned harder on the rig, busting one of Lem's ribs.

The bullet from Chaney's gun exited out of Lem's dead eye.

Bishop fell back, as Chaney moved on him, a Wesson two-shot Blade Derringer in his hand. "They call it the Gambler's Gun, and wasn't Deadeye surprised? Now, you're my prisoner, and going to take me to that goddamn gold."

The blast of a dynamite bundle shook the ground with cannonball force, tossing more Riders, setting one of them aflame. Their skull horses ran from the canyon, dead men dragging in their stirrups.

Bishop and Chaney faced each other's guns and eyes, the battle around them raging someplace else. Bishop said, "I've got no interest in you. You weren't with Beaudine the night this all happened."

Chaney flicked his gold tooth. "I ain't with him now. This is strictly a two-person game, and no one's sitting in."

Bishop eyed the palm-fit gun. "Give yourself a chance, son. Ride out. I'm on my own mission."

Chaney held out the Derringer. "You forget, I seen that thing in action," he said before plugging the shotgun barrel with the gun, and pulling the trigger. The small caliber bullet screamed up the barrel, before ripping into the black powder shell in the chamber, blowing the weapon apart at the breach.

Bishop spun off his feet as if he'd been hit with a sniper's bullet, his jacket and the rig's leather harness in shredded pieces. Blood began soaking the sleeve of his half-arm. Bishop tried standing, fighting against the numb feeling that was blanketing him, that he knew was shock.

Chaney said, "You don't even have an arm, and right now it hurts like hell."

The echo of the shotgun's bursting apart hid the sound of the arrow as it struck Chaney between the fourth and fifth ribs. He lurched in surprise before collapsing, the gun snug in his hand.

White Fox leapt the painted over Chaney, the reins to the bay in her teeth. She dropped from her own horse as Bishop tied off his bloody sleeve, the destroyed rig hanging loose from his elbow joint. He stumbled. She put her arms under him, giving him a boost onto the bay. Both horses snorted, ready to run.

Bishop had settled onto his saddle when the first set of mine supports along the canyon wall exploded, the force of the blast a sledgehammer blow to anyone standing.

The buried fuse burned from bundle to bundle, each support shattering with their detonation, sending burning wood, and metal in a wild burst across the mine, the four-by-fours becoming flying battering rams. Riders in red dove for cover, their horses cutting loose.

The old shed was next, the roof thrown into the air, then coming down on two Fire Riders, shards ripping them as jagged darts, a flaming cave-in from the sky.

Another blast tore the mine walkway from the canyon wall, huge sections tumbling, crashing to the ground, bringing tons of stone and gravel with it, blowing a hole in the earth.

White Fox and Bishop galloped through a thick curtain of violent dust, dodging the fallen and the debris, riding blind for the canyon entrance.

Howard took a draw on his cigar, and lit the fuses on two sticks of dynamite, before thumb-stubbing it out. He held the sticks as they burned down, watching the red glow eating the fuse, when a cry erupted from his massive chest; first it was a laugh, then a scream for "goddamn gold!" that became a wild animal howl that was beyond words.

He leapt from behind the slag heap and tossed the two sticks, holding back the Fire Riders with their explosions, as he ran for the open shaft of the old silver mine. He dove away from their rifle fire, scrambling on his feet, always moving.

Chaney managed his knees, breaking part of the arrow from his side, the pain eating him. He yelled, "You going to leave me in this Hell? I'm your partner!"

Howard's broken-by-laughter howl continued.

On the road to the canyon, the howl was just another distant note, followed by more explosions and cries. Bishop and White Fox broke clear of the Goodwill, those damned sounds fading, before another huge blast rocked the ground.

The dynamite quake shook boulders from the top of the canyon until they slid down the walls, breaking apart into huge chunks, blocking the entrance in a dust and gravel eruption.

The sound was louder than the hundred blasts that had come before it.

Bishop and Fox looked back at the Goodwill, half buried, as their horses ran hard toward the down-sloped trail off the mountain. The Fire Rider sentry, guarding the way out, charged them, firing warning shots. Fox drew, and hit him with a warning shot of her own, the arrow puncturing the meat of his shoulder. It was pure whip-fast movement, and perfectly accurate.

The Fire Rider's red hood garbled his howling as he pulled back on his horse too hard, tangling his footing. They tumbled hard into the ditch alongside the canyon road.

The Rider kept swearing at Bishop and Fox as they leapt down an ice-slick hill, to a small cut in the trail. Not more than a break between rocks and dead trees, but it was a door to the other side of the frozen Colorado.

He pulled off his hood, and watched the last burst of flames and black smoke erupting from the Goodwill, feeling the sound of those final explosions, then shook his head. "God Almighty."

He bit off a plug of hard tobacco, ignoring the arrow protruding from his shoulder. He wasn't entreating the Lord, or seeing the Goodwill as a Biblical pit of sulfur, or doing any damn thing, but just sitting.

Having a quiet chew at the end of the day, a hundred yards from an open grave stacked with corpses.

The opium smoke was gossamer, a light fog that hovered close to the ceiling of Widow Kate's office. The dragon pipe next to her was lit, but she didn't draw from it, just took deep breaths of the air, working at her desk. She carefully wrote half of the last zero of "100,000," then urged the ink into the tip of her new Waterman with a quick shake, to complete it.

The columns of figures in the ledger were neatly entered, and their total was her testament. Kate took satisfaction from just looking at the numbers, not thinking about the money, only seeing that each total was greater than the last entry. She could lose herself in numerals.

The knock on her office door was precisely three times, and there was a wait until Kate called, "Enter!"

Soiled Dove slid the doors open, and closed them behind her before saying a word. She placed five stacks of bills, each with a name written on a small slip of paper on top, on Kate's leather desk blotter.

"I double-checked every girl, makin' sure they wasn't holding out nothing. That's everything, to the dollar."

"Any gold? Silver?"

"No, ma'am, this was strictly a paper day."

Kate smiled as she gathered the cash, counting it for herself. "You're doing very well, girl. This place is running like clockwork, and I'm obliged, since I still can't get up and down those stairs."

Soiled Dove nodded. "I just want to be of help. Here." She held out White Fox's torn skirt and top that had been wrapped and tied around something small.

Kate took the bundle. "I was just thinking about those two, wondering if they did what they set out to do. Or maybe got killed. That would be a shame. You should burn these."

"Yes ma'am. There's something inside."

Kate unfolded the bloody clothes, revealing an earthen jar of salve with something written on its side: For your scars.

Kate stroked the bandage protecting the stitches along her massive side, luxuriating in the opiate fog, and said, "Now, I'm obliged to the Cheyenne."

CHAPTER TWENTY
Escapes

The explosion gut-punched Howard, Chaney, and Beaudine against the mine wall, pieces of the rotting ceiling beams falling around them, followed by broken chunks of rock and tarry mud. They kept their heads down as the force pushed past them, grit raining into their eyes. The grit shimmered, with a taste of silver fog.

"Was that the last?"

Howard didn't hear Beaudine. He was holding his nose and blowing, to clear out his ears. Beaudine asked again, and Howard said, "I ain't sure. Should be though."

"Let me put it this way, are there any more charges that are closer?"

"You saw where I put 'em."

"I'm saving your life bringing you here. Want to answer me straight?"

Howard blew his nose again. "There aren't no more that are closer."

The three looked back down the shaft to the opening of the Goodwill silver mine, which was now blocked by collapsed timbers, and fallen-in walls. Chaney inched his way to his feet, holding his bleeding side. "It don't make no difference. We're trapped. My thanks for saving us, though."

Beaudine didn't respond. Chaney cleared his eyes with his fingers, looked at the flecks of silver on their edge. "But at least I'll die a rich man."

Beaudine, holding the long cleaver and one of the Fire Riders' red hoods, said, "Rich is what we're all working for, but your death will not be today. We've escaped prisoners to find, and we're wasting time. There's an air duct tunnel right up ahead, opens above the river."

Chaney and Howard looked to each other, bloody and tired. Beaudine said, "See for yourself."

Chaney and Howard hauled themselves up and followed Beaudine farther into the mine, the dark of it becoming even darker, as they felt their way along the narrowing walls.

"Don't get ideas about picking up nuggets. This was played out years ago, if it played at all. And that stuff on your hands is residue from the mucking. Worthless."

Howard said, "Forget the silver, I'd just a-soon get the hell out of here."

"We will."

Chaney wiped off the worthless. "How'd you know about an airway? I thought Creed picked this place."

Beaudine said, "My brother told me. He's buried in that miner's bone orchard that you blew to smithereens, Mr. Howard. When Creed suggested the Goodwill, I did what a good soldier does in the face of the enemy, and revealed nothing."

Beaudine stopped, with Howard and Chaney next to him, their eyes hit with a narrow slice of sunlight coming from the end of a small tunnel cut in a sidewall.

Chaney started around Beaudine. "Let's go!"

"Hold on. Mr. Howard, you first. There are planks at the end that need to be broken through to the outside, and your strength is mandatory. But before you do, Mr. Chaney?"

Beaudine handed Chaney the red hood. He held it for just a moment, feeling its curious weight. Chaney's eyes adjusted, focusing first on the blood soaking one side of the hood, then on the Rider's head still inside it, lopped cleanly at the neck with the cleaver blade.

Chaney dropped the hood, choking air.

Beaudine kicked it aside. "This was a difficult day, gentlemen. We fought hard and let the savage loose, but now we're an army of three. If we're going to find our way to Bishop's gold, there can be no mutiny, no disloyalties. If your heart is traveling in that direction, now would be the time to tell me."

Chaney held his wounded side with red-wet fingers. "I'll do what's needed."

"Mr. Howard?"

Howard regarded the head at his feet, then said, "You keep asking like I don't want that gold no more. I want it."

The ceiling shifted with a low rumble, a crack above them widening. Chaney half-crouched as Beaudine stepped to one side, pointing to the airway with the cleaver blade.

Howard worked his way through the stone cut, to the opening fifty feet in. The passage was too small for him to raise his arms, so he smashed through the boards with a single head butt, flooding the mine with sunlight and the fresh sound of the river below.

The finger of water coming off this side of the Colorado didn't have a name, but ran cold and fast down the mountain, before splitting into a dozen streams cutting through winter-bare woods. White Fox and Bishop stood on one of those stream banks, frosted with snow to the water's edge, tending themselves.

Caked with black gunpowder, dust from the Goodwill, and blood, they washed as best they could, with handfuls of icy water splashing across their wounds. Fox pulled the shotgun rig from Bishop's arm, the blasted-jagged section of the breach slicing her hand.

She sucked on the cut, started to unhook the leather straps across his back, pain eating at them both. Bishop kept his voice flat: "The gambler was going to give us Beaudine. Give us. You didn't have to shoot."

Fox pulled the leather free. "We don't have the word. You'd say it was 'a choice.'" Then she stuffed the broken rig into Bishop's saddlebag.

Fox took a deep breath and held it, feeling the mountain cool, before she said, "*Ametané'ôsené.*"

"You think you gifted me life?"

She smeared the blood from her hand onto the blood on her clothes. "We wouldn't have survived. Now, you can go on with the hunt."

She knelt by the water, pulling her shirt down over her shoulders, so he could clean the deep sore there, rubbed to the muscle by her bowstring.

Bishop looked through the medical kit. "Your salve would be good for that."

"I gave the last away."

"Another choice?"

The tiny voice from behind the trees chirped: "Mister, if you've got money hid, you need to give it over. Really slow."

The little girl was about four feet tall, with a flat nose that seemed to run directly from her mouth with no break, and blue eyes that were too far apart. Her hair was straight, cornstalk yellow, and in desperate need of a ribbon or a comb that would have helped it hide her enormous ears. She held a rusting squirrel rifle crimped against her, and she moved it around every time she spoke in a way that was oddly musical. Tuneful, even when she mangled her words.

"That there the money? I'll be wanting it."

Bishop's arm went into firing position, without his thinking, and without a weapon. His eyes met Fox, and his instincts cooled. "Really don't think you need a gun."

Bishop tried to follow the end of the rifle as it moved in circles while the little girl bobbed her head about, almost singing. "I do need it, to make you give over money. Or I'll shoot. You. And her. And then, maybe, you again."

"It'll probably hurt some, but that's not going to kill either one of us. Or even a squirrel for supper. Is that what you're doing out here?"

"Ask you the same question!"

"We're just riding through. Is this your land? Is that it?"

"No, it ain't."

"Then why are you pointing that? Are you a robber?"

The rifle started moving again, and so did the "voice music": "My sister's ailing bad, and we can't fix our wagon, and my pa don't know which end is up, so I'm taking charge. And you all are the first things I'm taking charge of."

Fox said, "Where is your father?"

"No business of yours! Show me your hands!"

Bishop raised his left hand, and half a right arm skyward. The little girl said, "Was you born that way, or did somebody take after you?"

"Somebody took after me. We can help you, and your sister."

"She's been dyin' for as long as I can remember."

White Fox said, "He is a doctor."

"You're like somethin' the devil coughed up! I seen doctors afore, and they didn't look nothing like you. Or her!"

Bishop smiled. "You're surely right, most don't look

like me, but I am a doctor. Let me try helping your sister, and if you don't like it, you can still shoot me."

Nodding, the little girl lowered her rifle, blurting, "Don't think I won't!" She repeated it as if it were a chorus.

The Conestoga was propped on a tree stump, leaving the back axle to freely turn, without the weight of its shattered wheel. At first glance, it looked to be the wagon of a broken-down circus: the canvas top had seen too many repairs, with patches of all colors, as had the too-large wagon bed, which was pieced together from half a dozen freight schooners by a carpenter with no skills.

The campsite could have dropped out of the sky to land in this most unlikely place: there was a small fire with a fine, polished steel cook pot and implements hanging over it, surrounded by two upholstered rocking chairs, a mahogany dresser with bottles of perfume scattered across the top, most of which had spilled down its side, and a large vanity mirror mounted in a standing frame.

Albert Tomlinson stepped from the back of the Conestoga, wringing out a washcloth, when he saw his daughter rifle-marching between Bishop and White Fox, as they rode from the woods to the campsite. Albert, whose body could barely support the clothes he was wearing, waved to his little girl with a tired, grey smile.

"Well, how're you folks doing today?"

The girl started running to Albert, turned midway to keep her bent rifle on her new prisoners, then backstepped the rest of the way to his side. Her voice was all highs and lows. "Look what I found in the woods, Papa! Caught 'em on my own, brung 'em in on my own. And you know they got money!"

Albert patted the top of her head. "Now, May Flowers, I think you were supposed to get us some dinner."

"But they're better!"

Bishop and Fox got down from their horses as Albert

extended a bony hand. "Albert Tomlinson, over to Arkansas. Surely am sorry about this. Hope you didn't feel too threatened." Then he whispered, "My May Flowers wouldn't really shoot nobody."

Bishop shook with his left. "She's a good protector. How long have you been here, Mr. Tomlinson?"

"Nigh on three days."

"And we're the first to find you?"

"This is a pretty lonesome spot, I guess. There was a Shoshoni scout party one night, but they didn't come in."

"What happened to your outfit?"

May Flowers said, "Have 'em empty up their pockets!"

Albert took the rifle from his daughter as he scarecrowed back to the wagon, settling by the empty axle. May Flowers jammed her tongue stubbornly behind her lower lip as her father spoke: "The axle started turning funny coming down the trail out of that low range, and then we lost the wheel."

White Fox looked underneath the wagon, pointing to the loose iron above the axle braces. "The brake rocker is broken."

Albert said, "Yes, ma'am. We couldn't control nothing the last bit, and crossed the water too fast. Darn near toppled over completely. That's when we lost the wheel, and I had to fish it out. But I was surely glad to get to this side, with the girls and all."

Fox moved to the wheel, which was leaning against the mahogany dresser. She rolled it in the grass, to the place where the iron flatting had peeled back, splintering the wood.

"The felly is split. This can't be fixed."

May Flowers singsonged, "She knows about all of this?"

Bishop said, "She knows. If you don't pull out of this mud soon, this wagon's staying put."

Albert said, "We're worse than the church mouse right now, can't afford a darn thing."

"You've got some fine furniture, Mr. Tomlinson."

"My wife's things. She's gone."

"Why don't you sell a piece, get a new wheel?"

May Flowers grabbed one of the bottles of perfume and began dousing herself. "That's how come I was getting us money." Then she stuck out her tongue at White Fox.

Albert said, "I got me another daughter who's with bronchitis. That's the baby, and I can't leave her to go to town, to do business."

"May told us. I'm a doctor."

Albert took a long look at Bishop, in tatters, before finally saying, "Really?"

Little May Showers had a Chinese abacas lying on her tummy, and she pushed the beads around trying to match the colors in a row. If she managed it, she allowed herself a thin smile between fits of harsh coughing. A slip of a girl, tucked up tight in a hammock strung across the back of the freight schooner, she rocked it defiantly when her father came close.

She looked a great deal like her sister, but her face was smaller, and meaner, with coarse black hair instead of blond. She shared the same blue eyes, but they didn't soften her features, or invite anyone closer.

Albert entered the wagon, which was filled with more furniture, including a spinning wheel, and moved carefully to his daughter. May Showers huddled in her hammock, racking the beads on the abacas, back and forth, clicking them together with every step Albert took, as if he were approaching a rattler about to strike.

"May Showers, this here's a doctor, honey. He's going to help you, so you behave and let him."

The little girl thrashed violently, as Albert pried the abacas from her fingers. She didn't yell, but burst into a fit of deep, raw coughing. Albert tried more water, which she couldn't swallow, the spittle running down her chin. Her chest finally relaxed, and she settled back into her sweat-dirty pillow. She never said a word, but thrust her hands out for the abacas.

Albert put it aside. "I'm a bookkeeper by trade, and I find this exotic device very useful. The girls think it's a plaything. They don't like no dolls or nothing."

White Fox opened the medical kit, as Bishop reached inside for a small mirror. "How long has it been since she's washed?"

"I try my best. We got a bathtub, but it's packed away."

"Part of getting her well is keeping her clean."

Bishop handed the mirror to Fox, who angled it to catch a ball of sunlight, which she focused on May Showers' chin. May hit her father with furious eyes, clutched the sides of the hammock, and was about to twist.

Albert stammered something about behaving, but Bishop cut into it: "May, I don't look like a doctor, but I am, and I know how to make folks feel better. All I want you to do is open your mouth just a little bit, so I can look inside with this glass. I promise not to sneak in any nasty medicine. And, I do anything you don't like your sister's going to shoot me with her squirrel gun. Okay?"

The girl's jaw was clenched angry-tight. White Fox ran her hand across her forehead, brushing her unwashed hair out of her eyes, and letting it rest there. May sagged her mouth open. Bishop adjusted an examining lens to see into her throat, illuminated by the sunlight reflected in the hand mirror.

"There's no infection."

"The Little Rock docs said it was the bronchitis."

"Her airway's blocked. That's different."

Bishop held out his hand, and Fox automatically gave him his monaural stethoscope. He placed it on May's chest, and listened, looked to Fox and said, "She sounds like you."

White Fox reached into the medical kit.

The reservoir of the oxygen pump filled instantly with running water from the stream. White Fox picked out slivers of ice, while May Flowers peered over her shoulder.

"What's that thing? It worth any money?"

"For your sister."

"What's it worth?"

Fox stood, checking the rubber tubes. "It will save her life."

May Flowers stayed on Fox's heels as they walked back to the wagon. "But what's it worth?"

May Showers' hands fought the celluloid oxygen mask, clawing at it until Bishop pulled it back. "May, this is what you need. You don't have to do anything but breathe. Won't that feel good? No more coughing?"

The little girl screamed, throwing a tiny, balled fist, before doubling over, her chest racking. Fox held her hands as Bishop fitted the mask over her mouth and nose, tightening the strap around her head.

"Turn it!"

Albert jumped at Bishop's voice, and started to crank the device, bringing the oxygen from the water through the tube to the mask. May Showers took the new air in, but her hands went to the mask again, her fingers clawing.

Albert said, "Daughter May Flowers? Mr. Foster's song, now."

May Flowers stood behind her sister, her downturned face sullen and dark, but she began to sing, "Slumber, my darling, thy mother is near,/Guarding thy dreams, from all terror and fear," bringing her voice up from someplace beyond her, filling the wagon.

May Showers settled in her hammock, breathing quietly, her sister's voice wrapping around her.

May Flowers carried Stephen Foster's lullaby out of the wagon on wings, to the edge of the stream and the horses, where Bishop and Fox were checking their saddles. They listened to that perfect voice, clear as mountain air, and a smile traveled between them. Albert shrugged at his daughter's talent.

Bishop said, "That's an amazing gift she's got."

"Like their mama. Not much to look at, but they do have those voices. Both of 'em."

"I didn't presume, Albert. Did your wife pass?"

"No, sir, she run off. So guess I'm divorced, but without papers. Uglier than a two-snout pig, but she found another fella."

The song hid White Fox's reaction, and she sneezed her laugh, as Bishop nodded toward the dresser. "Then, I suppose if it doesn't pain too much, sell one of her pieces, get that wheel? You can go to town now, your girls will be all right."

"Now." Albert dug his hands in his pockets. "That's just what I'm going to do, get fixed up, and to my new job. But I don't have no money to pay you, Doc. You want to take a chair? They're nice sitters. Frenchie imports from New Orleans."

Bishop secured his med kit in the saddlebag. "Your daughter's sleeping easy because of this young woman. That breather belongs to her."

"Then I thank you greatly, ma'am. Maybe you'd like to take something with you?"

White Fox got on her horse. "I am."

"There are a lot of good reasons to kill a man, but target practice ain't one of 'em," Fuller said.

"Is he being ironic? Is there a smile there?" Creed asked.

Hector gently gaffed Creed's Pride to quicken his pace, so that he was now riding parallel with Fuller. The sniper glanced at the boy and Captain Creed, who were saddled together. There wasn't a hint of a smile on Fuller's face, or anything to read in his eyes, except the burning from the bullet in him.

"Satisfied?"

Hector nodded his approval of Fuller's expression and response, a kid pretending to be an officer in a mirror.

Fuller returned his eyes to the horizon, and the storm roiling there, its light pre-snow just starting to reach them.

"Report?"

Hector spoke over his shoulder. "Sir, I'm looking at Mr. Fuller, and I think he's saying exactly what he means."

"I won't make it a direct order, but you'd be doing the company right, getting rid of that useless sack."

Fuller kept riding, his hands almost going to his sniper's rifle. Almost.

Creed's Pride whinnied. The captain leaned in, squeezing Hector's shoulders to the bone. "You're holding Pride back. Appreciate the honor of where you are; let him have his way."

Hector loosened his pull, trying to fall into the rhythm of Pride's gait, but was still a plowboy on a thoroughbred. The boy's awkward movements, sputtering and gangly, got a half smile from Fuller, but he stayed fixed on the flattening land, and the mountains that were changing shape and color the farther they rode into Wyoming.

Behind them, a ways back, Fat Gut was running his nag hard across the flats, trying to catch up. He yelled to everyone at the top of his lungs, but there was no attention paid to his mush.

Fat Gut tried calling again, and Creed said to Fuller, "You still favoring that shoulder?"

"I expect to for some time."

Creed considered the sniper's response by adjusting his sunglasses, new snow collecting on the lenses. "We still have a mission, and I expect every man to do his part."

"I will, sir." Fuller let that stand, and then: "I already have, as best I could."

"Thinking of your failure in the woods?"

"I'm thinking about my wife and son."

Creed's voice rose. "Want to do right by them? Then you need to know just how much your skills have been compromised, to make sure you can claim your fair share of that money. There's a target running up on us, and I'm giving you a direct order to fire at it."

"I'll get myself back up. You'll see."

Creed said, "Actually, I won't. But I'll know."

Hector yanked Pride to a sudden stop, jolting the saddle. Creed slammed the boy hard with a double-fist against his side, knocking him clean out of his stirrups, and landing him hard.

"What are you doing, boy? You don't treat this animal with disrespect!"

Hector stood, rubbing the feeling back into his elbow, his eyes trying to focus on a rider in the distance. "Truly sorry, sir. It's that, ahead. I-I never seen nothing like it."

He took a rosewood and dragon's blood rosary from his pocket, and held the simple wooden cross close to his lips. "My mama, she swore me a Catholic. Don't know why."

The horse was a living skeleton, skull head mounted on bleached bones, with fire pouring from its sides. A red, faceless demon, was running the animal straight out of hell, cutting through the grey of the horizon, to come for Creed, Fuller, and Hector.

"Report! What is it you're seeing?"

Fuller put his arm through his rifle sling, and brought up the weapon. "Man in a hood, sir."

"Sniper, I imagine you've already got your finger on the trigger." Creed patted his horse's neck. "It's not needed."

Fuller steadied the butt of the Morgan-James against his still, blood-wet shoulder, shutting one eye to site this new target. "We'll see."

Fat Gut short-pulled on his horse, bringing it to a stumbling halt beside Creed's Pride. Gut and the nag were both sweat-winded, and his words still beaten by broken teeth: "It'th about timeth you thtopped! Dinn't you hear me, cousin?"

Creed said, "We heard."

Gut squinted in the direction everyone was looking, at the Fire Rider getting closer. "Who the thell is dat?"

"Exactly."

The skeletal horse eased its run, the flames in its mane and tail relaxing, as it slowed to a perfect stop before Creed. Fuller kept his rifle steady, aiming at the place directly between the eyeholes of the crimson hood.

The Fire Rider waved. "Captain, you're fighting light."

Creed said, "These men are my handpicked best."

"Not all of them."

Smythe pulled off his hood, smoothing his wiry red hair with one hand, while keeping the other resting in his lap. He looked to Fuller, bit off a chaw, then rubbed his shoulder where White Fox had left her arrow.

"You look to have the same problem I do, boy-o. That shoulder? Little whore stick you with an arrow, too?"

Fat Gut got out between laughs, "Nopeth! A bulleth!"

Smythe looked directly at the inescapable barrel of the long-range rifle. "That's a beef-headed way of doing things, ain't it? You loaded? Capped?"

Fuller nodded, and Smythe said, "Then lower it.

You've all made too many damn mistakes. Don't make another. I'm taking you in, so you can alibi yourselves."

"Stand down, sniper Fuller." Fuller let a few heartbeats pass, then followed Creed's order, pulling the rifle up, resting it on his hip, arm still through the sling.

Creed said, "Did you get the prisoners?"

"No, Captain, we ain't."

"We sent a message, and you had a lot more men than I did."

"Beaudine brought the whole Goodwill down on their damn heads."

"I'm a military officer—"

"A blind man."

Creed continued as if Smythe hadn't uttered a thing. "—who captured Bishop, and held on to him. Most of my volunteers are left frozen in those mountains, but we were better than you. A hundred fighting a madman, and you lost."

Smythe ran his fingers through his beard, thoughtfully eyeing Fat Gut before saying, "Looks to me like *you* lost, mate. She kicked your teeth out? You know, there are a half dozen I could name that I'd rather see on that horse than you."

Creed said, "Now, I can agree with your blather."

Gut swallowed his spit, forcing his words out slow and dry: "I-am-a-good-fighter. Always-do-wath-my-cousin-saith."

Smythe said, "You can't even defend how worthless you are. Ride on, I'm not taking you in."

"You're justh a pristhon guard! You got nothin' to thay about nothin'."

"I was a guard, and what I am now doesn't matter. What you've got to remember is that whether I'm wearing a uniform or a hood, I'll kill you just as soon as sneeze."

Fat Gut tried a busted-teeth smile, to show he wouldn't be backed down, so Smythe drew a Colt six-shot with a worn handle from his red tunic. "I said, ride on. Or be dinner for the wolves. Either way."

"Whath abouth my thare of gold?"

Creed said, "You're family, I carried you. But the prisoners' escape is on your head. That's what happened to your share." Creed turned his eyes to the sound of Fat Gut's heavy breathing. "I had other plans, but these men are saving your life. You should appreciate that. Now get the hell out."

Gut was about to say more, but thought better of it, as he brought the nag around, spurring her side too hard, and taking off at a run. Heading into Wyoming, leaving the rest behind.

Smythe looked down at Hector, who was amazed at the events of the previous minutes. "You're gonna catch flies in that mouth, you don't close it."

Creed, settled into his Pride, said, "He needs a ride."

Smythe said, "That horse's your eyes?"

"Better."

"Okay, boy-o, let's see what mama feeds ya."

Smythe extended his good arm, and pulled Hector onto the back of his saddle with a single, sweeping motion. Pain gripped him, but he didn't give it away. Fire Rider Smythe angled his skeleton-horse around, heading back toward the horizon, as Hector settled in. Creed's Pride followed, the captain holding the reins easy, with Fuller behind the bunch, keeping everyone in his sights.

No one was in a hurry against the snow and the darkening sky.

Smythe smiled at Hector. "You look like a veteran. Been with the captain a long time?"

"Pa rode with him, and he got killed, so he took me in. I'm his eyes and ears sometimes. Other times, he ain't too happy with me."

"I imagine you'll have a few more years together, yet."

"If I can ask, how you know each other? You don't sound like anybody else who rides with him."

"No, you can't ask that. But I'll tell you I hail from the coast of England. You know where that is?"

"Across the ocean someplace. That's how come you talk like you do?"

"Right."

"And does everyone there paint up their horses?"

Smythe reached behind his back, giving Hector his red hood, "In my business, sometimes it works best if people are a little scared of you. Throws 'em off their game."

"I never seen nothing like this before."

"When I was your age, my dad told me about the demons of Romney Marsh. You never heard of that one, right?"

"No, sir."

"They were pirates, did up themselves and their horses like demons, raiding French ships for booty. Come riding right out o' hell, scaring everybody to death, sometimes taking a shipful of goods without firing a shot."

"What happened if anybody tried to fight back?"

Smythe made a slashing motion across his throat. Hector's voice was small. "And you're the leader here?"

"Not the leader boy-o, but the painting-up was all mine."

Hector nodded, as a sting of wind rushed by his ear. There was a sound like bee wings, and a tiny pain. The snow blew heavier, and he brushed the cold from his ear, coming back with bloody fingers.

"H—Hey, I think I been shot!"

Fat Gut's second and third shots were distant puffs of smoke that ended in ground strikes. He pressed the nag full-out, galloping toward Creed and his men, with two pistols firing. His hands flailed in all directions, sending the bullets every which way.

Creed called out, "Hector!"

"I'm okay, sir! I can still do my duty!"

"Good. Sniper!"

Fuller had the Morgan-James, his thumb locking the hammer in place, steadying his shot.

Fuller said, "He's a mighty big target," before pulling the trigger, and exploding Fat Gut's chest. The slug passed clean through, hitting the trunk of a bare tree some yards behind him.

The nag carried Fat a while longer, before he slipped off her back and hit the ground, eyes locked open.

Creed said, "I could hear it. That was a clean shot."

Fuller lowered the rifle. "Yes, it was. And at a good distance."

"Hector! Report!"

Hector was blotting the blood from his ear with Smythe's hood. "I'm fine, Captain. Had to earn my wound sooner or later."

"You're a good boy." Creed gently nicked Pride to start again. "Sniper Fuller, why didn't you take the target when I asked the first time?"

Fuller eased alongside Creed. "The fat bastard never shot at me before."

The snow was gentle in the air, large flakes dancing around Bishop and White Fox, as they rode along the edge of the stream, thin bits of ice cracking under their horses. The sun was dipping, bringing a snap to the cold coming out of the woods, but Bishop didn't shield his face with collar or scarf; he wanted to feel the purity of it. The clean.

Bishop said, "That was a good thing you did, helping that child."

"Ugly child."

He laughed. "Like a two-snout pig. Never argue with a father."

White Fox smiled. "*Néhnéšétse.*"

"Yes, I guess it was both of us."

"She needed a doctor, not just me."

Bishop let that thought hang for a moment, and then: "We helped her, and a few hours before, we killed a man. More than one. A hell of a lot more."

Her voice was flat. "Your journey became a war."

"And you knew it was going to happen."

Bishop looked at her. "We're riding in the wrong direction. We need to go back to the Goodwill."

Fox didn't return it. "This is right. *Anôse.*"

"It isn't right. We don't know where the hell Beaudine went. We almost did."

Fox finally met him. "Their horses had an army brand."

"So, they were rustled."

"There's a man, past the deep trees, who'll know about the stolen horses, and the red ones. Everything."

"*Ma'êhóóhe.*"

Fox didn't respond to her given name, she just repeated, "Everything."

They leapt across a small, leaf-filled gully, to an open break in the woods where a row of pines had been cut into a semicircle, their branches bent back, tied to stakes in the ground. The cones that had fallen around the trees were neatly stacked beside them.

Bishop brought up the bay, looked around. "Did we just cross a line?"

Fox turned, about to call out, when a large branch whip-snapped from the side of the largest pine, slamming Bishop in the chest, and knocking him hard, backwards off his horse. It was a trip-wire cannon shot that had the bay rearing, front legs chopping the air.

Bishop's head slammed onto the flat of a rock. He turned over in sharp pain, trying to find his way back to full consciousness, when the heavy rope slipped around his ankles, hoisting him into the air.

He was spinning.

He heard Fox's voice: distant, screaming, in Cheyenne. They were twisted half words that Bishop struggled to figure, if he could just hang on to the edge of the light. And stay there.

That's when the dark swallowed him.

CHAPTER TWENTY-ONE
Blood on the Claw

There were five talons to it, each pointed at the end and sharpened raw along the side. They were attached to a metal wristband by precise welding, with just a hint of a bump where the iron pieces were joined. The bumps actually looked to be knuckles on someone's hand, and not sloppy workmanship.

The spots marking the sides of the talons could have been blood, or flecks of rust. Bishop's eyes weren't focused yet, and he couldn't tell. The claw was mounted on a cut-stone wall just feet from where he was lying, between a Cheyenne warrior's shield crossed in black and white hide, and several long-knives, each in its own colorfully beaded sheath.

Bishop moved his head, and water tear-drizzled down his face. He bolted up, the bear rug covering him falling forward, as he pulled the wet cloth from his forehead, tossed it aside.

Noah Crawford picked the cloth up from the hard-dirt floor. "I keep a clean house, goddamn it!"

Crawford's voice was an explosion. His face, something carved from the side of a mountain, was surrounded by an acre of matted, grey hair. Brows were wild tufts over two lumps of coal, his mouth and nose shapes hammered to fit into this mess that'd been blasted apart, and put back together wrong.

There was a hogleg tied down to one thigh, and a Colt Lightning in his belt, almost covered by his wave of a belly. He slapped Bishop's feet to the floor with saddle-sized hands, "You took it hard, but I've had worse. What are you drinkin', and don't say well water."

"Anything."

Muttering thick in Cheyenne, Crawford lumbered to the other side of the rounded dugout, stopping to sniff at a cook pot in the fireplace. The curved ceiling and sides were rough-cut logs, cemented by sloppy mud and straw, while the wall Bishop rested against was bare rock, protected by animal skins crazily quilted across it.

Crawford said, "Sorry about the trap, but a man's got to protect his patch."

Bishop threw his legs over the bed, catching the edge of a spear with his foot. War clubs, bows, and blades of mountain tribes were all within reach, propped against the wall or under the furniture. By the door, there was a cabinet with ten books, all worn cloth binding, placed neatly on its top shelf. A double-blade fighting axe took up the rest of the space.

White Fox handed Bishop oily whiskey in a small bowl. "You can drink." She touched Bishop's hand, lifting the bowl to his mouth. He drank. She looked to Crawford, who brought a large knife down on a slab of salted beef he was cutting, the meat not pulling from the bone.

Crawford swore, and she said: "I'm needed outside, *ného'éehe.*"

Fox moved to the door, taking one of the books from the shelf before leaving.

Bishop waited for her to leave, then said to Crawford, "I know what that means."

The sun was actually showing its face as White Fox sat *on a rail of the corral fence, Tales of the Grotesque and Arabesque,* by Edgar Allan Poe, open on her lap. The corralled horses nickered and nudged, and she would absently stroke a mane, but stayed lost in the pages.

Crawford stood against the planked front door, watching, before looking down to Bishop, who was beside him, finishing the whiskey in the bowl. "Always the same book, always the same place on the goddamned fence. That's how she learned to talk, that book."

Crawford waited another few minutes for a look from White Fox that never came, then stomped around to the back of the dugout, grunting at the Morning Star and five-talon claws painted on its walls. Bishop followed him to the smith's shop tucked in the back. It was a clean space, with bricked stove, crated scrap, and tools of all types, some for finer work, neatly laid out. It reminded him of his medical office, not a place to forge horseshoes.

"I didn't even know all this was back here 'til a month after I settled in."

"I thought you built this house."

Crawford took down a hammer and tongs. "Hell, no. I been living above the Platte River for a couple of years, and come down to get away from the goddamned Indian wars. Came out of them woods, saw this place and thought it damn nice. I figured to kill whoever was inside, and take it. These other boys beat me to it, hanged the foreigners what built it. So I took care of them, moved in. I guess the foreigner who put it up was a smithy, so after drinking everything in the house, I wandered back here and learned myself. Come on, use that one hand you got, give it some air."

Bishop pumped a small bellows to feed the coals in an iron scuttle. Crawford watched him. "You get why I'm tellin' you this?"

"I think I do."

"I know she never says nothing about me; what about her mother?" The coals began to glow, and Crawford inserted the tongs and several iron punches into the heat.

"She doesn't speak about herself."

"Well, she's back on that fence, and if I believed in anything, I'd say that was a miracle."

"She came here on her own, to talk to you about horses."

Crawford's beard shifted with his face, almost revealing a smile. "I think you're here for this." He dropped the blasted-open shotgun rig on the workbench.

"I know what happened to you. That son of a bitch she married build this thing?"

Bishop couldn't hide his surprise. "Yeah. I told him what I needed."

"A new arm." Crawford inspected the weapon, before shoving the barrel into the hot coals. "Piss-poor job, but I ain't surprised. Worked for me right here. That's how come she knew him. When he said he wanted to marry her, her mother said no, but I figured it was better than the other trash that was hangin' around."

Crawford turned the rig over, as the barrel started smoking. "How many times you sew her up, Doc?"

"Twice. Set a few broken bones. My wife always helped."

Crawford pulled the rig from the scuttle, breaking apart the last of the barrel and breach, the pieces dropping. "If I'd known what was going on, I would've had a great time killing that streak of piss."

"She did it all right."

"He suffer?"

Bishop's silence was answer enough for Crawford.

"Nice to know she took something from her daddy. This how you firing these barrels?"

Crawford held out the rig, so Bishop could grab hold of the leather harness and pull it away from the scorched remains of the gunstock. Crawford snatched the leather back. "I don't like this trigger line. Get tangled, move the wrong way, kill the wrong man."

Bishop said, "It does the job."

"Not good enough, and you know it. I'm a white-smith, too. Work in cold metals, and damn good at it. I'll rig it new."

"I've seen your work. They still call you *Vóhpóóhe*?"

"She's teaching you, right? Painted them symbols on the side of the place when she was a kid."

They both looked back at Fox, who remained buried in Poe's words, never glancing up. Her father continued, "Before I ever married her mother, Crow warriors would come down, snoop around, and I gutted a few. That's when the Cheyenne started with that White Claw. Had to get special permission from the chief for the wedding, but we got it because I'd killed his enemy. Nobody's bothered me since. Helps to have a reputation."

Bishop said, "Yeah, it can."

"I already know your'n. You made that breather for her. We ran out of medicine to help with that when she was a kid, but you figured something out. Probably saved her."

"She gave it to a little girl she thought needed it more."

"Gets that from her mother."

Crawford threw the pieces of the double barrel onto the scrap pile. "Doctor, I'm going to build you a weapon you can use."

Howard held old man Kirby down, one massive arm across his chest, and a hand tight on his mouth. Kirby twisted and kicked as Beaudine withdrew his blade from the man's belly, while Chaney pretended to check the dynamite wagon. He sorted through a few boxes of fuses and caps, found a dead mouse and tossed it—did anything not to hear the last bits of that old man's struggle.

Kirby finally went slack, and Howard let out, "Was he stronger than I thought, or just being stubborn?"

Beaudine said, "I gave the right order, not to shoot. Who knows who'd hear it? It was good strategy."

"Damn, it took a long time for Kirby to give it up."

Chaney stepped up to the wagon's driver's seat. "All he had to do was drive us, didn't have to fight."

Beaudine took a place beside him. "That wasn't Kirby's way. I've known that old man a lot of years, and he'd want paying, or go to the law. He always had his hand out."

Chaney said, "His dynamite sure helped the fight."

"As long as I was throwin' it." Howard counted the cash from Kirby's pocket, stretched out in the back of the open wagon, comfortable between two dynamite cases, his legs dangling over the side. "And those idjit buddies he sent us all got dead."

Beaudine slipped the cleaver beneath the driver's seat, "Kirby lived his life in the rough country, and this is how he knew he'd end. I feel good not to disappoint him."

Howard said, "Hey, he's got a plunger back here! Use that instead of them damn cigars. Made me sick as hell."

Chaney looked to Beaudine. "Now what? Who do we throw the dynamite at? Or shoot at?"

Beaudine measured his words. "Lem always claimed you to be a gambler, but you don't know strategy. You must not be a very good one."

Chaney said, "Lem mouthed off. A lot. This capture did not go as planned, so I want to know about the new plan. Major."

"It's simple. We are the target and Bishop wants us. So we'll let him come, and be ready to meet him."

"Like all that craziness that just happened? What about them riders?"

"You don't get that many attacking for nothing. That's more proof the gold is there for taking."

Chaney pressed. "By who? And when?"

Beaudine shut his eyes. "If you want out, we can leave you with Kirby."

"You're not answering the question. Try and game me now? I'll kill you."

Chaney looked at Kirby and didn't answer Beaudine, who was now rubbing his temples, his head rocking back. "If you're driving, Mr. Chaney, head the team for the next town and wake me when we're near a clean bed and hot food. And we'll strategize to your satisfaction. I believe you want to be going northeast."

Chaney snapped the reins on the two mules harnessed in front of them, heading the wagon down a half-frozen trail leading out of the foothills.

Bishop dipped into the cook pot, trying to balance a clay bowl on his knee. Fox swatted him away. "You're no help, so sit and enjoy it."

Bishop settled on the floor in front of a small tree-stump table, tucking his shirt behind his back, then running the palm of his left hand over his clean-shaven face.

"A man shouldn't hide behind a beard."

"I've had it for so long, it feels strange."

"Because you've changed."

Bishop couldn't deny it. His fingers told him the soft roundness of his face was gone, the scar from Chester Pardee's knife as much a sign of who he was now as the shotgun rig on his right arm.

Fox smiled. "From now on, you shave yourself. Do you want my vanity glass?"

She ladled jerky soup and dumplings into clay bowls with intricate designs of deer running around the edges.

"This is all he lives on. All he ever lived on."

Bishop took his bowl. "And whiskey."

"And whiskey."

Bishop said, "*Vé'ho'émahpe.*"

Fox sat opposite. "That's right. You can eat."

"Shouldn't we wait, for your father?"

Fox set out a plate of cornbread. "He's at my mother's grave. He'll be back in the morning." She held out her right hand. "You can give thanks."

Bishop squeezed her hand, and they gave silent thanks, for the food and the warmth. Bishop squeezed her hand again, and Fox broke his grasp, started eating.

"Why didn't you tell me about Edgar Allan Poe?"

She said, "I read to learn, and haven't learned it all. Yet."

"'Morella'? I go back to that one most."

"Still, not perfect."

Bishop smiled. "You don't speak so you can find out what everyone else is thinking."

Fox cast her eyes to Bishop, ate a dumpling from her spoon. "When I'm perfect. When will you be perfect?"

Bishop grinned. "*Nenóveto?*"

"Good. Then soon, we can both talk the way we want."

"Did your father buy those books for you?"

"No." Fox broke a piece of cornbread, put the rest in front of Bishop. "He killed a man for his horse. They were in his saddlebags. My father is *not* like your father."

Fox's words dropped off. Bishop gave her time before saying, "He knows about your life."

"Memories of what *náhko'éehe* said."

"Your mother told him, about when your husband hurt you."

"Right before she died." Fox poured the last of the

soup into Bishop's bowl. "You saved me. And I will do for you. Until I can't."

The lantern cast stale yellow on the two grave markers. One was flat steel, polished, with fine scrolling and the Morning Star hammered into its surface. Just below the star were the words, ARCHISHA. MOTHER AND WIFE. SHE LIVES ALWAYS. The other was a wooden cross with HORACE SMITH burned onto it.

Crawford stood before the Morning Star. "You won't believe what happened, Chisha. Hell, you probably knew before I did." He punched the ground in front of Horace's marker with his shovel, quick-turning the earth only a few inches before hitting the coffin.

Crawford tossed the shovel aside, pried the lid until it opened.

Batting the smell away from his nose, he scooped a pile of moldy hats and bloodstained jackets with his giant hands, tossing it all on Archisha's grave beside him. He added a tangle of kerchiefs, monogrammed things, and a sheriff's badge cut by a bullet hole to the pile, before yanking up the coffin's false bottom.

The coffin was actually built deep enough for four men lying on top of each other, which meant that Crawford could store at least fifty rifles and as many pistols as he could tuck in around them. Each weapon was wrapped in oilcloth, and he checked them carefully, searching for a specific shotgun he'd taken off a Swede who had been passing through years before.

Crawford found the Shuster double-barrel, and remembered the kill: the Swede was a family man, and surprised as hell when Crawford peeled two slugs into him after he'd just paid to have his horses shod.

Most of the others had fought back. He'd been chopped and shot, but one way or another Crawford got them, their horses, or their wagons. That's when he was White Claw, ripping through whoever came his way. Other times, he just did his work in the smith shop, lived a righteous life. It all depended on his mood.

He packed away the guns and clothes of the dead, covered the coffin up again. Tucking the Swede's gun under his arm, he picked up the lantern, and said to his wife's marker, "I'm giving *Vóhkêhésoa* a gift. She always heard you—get her to take it."

Bishop watched Fox from the rope-mattress bed as she knelt by the fire, pouring water for tea. Her naked legs were long, meeting her waist a little high on her body. They were muscular, the sinews working too close to the surface of her skin, as they did on her upper arms.

Her toned strength was almost masculine, except where it melted into the flat of her stomach, or the full curve of her breasts. Her hair fell in front of her face, until she threw it back over her shoulder, glancing back with a smile for him alone.

Her smile was so rare it felt like a privilege to see it. It always started with her eyes, warming from cold to welcoming, letting him inside. She stood, carrying the tea to the bed, walking proud, and just as fine exposing the multiple scars on her left side as she was with the flawlessness on her right.

Bishop sat up in bed, propped on his one arm, as she settled under the bearskin, holding out the tea.

"It surely tastes better than the whiskey."

She sipped after he did, nodded, put the cup aside, and then wrapped herself around his body. He could feel her scars among the softness, the rough flesh left behind after his surgeries and the signs of recent violence that were healing.

She murmured, running her fingers across his chest,

lightly kissing to his shoulders, across them. Bishop's half-arm pressed against her back, holding her tight to him. All she felt was his strength, not any sort of compromise. Her hands traveled back across his wounds, brushing his nose with a giggle.

Her laugh was something Bishop had heard only a few times, and he didn't want it to stop, but her smile was fading, and a different feeling was taking over her eyes.

He kissed her, and they lost themselves in each other again.

Bishop shifted to the other side of the bed, curling under the bearskin, reaching for Fox in his sleep, when the distant thunder jostled him. There was a second strike, and Bishop sat up and saw that he was alone, except for a pot of coffee boiling over.

Bishop stayed in bed until the blast faded, his thoughts about his wife and son.

Outside, Crawford shucked the spent shells from the double barrel, checked the dead oak he'd used as a target. The buckshot spread was good, and the damage severe. He set the gun on his workbench to adjust the special triggers he'd made, when Bishop limped around the side of the dugout, struggling to put on his left boot.

"So that's why God gave us two hands!" Crawford was still laughing when he grabbed the bootstrap, pulled it up. "Doctor, I guess there are still some things you need help with."

"A few, thanks."

"Your boots, not shooting this here."

Crawford moved to his bench, held up the new shotgun rig with tired, toothless pride. "Say somethin', damn it."

The weapon was swivel breeched-open to the side,

with the stock cut shorter to fit flush into the amputee cup. Jointed metal supports kept the gun steady in any position, while a catgut line looped around both the triggers, and was knotted to a small chain bracing across the cut-leather shoulder straps, and then anchored to the left arm at the wrist.

"That's fine workmanship, Mr. Crawford."

"Told you I was going to do it."

Bishop slipped his half-arm into the padded cup as Crawford fastened the new leather rig across his back. "This is a damn sight better than what that son of a bitch fixed up for ya."

"Did Fox see all this?"

"She's running her horse."

Crawford brought the trigger line from Bishop's right arm, and fastened it to a small, Cheyenne-silver band that he slipped on his left wrist, giving the line a little play. Bishop buttoned his shirt, rolled down his sleeves. He nodded; the rig was perfect under his clothes.

Crawford said, "This needs saying: we're not on terms, but I'm still her pa. Any kindness I'm doing? Because of her." Crawford held up two twelve-gauge shells. "So?"

Bishop loaded both barrels, snapped the breech shut.

"That's a Shuler swivel-breech for a quicker reload. And these barrels can take anything. Straighten your left arm."

Bishop straightened his left at his side, the chain from his wrist snapping tight across his shoulders, instantly bringing the shotgun rig on his right waist-high and steady, twice as fast as before.

"Position and shoot. So, who're you going to face down, Doctor?"

Bishop turned from Crawford, brought back the hammers, and snapped his wrist pulling the trigger line. The first barrel blasted the oak dead center like a man's chest, the metal braces absorbing the gun's recoil into Bishop's body.

Bishop said, "It really feels like a part of me."

"Over here!"

Bishop half-turned, and the rig reacted, swinging in the direction of Crawford's voice, and locking, but not firing.

Crawford laughed, "She won't do nothin' you don't want her to. Go ahead, shoot. The line's tight, use your shoulders."

Bishop spun on his heel, as if taken by surprise, and shrugged. The second barrel ripped apart two limbs. Bishop swung open the rig, popped the shells.

They clattered to the floor, black-powder smoking.

Crawford said, "That's faster than a lot of men can draw. And I made you this here."

Crawford held out a small bandolier, sized to fit Bishop's arm. "It'll hold six, so you ain't fumbling for shells. I also got a loader for you."

Bishop regarded Crawford. "If you've heard anything about money I'm supposed to have—"

"Because I'm White Claw? I know you had to get that insulting shit out of the way, but forget it. She picked you, Doc, and this rig's to keep her safe as long as she's with you. If you ride on alone, this pays back all you done for her."

"I wouldn't be alive if it wasn't for her."

"I settle my own accounts." Crawford stepped back to admire his work. "Either way, them dogs you're chasin' won't know what hit 'em. It ain't flapdoodle—I'm damn good."

Bishop checked the sights. "We came close to getting the leader."

"You'll get him, you'll feel the revenge for your family. But that'll go, and you'll go after more. Killing a man ain't nothing more than flipping a switch, and there's always some that's asking for it."

"I'll finish what I have to do, then put it behind me."

"The hell you say. You've already crossed the river. Look at the way you handle that rig. Like God's own power, ain't it? Some days you'll be the doc, other days you'll be the shotgun man. Then one day, you'll only be shotgun. And I hope she ain't with you when that happens."

Bishop said, "Maybe," the truth punching him.

He bent his elbow, bringing the rig up to him, as if it were on a precise gear-set. He moved his body, and the double barrel adjusted its height and position to compensate. "You have skills, sir, and at this moment, I'm a doctor and I need them."

"A week."

"What?"

"Rifled your saddlebag."

"Not much there, Claw."

"I saw what you sketched out for that breather box. She needs a new one, gave the old one away? One week, and it'll be better than what she had. But don't tell her it's from me, 'cause she'd rather choke to death than use it."

Crawford held out two more shotgun shells. "Ain't you gonna reload, Doc?"

White Fox ran the painted through the woods, heading for the clearing where her father had set his traps. She had a long blade tied to her thigh, and a vision of red hanging in front of her eyes like blinders.

It was dark red, as dark as the night sky above it, and spreading wide against the snow. It was the first thing Fox had seen as she'd ridden toward the little house with the porch and rocking chairs. She'd had a present for Dr. Bishop's son tucked under her jacket, away from the evening weather, and had been rehearsing a birthday song when she saw the circle of blood around the two bodies lying in the yard.

Fox pushed the painted harder, thinking of how she'd run to Amaryllis, who had been shot twice and had still been cradling her son. The boy, his face buried against his mother, had had a single bullet wound to the head.

They had been holding hands, gently.

The painted broke to a full gallop. White Fox was pushing against the images of Bishop's wife, but they kept coming. She remembered touching the side of her face, color gone, her skin turning with the cold, frozen tears on her cheeks. Fox had taken a blanket from her horse, draped it over mother and son.

That's when she'd heard John Bishop's voice from the house. He had crawled inside, arm gone, and had been trying to get to a rifle behind a shattered china cabinet. Bishop had pleaded about his family, but Fox hadn't known what to say to make him understand. She hadn't had the words.

He was dying in front of her.

She'd brought the painted right to the front door, helped him climb from the chair onto its back, where he'd collapsed. She'd swung on behind him, holding him on, and they'd galloped away from that ruined house, leaving wife, son, and a birthday present lying in the snow.

That was a year ago. She'd had the same painted then, running the same way, and she was now on her own mission to revenge that night. Her revenge. The Cheyenne word is óoxo'eéh, and it was the first she'd taught Bishop to say—the first he'd wanted to learn.

This moment, it was all she could think of as she got closer.

She leapt the small gully before reaching the clearing, and Fox stopped the painted feet away from the trip lines around the pine trees. She cut rope after rope with the long blade, releasing the tied-back branches, hurling packed snow and ice like flaming bales from a catapult.

She rode beyond White Claw's traps, to a small slope leading to a split of two tall-grass hills damped with snow, a stream running between them—a tiny valley. Fox heeled, and looked down into the split at fifty or so horses, all good stock, held behind a barrier of fallen trees. She pulled the lasso from her saddle, and headed toward them.

Bishop was packed and saddled, when Fox brought the painted down the small trail to the dugout, a second stallion tied behind her. There were small cuts and bruises on her hands and face, and her expression was dark. Bishop stayed by the bay, as Fox rode her horse to Crawford and stopped just inches away, looking down on him from the painted's back.

Crawford's beard and bearskin coat buried him in hair, with only his two black eyes showing through the tangle. Staring at her. "Thought you might head out to Wyoming."

"Don't know anyone there."

"That ain't always a bad thing. I got your man outfitted with a whole new deal."

"Don't call the doctor that."

"Doubt that he minds." Crawford opened the gate to the corral, looked beyond Fox to the horse tied behind her. "Catch one of my strays?"

"No stray, and not yours." Fox finally turned to Bishop. "Ready?"

"Whenever you are."

"Which way should we go? Follow the river? It's of no

matter." Fox looked to her father. "Were you going to warn them we were coming? Have us killed?"

"You got it wrong, daughter."

"I did not want to return to this place." Fox got off the painted and moved around it to the horse she'd roped in the hills, pointing to an FD brand on its rump. "The men in red hoods had this brand, and I knew it was you. An army horse, the kind you always stole. Two are in the corral."

"I've got customers coming. Not them red hoods, though."

"And you hide the rest in the same place you did when I was a girl. I was just there. You'll always be White Claw, and I'm forever *tanehe*."

Crawford said, "I know you're ashamed, but before you start jumpin', take a ride. I've got something that'll help you both." Bishop had the shotgun aimed, as Crawford threw his hands up. "If you don't like it, the doc can always use the new rig on me."

Bishop said to Crawford, "You built this thing to cut a man in half."

Crawford shook his head. "Oh, I know, Shotgun. Well? *Vóhkêhésoa?*"

The shadows of the grave markers grew longer as the winter evening settled in. The sound of the distant river was carried on a cold breeze that blew back Fox's hair, and the fringe on her leathers. She stood by Morning Star, but kept her eyes averted from her mother's name.

Bishop held fast by the horses, letting father and daughter settle their business, the hammers on the rig cocked, the bandolier with six shells tight on his arm.

Fox said, "What is this gift, *nomáhtse'héó'o?*"

Crawford stepped to the other side of the markers, said to Bishop, "Did she teach you that one yet, doc? It means 'thief.'"

Crawford held up a large bundle, wrapped in an old blanket and tied twice. He tossed it with one hand onto the snow-wet ground of Horace Smith's grave. Heavy as cast iron, it sunk in. Fox and Bishop eyed the bundle, but made no move.

"It's only right that White Claw's daughter recognize the branding on a stolen horse." Fox met Crawford's face as he continued: "I know it pains you to say it, but I'm your pa. A thief, and a killer, and every other damn thing you ever dreamed up."

She said nothing. Crawford blasted, "White Claw. Goddamned White Claw, and you're *my* child!"

White Fox would not shake. She rested her hand on the tip of her mother's grave marker, keeping her words low and flat. "What about the horses?"

Crawford yanked a bottle from his coat, drank half of it in one swallow. "There's a foreigner, he runs a bunch call themselves the Fire Riders. And I be dealing with them."

Bishop said, "Are you with them?"

"Hell, no!"

"Then what?"

"They're about money, new U.S. currency. And anyone who don't do business gets their house burned and their throat cut. Ain't no politics here. And they dress up crazier than a pack of wall-eyed mules, scare most folks to death. Reputation, right, Doc? That's how come they can do what they want."

"What about the law, the Marshals in this territory?"

"They love them Fire Riders, 'cause all they do is come down on scofflaws like me! Take a train, they want a piece. Rob a bank, you gotta pay!"

Crawford threw the finished bottle to the sky. It shattered someplace. "The foreigner's an Englishman. Never saw his face, just heard him. I've been supplying horses for six months, Army mounts from Fort Davis. The branding you recognized, daughter."

Fox said, "We fought them."

"Sure as hell did, and lived to tell the tale."

"It was a bloody war."

"That's what they do. I don't know if them Fire Riders are mixed up in your business, Doc, but that's really stickin' your head in a rattler hole. If I hadn't gotten them mounts, I wouldn't be here now, claw or no."

Bishop said, "You know I'm going to hunt down the men who killed my family. These Red Hoods know who they are well enough to attack them."

Crawford looked to Bishop, and the barrels leveled on him. "You don't have to threaten me, Doc. I'm the man who built you the best chance you got. I'll tell ya, they ride the Wyoming border, come in for raids. Paradise River don't have no river, but they got a rail station, and they've been hit more than once. Somebody'll give up that foreigner, if you swear to kill him."

Bishop lowered the rig as Crawford reached out to Fox, but didn't touch her. "This is too dangerous, daughter. You were lucky once—it may not happen again."

Fox kept her hand on her mother's name. "I can't stay here."

"You can go anyplace you want, but it don't have to be with the doc."

Bishop said, "You already saved my life."

Fox let her hand fall from the marker. "I told you I would be with you until I couldn't. That was my mother's way. That's my way."

Crawford crouched by the bundle, untied it. "I made these a couple of months ago, when I knew you two was riding together."

He threw back the blanket to reveal two more grave markers, one with Dr. John Bishop written on it, and the other, VÓHKÊHÉSOA—BELOVED DAUGHTER.

"That's my gift: freedom. If they think you're already dead, you can do whatever you want. And if anybody comes lookin', this should stop 'em. Or I will."

Crawford stood and looked to his daughter, who simply nodded. He said, "You better make tracks. I'll get these up in the morning."

Fox turned away from her father, running her palms over her face. Bishop stepped up, extended his left hand.

Crawford's giant hand smothered Bishop's. "Better that one than the other."

"You did a lot for us."

Crawford was still holding on, grip tight as hell. "The Cheyenne's a strong spirit, Doc, so you protect her, even if she hates you for it."

CHAPTER TWENTY-TWO
Good Deeds

Crawford pulled the punch from the coal scuttle, then pierced the edge of the breather box, before rounding the corners with small sections of sheet silver. Large fingers manipulated the cold-smith tools, fashioning an air portal around the pierced metal surface. Each move was precise, and the tools never slipped.

He was cutting the padded leather sections for the side of the box when he saw the small wagon with the flat top rumbling down the trail, and pulling up by the corral.

The Brakeman, all blond mustache and braggart's mouth, dropped off the driver's seat with a wave to Crawford as he walked out of the smith's.

"You ready to do some business, Claw?"

"I don't like that coming from you, but if you got money this time, I'll let it slide."

"Sorry, Noah. Them the ones you talking about?"

Crawford brought one of the stolen horses out of the corral for the Brakeman's inspection. He was making a show of checking the teeth and hooves, but actually knew damn little about horseflesh.

Crawford said, "Why you bother with that every time? I know you're gonna take 'em out on the trail and sell 'em."

"Not to blind men. I want to pay a fair price, but I have to make mine too." The Brakeman ran his hand across his mustache. "These still got the brand on 'em. I'm taking a risk."

"A hundred extra, I'll change the brand right now."

"One fifty for both, change the brand, and I'll give you a free turn."

The Brakeman nodded to the wagon, and a petite Chinese woman threw open the canvas in the back and peeked around the corner. She was in her early twenties, but had additional age beaten on to her. Her nightgown hadn't seen a recent washing, but she tried for beauty with a torn paper flower behind one ear.

"Ain't she left you yet?"

"Hard to get a divorce in the wild country."

"I don't want no time with your wife, but I'll settle for the price, if you take a package to general delivery up to Paradise River."

"Who's it for?"

"What the hell's the difference?"

The woman watched from the wagon, waiting for White Claw to tear into her husband, holding her breath and crossing her fingers.

The Brakeman said, "I'll do anything, Noah. I just don't want to get picked up. I've got a job in a couple of days."

"For my sister. My daughter passed away, and wanted her aunt to have a few things."

"I sure am sorry to hear that, Noah. I ain't gonna up my offer, but I feel for ya."

Crawford handed the Brakeman the reins on the

horse, as his wife dropped back inside the wagon, the canvas flap falling shut behind her.

Crawford said, "I'll heat the irons for the horses, you'll wait for the package to take."

"Whatever you need. We're amigos."

Crawford peered at the wagon. "She all right in there? Got jerky and dumplings."

The Brakeman shrugged. "She's fine. And don't never eat. That's one of the things I like about her."

Fox and Bishop had been riding in the Colorado silence for hours when they saw the buckboard coming from the opposite direction. The road they were on was well traveled, cutting along the base of some smaller mountains, but today, they had had it to themselves and the wind, until they saw the couple.

The husband was waving at them in a friendly manner, but the wife sat statue still, with her hands folded in her lap.

They pulled up.

Fox had seen it first, and she gave Bishop a look as she peeled away from him, riding the painted to the side of the wagon where the wife was sitting.

The husband tipped his hat. "Good 'morrow, friends! This is a lonely stretch. Are ye travelling far?"

Bishop kept his rig arm down, the sleeve of his coat covering the barrels from the husband's view.

"We're on our way to the next town, going to meet a friend, actually."

"The next town is Paradise River, and aptly named she is."

"How much farther is it?"

"Less than a day's ride, friend. We've just stocked up ourselves, this sky tells me we'll be seeing a long winter. You look a little light on food. Perhaps we can leave you with something."

"That'd be appreciated. Truly."

The husband tipped his hat, still smiling broadly when he reached behind the seat.

The rig blasted, tearing the husband in the side, hurling him off the wagon, onto the road. The pistol in his hand fired when he hit the ground.

The wife burst into tears, screaming, "Kill him!"

Bishop jumped from his horse, moved to the husband, and kicked the pistol out of reach.

"Sorry friend, but you're not going to make it."

The man was still showing long, perfect teeth. "Should have killed you before we stopped. What'd you get me with? How'd you know?"

Bishop tilted his head to Fox. "She knew. Your pocket."

The man felt his jacket, and the hood that was sticking out of the top of his side pocket, like a red warning flag.

"Did you really come from Paradise River?" Bishop asked.

"You know how many of us there are?"

"What about a man called Smythe?"

The man's smile was locked, and not going anywhere, when he said, "Dyin' isn't as hard as I thought it would be. Piss on you, brother."

Fox said to the wife, "What about your man?"

"He's been shot, left by the side of the road."

Bishop said, "How long?"

"Not half an hour ago."

"You really coming from Paradise River?"

"Trying to leave forever, because of those damnable night riders. My husband's a deputy sheriff." She choked on her words, but her face was calm now, and lovely. "And he was quitting."

The wife turned the wagon around, running the team back toward Paradise, with Bishop and Fox alongside.

CHAPTER TWENTY-THREE
Fortress of the Dead

"What's it looking like, boy?"

"Like a castle from a picture book, Captain. A burned castle."

Smythe laughed out loud at Hector's description, grinning at the boy over his shoulder, but not contradicting him. Hector craned his neck to get a better look at the grey ruin rising out of the Wyoming badlands in front of them: Cannon Mountain Territorial Prison.

The walls were more than thirty feet high, and sloped outward, with tons of smashed, jagged boulders protecting the foundation, like an ancient moat. Iron spikes with bent, speared edges lined the top of the walls, with stretched barbed wire connecting them.

Parapets stood as sentries at each corner, with eye-like windows for the sniping guards facing both the outside and the prison yard. Stout anchor chains hung from the windows, ladders for the men to climb into position.

And it had all been burned.

Scars of the fire disfigured the place, destroying large sections that were now falling in on themselves. A few men on horses broke around the charred front gate, riding toward the group at a full gallop.

Smythe said, "Nobody draws. These blokes'll kill you, even if they know you."

The men rode up, and gave a signal to follow.

A body dangled by the neck from one of the few bare and twisted trees near the place. Its hands and feet were bound with red cloth and a sign that read "He Didn't Pay!" had been fastened to his chest with a small dagger.

Smythe said to Hector: "That's to show the scoflaws that we mean business."

Passing through the front gates to the main prison yard, with riders and guns on all sides, Hector kept speaking to Creed, describing everything: the corpse, debris and rubble piled high enough to climb; twisted-apart cell doors stacked against the scorched remains of a guard's turret; and behind it, what had been the stables, now a pile of ashes and trash.

Hector watched as men in red moved among the wreckage with purpose, carrying weapons, furniture, and food supplies to tents that had been set up along the inner wall, forming a compound. The injured Fire Riders were laid out around the tents, waiting for a medic to fix them or pronounce them.

He stumbled in his telling, as this new, savage army prepared itself for some kind of war. Hector looked to the far end of the yard, and the entrance to the cell-block, where old cannons were being repaired, ammunition stacked, and a Gatling gun was being set up in the back of a freight wagon.

Hector said, "Sir, you've shown me a lot, but nothing like this."

Creed took in the prison with his dead eyes. "That's fine, son, but you don't have to go with the report. I can hear what they're doing. I know what's around me."

The remains of an iron fence served as a hitch rail,

where Smythe, Creed, and Fuller tied their horses. Hector dropped from the saddle to help the captain.

"You don't know it, son, but these are your brothers in arms."

One of the riders who'd brought them in noted Fuller and his rifle. "There's some new beauties. You're going to want to move up, if you fight with us, boy."

Fuller kept the Morgan-James on his shoulder. "I haven't decided yet."

"Maybe it'll be decided for you." The rider turned to Smythe. "He's busy now, but he'll want to know why so many got left dead at the silver mine."

Smythe held out his slinged arm, "And I'll tell him. What's he busy with?"

The rider spit, pointed to a multi-colored Conestoga wagon and its team, hitched to a post by the old cells.

Warden Allard had broken his chair more than once, and Devlin Bishop felt lost in its warped back, and over-stuffed seat. He adjusted himself several times as Albert Tomlinson opened a ledger on the hand-tooled leather-top desk that separated them.

Tomlinson admired the desk. "Nice piece. I understand this is already paid for, Mr. Bishop."

"I didn't pay for it."

"Regardless, it's a luxury, and if you get used to such things, it can make the adjustment of paring down difficult."

Dev's shirtsleeves were cleanly rolled up, revealing a tattoo of the flag of Virginia on his forearm, and his collar was buttoned to his Adam's apple. He sported suspenders and trousers cuffed above new, laced shoes. His prison manner had neatened with his wardrobe, but the casual threat behind his eyes was permanent.

Dev had Tomlinson's complete attention: "Tomlinson, this is the beginning of a great business, the first of its kind in the west, and it's important that it be run like a business. Now, I don't have a lot of formal learning, which is why you're here, to make sure our money is going where it needs to go."

Matching Dev, the timid, Arkansas scarecrow was now a seasoned professional, without a trace of stammer. Tomlinson took a pair of bifocals from a tortoise-shell case, slipped them on, and ran his finger down a column of numbers on the ledger page. "When you refer to monies, that's a problem, because your cash situation is, uh, compromised."

Dev leaned across the desk. "You understand what this is? We're robbers, Tomlinson."

There was a moment, as Tomlinson considered his response. "You're my employer, Mr. Bishop, as long as you want me. I pride myself on discretion. This business is a tad unusual, but I have two growing girls. You know how that is."

"Fine, then. You've worked for thieves before?"

"Well—"

"Railroad? Steamship company?"

"Yes."

"Then you've worked for thieves, just none honest about who they are. But they all have money to start with. We don't. Our investments are goods. We bring in a wagon, it ain't filled with cash. But the rifles, and tomato plants, the clothes, and Grandma's piano all have value, and I've got some pirates who're very good at trading."

"That's difficult to enter. I'd have to approximate, after seeing all the stores. Or wait, for the cash deposits to vault. Or whatever."

"Let's say whatever."

Dev leaned back in the large chair, finally settling in. "The cash is going to flow, and it's going to be a hell of a lot. Because every thief in the territory is going to be paying us tribute."

"Really?"

"If they don't want to end up dead, or worse, a place like this here."

"I saw the example outside."

"The men have left a few around the territory."

Tomlinson sniffed, "I'll be ready to make those entries," before turning the ledger around on the desk for Dev to inspect. Dev just looked straight at the accountant.

"What about gold?"

"Your gold is your foundation."

Bishop said, "That's good. Good to know, because I've gone through hell for that foundation."

"Uh, it would help a great deal if I knew how much gold there was."

"I had some, but that all went to bringing these men, this place, together. Very little left, but the total's about to go up. I'll give you a figure next week. We'll also be getting regular protection payments from a gal who'll be running some whorehouses between here and California. That'll be good money, and good company."

Tomlinson's head bobbed in agreement. "This is going to be colorful."

"You should see this."

Dev stood, revealing a bullet hole in the back of the chair. "That's where the slug went through Mr. Allard, came out his back. You didn't know him, but that's a hell of a trip. Now, I didn't fire that shot."

"I'm relieved."

"But I danced me a jig when I found out, not fifty feet from here."

"May I ask where you were, sir, when this all happened?"

Dev kicked the burned remains of the door aside. "Guess the territorial governor forgot to tell folks they was storing lamp fuel and powder under here. Figured if it blew, who'd miss this bunch of cow pies? Well, it did and nobody gave a tinker's damn."

Tomlinson stood beside Dev in the commons area, with its roof now burned through, the cells twisted apart by heat, and the stains of the dead scorched to the floor.

"We're just a burned-down nothing, until somebody from the territory decides to notice. Which they never will."

Tomlinson said quietly, "I've never even been in a prison before."

"This is a hell of a one to start with," Dev chuckled. "And hell it was."

"You were a prisoner, now it's your fortress."

"The warden was a snake; took a payoff to fake my execution, then double-crossed me when he wouldn't let me out of the cells! I paid him off to stay inside!"

Dev let it settle. "I was the king fool for trusting him, and there wasn't a guard or prisoner who didn't hate his guts. But we got him."

Tomlinson asked from the back of his throat, "Did you set the fire?"

"One of them jackass guards was sellin' black powder to a Sioux war party, so they could blow up a piece of the railroad. Got into a fight, set the storage on fire, and brought this whole place down. Lotta men killed, and the ones that were left had nothing."

Dev Bishop ran the toe of his shoe over the scorched outline of a prisoner who had been trapped at the bottom of the iron stairs, now collapsed.

Dev repeated, "Nothing."

Tomlinson stood up straight. "You had gold."

"A little. From a Union pay master. Never did time on that one, don't know if they've forgotten about it yet."

"They don't forget. You could end up in a place just like this again."

Dev faced Tomlinson. "That ain't gonna happen."

"I surely hope not."

"If you've got something on your mind, bookkeeper, you better say before we go any further."

Tomlinson stepped closer, his voice as low as he could take it. "I think I can work for you real well, but I need something extra."

"How much?"

"It's my wife. She's in the wagon. My eldest got into it with her, hit her hard, while we was on our way here. She's kind of stuffed in a dresser in the back. We've been traveling with her."

Dev took a breath. "You want her buried?"

Tomlinson took his step back. "Well, yes. I wasn't going to leave her in the woods, and the way she is, we can't take her to no Methodist cemetery without questions. She was Methodist."

Dev patted his shoulder. "I can have that taken care of."

Tomlinson heaved a sigh that came through his entire body. "That's a real burden lifted. Thank you."

The old whipping post blew apart on the floor, charred pieces flying, when Smythe kicked it over. Tomlinson was startled as the Fire Rider strode across the common area with a guard's swagger, his arm in a sling and his fist balled.

Captain Creed had Hector lead him in, right behind. "Tomlinson, this is Captain Creed, and Smythe."

"I'll note they're a part of this organization?"

"We'll see."

Smythe loomed over Dev and said, "Oh, you have something to say to me, boy-o?"

"In the old place."

The kid at the telegraph was thinner than a homeless dog, hunched over the receiving key, downing his third cup of belly wash, when he heard Smythe's voice. He turned as Dev, Smythe, and Creed made their way down the metal stairs to the Tomb.

Creed said, "The stink of death."

Smythe leaned in with, "And more than a few. Your kid thinks he's in a bloody haunted house."

"Hector!"

Hector descended the stairs, inches at a time. "Sir?"

"Stand with me, boy."

Hector found his place with Creed as Dev slapped the telegraph operator on the back. "It's all right, Lemuel. We won't get no messages in the next few minutes."

Lemuel mumbled, "You never know," and took the stairs two at a time to get out.

Smythe stood by Dev's old cell, which was now being used as a store for old single-shot rifles. The other cells were filled with crates and stuffed burlap sacks, the metal bunks stacked with supplies.

"I was right here while you set up your brother, boy-o. That was quite a bit of business."

Dev said, "And why didn't you follow on it?"

"Because I was keeping me eye on the lot of you, in case I had to beat somebody senseless."

"And you always liked that. So what happened to your arm?"

Creed's voice was first: "He was ambushed, because he was following your orders."

Dev moved between Creed and Hector. "Captain, you're the one who truly failed. You wanted to settle a score with John, and still let him get away."

"We followed protocol. Let you know as soon as possible."

Hector said, "Yes, sir. I was at the key."

Dev said, "And the message came through right here. Failure is your word, how you described letting him escape."

Creed said, "And to make up for it, you sent all those men to slaughter. All you want is your brother and Beaudine dead, and you can't manage it."

"You're really overstepping yourself, blind man." Dev walked into his old cell, touched the ceiling with his hands, his palms flat against it.

"It really is like being buried alive. It's because we were in the Tomb that we weren't killed in that explosion."

Smythe blocked the cell door with his enormous frame. "You don't have to remind me, boy-o. Just like you don't have to remind me what a hog screwing we took at that silver mine. Beaudine's crazy, but it's what keeps him alive. That place was rigged like you couldn't believe."

Dev said to Creed, "Rigged—expecting you, Captain."

Smythe cut back, "You can't predict him. You should know, all those letters you had him write. What you figured he was going to do."

Dev said, "He was my voice down here. And I knew as soon as I put it in his mind about me and John and some robbery, he wouldn't be able to let it go."

"Your brother never had anything to do with anything."

"Of course not, but he had to be gone if we were going to build this empire."

Smythe said, "You should've stopped him, boy-o."

"I couldn't raise a hand against him myself. Never once, even when we was kids. Thought Beaudine would take care of it for me. Or you, Creed."

Creed said, "Your brother owes me, and I will collect that debt."

"John survived the conflicts, Beaudine's attack, all of it. One thing you learn in here, some men die easy, and some don't."

A small voice said, "With that special shotgun of his."

Dev stepped from his cell. "The boy has something to add?"

Hector coughed, looked to Creed, who put a hand on

his shoulder for assurance. Hector finally said, "Just that I've seen him use that gun. I'd be real, extra careful, sir."

Dev said, "That's the smartest thing I've heard today."

"All she must do is say the words. She must."

The Brakeman grinned at Beaudine. "She's a chink. Don't know no English, buddy. Just do your business. She don't care."

The canvas walls of the tent wafted as the Brakeman stepped outside, leaving his wife alone with Beaudine. She sat on the edge of a tiny, wooden-slat cot, Beaudine before her, suspenders off his shoulders but still dressed, including his boots.

He said, "You can't say you're Nellie Bly? You have no idea, you poor idiot."

She smiled politely, and shrugged, reaching up to unbutton his trousers. He swatted her hands away.

"I do lose myself, sometimes. You have to help me, and you can't. Or won't. If you're refusing me, that would be an insult, wouldn't it?"

Her smile continued, even as he raised his hand. She did not flinch or turn away.

Outside the tent, Chaney and Howard sat on the empty dynamite wagon, counting the last of their money, all coins. Chaney's shirt was caked with blood, and he had a bandage wrapped around his ribs. Behind them, the muddy trail stretched for miles, and in front of them was more of the same. The bursts of wind from the Colorado north felt like broken glass.

The only thing for miles was the Brakeman's tent, and them sitting beside it.

"Everything we got from old man Kirby wasn't worth salt for peanuts."

"And you choked him for it." Chaney shoved the change back in his pants. "This working out the way you thought? You made more hammering coffins. Hell's fire, I'd join you."

"I was set, and you all came in and turned me upside down."

"Along for the ride. That was Lem."

Howard shook his head. "It wasn't Deadeye. Don't be saying that."

Chaney winced. "Beaudine's holding a bluff hand, and we fell for it. Now we're an 'Army of Three,' whatever the hell that means. Now what? Gonna keep following that maniac? He's got to get his bell rope pulled, and we're out here freezin' to death. At least the cold makes my side feel tolerable."

"You said you'd kill Beaudine. Seems like that's your bluff."

"You'll find out."

"Maybe I should have let you die back there. You ain't my friend. Lem was."

"Well, I sure wish he was with us now."

Howard said, "I never seen who shot him."

Chaney pulled at his bandage, adjusting it, not missing a beat. "It was that Bishop, but I blew that double barrel to pieces."

"Looks like he did more to you."

"The Cheyenne! And just what are we gonna do about all that?"

They looked up as the Brakeman set out a stack of jars of milky-white grain shine, and a few with moldy preserves floating in sugar-clouded juice. He arranged them on an old ammunition crate beside the torn canvas, with a large sign declaring A DOLLER FOR ALL THE HAPYNESS YOU CAN STAND!

"Thirsty? If you don't have the dollar, you don't have to answer."

Howard said, "I like store bought."

"Store bought ain't got this kick, and I don't see no saloons nowhere."

Chaney took a deck of cards from his jacket. "Would you play for it?"

The Brakeman ran his fingers through a thick blond mustache. "The lady of chance is a whore I don't favor."

Howard grabbed the last stick of dynamite from one of the crates. "It's gettin' damn cold. You just gonna let us sit here?"

The Brakeman said, "You don't have a primer or a fuse for that, friend."

"You know your TNT?"

"Work with it all the time on the Colorado Line."

Chaney said, "This ain't your work?"

The Brakeman laughed, "Her? That's my wife! We travel these teamster trails, set up for a week, then move on when the railroad needs me. You'd be surprised how many she can handle in a day."

Howard said, "Lotta money. Sounds like you could spare a drink."

"It does, don't it?"

"So what is your trade, friend, other than your wife?"

"Stand-by brakeman."

"On the Colorado?"

"That's what I said. I don't repeat."

The Brakeman took a sip of homemade, while Howard was rubbing his arms to keep warm. Howard said, "Which work do you like better, that or this here?"

"The same. She pays, they pay. And sometimes the Colorado kicks it up a bit."

"When's that?"

The Brakeman checked his watch. "Your friend has three minutes."

Chaney said, "Won't let us put anything on the cuff, so what's the harm in talkin'? I'm looking for work. So when does the Colorado kick it up? You ever work a run from that mint?"

The Brakeman took another sip. "Not that they ever told me."

"Friend, you could be a couple of train cars away from a fortune."

"I don't think about that. I do my job."

Howard said, "When's your next run?"

The Brakeman pulled a folded schedule from his pocket. "Whenever they say. We're packing out of here tomorrow. Either of you want a crack, best speak up."

Beaudine stepped from the tent, holding a small package, addressed to Mrs. Bishop. He shoved it at the Brakeman, who grabbed for it.

"How the hell'd you get that?"

Beaudine kept it out of reach. "It was by the woman's bed. Who is this for?"

"Your time's up!"

Beaudine tossed the small package to Howard. "Look at that name. Where did you get this? Believe me, you don't want to set my blood to boiling, friend."

The Brakeman screamed, "Lotus! Get your ass out here!"

Chaney tossed Beaudine his long cleaver, and he advanced on the Brakeman, turning the blade. Chaney and Howard both had their guns out.

Beaudine said, "All I need is the truth. Who is this Mrs. Bishop?"

The woman stepped from the tent, but made no move for her husband. She stood, watching.

Beaudine brought the cleaver to his throat. "The truth, or you will spill on this ground."

"I don't care who it is, goes to general delivery in Paradise River before I take the train out. My old buddy's got a daughter, and she died, and he's sending something to family."

Chaney said, "Is that daughter a Cheyenne?"

"How'd you know that?"

Beaudine said, "And where is this friend?"

The Brakeman straightened, met Beaudine's stare.

"Now information like that's gonna cost. In fact, these last five minutes are going to cost."

The woman said, "I know him."

Chaney shot the Brakeman in the chest with the Derringer. He fell back, busting some grain shine jars, then slopped into the side of the tent, ripping part of it to the ground.

He sprawled, gurgling. "Bastards . . . do anything for money . . ."

Beaudine said, "No, that would be you."

Chaney hopped down from the wagon and went through the dying man's pockets. He found a razor in his belt, a wad of singles, some coin, and a rail worker's schedule. He pocketed the schedule, peeled twenty dollars, and handed the rest to the woman.

Beaudine said, "If you hurry, you can get him to a doctor. But you'll have to tell me what I need."

The woman said, "No, I won't hurry."

Chaney fired one more slug between the Brakeman's surprised eyes.

The woman quick-stepped around Beaudine to where her husband was lying in a mess of canvas, 'shine, and icy slush. She bent down to look at him closely, neatened his mustache with her finger, pausing for a moment to feel his breath. There was none. She stood back up.

Beaudine said, "Miss Lotus?"

"My husband would get lost. We have a map."

Howard said, "He must've been a lousy railroad man."

She went back into the tent.

"Howard, take the map, see who this is. Gambler, you're coming with me to Paradise River."

The woman handed the map to Beaudine. She pulled the paper flower from her hair, dropped it on her husband's chest, bowed to the three men in the dynamite wagon, and said, ever so quietly, "My thanks."

* * *

Dev Bishop was careful with the last of Allard's whiskey, pouring it into two glasses on the desk, the final drops hanging on the lip of the bottle. The soldier was dead, and Dev corked it. Smythe sat in front of him, raising his glass.

Dev wasn't returning the toast. "Smythe, how bad was it at the Goodwill?"

"You lost a lot of men, most to the dynamite Beaudine planted. And that was all done for the meetup with Creed. Beaudine wanted to make sure nobody walked out of there."

"You said most, how did we lose the others?"

"Your brother. But you know that, don't you?"

Dev took a drink. "We've got something big coming up in Paradise River in two days, and it can't be thwarted."

"That train job could really set us up, boy-o. We need it."

"It's always tough to get started."

"Or reconstructed." Smythe laughed as he took another pull, leaving the last bit. "I know my history, Dev. New country can be a great playground, but only if you get in early."

"That's what this is all for."

Dev unfurled a map showing sections of the Colorado Line, and its stations, including Paradise River. The railroad was a curving snake of red across miles of green and blue mountains.

"And there's the problem," Smythe said. "How many miles? What you want to do is already being done in New York and by my old man in London. Villages and cities, mate. You can control that with a few men on every street. There's too much land—how can you keep track?"

"That's why we need an army."

"The one we almost lost."

"I kept you on the road. All you got is that scratch."

Smythe snorted. Dev continued, "You'll heal. That accountant's going to help us get organized. The money from this train will get us men, equipment. Maybe even buy us a sheriff or two. Whatever we need to stay in control, and you're going to be the man in the towns and villages, making sure everything's running right."

"The Indians might have a thing or two to say about these plans. And the real Army."

"Wouldn't it be something if the tribes lined up on our side?"

"Oh, big dreams, boy-o."

"This train is no dream."

"That's a hell of a job you're handing me."

"You're important to this."

Smythe finished his drink. "Because I shot the warden?"

"Because you listened to my ideas."

"And you're paying me well for it, but it doesn't mean I agree with everything."

Dev leaned forward, his injured arm resting on the edge of the desk. "One more Goodwill, and we're done.

"John doesn't know I'm alive, and wants Beaudine dead. Let 'em tear each other up, and we'll take care of the man left standing. But nothing comes before these plans."

The bounce-back of a rifle's report moved Dev to the window, where he looked down into the prison yard. Fuller was drawing down on targets beyond the front gate—loading, shooting, and hitting straight, every single time.

Captain Creed sat his Pride near Fuller, with Hector by the stirrups describing the shots. Dev watched for a few more moments, then turned to Smythe. "Creed's got that buffalo soldier. Good sniper. We can use him."

"What about the blind man himself?"

"This is going to be done right. Cut him loose." Dev drank the final drops of the warden's fine mash. "We're taking this train."

"Never thought any different, mate."

CHAPTER TWENTY-FOUR
Bad Deeds

"I've been shot before, and can't say it ever gets any better."

Miles Duffin tried a smile, but failed, as Bishop and Fox swabbed the bullet wound just above his hip. He was lying on a stack of blankets in the back of a buckboard, surrounded by suitcases and packed boxes, the bay and the painted tethered to the side.

His young wife was driving, and not looking back at her husband as he tried again, "I wish I could say the other fellow looks worse."

Bishop said, "He does."

"You get him with that Shuler double?"

Fox took cotton from the medical kit, combed it out, before pressing it onto the bullet wound. Miles screamed, and his wife looked back. Her face was streaked, but didn't give up a word. Fox bound the cotton tight; the wife kept her jaw clenched.

"You two are the doggonedest doctors I ever seen. But dying men can't be choosers. I'm truly obliged."

Bishop smiled. "You talk too much, Deputy."

"Not my only failure. I was serving papers when this happened, wish I could say it was a shoot-out."

Miles's wife looked at him again. Furious.

Bishop said, "Be glad it wasn't, and you really talk too much. You've lost a lot of blood, and half the slug's in there. You know the doc in Paradise River?"

Miles's wife spoke from the driver's seat. "Yes, we know him. He's worked on Miles. A lot."

"He's going to be working on him again. It's not deep, but it's got to come out."

Miles whispered, "Okay. If you tell me how you got that all fixed up."

"I lost the arm a year ago, and her father made it."

Miles turned to Fox. "Real good job. Don't make you look like a doc, but I sure as hell wouldn't mess with you!"

"We're trying to find other men like the one who shot you. The Fire Riders."

Miles's wife said, voice rising, "That should be easy enough. They've raided the town half a dozen times, and I don't know how many they've killed."

"Rachel, it wasn't that many times, or that many people. And I took down a lot of 'em. Give me a little credit, honey."

She said, "Fine. And they kept coming back, with more men. And now look at you."

Miles said to Bishop, "We best drop it," while scribbling a note on a piece of a wanted poster, with a pencil he had in his pocket. He pressed the note into Bishop's left.

Rachel guided the buckboard into Paradise River, following the one road that turned into a main street that met three more streets in the center of town. Paradise had a worn look, with shingles missing from roofs, split glass in store windows, or railings broken on hotel balconies. Yet, it was all freshly painted, as if the entire town had been dressed up for some quick influx of people or money that hadn't happened.

Paradise was a spinster, still waiting for a beau.

The one building that was newly built was the rail station, with a full loading area for cattle, and a water tower. There were no cattle. A few people lounged on the platform.

Fox and Bishop climbed from the buckboard, and grabbed their horses, as Rachel drove on to the doctor's down the street. Miles waved his best and shouted his thanks, which only made Rachel snap the team to drive faster.

She had given Bishop a look of gratitude, but nothing else, and he understood. She hated that her husband was lying with a bullet in him, and wanted no part of this kind of life. Not anymore. He'd seen that look in a woman's eyes before and, following Fox into the shabby hotel, wondered about seeing it again.

"We don't usually accept . . . unusual guests."

Bishop looked from the deskman, trying to focus on his small, pink rabbit eyes, then to Fox, and then to himself, before saying, "So who's unusual?"

"I don't know how comfortable you'll be here."

"The ground's frozen, and there's a storm heading in. You've got a lot of keys on that pegboard. You want to ask me about my arm? Ask."

Bishop dropped the double-barrels in front of the deskman with a loud thud. Rabbit eyes jumped back.

"Believe it or not, I'm a doctor, so I can tell details of the operation, but most folks just want to know if it actually works. Would you like to see? Maybe that old couch?"

He turned, the shotgun snapping into position, when the deskman grabbed a key from the pegboard. Fox snatched it from his hands.

The bed was too large for the room, the door hitting it when you entered. There was a nightstand with a cracked pitcher and washbasin, both painted with blue roses, and one ragged towel. There had been a mirror on the wall sometime, but it was long gone, with only the dirty outline of it remaining.

Bishop put his saddlebags and med kit on the floor, and reached for something as Fox splashed water on her face from the basin.

"I'm sorry about that."

She turned to him.

"I don't like to act that way, but he was being stupid."

"He was."

He held out the note that Miles had slipped him. "That's the train that's coming tomorrow night. It's a gold transfer for the bank."

"Dev's gold? The treasure that everyone wants?"

"That's not real."

"The pain it's caused you is real."

"This shipment might bring out some of the men we're looking for. You saying I should leave it alone?"

Fox just said, "Things do not stay the same."

"They have to for a little while." He took the copy of Poe from his bags, and placed it on the bed. "You left that behind."

Fox regarded the book, but didn't make a reach. "Let's do what you need done. Then we'll see."

Bishop said, "*Hó'ótóva,*" wanting Fox to agree and say, "Yes. Someday." But she didn't.

Instead, she handed him the bandolier of six.

Howard was on the ground at Crawford's feet, holding his stomach that had been ripped by the iron talons of White Claw. The metal contraption was still fitted to Crawford's hand, spattering red whenever he moved. Howard screamed, but it only made it worse for him, intensifying the pain, as he felt his lungs and throat with his cries.

His face was slashed, and one arm taken down to the bone. Every move that Howard made, Crawford blocked with his boots, holding him down, making him squirm even more. And cry out again, to nothing, but the woods.

Crawford kept walking around Howard, kicking small piles of snow against his torn face, bringing the claw close to him, pressing the sharp edges against open wounds.

"Think you can come onto my place, threaten my daughter? Because you're a big fella? That ain't the way it works. You're talking about harming *my* blood, which means *your* blood is gonna run! You're gonna die here, and then I'm gonna feed ya to the next thing that comes down out of them woods! Because you needed me to talk? Brother, that's the mistake that killed you."

He slashed again, opening Howard's back through his jacket. Howard crawled, face pressing into the muddy snow. Crawford bent down, and snatched the deputy's badge from his shirt.

"I don't know if you're a real lawman, or just stupid, but I'm keepin' this."

Howard rolled onto his back, staring into the sky. Crawford held Howard's gun above his head. "Gun ain't a threat, if you don't know when to use it. And you sure don't."

Howard couldn't speak, and tears erupted from his eyes to his mouth. Everything else was soaked red, and burning.

Crawford aimed the pistol at Howard's head. "If you shot me a few times, at least you could'a gotten the hell away. I ain't gonna do anything more to ya, though. Now, I bet you wish I would, just to get her done. You made your choice to come after my family, and you're gonna die with it. And wherever you end up, remember, it was White Claw what sent you there."

Beaudine let the match's flame edge the tobacco of the cigar, heating it just right, before drawing deep. It was fine leaf, but tightly rolled in several layers. That made it last and gave it a firm ash, but it was difficult to light.

Chaney stood with him on the platform of the Paradise River station, watching the cigar process and checking his watch. The sun was red behind the mountains, and Beaudine had to shield his eyes when he spoke to him.

"Mr. Chaney, the window doesn't open for another three minutes. You should enjoy this time."

"If we get that money, the shares are a lot larger than when we started."

He drew on the cigar, and studied it. "Yes, I've done my calculations. Our earlier efforts were derailed by other forces. I always said the best way was to have Bishop come to us. Now he has to, or he doesn't get the little package, does he? Or even the bang-tail. We just have to have patience."

"That's getting short in supply."

"So you keep threatening."

The ticket window opened, and a pair of thick glasses peered out, with a man behind them. Beaudine gave the ticket clerk the package for general express, then unfolded the Brakeman's schedule.

The clerk said, "You work for the Colorado, young fella?"

"A good friend does."

"That's paperwork only for employees."

"He's trusting me with this information. Can you tell me about this train? Is it express?"

The clerk laughed. "Better not be. It's got to stop here and make a gold transfer to the bank. And the only reason I'm letting you know is—" The clerk brought a Colt 45 up from under the counter and pointed it out of the cage. "And mister, there are soldiers on that train, and they're carrying something a damn sight bigger than this."

CHAPTER TWENTY-FIVE
Keep My Coffin Open

The bonfires were set in three separate places in the prison yard, spreading a moving light that allowed the men to check weapons and horses. Some tried for night target practice: quick-drawing service pieces, or cracking off as many as possible with a Winchester.

Dev and Smythe moved among them, noting the weapons and their variable abilities. One rider tried long-shooting with a Colt, missing the wooden target three times out of six. Fuller stepped in, obliterating it with two perfectly placed kill shots.

"You're putting all these fellas to shame."

Fuller checked the hammer of his Morgan-James, blew it out. "Well, that's not my intention, Mr. Bishop."

"Just the same. You going to be riding tomorrow night? We could use you, and I'll see that your share's double these others."

"Double?"

"Triple."

Fuller looked to Creed, who was standing with Hector, brushing down Pride by the firelight, the flames literally dancing in the reflection of the horse's muscled, black coat.

"What about the captain? That's who brought me in."

Dev said, "I'll talk to him. He wants the best for you."

He walked over and put a hand on Hector's shoulder. "Watch the captain, son. Learn how to do things right."

Creed continued with the grooming. "What are we doing about your brother, Mr. Bishop? Is finding him part of the mission tomorrow night?"

"The mission's about money. My brother's close, Captain. And when he pops his head out of the ground, we'll chop it off."

"You agreed that would be my role."

"Not tomorrow night, sir."

"I have the finest horse here, and Hector for my eyes."

"It's not enough. There's too much at stake."

Creed stopped brushing and followed Dev's voice so he could be directly in front of him. His dark glasses looked like eyeless sockets in the firelight, transforming his face into a skull.

"You remember who you're talking to? I have more right to kill your brother than anyone. I helped you organize this ragtag, because I was told that I would get to exercise that right."

"And we followed him after his accident, so you'd know where he was for the capture. But he's not here, is he, Captain?"

Creed turned away, slipping the grooming brush into his saddle. "If we're a burden, then we'll ride."

"Mr. Fuller's staying on."

Creed stepped around his horse, Hector taking his arm as he tripped over a pile of stones and rotting wood. He stumbled almost to the ground, then stood, jerking away from Hector. "Fuller! Is this true?"

Fuller said, "I need money for my family, Captain. That's what you promised."

"Do you know what will happen if I find Bishop?"

"Yes, sir, I do."

Fuller extended his hand to shake, but Creed turned from him. "I had my hand out for you, Captain."

"I know."

Hector guided Creed to his horse, then stood away, as he swung onto Pride's back. Pride lowered his head, helping Hector climb on behind. Pride snorted, ready to run, but Creed sat the animal for a moment before walking Pride around the bonfires, circling the yard and the men in red and then breaking to a full run out the front gate.

From the back of the Conastoga wagon, Tomlinson's daughters began to sing. Their perfect-pitch voices carrying over the sounds of the prison yard, as Smythe, Dev, and Fuller watched Captain Creed and Hector ride into the enormous darkness beyond the gates. And then they were gone.

They said nothing when Smythe held out a new .56 caliber Spencer carbine. "Ready to go to work?"

Fuller took the rifle, hefting its weight.

"Feel good?"

"A fine weapon. Balanced. Never shot it before. Looks like I'll be practicing." He slammed home an ammo magazine.

Dev said, "After the raid tomorrow, you'll be able to give your family a future. Better than these others. Money in the bank, and it's only going to get better. You're a Fire Rider, now, sniper."

"Maybe, but—" Fuller picked up a red hood from the ground, tossed it on the bonfire, and watched it burn.

White Fox was curled up on top of the bed, not even a blanket covering her, as Bishop sat in the corner, checking the motion of the rig. He snapped his wrist, and the barrels responded instantly. He turned, the gun turned. Every move, and the weapon responded. He let the hammers drop. Click.

Fox murmured, and Bishop tucked a blanket around her.

The break of morning was shrouded by blowing snow that moved thick in the air, the heavy powder of the mountains being swept up by cold bursts of wind. For Smythe, it was like grey evening, as he tied his horse and walked around the side of the Paradise River Rail Station, noting the platform and tracks.

The station was deserted—no crew or distant whistle of a locomotive. Just the cold that deadens the back of the neck, which is why he didn't feel the barrel of Beaudine's Colt against him.

Beaudine kept his voice steady, though his hand was shaking. "Mr. Smythe, killing you the worst way possible has been one of my dreams, since we were in the Tomb. But I think I'll allow you to stay aboveground, while we discuss our new partnership."

"Oh, you're making a whopping mistake, boy-o."

"My mistake was not killing you all those times I had the chance."

Beaudine nudged Smythe with the pistol, and they both moved off the platform, toward the cattle pens.

White Fox woke in the room, stretching her arms, and wiping her eyes. For a moment, she felt that someone would be next to her. But she was alone.

Rachel Duffin tried to hide her displeasure when Bishop knocked on the doctor's door, but she was unsuccessful. Her face was newly tear-stained, and her expression, dark.

Rachel said, "We're not staying in this town. I don't want you saying anything to change my husband's mind."

"I won't do that."

Bishop wanted to extend Rachel a bit of comfort and tell her that she reminded him of his wife, when Dr. Benson stepped from the back room and introduced himself. He was pleasant and old school, and probably had a drink or two with his breakfast. Benson walked Bishop to a small side bedroom where Miles was recovering. Bishop kept his arm down, his duster hiding the barrels of the rig.

Benson gave Bishop a sidelong look over his glasses. "Miles told me you fixed him on the road. Where did you serve?"

"Out of Virginia."

"That was a good field dressing, doctor."

Benson's office and the patient's room were clean. Organized. And he carried himself with that rare combination of sawbones and educated physician. There was a little more small talk, but he knew when to leave. Another good sign of a good doctor.

Bishop sat by Miles's bed and told him so. Rachel stood in the doorway, arms folded, struggling.

Miles said, "I'm glad to hear you think he knows what he's doing."

"You're the best judge. How do you feel?"

"Like hell. But less like hell than I did yesterday."

Rachel said, "This is the best thing for him, but he can't get overtired."

"Honey, I sure would like a cup of coffee."

"Tea."

"Fine. Anything for you, Doctor Bishop?"

Bishop turned to Rachel and said, "Tea sounds very fine, I haven't eaten this morning."

Rachel left, but didn't shut the door. Bishop tapped it with his foot, nudging it almost shut. "I need to know about the gold train."

"You gonna rob it?"

"Not me, but someone might have plans."

"That's what the soldiers are for, I guess. They didn't really include me in it, except as an extra gun, when they carry the money to the bank from the station. They've only done it twice before, and nothing happened."

"With the money or the town?"

"Both. They deposit here because shipping companies keep threatening to build, and they need loans. The mayor gets excited for the boom he's been counting on for twenty years, and then nothing happens, and they pull the deposits. Last time it almost wiped the town out."

"What about the sheriff?"

"Up territory someplace. I heard he has another wife. Anyway, he's not around much anymore, so when I get laid up, it can be a problem."

"And what about your wife?"

"She don't like what I do, and something like this makes her hate it."

"She might not be wrong."

"Doc, I have considered that about twenty times a day."

"Miles, no one can hit that train at the station if they've got men on it."

"I know a little spot, just a gopher hole about ten miles down the tracks. That's where I stake out. Perfect view of the Fire Riders, if that's what you're talking about."

"One man, one badge, huh?"

"That's why we're lame ducks. If you can find anybody from Paradise to help, you're a better man than me."

Bishop stood. "Doubtful, but here's some advice. Do what she wants, and go build your life."

"But, ere long the heaven of this pure affection became darkened, and gloom, and horror, and grief swept over it in clouds."

White Fox read the line from "Morella" aloud several times, the words coming easier and easier to her, even if their true meaning didn't. She said, "Not perfect," to the empty room, flipped through some pages, and let the cover drop shut.

The knock on the door came immediately afterward. Her hand turned the knob; then she was thrown back hard. Chaney had shouldered the door into her and was now slamming it shut behind him.

Chaney flicked his gold tooth before speaking. "Where is he? And don't look at me like a squaw pissing in the dirt."

Fox separated her words: "I—don't—know."

Chaney's Derringer was out of his jacket, and he brought it up to her temple. "We know about that little package from your pa, and I paid three clerks to let me know if they saw you. I stacked the deck a little, especially since you cut my rib in half with an arrowhead."

Fox let Chaney lean in close; she could taste his breath, even as he kept the gun pressed into her, leaving a mark.

"Your man has money, the railroad has money. Everybody but me, and we're going to fix that right up. Tell me where he hides his cash, or I'll kill you. Understand? Or do I have to talk in dog-tongue?"

She closed her eyes. "*Tó'ovenohtsé.*"

"Not an answer."

Fox locked eyes with Chaney, staring. He almost smiled, as she reached over her head for the water pitcher, and shattered it against his skull. The scream of the breaking china and the scream of the gambler were a garbled one as he fell to the floor.

She lunged across the bed for her saddle, grabbing a sheathed knife, as Chaney came up shooting wild, blood washing his eyes from the cuts on his head.

The slugs hit the wall behind her, as she threw the

knife. It hit his chest, but broke off at the tip. Chaney fell forward, catching himself on the edge of the bed.

"God, get me some help, and I won't do nothing else to you again. I swear. Just help me, please."

Chaney lurched as Fox took a step toward him. The knife blade in his gun's pistol grip jutted out, and he slashed, catching her arm. Fox smashed him back with both elbows, the bone punching his face, then brought up her knees to send him slamming against the wall.

The knifepoint was pushed deeper into Chaney's chest. He dropped to his knees, and then collapsed. The room seemed darker for a moment, as Fox sat on the edge of the bed. Chaney was nothing now, just an empty shell lying on the floor. It had all taken less than five seconds.

Fox wiped at the tears she hated.

The roof was nothing but an overhang, but it kept the now steady snow off Smythe and Beaudine. Smythe's hands were tied, and he was sitting with his back against a wall, long lengths of chain and butchering hooks hanging behind and above him. Sledgehammers to knock out the cows were gathered in a large barrel by the door that opened onto the always empty cattle pens.

Beaudine settled on a bench, holding the long cleaver.

"Another business in Paradise that isn't doing well. Ask anyone in town and they'll be happy to tell you. I understand their need, as I have it myself. Money comes so easy to some, and the rest of us can chase it forever, and not catch a dollar. What do you think, Smythe? About money? Do you know anyone who has any?"

"Come on, boy-o. Doc Bishop's got nothing! All that gold talk was a trick to get you to go after the brother, so Dev could work his own thing."

Beaudine studied the blade, letting the light from an

oil lantern bounce off of it, into his eyes. "You keep saying that, Smythe."

"Because it's the bloody truth. He's got big plans."

"I was closer to him than anyone, helped him."

"But he played you, mate. He didn't want you anywhere near this."

Beaudine took a few steps with the blade chest-high, as an executioner would hold it before going to the chopping block. "Yet, he trusts a prison guard, and not his own cellmate?"

"So what do you do now? Kill me? Or go after him? You've talked to the station master, you know what's happening with this train."

"Those men in red who attacked me, they belong to Devlin?"

Smythe threw away, "They're his men, yeah."

Beaudine lowered the blade. "That can't go unpunished."

"There's money on that train. Real money, not some kind of trick. I don't give a damn about Dev Bishop, but you can't take it alone."

"I don't trust you a bit."

"I'll show you, then you decide. I'm not running, boy-o."

Beaudine hauled Smythe to his feet with a grunt. "You know this is going to end in his death."

"And I'm in for shares, Major?"

CHAPTER TWENTY-SIX
Dead Men Kill, Too

The tracks of the Colorado Line ran through a narrow gorge that opened onto flatlands on the other side of a small grouping of mountains, before reaching Paradise River. It was like a natural tunnel, heavily treed, and a beautiful cousin to the Rockies if seen during a new spring.

But the first snows settled and stayed, slicking the mountainside, and weighing the trees until they bent almost to the ground. The gorge was covered with jags of ice, from frozen rain and water coming down from the higher range, only to be captured and paralyzed here.

Dev Bishop and Fuller stood by on their horses, just above the gorge, watching as dynamite was bundled to the trunks of some tall pines just above the tracks.

Fuller said, "That stuff almost killed you and your men once."

"Well, now you're riding with us, so you best pay attention. What position are you going to take?"

"You want me to hit the engineer?"

"Just take care of what the trees and the boiler don't."

Someone yelled, "She's goin!" and all broke for their horses, riding quickly away as the first charges exploded, throwing tree trunks in the air, and breaking them into huge pieces, tumbling down onto the tracks, blocking them.

A wave of snow and ice followed, rolling from the hillside, covering the blockade. After a few moments, the air calmed again, as the last bits of wreckage found its place.

Fuller said, "Now, that was a hell of a noise."

"There's not a train due until the one we want. This bunch will take care of anyone who comes sniffing around. You're too valuable for guard duty, stay with me."

Chaney's body was covered with a blanket, one of his hands peeking out from under. Spots of blood had soaked through across his chest. Miles walked around the side of the bed with the help of a cane, lifting the blanket for another look, then dropping it again.

Bishop and Fox stood by the open door, the rabbit deskman with them, his arms folded as tight as his expression.

"I knew I shouldn't have given them the room. I'm not letting this go. She's gonna feel the law!"

Miles said, "This is a killing, and you're going to have to go to trial, miss."

Bishop said, "Chaney tried to kill her."

"Miss, you self-defended this one all over the room and I'm sure a judge will see it that way."

The deskman said, "But you'll be rotting in jail until then!"

Miles stepped to Fox, his voice low. "I understand what this is about for you two, so if you swear you'll appear, I won't arrest you."

White Fox said, "I swear."

"I'll do up the papers for a territorial judge."

The rabbit said, "That's it?"

"For right now. If she don't come for trial, I'll have a warrant sworn out."

The deskman was still fuming, his forehead changing color, as Bishop and Miles moved into the hallway. Miles hobbled toward the stairs, his voice low. "I should be doing a hell of a lot more."

"I know. They'll probably take your badge."

"That's not the worst thing to happen. Doc, I couldn't be more grateful to you and the miss for what you've done, but please, don't test it. You have to come back and face this. I won't be the law anymore, but you don't want this hanging over you."

Bishop said, "Miles, if we're able to make it back, we will."

"One last bit of advice? You're a civilian. Let the troops do their job."

Bishop gave Miles a shake with his left, before turning to Fox. She started down the stairs ahead of him, walking across the street to the livery, her eyes dry and fixed ahead.

Bishop fell in next to her and said, "You don't have to go. Now I'm giving you the out, if you want it."

Fox said nothing. Light, fresh snow stuck to them both as they moved to their horses, checking for the weapons they'd need. She held out a knife, the same size as the one she'd used on Chaney. Her hand started to shake.

Bishop didn't see it, and said, "Have it ready."

He filled the bandolier with shells, and more in his pockets, then slipped a small-caliber Smith & Wesson into his jacket, and gave Fox a Colt. She checked the weapon; all their moves were measured, just what he thought they should be. Automatic.

Bishop said, "I'm ready. Are you? Last chance."

Fox swung onto the painted's back.

They broke from the livery, running the painted and

the bay down the road parallel to the tracks, heading for the trail in the hills above them. The snow was coming harder now, blowing heavy, and sideways.

"It would be unwise to fabricate."

Smythe was on his horse, riding alongside Beaudine, his hands still tied behind his back. "I'm telling you this is the place that we've chosen. They've already brought down some trees up the tracks, and here's where we'll ride out to take the cars."

Beaudine maneuvered farther along a ledge high above the tracks, ice patching the rock, before taking a spot next to a sparse blue fir.

Smythe said, "What about me?"

He didn't see the gun in Beaudine's hand, or hear the shot. He saw the muzzle flash, and then it was too late.

The distant shot echoed, as the Fire Riders gathered at the edge of the woods, some taking their attack positions above the railroad tracks, while others towed more split trunks and giant limbs into place. The wall they'd built was over ten feet high, and beyond the height of the engine's cowcatcher.

Fuller watched as they worked, all wearing their crimson tunics, and a few, their hoods. All the sniper could think about was family, and money, and the worth of the risk.

One of the Riders barked at Fuller, "Hey, how many times you kill for money, son?"

Fuller didn't answer, checked the action on the Spencer.

Dev Bishop called out, "We've got less than ten!"

Down the tracks, the train whistle called out, and

echoed back through the hills. The snow was now a thick curtain, whiting everyone's vision.

John Bishop and Fox rode their horses up from the tracks to a small space in the rocks, looking down on the gorge. Deputy Miles's cigarette makings littered the ground where there was a tin cup solid with ice, and flat stones for a small campfire.

The whistle called again.

Bishop looked to Fox. "We can't stop this happening, but we'll avenge my wife, my son."

She finally said, "That's what we're here for."

The train whistle became a pained cry, and the crash that followed was so loud the bay and painted buckled at the knees.

The gold train was five cars long, led by a Baldwin steam engine, powering through the storm. The engineer had pulled the brakes half a mile back, but the downward grade and icy tracks pushed the train faster, with its large power wheels throwing hot, yellow sparks as they skidded, fighting to slow. Failing.

Half the trees and rocks were blasted out of the way on impact, but the rest held fast, jammed beneath the rails and pushing against the boiler until it exploded. Bleeding iron. The rest of the engine crumpling into itself, blowing off the wheels, sending them still-spinning into the frozen mountainside.

Bolts were bullets, blowing off in all directions, while the brass fittings twisted from the engine and ripped back through the cab, killing the engineer and fireman.

It was all screaming metal and steam, as the rest of the train spun wild off the tracks, the cars tumbling, colliding with each other, glass and metal erupting before smashing into the snow drifts—dominoes thrown by God.

Bishop and Fox charged the small cut through the hills, down to the tracks. Metal was still bending, whining, as steam exploded from safety valves and brakes. The falling snow cooled the boiler, which sizzled as the winter fought to put it out.

The soldiers in the passenger and mail cars cried through bloody injuries. Bishop and Fox climbed on top of the mail car, peering into the door that had been ripped open like wet paper. Two young soldiers were huddled in the tipped-over corner, bleeding and wide-eyed, clutching their rifles, but not knowing what or where to shoot.

Bishop called to them, "Boys, we're here to help! Stay down!"

Slugs ripped at Bishop and Fox. They dove off the car, the shots tearing close.

In the trees, Fuller's position was good, as he lay cover fire for the Riders. He drew on Bishop, and fired. Bishop rolled, the slug ricocheting off the rig, and the steel taking it. Bishop grabbed Fox and dove from the wreck, as the shots tore into the train cars around them.

The sniper fire kept Bishop low, behind cover, as a Fire Rider bore down on him. Bishop jostled his arm. The rig was instantly up and loaded, and he sprang, blowing the Rider clean out of the saddle. The Fire Rider spun with the impact, then landed dead, on hot-metal debris.

Before his body tumbled into the snow, another Rider charged, and Bishop let fire with the second barrel. He shucked the shells, pulled down two more, and turned on another, who was coming up over the wood tender. He fired, turned, fired again.

The Riders lay wounded and dying, the snow offering a new shroud as they bled out.

Four Riders rode fast along the tracks, leaping around

wreckage, and hurling Ketchum Hand Grenades. One, two, blasts sent ice, mud, and fire into the air.

Two young soldiers dove from the wreck of the passenger car, scrambling to get a good shot, as a grenade landed between them. One panicked a throw, tossing it into the air, where it exploded through the falling snow.

Bishop shot two Riders with a pull of the trigger line, sending them sprawling from their horses and still shooting as they hit the ground. Bishop reloaded from the bandolier, and wounded one more as he rode by.

White Fox got the last one, hurling a knife into his gut.

Bishop called out to the mail car, "Boys, you okay in there?"

A soldier yelled back that he'd been hit, but was all right.

Bishop worked his way to the top of the car when the Gatling gun cut loose from the trees. The thousand rounds hit the train wreckage, beating hell out of it, as Bishop and Fox took cover behind the old boiler. A few of the young soldiers shot back from the passenger car, which was riddled with bullets.

The gun stopped as two Fire Riders hurled dynamite, blowing off the back of the mail car. Hot metal and fire sliced the air. They kicked their way inside, grabbed a large strong box, and shouldered it out to a wagon. The Gatling laid cover fire as the horse team bolted, carrying the Riders and the strong box away from the battle.

Bishop signaled Fox.

He ran around to the far side of the locomotive, keeping behind the wheels, bursts of steam still gutting from the engine. The Gatling let loose again. Bishop made for his horse.

Fox worked back to the wood tender, and the fireman's station. A drum of coal oil hadn't burst in the wreck. Its seams bulged as she rolled it into the half-ton of firewood that was spread from the tender. She grabbed a fireman's ax and cut open the lid, soaking the wood with oil.

The snow was falling solid now, frosting the wreckage, and the dead. Wet. Cold.

Fox watched, as Bishop climbed back toward the trail, trying to reach the ledge where the Gatling was protected. Fox ducked as another burst of fire raked the metal and glass.

She grabbed the brakeman's lantern, lit it, and waited. Bishop got to the ledge, dropped silently from the bay. Fox smashed the lantern into the wood tender, lighting the pools of coal oil, and the wood. The flames ate the oil, spewing black.

Thick plumes of smoke instantly choked the sky around the locomotive, then blanketing the train. The Gatling opened up from the hills, shooting blind.

The smoke rolled from the train, as the wood fire grew. Bishop kept low, moving on the Gatling, the grey smoke mixed with the snow his cover. Both barrels were ready, the Fire Rider feeding the ammo into the machine gun, raking the train over and over.

The Rider had no time to react when both barrels of the shotgun lifted him off his feet, and tossed him down the icy side of the mountain, to the wreckage below.

The last sounds of the machine gun died in the distance, and Bishop stood, listening to the final reports. The snow was thicker, a curtain of white beads, as it began dousing the flames around the train. Bishop pulled the firing mechanism and ammo clips from the Gatling when a voice said, "I could have killed you a dozen times."

Bishop turned to see Fuller step from the trees, with his Spencer rifle in his hands, but not aimed at him.

"Why didn't you?"

"You see all that down there, doc? I guess I've had enough for a while. How about you?"

Bishop brought the shotgun rig up.

"I never was after you, but you and Creed stopped me from finding the men who killed my family. That's all I wanted."

Fuller said, "If you'd let me, I want to get back to mine. You'll never see me again."

Bishop lowered the rig. Fuller turned and walked back to where his horse was tied in the trees. He got on it, his rifle on his back, and gave Bishop a last nod before riding into the deeper woods.

John Bishop took some deep breaths, the rig now weighing him down. He stepped around the bodies of the Riders he'd dropped, and looked at the burning damage below, the field of battle.

Bishop made his way off the ridge and rode toward the mail car, as the soldiers began climbing from the wreckage. He got off his horse, and walked it to the other side of the wood tender. The fire was now smoldering, but the smoke from the coal oil was still thick, and choking the air.

Bishop couldn't be sure of what he was seeing as he moved through the cloud of grey. He stopped, the cloud breaking apart. It was a man, holding a woman, with a large blade pressed against her throat.

"Dr. Bishop, wouldn't it have been so much simpler to give me what I wanted a year ago? Think of the lives you could have saved. You're still a doctor, correct?"

Bishop's answer was to take a step, the rig snapping into place. He pulled back the sleeve on his right arm completely, to expose the gun and the extra shells: two chambered, and two ready.

"What do you think this is going to get you?"

Beaudine held the blade tight. "My fortune."

"They stole some."

"Your brother promised me a fortune in gold."

"You should have gotten it from him before they hanged him."

Beaudine laughed. "They never hanged him, you fool."

Bishop took another step, the smoke and snow shifting in front of him, making him ghostly. An apparition. The shotgun rig shifted with his every move, keeping its aim on Beaudine's chest.

"Take that blade away."

"And what will you give me? You know what happened last time, and I have no problem doing the same thing again."

"I don't have any gold. But I can give you your life."

Beaudine was fixed on the figure in front of him, advancing.

"You asked if I was a doctor, and I'm really not. I'm something else, that is going to kill you in ten seconds if you don't let her go." Bishop extended the rig. "We both have something the other one wants."

"I know."

Beaudine said, "I'm the man who turned you into what you are, and I think that deserves compensation."

"You're right."

Fox brought her heel down, breaking Beaudine's foot, before smashing his windpipe with her elbow. He stumbled, the cleaver blade falling away. The first barrel caught him in the leg, dropping him.

Bishop moved on Beaudine, screaming in the snow.

"Why did you say my brother was alive?"

"Because he is! Oh, sweet Lord—"

"Tell me!"

"I don't know much—!"

"You've made me very angry."

The next barrel blew half of Beaudine's right arm off, leaving it to dangle. Beaudine screamed, and prayed. Bishop loaded the weapon again.

"I'll leave you in the snow to die unless you tell me everything."

Beaudine looked up; he was choking now, Bishop's

figure in front of him darkening even more behind the smoke and snow.

"The Riders . . . You're not who you were. . . . You're the Angel of Death."

Bishop fired two more barrels into Beaudine. Fox turned away, started to run for her horse. Bishop ran for her, grabbing her with his left, and spinning her around.

Fox twisted away. "Let go of me!"

"I deserved that! You know what that man took from me! You've been with me for a year, leading to this!"

Fox looked at him, said, "I told you I would help you until I can't. Now I can't."

The young soldiers had finally climbed from the wreckage, laying some of their comrades in the snow while wounds were tended to. A young officer took a head count, while the two soldiers from the mail car handed over the cache of gold.

Bishop watched all this from a distance. Fox had climbed onto the painted, and brought the horse around. She looked down at him, and said, "Aren't you going to help them?"

Bishop said, "Yeah, I'll try, if I can."

"This is what you need to do now."

Fox eased the painted away, and Bishop watched her as she followed the tracks, before climbing a small trail that led into the mountains.

"Are you a doctor? We could use you over here!"

Bishop nodded, following the young man to the remains of the passenger car and the caboose.

The soldier looked at the shotgun. "I've never seen anything like that before."

"I had it made special."

The soldier stopped in his tracks, was peering into the distance, snow collecting on his face.

"What's wrong?"

"The guys in the Red Hoods, there are two of them

on the ridge. If they go for another wave, that's the end of us. We've already lost the shipment."

Bishop looked where the young soldier was pointing to see two men on horseback, both wearing crimson tunics, one sporting a red hood, while the other was not.

The young soldier was calling his friends to arms, as John Bishop saw what looked to be his brother flanked by the other rider.

Bishop took a step, and Dev's face came more and more in focus. Through the snow and screams, he recognized him, and his name tore from Bishop in a demonic cry.

The rig snapped instantly into place. The hooded rider threw something, as Dev reared on his horse, and galloped away.

The grenade landed at John Bishop's feet.

Bishop's eyes opened, just as the Benson finished rolling his cigarette. He lit it and drew deep before saying anything to his patient.

"They tell me a grenade blew you ten feet in the air. You've got some bruises and a broken ankle, but I didn't find any sign of hemorrhage. Pretty amazing. There were a lot of dead men at that wreck."

"How many have you treated?"

"About twenty, shipped them out to an army hospital yesterday."

"How long have I been out? What have you been giving me?"

"Light morphine so you could sleep. Two and a half days."

Bishop edged his way onto his elbow, "Great. I'll have soldier's disease on top of everything else. How'd I get here?"

"A boy brought you on horseback. Said he was a

friend, but that no one could know he helped you. He brought some of your things, too."

Bishop looked to the dresser by the bed to see the shotgun rig, his medical kit, and a worn volume of Edgar Alan Poe setting on top of it.

The doc moved to the dresser and picked up the shotgun. "That's quite a contraption. Had a hell of a time getting it off you, but you don't need it now, understand? You should, you're a doctor, too."

Bishop lay back in the bed, enjoying the feeling of the cold, clean sheets. He nodded his cooperation.

The doc said, "Sleep for another few hours, and we'll get you some good supper. You're lucky, my wife can cook."

Bishop smiled. "Yeah, I'm lucky."

The doc stepped from the room, pulling the door behind him. Bishop threw back the sheets and sat up, a jolt of pain hitting him. He caught his breath, and then looked to the gun, book, and med kit on the dresser.

John Bishop reached for one of them.

THE BLEEDING GROUND

INTRODUCTION

From a journal left by Dr. John Bishop:

I write this as a dead man. My own life ended with the death of my wife and son. I existed only to find their killers and see them draw last breaths. It was a long and bloody trek, and with the help of White Fox, I have done it. But revenge has led me to my own family, and to my own brother, and a group of terror-riders worse than anything I saw in the War Between the States.

My mission is to stop my brother—and his followers.

I used to be a doctor, and now I'm a killer, with a gun where my right arm used to be. I am a monster of my own making, stitched together when I should have died. I have become what I am because to win this fight I must become something feared by the outlaws and killers who plague the decent families like my own used to be, and I must wipe that plague out any way that I can.

I set this down so that others will understand that I spilled blood, so that no one else will have to exist as I exist.

That is my mission, as a dead man, until I find my final peace.

CHAPTER ONE
Dead Memories

The special bandolier was designed perfectly. Cut from beaver skin and holding six .12-gauge shells, it fastened tight around the upper part of John Bishop's half-arm with two leather ties. The oil from the pelt let the shells slide easily from their pockets into the double-barreled, swivel-breech shotgun that replaced the rest of the right limb he'd sacrificed defending his family.

Bishop's one-handed prep of the weapon was all skill and adrenaline; quick motion to open the breech, pop the shells into place with his thumb, then a jerk of the wrist to snap it shut. It was load, fire, shuck brass, and load again. He could do it in fifteen seconds; less, if he fell into a rhythm, facing enemies from any direction.

At the moment, only one enemy was facing him, but with two guns. A shadowed figure stood on a frozen ledge jutting from the side of an unforgiving mountain, its peaks twisted like diseased muscles.

The sun was behind him, making him a dark specter. Blowing snow masked his face, but he held a Navy Six in each hand, his stance daring Bishop's approach from below. A horse couldn't make it that far off-trail, and a man, just barely. He kept the Navies hammered back, waiting. He knew Bishop was there, someplace, waiting for his chance.

Bishop stayed out of sight in a deep wound in the mountain's side—an opening in the rocks, hidden by tufts of dead grass. Without showing himself, he could see the man on the ledge twenty feet above him. The wound was good cover, but lousy aim, especially for a shotgun. He scrubbed the snow from his eyes with his left palm, looking for a better position, judging his odds of making it.

Shreds of winter light threw a hint of the man's shadow at Bishop's feet. He watched him inch to the other side of the ledge, ready to open fire as soon as Bishop stepped away from the mountain's protection.

Filling his lungs with the cold, Bishop followed the shadow. The enemy on the ledge had the advantage, but at least he was finally a clean target. Bishop raised his half right arm, the elbow joint bringing the shotgun rig instantly into place, the metal supports on either side of the prosthetic locking its firing position.

Flexing his shoulders, he drew tight the silver chain that ran from the gun's two triggers to the leather harness that fit snugly across his back. The chain looped through the leather and was anchored to a band on his left wrist so the triggers could be pulled with a simple tug or a half-move of the body. His body and the special weapon acted and reacted as one.

To goad Bishop out of the wound in the mountain, the figure yelled, "Your ma never . . ." but his words were murdered by the high wind. The second attempt was a shot into the sky, followed by whoops of laughter.

Bishop blocked his howls and screams, letting the sound of his own calm fill his ears, while keeping his eyes fixed on the man's shadow, his moves.

The man leaned forward, trying for a glimpse, and then fired twice more, angry wild ricochets. He straightened, howling for Bishop over the storm.

Bishop charged from his cover in the mountainside, letting loose with both barrels, shooting upward, burning the air.

The man shot back at the same time, flame from the pistols flaring wide, a slug opening Bishop's throat, spinning him backwards into a deep pit. He grabbed for a limb to brake himself. No use. He fell without screaming, hitting bottom with a head snap, the shotgun barrels smashing piles of jagged rock around him.

But it wasn't rock.

Bishop lay still, snow cooling his face, life seeping through the fingers of the left hand he'd clamped on his windpipe. He tried moving. What he was lying on moved with him—little bits and pieces, crunching under his weight. He turned his head barely an inch, and his eyes met the shattered half-face of a human skull.

Beyond it, another, and then still another. Empty eye sockets, half jaws, and shells of broken teeth were scattered among the snapped, hardened bones of thousands of skeletons piled atop each other. Bishop forced himself up, his bloody fingers smearing wet on the dried remains surrounding him.

All that created the mountain.

Not stone and earth, but body upon body. It was as if a mass grave erupted its corpses and stacked them miles high. Muscles, ribs, spines, arms, and legs of the dead formed its hills, crags, and ledges. What should have been granite was gristled flesh, the mountain's plants only tangles of rotting hair.

A patchwork of petrified skin made the steep walls of the pit. The stretched faces of men, all ages and types, were locked in agony, screaming silently.

Bishop's mind reeled, the stench burning his nose and eyes. He tried to whisper to God while managing to get beyond his knees, standing on bones and hardened flesh.

A slug hit him in the back, then two more tore each leg.

Blood sprayed, and he dropped again, his face beside the bodies of a young woman and a boy. They were curled together in an eternal embrace.

"Your family's been waiting, John. Just for you." The man with the Navy Sixes stood high on the rim of the pit, looking down, reloading. "I know you want to be reunited."

Without the sun's glare, Bishop could see his clothes were shades of red. His face, which he kept lowered was more distinct, but still curtained by ice and snow.

Bishop cradled the delicate bodies of his wife and son, protecting them as he heard the pistols cock. They crumbled to dust in his arms. The shots from above were a roar.

The water hitting Dr. John Bishop tasted of lye soap lumped in with chewed tobacco and spit-back. He rolled out of his bunk, coughing like hell. Sheriff Tucker stood by the cell door with an empty wash bucket, his flannels barely covering his whiskey belly. He pushed his bifocals up on his nose with a snort. "Christ on a crutch, you got to shut up!"

Bishop yanked the soaking wet dirty sheet off the bunk's hay-bag mattress. He coughed more gray water, slopping his beard, then settled on one knee, fighting for air. "Same dreams again."

"You ain't gettin' nothin' dry tonight! I've had prisoners mess the bed, piss the walls—"

"Clean up since?"

Tucker's voice got louder. "They've killed each other, killed themselves, and none was more trouble than you!"

"My sincere apologies."

An arm sprang between the bars of the adjoining cell, locking Bishop in a choke hold. It was massive, covered with ape-like hair, and its owner stunk of sweet-jack rye from two nights before. "I'm a man what values his sleep!"

Tucker traded the bucket for a tarnished Colt pocket revolver and pointed it at the prisoner who was squeezing Bishop's windpipe through the bars. "Let him go, Harvey!"

Harvey kept Bishop locked. "Gonna shoot me? Make your sister a widow?"

"Best gift I could give her."

Bishop pulled at Harvey's huge arm with his one hand, but it was made of God-steel.

Harvey's laugh was like a mule braying. "A one-armed man! Can't do nothing!"

Tucker took a step to Harvey's cell, aiming the gun directly at the back of his head. "But I can. Let the man go, Harv, or Esther'll have a lonely Christmas."

Harvey relaxed his grip, dropping Bishop to the wet stone floor. "Hell, he's gonna hang anyway. What's the difference?"

"The difference is you're an inbred ass, and I'm the law. All right there, Bishop?"

Bishop worked some feeling back into his neck with his one hand. "I'll make it to the hanging."

"Don't you have no more of that stuff to keep you quiet?"

"Chloral hydrate."

Besides the bunk, the only other furniture in the cell was a three-legged stool where a slop-drenched Bible and a small amber bottle were placed. Bishop's cell was one of five, separated by a slab of waist-high iron plating and bars to the ceiling. The privy was a hole cut in the stone floor covered by a busted lid.

Unlike the rest of the town, the jail was sturdily built, something that didn't escape Bishop when he'd ridden into town five months ago. Surrounded by clapboard and false fronts, it was the only stone building on the main street. The only sure thing about Paradise, Colorado, was its bad temper.

Bishop had met a proper lady, and she'd called it, "The mule pie of Colorado."

He'd laughed at those words coming from her mouth, but that was before the robbery and the massacre. Before the blast that turned him inside out. Before being left to die. All the things that were a jumbled fog of memory.

Sheriff Tucker said, "Hey, I gotta ask again."

"I heard you." Bishop gave the empty bottle a shake. "All gone."

"That stuff got you through the nights, at least. Doc Benson claimed these dreams 'd stop in a week. He lit out, leaving you and your tortures behind. It's been months like this!"

"Longer than that for me."

Harvey bellowed, "That ain't no comfort for the rest of us, you screamin' like a virgin on her wedding night!"

Bishop said, "Seems to me that men and women scream the same way." He absently rubbed the stump of his right arm with his palm, his fingers tracing the elbow joint and the roiled flesh around it. He stopped himself when he almost clasped his missing right hand.

"Look it! Crazier than an outhouse rat! Scratchin' at an arm that ain't even there!"

"It's called phantom pain. You wouldn't understand."

"See, I know about real pain, the kind what sets your insides on fire. How 'bout feelin' something real for a change? Something for all them men you killed?"

"You or Tucker ask me that three times a day."

Bishop flopped on his bunk, tired of conversation and ready to try sleep again. Just *try*. Water squirted and bits of wet hay dropped from the mattress bag as he stretched out, eyes shut.

Harvey said, "So let's hear it."

"I guess it depends if they were trying to kill me. You know more about it than I do."

"I can see lots of people wanting you dead."

"Leave my prisoner alone." Tucker opened Harvey's cell door with a large brass turnkey. "You're sober enough. Get the hell home."

"But Esther said she didn't want to see me for a week."

"Can't blame her for that. Find a stall at the livery. It's

no matter to me. And you borrowed my good Sears, Roebuck."

Harvey grabbed the rain slicker he'd been using as a pillow, then stepped around his brother-in-law, who was holding open the cell door with one hand, keeping the Colt in the other.

Harvey said, "You're coming for Sunday supper?"

Tucker wiped his spectacles on his sleeve. "We'll see. Now get on to the stalls, sleep with the horse pies."

"That suits me right to the ground. I can't abide to be around no half-a-man anyways."

Bishop regarded Harvey. "How do you feel about the boys who fought in the conflict?"

"What the hell's that supposed to mean?"

"I'm just trying to learn about you, Harvey."

Tucker stepped in front of his brother-in-law, jamming the pistol into his chest. "Out."

Bishop had his left arm behind his head. "I apologize again, Harvey."

"He's gone. Notice how much better it smells?" Tucker opened the door to Bishop's cell, the Colt still leveled. "We've been together a while, Doc."

Bishop's kept his eyes shut and didn't move.

Tucker continued. "Since the so-called massacre I mean. You're going down in the history books for that one. Train sailed off the tracks."

"All I know is what you told me."

"The newspapers."

"Them, too."

"You saved some lives that day, Doc, but you left a lot of blood 'n hair behind. That was some real killin' you did."

Bishop broke his words, trying to end it. "I—don't—remember."

Tucker said, "Not while you're awake. That's because you've gone crippled in your head."

"You're not going to let me sleep, are you?"

"Trying to help is all."

Bishop showed his impatience and sighed. "Tucker, I can't remember clear the last ten minutes, last week, or last month. But funny enough, I do remember a thing or two about medicine."

"Hell, I know you're the real deal. Your field kit's in the closet. I'm not saying I know more about what's wrong with you than you do, but see, I'm lookin' at you from the outside. Maybe that gives me something, huh?"

Bishop didn't answer.

Tucker pressed. "I've figured out a few things, like what's making you tick."

"I always like to hear from an educated man."

"Funny. It's usual for prisoners to look down their noses at the lawman. It's their nature. I'm surprised a doctor would run his mouth that way."

"I guess I can't do anything right today."

"Maybe you should give me a listen."

"I just want some sleep."

"Yeah. You're praying for it."

Bishop opened his eyes. He tilted his head to see Tucker standing over him, wearing a crooked kind of smile, the Colt an inch from his temple.

Tucker quick-touched Bishop with the gun. "Now, I don't have your fine learning, but you live long enough, you pick things up along the way. I can fix your problem."

"With that old .44?"

"I seen men break at Shiloh. Bawl like a newborn and never come back. See, mixed up in your head as you are, I don't think it's ever gonna leave ya alone."

"Probably not."

"You can't sort nothing out if you can't recall it."

"I can't call things up the way I could, but it seems I had a patient once, shot by his drunken wife. After that, he couldn't remember his own name." Bishop let it sink in. "The doc with no memory remembers the patient with no memory. That's what Harvey 'd call outhouse crazy."

Tucker said, "Maybe he's right. What you went through was like the war a second time. Fighting off the robbers who blew the train off the track; helping those soldiers protecting that gold? Even when they were being shot to pieces, you were in there."

Bishop gave a moment before saying, "Killing a lot of men, I guess."

"That's what's doggin' you . . . because you was doing both. Being a doc and a killer." Tucker's voice stayed a hiss. "Can you live with that torture?"

"You claim they'll hang me as soon as the circuit judge rides in."

"Who knows when that'll be? Maybe months? You really want to go on like this? Hell, I wouldn't. Bein' no use to myself or anybody else. Doc, you know how bad it's gonna get."

Bishop smiled. "So, what's your thinking, Tucker? That maybe I won't get hung? That'd be a problem?"

"Not for me. Not really." The lawman dropped his voice to barely a whisper. "If you tried an escape, I could shoot you with cause. I'd do it right, too, and all your loco talk'd be over for sure. Now, that's peace, ain't it?"

Bishop shut his eyes again and gave a quiet laugh before he spoke. "Right now, that doesn't seem like such a bad idea, but I'll wait for the judge."

"And tell him you don't remember all the blood you spilled?" Tucker was only a step away from Bishop. Sucking in his gut, he suddenly took an official tone. "I was offering a real way out of your suffering, but if you ain't going to take it, let's look at it another way."

Bishop lay still, knowing what was next.

Tucker said, "The judge don't care if he kills you or if I do. It's the same sentence."

"Going to try this play again?" Bishop brought his

right arm down to his side, measured his words. "Either I pay to end my intense suffering—"

"That smart mouth again. *That* you remember."

"Or I pay to get to trial."

Tucker said, "You've been a lot of bother, Doc, but I'm a good man. Merciful. You got a lot of them train robbers, but they still got away with a strongbox of cash. And what about that gold you got squirreled off someplace? How 'bout all of that?"

"You listen to too much barroom talk. I couldn't give God a dollar if he struck me with lightning." Bishop felt the barrel of the Colt against his temple again, the vibration of the hammer locking into place.

Tucker leaned in whisper-close. "You really want to go out a liar?"

Bishop didn't blink.

Tucker said, "Wait for the judge? Live with night terrors? Your business, but the only way that's gonna happen is if you pay to stop the pullin' of this trigger."

"We all pay, Tucker, one way or t' other."

Tucker's words edged like broken glass. "Smart mouth and damn stupid."

The balled fist of Bishop's left hand sledge-hammered Tucker just below the earlobe, pounding the bundle of nerves next to his jaw. The sheriff heaved over, stumbling away from the bunk, knees unsure.

Bishop jumped from the bunk. "My ending isn't coming from you!"

A spasm travelled down Tucker's arm, but the Colt stayed in his fingers. He tried to raise the gun, eyes refusing to focus. He blinked, tried again. His hand twitched, but pulled the trigger. A shot spit off the wall, before tearing into the wet Bible, thudding between the pages.

Bishop brought down his left arm again, a wide blow using all his shoulder strength. Tucker hit the floor hard, bifocal lens shattering, his face slopping into the mess he'd thrown from the wash bucket.

A bullwhip cracked.

The knotted leather snake wrapped around Bishop's neck, jerking him to the floor. He grabbed for the long tail as it snapped back, splitting the air. The whip came down across his eyes, then again on his chest, face, and arm. Sharp-edged leather sliced muscle deep, then peeled off.

Crack.

Bishop fought back with his left, shielding his eyes. The lash kept ripping, spattering his blood in a fine rain. He didn't see Sheriff Tucker stand or pick up his gun. He only felt the whip.

Crack.

Harvey said, "He ain't dropping!"

The barrel of Tucker's gun smashed the side of Bishop's head, washing his eyes red, the blow pounding him down.

Bishop heard one of them say, "Ain't nobody can take that much punishment. Nobody."

CHAPTER TWO
Blood on the Horn

Colby had gone by so many names he'd forgotten most of them. It was usually something he picked at random from the Bible and then mumbled to the trail boss, hotel clerk, or whoever. Folks never seemed to question him, but sometimes would mention that he had the same Christian first name as their pa or grandpa. The only problem was that he had to remember to answer when the name was called out.

Everything else, including who was the priority kill if there was more than one target, always came off like clockwork. But he had trouble with damn names. That was something to work on.

He was rolling his cigarette too loose, the makings sprinkling the tops of the new boots he'd scarred with a heated edge of a bowie. His hands refused to cooperate with the task, the paper tearing between his thumbs and fingers until he finally managed to patch together something that was close to a misshapen cigar, bulging in the middle, ragged tobacco peeking out from both ends.

Somewhere behind him, he could hear whiskey-snickers from a couple other rope hands, lighting their own smokes and shaking their heads at his incompetence.

He called out, "Any of you fellers spare a match?"

One of them, older, with a Winchester repeater resting across his lap, rode over, still having a joke, but trying to be good-natured. "Andy, I never seen nothing like you."

Andy! Why the hell did he think it was from the Bible? Colby took note of the name, tipping his hat and grinning wide.

Holding on to his laugh, Winchester handed him a match. "So, you're drawing wages?"

The poor excuse for a cigarette didn't want to be lit. Colby struggled until it finally flamed. He coughed, "Yes, sir. I surely am."

"Not wanting to offend, can I ask what for?"

"Same as you, I guess."

"Not the same as me, son. I'm on a special contract with Mr. Chisum." Winchester's voice was deep but quiet, commanding attention in the way he gave each word its proper measure.

Colby thought that if Winchester ever delivered a sermon, he'd listen to it. "Well, I'm here to take care nothin' happens that's not supposed to, sir."

"Make sure Chisum's cattle get to the railhead." Winchester motioned to the herd of cattle behind him, 1,944 at the supper count.

They were decent stock, not spongy but not musclebound either. Settling down for the night, a couple heifers were pushing each other, rubbing hair, but nothing serious. It was a good quality herd for a rancher who wanted to build something for himself. A starter.

Colby had actually thought about having a nice place, a little extra security. Something like what his folks had.

That notion had nothing to do with the job at hand, and he stopped it as soon as it entered his mind. No *imaginings* was his rule, so he wasn't listening when Winchester made another statement about the cattle and their value.

Colby's grin took up his entire face when he replied, purposefully stumbling over his words. "Yes, sir. That's as fine a bunch of that shorthorn breed, you know, that I ever seen."

"Durhams can fetch an all right dollar."

"That's a for sure, and I'll be keepin' a good watch on 'em."

"But what about those men yonder?" Winchester let the question hang, jerking a thumb toward the riders trolling the edge of the herd, listening for incomers and scooting back the strays. No muss, no fuss, just earning their pay.

Soon they would share the one low fire and take their grub quietly, with voices down, so the cattle would stay settled. It was the way professionals did it, and those men were all pros. It was the point Winchester was trying to make, but Colby already knew it. He'd been watching them closely, making note of who did what, and how.

And the guns they carried.

Winchester said, "I've known some of them since they were kids, and they've grown up to be damn handy"— he looked back at Colby—"and all good with a gun. Good men."

Colby's strained grin had gone lopsided, and he kept nodding his head in agreement, even when it wasn't needed. "Yes sir, you can see it. That's why they're drawing top wages."

"You must have something on the ball, too, or you wouldn't be ridin' with us."

"Well, I surely want to do a good job. I'm eager."

Winchester drew out his words. "That's fine, but you're all elbows and thumbs. Seems like you should have more experience, given your age."

Colby inhaled deeply on his misshapen cigarette. "The other fellas been talkin'?"

"They're looking at you. So am I."

"I surely don't want to disappoint nobody."

"Then step up. Throw a rope or show yourself with a gun. You have to do something, son."

The twisted cigarette went out. Colby tossed it before opening his stained jacket to show a shirt that had been patched so many times it didn't deserve wearing and that he had no gun belt. By contrast, Winchester's shirt was fresh, and buttoned to his neck, his new hat held in place with a chinstrap.

Colby said, "I don't carry no gun. Maybe you can teach me? I admire that rifle."

"If you're serious, we can give it a try. But"—Winchester's eyebrows came together, forming a gray question mark over his sandpaper face—"if you can't shoot, how are you standing guard over anything? This isn't adding up for me, son."

"Actually, I misspoke."

Colby held up a hand to pause Winchester's next remark and took a gold pocket watch from his dirty jacket. The watch was polished diamond-clean, and he handled it delicately, snapping the engraved face cover open to note the time. "I make sure things go the way they're supposed to."

Winchester covered the hammer on the rifle with his palm, easing it back. "What in the Sam Hill does that mean?"

Colby held the watch, smiling at a cameo on the inside of the cover. It wasn't a silly grin, but something real and satisfied. He snapped it shut. "Swiss works. Always perfect. My meaning is, that you have a choice to not use that rifle, sir. I hope that's the choice you make."

Winchester crooked his elbow, settling the rifle on Colby when shouts from the other cowboys startled him.

They were loud cries, and one had some panic. "Whoa, Lordy, do you see that?"

Winchester turned his attention for a heartbeat.

That heartbeat was all Colby needed to slip the blade down his arm into his palm and launch it, bullet-fast and sure, burying itself completely into Winchester's chest. The blade had no handle, and plunged so deep, Winchester's body seemed to swallow it whole, the wound just a slit above his heart, spraying a geyser of red.

Colby had hit the artery he was aiming for. It was perfect. Surgical. Winchester looked down at the blood soaking his starched-white shirt, then back to Colby, wounded surprise in his eyes. He tried to crack off a shot.

It was only a grazing as Colby dove from his horse, rolled, and came back up to his feet in a single acrobatic motion, before yanking the rifle from Winchester's hands. There was no struggle; his fingers just let it slip away. The older man settled forward, clutching his chest. Colby pushed him out of the saddle with the rifle barrel and watched him tumble.

The sound of the body hitting the ground was a confirmation. Colby gave Winchester a few moments to see if he'd move beyond twitching. He didn't. That satisfied Colby.

The shouts of the cowboys trying to figure what the hell had happened and the sound of the cattle stirring rose together like orchestrated music. Colby felt the thundering under his feet and faced the wide slope of grass that led into the small Kansas valley to see the demons crossing it at full gallop, charging toward the herd.

Their horses were phosphorous white skeletons with bursts of flame rippling from their manes and tails. Cloaked and hooded in red, the Fire Riders numbered twenty. They rode in a tight military formation, almost shoulder to shoulder, out of the spring night. Half held torches high, with their rifles in saddle scabbards. The others rode with pistols in their free hand, keeping their reins tight with the other. Several brandished cavalry sabers.

Some cowboys broke wide, getting off their shots, while the rest kept the herd in check. Colby positioned the Winchester to his shoulder and took aim, shooting the cowboys from their horses as if he were knocking old cans off a fence post.

He had seen one show off his quick-draw, so he killed him before angling the rifle around and shooting an older fellow who kept his gun in the belt loop of his pants. The revolver was drawn, and he was trying to steady it, when Colby put one through his throat.

Colby had talked to him over morning coffee, learned about his grandkids and his reputation as a man who could kill six men with five shots. He'd gotten a kick out of the old man's bragging, so he hoped the cowboy hit the ground dead, not lingering.

The one who laughed at Colby the loudest?

He rode fast around the herd, drawing down and screaming at the rustlers, letting loose four rounds from a Henry rifle. He managed to hit one Rider in the leg and a horse in the rump. Colby cracked a slug into the laugher's chest, saw him lurch back in the saddle but still holding on, then fired again, taking him out through his left eye.

They'd been difficult shots, each one a flame with an echo that Colby didn't let die before shooting again. He made it all one clean action, one continuous sound, and then it was done. He felt satisfaction as the Fire Riders circled the cattle and began moving them off, with no one putting up a fight.

Colby touched the side of his collarbone where he'd been bullet-kissed. The tiny wound burned as if someone had slapped him with a hot spoon, but the pain of getting shot was nothing. What Colby hated was that a bullet wound of any kind was evidence that the job had gone sloppily.

This job had gone well.

He stayed his tall chestnut stallion, patted the sweat from the back of the animal's neck as a steer butted his way out of the herd and started to run. His cries were loud, getting louder. The other cattle stirred, brayed, began pawing the ground.

Colby angled his horse around, the rifle at his shoulder, just in case. A cloudless moon gifted him just enough light to watch it all over the sights of the Winchester.

The Fire Riders signaled each other to ride out for a larger circle, giving the cattle their room, then moving ahead of the herd. Cloaks were stuffed into saddles and belts cinched tight to prevent excessive movement of their clothes, to prevent the cattle from spooking any more.

Eyes in the herd were wide, heads bowed to fight, and cries getting damn loud. Their weight and near panic could be felt as the cattle slammed into each other, ready to run for nothing.

One of the Riders, just a towheaded boy with his hood pushed back, galloped past Colby, charging for the running steer. With a good grip, the boy seemed part of his horse as he rode alongside the steer but not too close. He let his pinto and the shorthorn share movement before slipping his lasso over its head and pulling it easy. The steer bellowed, twisting at the rope.

The herd reacted to the cry. A few more started to break. The Fire Riders chased them down.

Colby stood in his stirrups, watching the boy lean from his saddle, stretching as far as he could to grab the steer's tail and bring it up toward his shoulders. He held it there, his skinny body straining, but legs locked around his horse.

The steer slowed, feeling the pressure on his tail. The

kid pulled up, dropped from his saddle, brought the steer to a stop. He dug in his heels, tightening the lasso, and turned the huge animal around, leading it back to the herd.

The Riders had moved in front of the other cattle, slowing them enough to push them toward the trail break. The boy let the steer loose, and it fell in with the others.

Colby settled back in his saddle as the other cows and steers were brought into line. The boy showed the other Riders how to work them, make them move together.

A Fire Rider pulled up his white-skulled horse and spoke through his hood to Colby, his words catching in his throat. "We almost lost it, but you did it good for us."

"You were late."

"We're riding in, not coming on the Kansas Express."

Colby kept the rifle cradled in his arms. "I'm just saying that when there's a plan, I like to stick to it. I'm not inflexible, as you can see."

The Rider's voice was easy, the Eastern Europe bleeding through. "That old man was a dead shot with a rifle. He was a worry, I can tell you. But you got them all."

"I like a job done thoroughly. This is a good herd, and you got it without a fight, which was the point of my being here."

With the Fire Riders pushing them, the sound of the cattle moving out was solid in the air. The towhead was in the lead, guiding the herd with expertise.

Colby had to shout over the din. "That's a good boy, knows more about what he's doing than anybody."

"He's a kid. He is learning."

"Just an opinion." He held out his hand. "My money. The rest of my fee."

The Rider just looked at him from behind the red hood, his barrel chest straining against the matched tunic. There was no expression that could be judged, no sense of emotion in the eyes, so Colby angled the barrel of the rifle toward him.

The Fire Rider said, "You going to kill me?"

"Not part of the strategy, but if it needs to be altered, I can accommodate and get my fee from your superiors." Colby frowned. "Did you understand anything I just said?"

The Rider had a Peacemaker in his hand. "I can't never tell if you're an educated ass or just an ass." He took a stack of bills bound with paper bands from his saddlebag and tossed it.

Colby caught it with one hand, keeping the other on the rifle's trigger.

"You want I should stay while you count it?"

Colby slipped the cash into the pocket of his filthy disguise. "We'll be working together again. If it's short, we can settle our debts personally."

"You talk like that, but my face, you haven't seen it."

Colby said, "Not in person, but you have a wife—dark hair with blue eyes, which is very unusual—and two daughters. In Havalock County, isn't it? And you're Romanian?"

The Rider managed to spit through his hood, turn his horse, and run it to join the others as they herded the cattle across the small patch of grazing land, toward their new water and new brands.

Colby just shook his head in wonder at the quality of the people he was forced to sometimes work with. It almost wasn't worth the feel of the cash in his pocket. Almost.

He watched as the last of the Riders followed the herd and was lost in the night shadows. He dropped from his stallion and walked it to the small cook fire, poured himself half a cup of reboiled coffee, then topped it off with premium Evan Williams from a silver comfort flask.

He could still hear the cattle making their way over

the hill, just a distant jumble of sounds. The stallion snorted in the night chill.

The fire was dying.

Colby looked at the cowboys scattered about the camp, lying facedown, their lives spilled wet around them, their blood black in the moonlight. He lifted his cup of coffee and bourbon, toasting his targets, "Gentlemen, to a hard life lived well."

The voices were fragments, drifting through the barred window above Bishop's bed. He knew one of them was Tucker, but the other was someone younger, with a thick Louisiana accent, talking so fast his words swamped into each other without a pause in between. He kept repeating Bishop's name, but the rest was blather to him, as he fought himself awake. Bishop tried sitting up, but his right hand jerked him back. He'd been handcuffed to the iron frame of the bed.

Harvey laughed, his braying coming from someplace Bishop couldn't see. "How'd you like it? Can't open your big mouth now, can ya?"

Bishop hadn't been asleep. He'd been unconscious. Coming back was like putting together pieces of a broken mirror—sounds and faces not quite fitting, slivers missing. And the pain. The more Bishop was aware, the worse the pain hit him, but he wasn't going to slip back. He wasn't.

Harvey dangled the bullwhip on Bishop's swollen face, just letting the frayed tip rest on one of the wounds. "I started with the Cattleman's Crack to put you down, and then I used the Snake Killer. Just a little flick to bring the whip back, that's the trick. Supposed to take the head off a rattler. Must sting like hell."

Bishop managed, "It does."

"You're gonna have some scars."

"Already have some."

Harvey teased the end of the whip by Bishop's purple . . . and shut . . . eyes. "Maybe you'll have, uh, bitchin' pains in your face," he brayed, "if you live that long."

Bishop twisted away, throwing a kick at Harvey. "You never dropped me with that whip."

Harvey punched Bishop in the chest with the whip handle. "Keep tryin' half-man, 'cause your time's coming."

"Kill a one-armed man while he's chained, maybe when I'm sleeping? Brave as hell."

Harvey slammed the edge of the bunk with one of his size twelves, knocking Bishop off, wrenching his left arm behind him, stretching the wrist that was anchored to the iron frame.

"I don't have to do nothing. That guy out there with Tucker? He just claimed the body of one of the men you and that squaw killed. Chaney? I dug him up, threw him in his wagon. He's a relative, and damnation, does he want to see you."

"I'm sure." Bishop stood, slowly turning to release his arm, almost popping his shoulder. The whip marks seemed joined as one blister across his face, the purple cuts splitting up his cheeks, eyes, and throat.

Harvey said, "Tucker won't let him in 'cause he might blow your damn head off."

"Want to save that for yourself?"

"Hell, it won't take that much to finish you."

"Harvey, there's nothing you can do. You'll never match what I've known."

Harvey coiled the bull whip. "You really askin' for more?"

Bishop's broken face came together in a go-to-hell smile.

* * *

Albert Tomlinson didn't fill up a quarter of Colby's hotel room doorway. He stood there clutching a leather satchel and waiting for permission to enter. His new suit hung too loose on his stooped shoulders and couldn't hide the single-shot Marlin Standard pistol in his inside pocket. The weight of the gun actually made him favor his left side a bit.

Colby, in a satin robe piped along the collar and sleeves, noted the outlined shape of the Marlin and guessed its make and model.

"You're quite a man with weapons, Mr. Colby."

"One of the reasons you hire me. Shut the door. The drafts in this place are this side of intolerable."

Albert shut the door, pressing his hand flat against its parquet inlay that was in keeping with the rest of the room. The furniture was new. A bookcase took up one wall and a personal-sized desk was built into it. The large bed was angled between a standing fireplace with scuttle and bed warmer and French doors that opened onto a small balcony overlooking the street. A pair of rocking chairs waited in the balcony's shade for whoever wanted to enjoy their comfort.

"Have you taken advantage of your balcony, yet?"

Colby said, "No reason to," as he took pressed pants and clean shirt from the closet and started to dress.

"It's paid for . . . at the maximum rate. Seems a shame to waste it."

Colby checked a loose button on his shirt, feeling no need to respond.

Albert said, "Me and my girls were making do in a prairie schooner, trying to get down Wyoming-way, for my new position and all. Ever travel like that? I think we found every piece of bad luck you could trip over, but finally made it."

"Congratulations on your tenacity."

Albert's eyes couldn't help but envy the shaving kit

laid out on the dresser. An ivory-handled razor lay open on a fresh towel. Specialty lathered soaps were stacked neatly next to the washbowl, alongside a bottle of imported after-scent.

"A place like this would have been a fine break from the way we were getting along."

"You're working now, Tomlinson. Why not treat yourself?"

"I've never felt comfortable doing that."

"All business, yes?" Colby noted. "There's a tub behind that folding screen. I just used it. The bottom's still wet if you need to check, but the bed has more lumps than a swaybacked mule, so I'd ask for a partial refund." He tossed Albert the too-patched shirt caked with dust, sweat, and a little blood. "Put that in the stove."

Albert checked it for rips before stuffing it into the belly of the room stove.

Colby looked at him. "Thinking you could get more use out of it?"

"Not as a shirt. Maybe to patch something else."

"Thrift comes part and parcel with your work, but that's evidence I was the bumpkin who couldn't lasso a sleeping coonhound. An embarrassing guise, so we'll let it burn. But, it did win me this." Colby held up the Winchester, his fingers tracing the silver scrollwork around the stock and cheek piece. "That's a twenty-four-inch, heavy twisted barrel." He cocked the rifle. "Do you hear that perfection? The finest that Winchester makes, and this is even finer still, the '73. Owned by a gentleman of breeding. I wish he hadn't chosen to use it, but he had his job, and so did I."

Colby placed the rifle on the bed as if putting an infant down for its nap, then laid out a thick, rolled saddle blanket next to it. It was a Navajo pattern, fastened at both ends and the middle with buckled leather straps. The bed sagged under its weight.

Albert asked, "So, you didn't carry a gun with you on this job?"

"Questioning my methods?"

"No, we're very pleased. Just wondering why you take the chance."

Colby regarded him for a moment before unfastening the straps and unrolling the blanket, revealing his weapons cache. Four rifles of various make and caliber were fitted into special sleeves. Six pistols were arranged around them, held in place by small leather ties, and a pocket held ammunition. An assortment of knives lay flat along the blanket's edges. He looked at Albert. "What chance?"

Colby took the three throwing blades he hadn't used and put them back in their own pocket. "I have these made especially for jobs like yours. Very balanced, very effective. The edge sharper than a Japanese katana."

"I see. Very nice."

He heard Albert swallow and smiled. He slipped a long-barrel Buntline from its ties, and checked its action. "This beauty hasn't seen use in too long, which is never a good thing for a gun, and that leads to your question. In some cases, I don't carry because no one feels I'm a threat if I'm unarmed. I can always take a firearm from someone—they're all around me—but if they think I'm wandering around without . . . well, people are more inclined to write me off. That's my element of surprise."

"You definitely surprised the hell out of them. It's appreciated."

Albert opened the satchel and removed an envelope that was straining with contents. He held it out to Colby.

With a look, he said to drop it on the bed.

Albert did. "There is another job in the offing, but it's got to be done quickly. You'd have to leave right away."

Colby was wrapping his new prize Winchester in lightly oiled cloth. "It's always urgent."

"And as always, my employer would like to put you under yearly salary. It's rather generous."

Colby smiled at the way Albert's voice dropped when he spoke of salary. "I'm sure, but I prefer to continue on a situation-by-situation basis."

Albert took a second envelope from the satchel, this one long and narrow with an oval family portrait attached to it. Colby took the picture, studied it for a moment, his eyes fixed on the young couple and their son. The husband and wife were blond-headed, wearing their Sunday best. Her features were plain but better than his. Both had one hand on the shoulder of their blond son, who stood in front of them, smiling.

Colby turned the photograph facedown and said, "The child looks to be about ten. Isn't this the boy that rides for you?"

"If you're asking if he's a Fire Rider, yes."

"He worked last night. He's good, has good control. Better than the rest. Why are you giving him to me?"

"They stopped to water the herd and were set upon by John Chisum's men. The boy got himself captured."

"Do you want the Chisum men also or just the boy?"

"The amount in the envelope is the answer. They were camped ten miles past the Little Fingers and moved on from there."

"That should be an easy track."

"Just so long as it's done quickly. Those are the instructions, and I've delivered them."

"And very precisely, too. In a case like this, I think a message needs sending. To discourage Mr. Chisum's men from trying this again." Colby pulled a rifle from its blanket sleeve and replaced it with the Winchester. He held up his new selection. "My choice would be the Colt's Dragoon revolving rifle. Do you agree?"

Albert had a pencil in his hand and wrote in a small ledger he'd produced from his inside jacket pocket. "Whatever you want, I'm sure will be appropriate."

"That ledger suits you better than the pistol."

"All business expenses are noted."

"What do you have me down as? What do you call me?"

"No name. Just the job—regulator."

Colby loaded the Dragoon. "God, that term's just a pretentious disguise. Enter what I am—an assassin. You pay me to take human life. I'm not ashamed."

The depot clerk they called Junior struggled to write as fast as the stranger was talking, but was losing the fight to age-failing eyes and ears. "Sorry, sir. You're gonna have to say again. From the top."

The stranger, finely dressed in tailored wool with a matching hat, and only the grime on his boots spoiling the image, leaned into the window and slowed his thick, New Orleans speech. "Whatever happens to that prisoner yonder, make sure to wire me straight away. Now, if he gets himself hung—"

"Well, they got him up for murder. Quite a few," Junior interrupted as he scribbled with swollen knuckles.

"If he gets himself hung in or out of his cell, or shot by anyone, or trampled by a runaway stallion, or struck by lightning, you wire me through Western Union, general. I'll check frequently during my travels. I'm fully aware of Doctor Bishop's situation, but must know immediately if they're any changes."

"Yes, sir, Mr. Chaney. I got it all."

"Actually, this might have been easier on you. My apologies." Virgil Chaney pressed an embossed business card and ten dollars into Junior's palm. "You should know there's a lot of fellas interested in Dr. Bishop. They have asked me to do them the same service." He nodded without changing expression and handed Junior a new fifty. "I trust this takes me to the front of the line?"

"Yes, sir."

Junior sneezed at the ripe perfume rising from the corpse slung on the back of Chaney's freshly groomed horse. "If you and your friend are off to Louisiana, we should box 'em up, straight away."

Virgil Chaney said, "Hardly a friend. He was my third cousin. He died at Dr. Bishop's one hand. We won't be taking the train, but I believe people will know we're approaching, especially if the wind is behind us."

Junior laughed like he should as Chaney climbed onto his horse, then took a fine handkerchief from his breast pocket with a flourish and tied it around his head, covering his mouth and nose. "Whatever happens to Doctor John Bishop?"

"I'll send the wire. First thing."

"Good man." Chaney tipped his hat with the silver band before turning his horse away from the Paradise rail station and riding the scant mile out of town. The corpse was lashed behind him.

Junior sneezed again.

Bent over his desk, a blood bruise from Bishop's fist mapping one side of his face. Tucker regarded three separate envelopes in front of him. Each one had different initials on it. From the cell, Bishop made a pained sound.

Tucker kicked his chair back "Goddamn, I don't want to hear nothing from you!"

"Hurting."

"You hurt 'cause you got a smart mouth and you're jackass stubborn! You gonna come across with that money you got hid?" Tucker waited for Bishop's answer, hand on his gun.

Finally Bishop answered. "No."

Tucker grabbed a bottle of whiskey from his desk, tore open the cell door, and poured the alcohol over the near-open wounds lashing Bishop's face, "Maybe a drink 'll make you feel better."

Bishop threw his head back as the whiskey soaked the cuts. Searing fire rolled him from the bed, dropping him to the cell floor, his left arm still chained.

Tucker said, "You ain't gonna get the best of me twice!"

Bishop managed a grin. "I can live with this, Tuck. I couldn't live with the infection that the whiskey just killed off. Thanks, Sheriff, you did me a real service."

CHAPTER THREE
Prophecy

Across a stretch of beauty more than four hundred miles away from Paradise, Colby was enjoying a morning ride, feeling the sun, and thinking of sending Albert Tomlinson a complimentary note. The bookkeeper's information about Chisum's men and the Three Fingers had been absolutely right. They'd made camp there, leaving a lot of sign behind. Colby knew it wasn't a matter of sloppiness. They worked for Chisum and assumed no one would be damn fool enough to follow or challenge, especially with a prisoner in tow.

He'd ridden up on the first campsite, ashes in plain sight, then tracked them for a few miles, their horses leaving a perfect trail in the soft earth of the riverbank they were edging. The trail made sense since this finger of the Arkansas River led directly to a railhead where they could board the train for New Mexico and then on to the big J.C. ranch in Roswell.

They were taking the back way, quiet, with a false sense of security. Colby always liked that. He'd once told an employer, "The easiest man to kill is one who's sure he's beaten the odds."

He stayed casual in the saddle, letting his stallion follow his nose. The Dragoon Revolving Rifle hung in a scabbard by his left leg, with the Navajo-blanket arsenal secured behind him. Just to be thorough, a new Smith & Wesson Schofield that had belonged to a big mouth was holstered on his hip. That was an enjoyable kill, and Colby liked the pistol for luck, if nothing else.

He found a shallow and crossed over to the other side, riding upward onto a small trail that gave him a good view of the river and the opposite shore. The air was pine-sweet, and the taste settled in his mouth like a drop of honey. His relaxation was total, even as the Chisum men came into view. Using a spyglass, he counted five cowboys with six pistols, and three rifles.

Another man in a tall felt hat and finely tailored long coat rode alongside the group, sometimes speaking to the older cowboy riding point. They exchanged a laugh the others didn't share. The man in the hat had a face as pink as an infant's, with no hint of hair on his head at all.

Colby noted the aberration, then swung the glass to the others.

The young Fire Rider rode in the middle of the group, hands hog-tied to his saddle horn, head bowed, and blond hair tacky with blood. Colby focused the small telescope, bringing in sharp focus. The boy had bruises around his eyes and a purple lash along his jaw where he'd taken a hell of a punch.

Colby pocketed the scope and urged his horse on. Moving ahead to a small outcrop, he pulled up, hidden by a gathering of red maple trees. It was a perfect ambush point. Bedded with new grass, the trees provided cover and the river trail was a clear shot in either direction.

The Colt's Dragoon slipped easily from its scabbard.

He wiped it down, humming as he looked around. The place would be perfect for him and his son to picnic one day. Maybe do a little fishing. Colby allowed himself the thought for a few beats, then cleared his mind as he took a crouching position behind the maples, the rifle flush against his shoulder.

He touched his neck where the bullet had kissed him. The quick shot of pain was small, but a reminder.

He narrowed his eyes at the Riders. The man in the felt hat was still riding close to the older cowboy.

Colby shifted his body, the weapon settling, feeling right. Completely comfortable. Somewhere above, a gathering of mountain plovers spoke in low music as he took aim, began his calculations for distance, and assigned a killing order.

The group rode into his bull's-eye range.

He watched as the man in the hat and the cowboy shook hands. He drew a breath, focused on the man's back, ready to shoot.

Someone shouted.

Colby's eyes shifted. The boy kicked at one of the flanking riders and took off running, his horse breaking for the woods along the river.

Colby followed the boy with the barrel sight and fired once, blowing a hole clear through him, throwing him hard from his saddle, hands still tied. The sound of the Dragoon was thunder, eating the boy's scream and not dying for miles.

The other cowboys opened up on what they could see—a blast of smoke from distant trees. They popped off shots in Colby's direction, the sound and the flash of their pistols moments apart. A slug tore into the maple trunk behind him as he leveled and shot one, two of the cowboys.

All in the head.

The slugs took them off their horses and delivered them to the riverbank. One spun in the air, landing face-first in the water, his blood swirling away pink. A cowboy with two pistols tried laying down a quick barrage. It was nothing but a nuisance as Colby hit him solidly between the eyes, leaving half to be buried.

Colby swung the Dragoon around as the older cowboy brought up a repeater. Colby took his face before he could get anything off, and his horse galloped away, the cowboy's body hanging in the stirrups.

The man in the felt hat was gone. Only a whisper of dust was left behind as he ran his chocolate mare away from the river, up a small logging trail, and into the woods.

Colby cracked the last rifle shot in his direction, the echo from his others still rolling along the hills. Nothing. No scream. Nothing. He jumped to his feet, tore the Smith & Wesson from its holster, and pulled the trigger four times, cutting into the trees that framed the logger's trail.

The shots were precise, aimed at movement between branches—the possible shadow of a rider. He waited for return fire or the sight of Felt Hat's mare running without a rider.

There was neither.

The kid charged from the train depot, the telegram wrinkling in his hands. He jumped from an old wagon tongue to a small pile of bricks, staying above Paradise's ankle-deep mud. Steering around a tethered mule, he ran past the prisoners' graveyard, then crossed himself before knocking on the sheriff's office door.

Tucker answered, his face looking like pounded beef. He gave the kid a dime for the telegram. "This is for swallowin' your tongue." He slammed the iron door and bolted it.

Still cuffed, Bishop was on his bunk, Bible out of reach, staring at nothing. He glanced when Tucker came to the cell with a bowl of soup from the night before.

Bishop's nose and eyes were still whip-swollen purple, his teeth pushing against his lips, but the whiskey shower had helped.

"Gonna feed that to me?"

"You haven't had grub for almost two days. You're not gonna starve yourself in my jail. Sit up."

Bishop sat up, his only arm straining behind him. "I could use a spoon."

"You think so?" Tucker stood before him, holding the bowl of soup. "Cut off both your arms, and I wouldn't trust ya. Lean forward.

Bishop lowered his chin as Tucker lifted the bowl. "We both look like hell."

The soup was thick with old chicken fat, but went down.

Tucker took the bowl away and held out the telegram. "You're gonna have a visitor tomorrow. A woman. Maybe she's coming for all that money you're hiding?"

Bishop let it lie, then said, "Any chance for more soup?"

"Chow time's done."

Bishop didn't hear Tucker, didn't care about chow. He thought about the woman who was coming. Something flashed in his mind. A streak of lightning behind his eyes. A beautiful young woman on a painted horse, leathers torn, bloody tears on a proud face. Raging in Cheyenne, surrounded by twists of steel, blades of fire, and a pile of bullet-riddled bodies.

It was nightmare and memory colliding.

He struggled to remember something else, a memory of seeing something else . . . but it was lost as a rain of blood flooded his mind's eye.

Tucker said, "You look like you went someplace, Doc, but you didn't."

Bishop gave his cuffed hand a jerk. "You heard the man, Sheriff. Outhouse-rat crazy."

* * *

The steam whistle shrilled then sputtered into a coughing fit, thanks to a bullet hole in its brass. The old Baldwin Locomotive churned through the low Colorado hills, wood smoke pluming. It was not making good time, and the engineer had to announce its coming over and over.

In the only passenger car, Frank Farrow covered his ears, trying to find a comfortable spot on the hard bench seat. The whistle finished, and the car heaved, knocking his tall felt hat to the floor. He picked it up and set it on top of the suitcase resting beside him. Handling the case as if it were spun glass, he carefully adjusting its position.

Sitting directly across from him, the woman in starched gray that matched her manner was unaffected by the whistle or the rough ride. She kept her attention on a copy of *The Woman in White* by Wilkie Collins. It appeared she had an idea about herself, about her image, that was so precise, anything that forced her from it would probably make her shatter like Grandma's vanity mirror.

That was Farrow's first assumption about the woman . . . and it was wrong.

On the seat next to her was large squared birdcage with a domed top and draped in barkcloth. Without taking her eyes from the novel's pages, she reached into a purse, took out a small robin's egg wrapped in tissue, and held it next to a slit in the cloth.

Farrow didn't find her unattractive and leaned forward on his elbows, watching. A sharp-edged, black bill snatched the egg, then instantly retreated back into the cage.

Farrow said, "Is that a raven? If it's a crow, he's as big as a hoot owl."

"But it's not."

"Ravens. Very intelligent birds."

"I've found him to be so, yes."

"The eaters of the dead."

His last remark made Ophelia Wylde leave her book with annoyance, not moving her head. Her expression remained locked, even as she wondered about Farrow's complete lack of hair, which made him seem eerily faceless, except for his black eyes fixed on her.

The car jostled again, the tracks groaning under the train's weight. Farrow ran his forefinger across his upper lip as if a waxed mustache were growing. "If I were him, I'd think I'd rather be flying."

"Sir, are you accusing me of being cruel? I could open the cage door, and Eddie would remain inside. I don't impose myself on him."

"Not at all. I just know birds a little bit. I had a parrot for a time."

"Hardly the same thing."

"Parrots can be mean. Mine was. The raven's more docile, isn't he?"

Ophelia finally looked up. "Eddie can be provoked."

Farrow said, "I didn't mean to interrupt your reading, ma'am. My apologies."

Ophelia put her book aside. "I'm slightly irritated because you did mean to interrupt. You're curious about something, so go ahead and ask. Then I can return to my book."

Farrow gave himself a moment. "I heard you ask the conductor about our arrival in Paradise."

"And why is that your business?"

"That's my stop, too. I guarantee there aren't two more passengers on the next five trains with Paradise as their destination."

"I ask my question again."

Farrow shifted just enough to reveal the shoulder holster under his jacket, and the .38 revolver tucked in it. "It's just that there's very little in Paradise, nothing in fact. But I can't imagine we're both going there for the same reason."

"I would seriously doubt it."

"Or the same person."

Ophelia picked up her book. "You're being intrusive, sir."

"My name's Frank Farrow, ma'am. I work for the Chisum Cattle Company, and I'm familiar with you, Miss Wylde. Very. That raven's your calling card. You've achieved some fame for your abilities."

"And whatever you've achieved, is it infamous? I see the condition of your hat."

Farrow picked up the felt hat and put the tip of his finger through the bullet hole in the crown, before giving Ophelia a nod of surrender. "That was a close thing. I've worked both sides of the law, yes."

"And what side are you working now?" Before Farrow could respond, Ophelia continued. "Don't bother. I can—perceive—who you are, sir. I assure you that our reasons for visiting Paradise are entirely different."

"I've never met anyone before who'd ever summoned a ghost."

Ophelia's words were separated by moments. "That's . . . not . . . what . . . I . . . do."

Farrow let the train's voice take over—cars banging into each other, steel groaning, then settling as the track smoothed—then he said, "It would be a real humdinger of a coincidence if you were going to Paradise to see Dr. John Bishop. He's become notorious in his own right, hasn't he?"

Ophelia turned a page before finishing it, refusing to meet Farrow's look. She went to her purse for another robin's egg and held it in front of the cage. "*Sauvez-moi des idiots.*"

The egg was snatched.

"My French is poor, but certain words I do recognize.

My apologies. I'm just a businessman with a curious nature."

Ophelia said, "No, you're not. I won't be manipulated by conversational cues and games, Mr. Farrow. Believe me, I know them all."

"Understood."

During the conversation, Farrow's hand rested on the suitcase next to him, palm down, making sure it was there. He shifted his attention out the window as the car swayed, passing the twisted remains of a derailment.

Soot smeared the glass like a fine, dry cloud, blurring his vision as if he were seeing tintypes of the ruins, specters of the train wreckage. Huge sections of the mail- and boxcars were blasted apart, partial roofs and doors scattered along the hillside, all scarred with bullet holes. Steel wheels, axles, and corroded iron lay by the tracks, rusting in giant heaps for scavengers to pick over and the weather to eat.

The train slowed into the curve before the Paradise depot, passing the gigantic, burned corpse of the locomotive lying on its side where it had jumped the tracks, its steam belly torn in half.

Dead and useless.

"God a-mighty, who could have survived that?" Farrow glanced at Ophelia for her response to the deliberate question he left hanging.

She gave away nothing. Head barely turned, she stole a look out her part of the window, but her eyes were fixed on the wreck as if she were sighting it down a long barrel. Then she turned back to her book, refusing the distraction.

The awful whistle got them out of their seats.

The train rolled into Paradise, almost overshooting the small station, wheels skidding across poorly repaired tracks. The engineer peered from the cab, swearing like hell as Farrow and Ophelia Wylde stepped from the only passenger car.

He helped her onto the platform, she holding the raven's cage high with one hand and a large carpetbag in the other. A burst of brake steam caught them both as the engine chugged, not waiting another minute before moving on to a better town.

Farrow said, "So, this is Paradise."

"Your irony is not biting."

Farrow did his best to block Ophelia from any more of the train's grime. She nodded and stepped around him, walking deliberately to the edge of the platform and the planking that crisscrossed Paradise's muddy streets. He stayed beside her, carrying his briefcase and offering his free hand, which she would not take.

Ophelia kept moving. "You must know, Mr. Farrow, that your manner is off-putting to me."

"Oh, I'm very aware. I bid you good afternoon." Farrow stepped back, made a grand gesture with his felt hat, and allowed Ophelia a considerable lead.

She maneuvered the planks toward the jail, the raven's cage leading the way. As she paused to take in the place, her back stiffened even more. Silently, she agreed with Farrow that Paradise was ill named.

The town was rotting from the streets up.

The scatter of buildings had been washed dirty brown by the swamping spring floods, the high waters soaking everything through before leaving behind piles of silt and filthy debris that fed the termites. The needed repairs were stacks of green lumber splitting apart, windows without glass, unfinished stairs, and never-shoveled walls of mud.

The livery was empty save for a buggy missing a wheel, but the small corral beside the depot had two played-out horses and one tall bay that kept head and tail high while walking the fence.

At the end of the main street, an old two-story was trying for resurrection as a couple of grunt-backs struggled to hang a double front door with a Chinese symbol for love in its center. The rest of the house was in dire need, but the symbol was fine stained glass. Paradise's only touch of opulence.

Ophelia glanced over her shoulder as one of the men swore at a hammer-busted finger. She recognized the stained-glass symbol, watched Farrow quickstep from the planking to the front porch of the place. A heavy girl in bodice and nightgown was on the balcony, sipping a cup of tea.

Marge leaned over the railing, spilling the tea. "Are you Mr. Farrow? They're waiting for you in the parlor."

Ophelia muttered, "So obvious," and added a phrase in French before continuing along the planking to the squat stone building that was the Paradise jail.

The raven squawked, "Nevermore!"

Farrow heard it and laughed as he went inside.

Wearing a velvet suit with a lace collared blouse, Soiled Dove led Farrow into the House of Pleasures parlor. He thought it less desperate than the rest of Paradise. Sheets shrouded moldy furniture and water-stained walls waited for paint, but a new pool table still in its crate took up the center of the room and several carpets were rolled into a corner. All that offered a bit of hope.

He was impressed with Dove, the way she moved in her clothes. Her valentine-shaped face with the knowing smile, tight strawberry curls, and barely five feet of height, made her nymph-like. A knowing innocent.

An explosion of a voice turned Farrow around.

In his thirties with a broad chest and smile, Mayor O'Brien roared into the room. Sleeves rolled up, he held out a big hand for the shaking. "Mr. Farrow, this is a fine thing to meet you!"

Farrow held back. O'Brien's hand was streaked with blood from a badly cut thumb.

O'Brien jammed the thumb into his mouth. "Stings

worse than a Sunday hangover. I'm not much of a carpenter."

"You're putting up the doors?"

O'Brien gestured for Farrow to sit in one of two satin chairs. "Well, somebody has to. And the girls are always busy." O'Brien guffawed as he took a seat.

Soiled Dove wrapped his bloody thumb with a handkerchief. "He's the nicest mayor I've ever known."

Farrow nodded. "I'm sure."

O'Brien said, "Honey, see about my private sour mash."

"Actually, a glass of port would go down better, if you have it."

Dove smiled. "I'll bring the whiskey and see what we can do about the wine." She gave the two men a little bob before pulling the parlor doors shut. They didn't hang straight, but she finally got them closed.

O'Brien said, "I have to work on those, too."

Farrow let his smirk play. "You're not what I expected."

"Sometimes a man has to roll up his sleeves." O'Brien opened a box of cigars. "So, working for Mr. John Chisum? Folks claim a lot of things, so I don't know if you have responsibility or you're mucking stalls. Either is fine with me." He offered a cigar.

Farrow declined with a wave of his hand, bringing a silver cigar case from his jacket, popping it open. "Wouldn't you enjoy something of a little more quality?"

"I'm satisfied with my own kind, thanks."

"You might want to improve your lot." Farrow set his suitcase on the covered couch and opened it with a small key on a chain. He stood back, his own cigar clenched in a Cheshire smile, revealing stacks of neatly bound bank notes, numbering thousands.

O'Brien said, "I'll hear your proposition."

Ophelia Wylde had stepped off the planking before reaching the jail, hiked up her dress, and walked around the low-slung building to a small patch of weeds in the back.

It was a place forgotten behind the jail, bordered on one side by a falling-down fence where the unclaimed murdered of Paradise found some kind of rest. A smattering of slapped-together crosses stood as markers. Numbers had been scrawled on them, but no names or dates.

Sheriff Tucker had that information in a little book, listing all the numbers and who they were. Also, who'd killed them or who they'd killed. It was simpler than keeping track of names or making new markers. If family wanted to claim number forty-six, all they had to do was dig him up.

Ophelia dropped her carpetbag, hung the cage on a bent nail sticking from a fence post, and lingered by a grave that had been freshly turned. She closed her eyes for a moment, shoulders lowering, the rigidity leaving her posture.

It was silent—no sound around her. Nothing.

The raven cried, snapping her eyes open, a wave of feeling bringing her body instantly to attention.

Watching the whole time from the small window in his cell, Harvey hacked as she took a pad of foolscap from the carpetbag and quickly drew on it with a piece of charcoal, her hand moving furiously.

Ophelia took the cage and stepped deliberately, passing Harvey's window. He spit, catching the hem of her dress. She took no notice and continued to the front door of the sheriff's office, each step a punch.

"You're drooling. It wouldn't matter if I wanted to buy your mother," Farrow said as he dropped the lid on the suitcase, then struck a match, relighting his Havana Robusto. He took a seat opposite O'Brien, drew deep to make a showing, ready for the mayor's immediate grovel. That's what he was used to.

O'Brien leaned forward on his large arms. "Don't be fooled by the sweat on my neck. You want results from me, present yourself and your business like a gentleman."

Soiled Dove entered with a glass of ink-dark red wine and a whiskey decanter. She silently poured.

Farrow said, "Sometimes you have to push to know who you're sitting with. My apologies."

O'Brien said, "Maybe."

Dove's eyes were on the case, even as she set out the drinks. "We didn't have any port, but this is a decent red from Williamsburg that I think should go down nicely."

Farrow couldn't hide his surprise.

Dove gave the men a smile and a little curtsey before leaving.

Farrow tasted the wine, approved.

O'Brien said, "If the cards cut right, she's going to do very well."

"I imagine some of the town ladies aren't welcoming that, but every business is important."

"Especially when you're trying to come back from the dead. That why you throw open that suitcase like you're dangling a carrot in front of a mule?"

"I meant no offense. I understand now." Farrow raised his glass. "To the mayor of Paradise! A man who knows how to do business."

Mayor O'Brien tipped some sour-mash into his glass. "You never know, do you?"

Ophelia was before Tucker, her body and manner thrust forward, the raven's cage on his desk. Harvey sprawled in an empty jail cell, running the whip through his hands, snickering.

She said, "You were given proper notice of my arrival. That prisoner has a right to visitors."

"I ain't saying you can't see him. Just tell me what it's all about."

"Private family matters."

Tucker held his bifocals like a monocle, squinting through the one unbroken lens. "But you ain't family. You're just some crone come buttin' in here, shrieking orders."

"If I violate the law, do you think the two of you could handle me?"

This last made Harvey bray, "You gonna try us?"

Ophelia said, "Dr. Bishop has a right to see me in his cell. You can inspect anything I give to him, monitor our visit."

"I don't think you're here to bust him out, but we'll check you out. Harvey'll be on guard. I got business, and you got fifteen minutes."

The raven made his voice heard.

Ophelia moved to stand by the cell door. "Dr. Bishop, I am Miss Ophelia Wylde, and I've travelled to see you. Would you object if we visit?"

Bishop stood, the handcuff slapping the iron railing. His hair was combed, and his bloodstained shirt was buttoned to his neck. Trying not to grin because it pained too damn much, he grinned anyway, his whip-swollen face turning in on itself. "Just watching you these last five minutes has been a great pleasure, ma'am. I'd be honored to make your acquaintance."

Ophelia looked at Tucker. "Open it, then you can go to the bordello. That's correct, isn't it?"

Tucker swallowed his words. "No ma'am, it ain't." He made a show of rattling the keys before unlocking the door.

Ophelia stepped in as Harvey peered through the bars of the adjoining cell.

Harvey said, "Stinks in here, don't it?"

Bishop did his best to stand. "I'm sorry about these conditions."

"I've been in jails before." Ophelia turned to the sheriff. "A disabled man, compromised, and you have him chained like a wild animal?"

Tucker said, "Yep, and that's the way it's gonna stay. Fifteen minutes, Harvey!"

Eddie disagreed. "Nevermore!"

Ophelia took a few steps closer, smearing the fresh spots of blood on the cell floor with the toe of her shoe.

Harvey pressed his face against the bars, his tongue wagging. "That bird got a name?"

Ophelia stood quietly for a moment. "Eddie."

"Funny."

Bishop said, "Then why don't you two have a laugh?"

Harvey sauntered from the open cell, giving the bull-whip a loud crack. "Don't do nothing I wouldn't do, and that ain't much."

Ophelia looked at Bishop. "Another warning? You have these men on edge, Doctor."

Bishop said, "Harvey'll lean by the window, listening to every word. Then he'll repeat them wrong."

"That doesn't bother me a whit." Ophelia took another step, stopped. She felt something. Her arms stayed close to her side, but she allowed her fingers to part an invisible curtain, a small gesture she tried to obscure. Her voice broke just above a whisper. "*Vóhkêhésoa* told me there was black surrounding you, your aura."

"White Fox." Bishop mulled the name, was lost in it for a moment, then said, "She would know," before reaching out his right half-arm as if to shake hands. "Miss Wylde, you have me at a disadvantage."

"I've never felt anything like this. Violent death is all around you."

Bishop pulled on the cuff. "It's why I'm here. What do you mean, *you feel?*"

Ophelia said, "I'm here to offer you some relief." She took a letter from her purse. "This should serve."

Farrow emptied his glass, nodded toward the still-crated pool table in the middle of the parlor floor. "What's your game, Sheriff? Elimination? I prefer three-cushion, myself."

Tucker stood behind the mayor, waiting for the offer of his private stock. "Oh, I just hit a rack straight. Maybe wager a drink."

Farrow said, "I'd guess you win free drinks all night. Pool table, the ladies—this will be the place to be, provided the mayor gets all his work done."

O'Brien just smiled. "It's not easy. Take a drink, Tuck. Find a seat."

Farrow handed Tucker a cut Havana. "Not next to the suitcase."

The sheriff poured himself a shot and held the cigar as if it were solid gold.

Farrow said, "Those are Mr. Chisum's special imports."

O'Brien said, "Bring out Chisum's cigars or silver coins dropped from his hind end, you're not getting anything up on us."

"Ran the bank here, didn't you Mr. Mayor? Until it failed?"

"By many acts of God. The railroad was supposed to bring business that it didn't, a couple good horse ranches were taken over and moved upstate. That hurt, but didn't kill us. We're strong people in this town, Mr. Farrow."

Farrow threw a glance at Tucker's damaged face. "That's very clear."

"We faced raiders—"

"Actually, you didn't." Farrow sipped his port.

O'Brien continued. "And flooding from the snow-melt up mountain damn near wiped us out."

"Damn near? You said you were dead."

"Coming back from the dead. Towns come back. We obviously have some value to you. What exactly is all that money supposed to buy?"

"Doctor John Bishop."

Tucker laughed. "Right after we hang him! I'll even let you keep the suit he wears!"

Farrow said, "His release."

O'Brien said, "There's no bail."

Tucker pulled some tobacco off the end of his tongue. "You know how many murder charges he's got on him? Hell, don't you know what happened here?"

"I read about it, saw the wreckage coming in."

"Them damn terrorists attacked that train, must of left fifty men dead before riding out!"

O'Brien said, "Except Bishop."

Farrow took a last sip. "But he wasn't with them. In fact, he was about the only person in this dog-pile who fought back, isn't that so, Sheriff?"

Tucker shook his head, saying, "I wouldn't put it that way myself."

"That's how your deputy put it. He's down in Texas, speaks very highly of the good doctor, but not much else." Farrow brought his words in close. "Have you seen that shotgun rig? Seen him use it?"

Tucker said, "I've seen what happens when he does."

"Lots of dead men." O'Brien took his drink. "And when Bishop goes to trial, that means the hotel will be full up with reporters and rubbernecks. They'll all need a place to sleep and keep their horses and have a nice time. That's money to every business in town."

Farrow nodded. "Including this one. Anything else?"

O'Brien said, "The charges have already been filed. To reverse these plans won't be easy. Or popular."

Farrow asked, "All of these issues are solvable?"

"Dr. Bishop is no common outlaw, but there's a lot to consider."

"We've made all considerations."

Tucker drew in the taste of the fine leaf, let the smoke dance around his nose, but his mouth was dry, his heart racing as he rubbed a gold coin between his fingers.

O'Brien said, "You can't put a price on justice."

"Justice like letting John Bishop swing for fighting your fight?"

"I have to think of the town of Paradise, not just one prisoner." O'Brien finished the bourbon in his glass. "I'm trying to build something here."

Farrow regarded O'Brien. "A responsible elected official. It's nice to meet you, sir."

Eddie's "Nevermore" scraped the air as Bishop read the letter for the last time. Ophelia stood in her spot near him, but keeping a few steps away so she could observe. The darkness of his soul shadow had left her genuinely rattled, but she wasn't going to show any more emotion than she already had. That was a mistake.

He held out the letter to her. "I can't fold it."

Ophelia manipulated it back into an envelope and put it on the upended table with the leg that had been shot off. "I watched your eyes. You couldn't read everything she wrote."

Bishop said, "Half was in Cheyenne. I could read it once, but now I can't make heads or tails. My memory's spotted, at best."

"But you remember her, and her given name. Also, that she's considered beautiful."

"Yes, I remember."

"And your wife and son? Fox gave me details."

Bishop's voice was low. "That will never leave me."

"What about the rest? Soldier's disease?"

"Concussion from a grenade. The town doc sewed up my head then took off."

"I don't wonder. A very poor job, indeed."

Bishop pained through a swollen smile. "This is all new. This, I remember pretty well."

Ophelia said, "When you heard you had a visitor, you thought it was going to be Fox."

"The sheriff wouldn't uncuff me, so I got Harvey to comb my hair and button up my shirt."

"I'm sorry to disappoint."

Bishop said, "Miss Wylde, you delivered the letter. I appreciate it, and I'll try to read it again, but do you understand I'm a man they want to hang? All I know about what I've done is what they tell me. Maybe that's a strange kind of blessing."

"You may not recall a man named Chester Pardee. He was a ne'er-do-well who died in a gunfight against you. He had a link to your past."

Bishop said quietly, "I did fight Chester . . ."

"You killed him. His family asked me to bring them comfort, and I could do very little, given the kind of man he was. It's better you disposed of him. My journey took me to White Fox, who was with you, and now here."

"You get paid to follow the dead?"

"To assist the grieving, the troubled." Ophelia unbuttoned her sleeve and rolled it up to show a bracelet with four interwoven beaded strands joined together by a silver and turquoise clasp. "From White Fox, for helping you. I've never had anything so fine. That's an inherited skill. I believe her father is a gunsmith? Didn't he fashion your bizarre shotgun that's now so infamous?"

Bishop nodded. "Probably so."

"White Claw is also a thief and killer. She told me." Ophelia rolled down her sleeve to hide the bit of vanity. "Don't let your medical training reject what I have to say. I've found men in your profession can be very closed off."

"Nevermore!" screeched from Eddie's cage.

Bishop said, "I'll try. I want Fox to get what she paid for."

Ophelia let his words settle. "Dr. Bishop, what do you know about otherworldly phenomena?"

Bishop's swollen expression said it first. "Not much now, and damn little when I had my complete memory."

"You don't believe the dead have any influence on the living? You've left a lot of dead men behind."

Bishop jerked at his chain and angled his head toward the small window above his bunk. "Those are the graves of men I shot. Tucker can give you the names. I don't remember them."

Ophelia said, "They remember, and they've told me about it."

Harvey's bray erupted just outside the cell window. He glanced in with an all-crooked-teeth smile. "You buyin' this horse manure, Doc?"

Ophelia said to him, "We still have nine minutes . . . if you can tell time." To Bishop, she said, "You're not that much of a fool, are you?"

"Not like Harvey, no."

Ophelia moved closer to Bishop, tentatively placing her hand at the end of his left arm. It flexed, as if it were all there.

Ophelia said, "You can't explain that feeling, but it's real."

"There's a reason the body acts the way it does."

"And there are reasons the spirit behaves the way it does. Doctor, I was a charlatan who became a believer. I've used every trick in the book, sometimes to give someone a little hope, sometimes to bleed a fool dry. I know intimately the difference between what's fake and what's not. I walked in here and never felt anything so bleak in my life. If I was more romantic, I'd say you were an Angel of Death."

"You do know how to sell it, madam."

"When someone has an epiphany, they want to share it."

Bishop said, "But I'm just a man waiting to be condemned. Or so they tell me. Lot of prisoners in this country in the same fix, I imagine."

"But I wasn't sent to any of them. Are you saying you don't have nightmares?"

"You've earned your bracelet."

"I want you to see something before I go." Ophelia reached into her bag and removed a rolled sheet of paper. She opened it, holding it up so he could see her sketch of a man at the bottom of a deep pit with another man standing above him, aiming a gun.

"I drew this minutes before I walked in here . . . after standing at those graves. What does this mean to you?"

Bishop regarded the sketch but couldn't bring forth any words.

She said, "The only way your torture ends is when you kill a dead man."

"No, I think my torture ends when they hang me."

Ophelia was planted before him, holding out the drawing as a challenge. "Your quest was revenge against those who wronged you the most. Some are buried fifty feet from here. Is Beaudine the name?" Her words echoed.

Bishop said, "Tucker knows who's out there. He has the names."

"Beaudine."

Bishop coughed when Ophelia repeated the name. He thought he tasted blood in the back of his throat, erupting from an injury. His face numbed as if being covered with snow. He felt a sudden rush of cold. A picture of a man standing over him with an axe appeared in his mind.

He could feel both of his arms and sensed being held down.

Coming from somewhere was the sound of his wife

and son . . . screaming. It was distant, like birds calling in far-off trees. The feelings and images lasted only a few heartbeats . . . like a slash of heat lightning.

Quickly, Bishop was back in his cell.

Ophelia locked into his eyes. "I knew that would stir you. I learned that name standing by those graves, and it took you someplace, didn't it? You remembered?"

"Amnesia turns the brain upside down and shakes it. Everything's displaced."

"That sounds like a doctor explaining to a patient."

It hurt like hell, but he had to smile. "I suppose I still am a doctor. Someplace."

Ophelia said, "And an avenger, right? This specter you're dreaming of is the worst of the lot. He wronged you more than anyone. I don't know who it is, the messages weren't clear, but you will confront him, and that'll be your peace."

Bishop said, "You give me all this nonsense as if I was getting out of here."

"I'm just giving you the messages I receive."

The light in the parlor had dimmed with the afternoon. A streak of sunlight focused on Farrow as he lifted the shelf out of the suitcase, revealing a compartment underneath containing two cloth sacks. His Cheshire grin returned. "Go ahead, Sheriff."

Tucker grabbed the two, tearing into one with stubby fingers. He almost burst out, but kept his voice low as he turned to O'Brien. "God a'mighty, I never seen so much money."

O'Brien said, "I have."

Tucker emptied one of the sacks of gold coins into his hands, dropping several on the floor. He grabbed for them as O'Brien watched.

"You get everything here, if you choose it." Farrow closed the case and locked it. "That's a hell of a lot for

the two of you or enough for Paradise to get on its feet
again. And, I might be able to arrange for a cattle shipment or two to work through your depot."

Tucker said, "It'd be a damn great thing for the town.
You can't say that ain't true."

Farrow's smile was constant. "And it means you don't
have to build a gallows, Mr. Mayor."

O'Brien stood. "What the hell makes this man so valuable?"

Farrow shook his head. "You only have to know that
he is."

O'Brien looked at Tucker thumbing the stack of bills,
loving the feel, and soaking in the deep perfume of new
money. The sheriff couldn't hide his grin or pathetic
giggle.

O'Brien studied his drink, thinking about a different
sheriff.

Farrow said, "Gentlemen, we're in a house where
everything's for sale. I need an answer."

Bishop brought up his cuffed hand as far as it would
go to extend a courtesy to Ophelia. "Honestly, I think
you've been playing a cruel game, madam, but I'm still
obliged for the letter."

Ophelia didn't shake. She rolled up the sketch,
placed it in Bishop's left hand, and let each word carry
its weight. "Trust the dead."

Tucker slipped off the planking, and sank deep into
the mud. "Maybe we could put some damn sidewalks in
on Main Street. That'd be a nice change!" He freed himself with O'Brien and Farrow's help.

The mayor said, "Don't spend what's not yours, Tuck."

"The money's yours, the prisoner's mine." Farrow

said, "If Bishop did that to your face, you must be awful glad to be rid of him."

"He looks worse." Tuck shook slop from his boots. "These are from Sears, Roebuck, and only a month old!"

O'Brien said, "Why does Bishop look worse? What have you been up to?"

"Doing my damn job."

Farrow was the first to reach the sheriff's office door. "Doing his job in an interesting way. Even allowing a carnival humbug to see your prisoner."

"What?"

"Want to have your fortune told, Mr. Mayor? She might even do it for free."

Tucker reached around to unlock the cell. "I didn't know who the hell she was!"

O'Brien said, "Why bring this up, Mr. Farrow? Sounds like you're trying to talk your way out of our agreement."

"Just the opposite. I want you to see how our deal solves many problems, including incompetence."

Harvey's nose was inches away from Eddie's beak as he squinted into the raven's cage, its cover pulled back. "Go on, be smart again, you sumbitch."

Eddie tilted his head, blinked twice at Harvey.

Out of Bishop's cell, Ophelia recovered the cage. "I've never before seen a man challenge a bird to a contest of wills and have the bird win."

Harvey frowned. "That little bastard's nothin' but a smart-ass!"

"Well, smarter than some."

Bishop laughed from his cell, which brought Harvey to the bars. His hand went to the coiled bullwhip that dangled from one of his belt loops. "You still think hangin' later saves you from pain now? You ain't learned your lesson?"

Tucker moved to Harvey. "Back out of there, Harvey."

Harvey said, "You want to hear what they was talkin' about? These two are crazy!"

Tucker elbowed him out of the way as he opened the cell door. Farrow tipped his felt hat with the bullet hole towards Ophelia.

Bishop said, "More visitors? Is this my lucky day or my worst?"

Farrow said, "I think you'll be celebrating this date for years, Doctor. You're a free man. Get that chain off him."

Bishop brought his arm up, pulling the cuff out straight as Tucker went to him, keys jangling. "Going to have Harvey take me out back, Tuck?"

"It's no joke, Doc." Tucker unlocked the cuff, then stepped back. He touched the side of his face. "I ain't even bringing charges."

Harvey filled the jail. "What the hell, Tuck?"

Bishop stood up straight for the first time in weeks, his legs searing, but the pain was good, giving him relief as he walked it off. Tucker didn't go for his gun, and the door to the cell stayed wide open.

Farrow said, "Doctor, arrangements for you have already been made."

Bishop still didn't move toward the door. He looked to Ophelia for a clue of some kind. She nodded, not breaking a smile, but satisfied. She held the raven's cage high, stepped around the group of men, and walked out the front door.

Farrow watched her go. To Bishop, he said with a grin, "I'm sure she predicted this would happen, so let's not make her a liar."

Bishop leaped to the window and looked out between the bars. Ophelia walked steadily on the planking, stepping around the slightest hint of mud on her way to the station.

He called out to her, but she had no interest in looking back.

CHAPTER FOUR
Related by Blood

My only son,

    First, let me wish you the happiest of birthdays, and say that I hope this letter reaches you in time. It is hard for me to believe that it was thirteen years ago that I held you in my arms and couldn't imagine what a fine young man you'd grow into. I can only add how sorry I am that I won't be able to join you, but please take your classmates for a party celebration on your father, leaving behind a little bit for yourself.

    Work continues, with jobs being plentiful, for which I'm thankful. It is dull and offers little reward beyond the money which affords us your schooling in England, giving you the best possible education.

    I am planning for a great Christmas holiday for us both, perhaps with me making the trip to you, rather than you coming here. I can't think of a better Christmas than to be in London with my son, but that is months away.

Your current job is to have the happiest of birthdays.
                              Devotedly,
                              Your father

Colby finished with a little swirl below the r *in father, as was his habit, and then made an ink slash through it in the style of John Hancock's signature. He blotted the letter, then placed two hundred dollars in its center and folded it into thirds before putting it into an envelope and sealing it with the wax from a red candle burning next to him.*

The wax dripped, and he pressed his signet ring into it, letting it cool before turning the envelope over and addressing it to his only son. When he was done, he blew out the candle, turned in his chair by the small ornate desk, and enjoyed the embers in the hotel fireplace, burning warm and orange, as he thought about the preparations for his next kill.

John Bishop sat up in bed, the sheets bundled around him, and said, "Be still now, we're saying grace."

The woman's hand was on Bishop's chest, and she whispered, "What? Are you okay?"

Bishop looked to the doorway, but there was nothing there but an empty blue shadow. He rubbed his eyes with his left palm. "I'm sorry I woke you."

"You were dreaming."

He lay back in the large bed. "Better than most I have lately."

"Tell me."

"Go to sleep."

"If you say it out loud, you'll feel better."

He knew she was right. His voice was quiet, as if describing distant music: "It was my family, eating dinner, and my boy kicking the leg of the table while we said grace. It seemed very real."

The woman's voice was warm out of the dark. "Because it was. Now you can find your way back to sleep."

Bishop shut his eyes, the voices of his family still echoing.

CHAPTER FIVE
Hired Guns

The house detective had knocked on the hotel room door four times, the last, a pounding of force. There was no answer, although he could hear the guest moving around inside.

"Mr. Andrew Barmuster, I'm with the hotel. Open the door, sir. There's a matter of a large bill that needs settling." The detective took enough time to draw a .38-caliber pistol from his jacket before using his passkey on the lock. The lock clicked. He thumbed the hammer back before turning the doorknob, his sweaty finger almost slipping.

The parquet door swung open into empty and quiet.

He stayed in the doorway, searching the room with the pistol barrel. "Mr. Barmuster, I know you're here, so better to show yourself. I am armed."

No response. The detective inched his way in. The bed was neatly made and packed bags stood at its foot. The flames in the fireplace had burned down to a glow. The air smelled warm.

He tried again. "Sir, you haven't paid your bill. You're trespassing. I have the legal authority to arrest you, but that doesn't have to happen. Please show yourself, and let's get this settled."

He took a few more steps past the dresser and opened the closet door with his foot. Empty. He backed away, turning from the closet toward the bed, when he stopped, catching a glimpse of a figure on the balcony. It was a man standing against the far railing, masked by the curtains hanging in the balcony doorway, moving with the evening breeze.

Colby said, "Don't turn, not even an inch."

"What—"

Before the detective could get out another syllable, the knife had flown from the balcony, across the room, and sunk into his shoulder, cutting to the bone. He dropped in a rain of blood and pain, the pistol clattering into the washbasin.

Colby moved to the detective. He watched him twist on the floor, holding his shanks to his chest, rocking back and forth, smearing himself on the Persian rug.

He yelled, "Lord on fire, I wasn't going to kill you, Barmuster!"

Colby knelt next to him. "No, I'd never give you the chance, but I had to prove something to myself. You were a great help." He packed a damp washcloth around the blade and the wound, soaking up the blood. "Really, thanks very much."

"Where's my gun? I'll come back proper!"

"It's soaking wet, and coming back at me would be a mistake. Now, because you'll get medical attention you're not going to die. I'll leave the money for it."

The detective squeezed his eyes closed and took an enormous breath. "Barmuster, if you've got money, what the hell are you doing this for?"

Colby said, "You wouldn't understand, but recently I

was not able to do my job as well as I would like, and I was afraid I was losing my abilities. Putting that knife into your shoulder, from that distance and in that exact spot, with your body in the position it was in, half-turned away? That wasn't easy, friend, but I did it. Clean. You've given me back my confidence, and I thank you."

"This was my first day on the job. I can't lose it. . . ."

"You need to bite on this." Colby forced a hairbrush handle between the detective's teeth before pulling the knife from his shoulder with one fierce yank. The meat tore, but it was out. The detective choke-screamed, the sound lost behind his tongue, then rolled onto his side, unconscious.

Colby placed a hundred and fifty dollars in silver on the dresser, picked up his bags, and stepped around the detective curled on the floor and spreading red. "Barmuster? I didn't remember I'd used that." He walked from the room, leaving the door slightly open so the desk clerk and bellman could make their discovery.

The detective screamed.

"The last time you saw me, I was something you'd find in the shed with my legs open."

"I wouldn't say that."

"You don't have to, 'cause I just did." Soiled Dove had carefully shaved off Bishop's scraggle of a beard. Her fingers dug into the earthen jar, gathering the yellow salve, and then travelled across the lashed wounds on his face.

"That Indian you was with? She left this for Kate, so she's the one who's really helping you, not me."

"The day we got the weapons." Bishop felt the cool, as the salve found its way into the lacerations on his cheeks, nose, and chin, then settled there. "I'm surprised you remembered."

"Because I was too dumb or had laudanum pouring out my ears?" Dove pulled the handle on the side of the barber chair, angling it toward her, bringing Bishop back flat, his head slightly raised on the cushioned rest. "I was just dirty feet and a nightgown."

She stepped back to look at him then dabbed a tiny welt with the last bit on her index finger. "Even with this, you're still a good-looking man, just not put together right."

"That's pretty much how I feel." He tilted his eyes to her. "How did you ever end up in Paradise?"

Soiled Dove put the jar on an upended crate next to the bed and wiped her hands on a towel. "Widow Kate's is the best house in two states. You've been there, and you all talked about big plans to open new houses from here to California."

"That's gone out of my memory."

"Do you remember you made a deal to kill Major Beaudine?"

Bishop regarded her for a beat then said, "I remember enough of Beaudine."

"Well, you did it. Word was they buried him in pieces. As soon as Kate heard, she started making her moves with lots of money at stake. I told her I was ready to take charge, open the new places. It don't look it, but big things are going to happen in this town. We just wanted the first taste."

"No more dirty feet."

"No, sir." Soiled Dove curtsied. "The trick to movin' up is not to let 'em catch you listening."

The chair sat Bishop up. "So, you're going to be quite the madam."

"Of five new houses, and no hog ranches neither. The best you'll ever visit. I'm training Large Marge. She'll do all right."

"Well, I love the chair."

"There was only one thing my daddy loved more than getting his hair cut. This is the master's suite. You're the first guest."

The room was L-shaped, wrapping around the second floor of the house, and as unfinished as the rest. The upholstered barber chair and the Victorian bed with carved headboard were the room. As in the rest of the house, the rugs were rolled up and the walls were bare.

Bishop wanted to swim in the huge bed but settled for six hours of sleep with no nightmares before Soiled Dove and Large Marge woke him with coffee and comfort.

He was cleaned, pressed, and his face doctored. "This has been a fine stay, and I'm genuinely honored to be the first."

"Don't worry. Your name won't go on the wall. Mr. Farrow really put out, though."

Bishop looked at Dove. "Did you know I'd be getting out of jail?"

Dove's response was a smile.

Large Marge, spilling from a different pair of pajamas with pink bows on her hips and breasts, and dancing across her backside, walked in carrying a red hood in one hand and the double-barreled shotgun rig in the other. "All for you, Doc!"

Marge could barely lift the rig, and Dove grabbed it from her stubby fingers. Marge tossed the hood on the bed, and Dove put the gun rig beside it, arranging the straps and bandolier not to tangle. On the pillows were a hat and a folded duster.

Marge said, "That hood's from them Fiery Riders. Anyway, you're supposed to take a good long look at it and tell that Mr. Farrow everything you know."

"That's still not much. Now."

Instead of the hood, Bishop picked up the hat, a new Stetson the color of dried blood.

Soiled Dove said, "It suits you."

Farrow was at the door before Bishop could try it on. "Get him in the rig."

Bishop held his elbow joint steady, as Soiled Dove fit the prosthetic cup over the corrupted end of his right arm. She was cautious, sliding it up the arm. Bishop twisted it to make it fit. The lining of the cup was soft deerskin, a fine woman's touch. He thought of that as the inside of the cup formfitted around the hard tissue of his amputation. He made the adjustments, a few small twists, so the shotgun that protruded from the cup hung straight.

He leaned forward "The straps go across the shoulders, then tighten."

Dove didn't speak, just pulled the straps over his shoulders. He grunted in pain, and she stopped.

"It's all right. I think there should be a little pain as part of this." He put his left arm through the opposite strap.

She tightened them by fastening both sides to a small hook like a belt buckle that hung in the middle of his back.

Bishop used his left hand to snug the silver chain attached to the shotgun's double triggers, then Dove looped it through the rig's straps and brought it all the way across his back to his left side, where it was anchored.

He stood and brought his right arm up slowly. The gun felt heavy as he moved his body, favoring his right side, getting used to the weight and the way the weapon moved.

Soiled Dove held out a box of .12-gauge shells. "Do you want to or should I?"

The sun was dipping as they walked the uneven planking from Soiled Dove's to the train platform, Farrow in his tall felt hat with the bullet hole, Bishop wearing the black duster and Stetson that shielded his eyes and healing face.

The shotgun rig was now his right arm. Conscious of its weight and how it made him move, he was learning the weapon again.

The double barrels were barely visible below the cuff of his duster sleeve. A slit was sewn into it where his forearm would be, so the rig could be broken, reloaded. The special bandolier, with six shells, was tied high, almost to his shoulder.

Farrow said, "How do you feel, wearing that again?"

Bishop moved his shoulders, let the gun shift positions and react to him. "It's been a while, Mr. Farrow. I'll get used to it."

"You and Chisum share a common enemy."

"So you keep telling me."

"You're going to be in the front lines. You've got to sight down on the right people, don't you agree?"

"Just point me, and I'm supposed to shoot?"

"We saved you from the hangman, Doctor. I think that gives us a little bit of sway on your targets, don't you?"

"I'm not a hired gun."

"Half-gun?" Farrow smirked at his cleverness.

Bishop said, "How old were you when you got the fever?"

Farrow stopped, tipped his hat. "Nine. Lost every bit of hair I had. You think you're a doctor. With that special rig, I can't figure exactly what the hell you are, but my job's to deliver you to Chisum."

"Don't worry. I'm getting on the train."

"Instead of being cuffed up in a jail cell?"

"Damn right about that."

Farrow had the red hood in his hands, poking his fingers through the eyeholes. "Cowards and killers. Am I right?"

"You keep waving that thing at me like a verónica in front of a bull."

"Maybe you'll remember putting a dozen Fire Riders

in the ground? Didn't one of them toss the grenade that scrambled everything?"

"That's what they say. You're a thorough man."

Farrow patted Bishop on the shoulder, pulled his hand away at the feel of the gun straps. "You'll know your enemies again. They're Mr. Chisum's, too."

Junior cracked his swollen knuckles before turning up the oil lamp on his small high desk by the ticket window. Arthritis in his neck fought him as he looked over his shoulder, watching Bishop and Farrow move onto the depot platform.

Hollis, a cowpoke with gravel for skin, sat on a barrel behind Junior, slicing an apple with a wide blade. "You see 'em? I see 'em."

Junior's head bobbed as he spoke, his neck paining him. "Yes, yes. I ain't blind or deaf! Fetch his horse. The train'll be here in ten minutes."

"So you pray. Gonna send a wire to that dude?"

"Fetch it!"

Hollis said, "You told me to remind you is all." Arms dangling, he walked out the back door toward the corral.

Junior shuffled dog-eared train schedules, old mail stained with rings from his coffee cup, and threats from a freighting company, before finding Chaney's embossed card VIRGIL LOUIS CHANEY. WORKS OF LITERARY DISTINCTION. PARIS, CHICAGO, NEW ORLEANS.

Junior took a pencil from his pocket, ran the lead across his tongue, and then set down his message for Chaney, double-checking with the Morse manual for every word. He cracked his knuckles again before tapping the brass telegraph key.

The gate to the corral beside the depot creaked open, its bottom slagging through the mud. Hollis walked Bishop's tall bay onto the loading platform. He was followed by a breed wearing a hat slouched low over his head, his braids tied behind his neck with a piece of beaded leather. Hollis wasn't wearing a gun. The breed wore two under a dirty fringed jacket.

Farrow said, "Your horse and the rest of your things will be on the train."

"Like I said, you're a thorough man." Bishop went to the bay, stroked his mane, patted his withers. The horse was clean, newly brushed. It nickered softly, angling its head toward him and instinctively nudging his left arm.

Hollis fed him the last bit of his apple. "You can see who he belongs to. I been seeing after him."

"Until I was hanged?"

Hollis dropped his face and scraped the wooden platform with his toe. "Guess that was the deal, yeah."

"No worries. Thanks for the work."

Hollis looked up. "You're the one with that special gun?"

Harvey snapped his whip at nothing, cutting the light in the air as he stepped onto the platform with giant, long-legged strides. "Hell's-a-fire, yeah, he's the one! And that gun sure is special. It can kill one man and save another from a hanging!"

Bishop turned to Harvey. "You're not coming near my horse with that whip."

"Didn't even cross my mind, because I got you." Harvey beat the air again, the bay recoiling at the crack.

Bishop handed off the reins to Hollis before facing Harvey, the shotgun coming up automatically, snapping into place. It was a quick move that surprised Bishop. Instinct was taking over.

Harvey's grin trembled. "Want to try me, Doc? I ain't got a gun like you. Don't need one. I beat you down once."

"No, I was cold-cocked. Funny what you remember."

"Don't matter. Without that rig, you're nothing. Maybe this fella should give me all kinds of money." Harvey barked to Farrow, "How 'bout it? I'm a better man. Got two strong arms. Why don't ya give me a job with Mr. Chisum? Hell, you don't even have to buy me out of jail."

Farrow said, "You're good with that whip, Harvey. I'll pass the word on to Chisum, so you can go on home."

"I got rights to be anywheres I want to be, and I want to say good-bye to my buddy, Shotgun. Make sure he gets on that train without a problem."

Bishop tilted his body just a bit, bringing the barrel of the rig above his waist, locking it for firing. "I don't like that moniker, but today, maybe it fits."

"That special gun is the only way you can beat me. Ain't that right half-man?"

Bishop said, "Harvey, this doesn't have to go any further. In about ten minutes, you'll never see me again."

"Half-a-man, and money falls out of the sky for you. Gun down a dozen men, and there's no rope. Doesn't seem fair, do it?"

Bishop said, "I've got my debts."

Harvey stepped closer. "That some kind of answer?"

"What do you want?"

Harvey shook the coiled whip in his fist like it was a warrior's spear. "I beat you to hell, and you still came back for more. The sheriff saved your ass, but he's not here, and these folks would like a look-see at a man what refuses to die."

Bishop shook his head. "That ain't me by a long shot."

"I deserve to watch you crawl."

"Your reputation as a man to be feared is safe with me."

Harvey let the bullwhip unfurl, the end hitting the ground as he brought back his elbow to snap it hard. "Lower that shotgun, I'll lose the whip, and we'll go. See what you really got." He shouted, "How about it? Our famous prisoner, the shotgun killer, in a fair fight for once?"

Used to Harvey's mouth, the few loungers around the depot watched without saying a word. Hollis and the breed walked Bishop's horse to the loading dock, not looking back.

Mayor O'Brien stood on the balcony of Dove's house, Large Marge beside him, sipping more of her tea. They didn't call out, just watched and waited.

Farrow said, "You can't waste time with this fool. You have a job waiting and have to be in shape to do it."

The shotgun unlocked, reverting to its position straight by Bishop's side. He took the few steps to where Harvey was standing.

Harvey held out the whip then let it fall. He smiled. "Take it off."

Every bruise and cut on Bishop's face burned, but he ate the pain, met Harvey's stare. "I don't have to lose the gun. I've got no need for it."

Harvey's next word was a gut-pulled scream as Bishop's heel smashed into his knee, tearing it sideways beneath the skin. Doubled over, Harvey tumbled to the platform. Tears and more screams covered his face.

"That's what half-a-man can do, Harvey." Bishop turned and walked down the platform to where his horse was standing.

Farrow stayed with him as Harvey's voice colored the air, his crying and curses all anyone could hear until the distant whistle of the incoming train wiped them out.

CHAPTER SIX
Hell Travellin'

Colby stood at the counter of the Butterfield Line station as the clerk updated the stage runs on a mounted chalkboard. He was precise in his writing, crossing the sevens in the European style. Colby checked the update against his own watch, approved, then presented his letter.

The address made the clerk ask, "Blackheath?"

"Yes, it's seven miles—"

"Actually, nearly eight kilometers beyond London, last stop of the railway." Colby's surprise gave him half a step back.

The clerk said, "I gauge London to be ten cents over five dollars. I'll have to confirm for Blackheath." He thumbed the postage rate book.

Colby was impressed and didn't hide it. Out of targeting habit, he sized up the other travelers in the small but clean waiting room.

A roughneck snored loudly in the corner, his hat pulled down. while a young fellow in new jacket and collar read a newspaper, despite the honking. Two older women took up the bench on the opposite side, speaking in strained whispers. They wore all-over gray. Colby assumed them sisters, but he was more interested in the young fellow and the Colt nickel-plated pistol he'd holstered in the top of his boot.

"Five dollars and seventy cents."

Colby faced the clerk, who repeated himself. Colby handed him one carefully folded bill and exact change. "How long for delivery? My son's birthday is soon. That's his card."

"Four weeks at the outside. The Royal Mail's very reliable."

"That's been my experience, as well."

The young fellow crossed his legs, pulling at his trouser cuff to hide the pistol grip.

Colby watched without looking at him then said to the clerk, "Where do you hail from?"

"Iowa. The Continent is what you dream about between stage runs."

"Dreams are what keep a man motivated." Colby moved to the waiting area and sat next to the young man holding the newspaper too close to his face. Smiling at his slight tremor and the drops of sweat that had fallen from his forehead, dotting the newsprint, Colby said to him, "Hot?"

The young fellow thin-smiled his "yes."

"I find it rather cool and pleasant. You should take some water. You might be coming down with something."

The scream in Bishop's ears was actually metal pounding metal as the train picked up speed, rounding the curve that led away from Paradise. He stood on the small grate between the coach and the boxcar, the coupling inches away, the tracks underneath passing faster and faster, and the rushing cool night air feeling pretty good.

The cars bucked and heaved, but he kept steady, his left arm crossed, holding the shotgun in place. The tracks jolted him, the iron chains holding the cars yelling under the strain, but he didn't move. He was fixed.

And then the destroyed locomotive was there.

It was blue in the random streaks of moonlight breaking the clouds, turning it into a huge, eerie death monument beside the tracks. Bishop kept between the cars, trying to lose himself in the blasted iron and fire-twisted steel of the train wreckage, to bring back some kind of memory. Trying to find something.

The cars picked up speed.

Bishop held on. There were flashes. Bodies tossed by explosions. Young soldiers torn by a Gatling gun. Riders charging to the slaughter. It was a chaos of thought that lasted less than seconds and brought him no closer to filling the lost stretches of his memory.

The cars were moving faster.

The train roared onto a straightaway through a mountain pass, then eased. Bishop opened his eyes. Memories were still jagged pieces, but at that moment they weren't weighing him down.

The taste and smell of the rotting sweet of Tucker's jail cell was gone from the back of his throat, replaced by the cold rush coming down from the mountain. He watched the landscape pass, the profile of the Rockies and the coyotes jumping at the whistle, their shapes darting for the trees.

The boxcar's access door banged open and Bishop stepped from the coupling. Peering in, he saw his bay secured between hitch posts in a stall at the shadowed far end.

"Vé'ho'évo'ha."

The door slammed heavy behind him, Hollis and

Breed blocking it. Breed had two revolvers. Hollis had a wide-blade that he shifted from left to right.

"Still taking care of my horse?"

Hollis smirked. "You know what Tuck said? That you had the craziest goddamned mouth of any prisoner he'd ever seen. Even when you was gettin' whooped."

Bishop backed up a few inches, taking in the movement of the two men, watching Breed more than Hollis. "You and the sheriff talked."

"Tuck yaks about everything, special about how crazy you is. Who were you talkin' to out there?"

"Ghosts. Now what?"

"You're crazy . . . and worth money. Dead, you're worth money. Half-dead, a little more."

Bishop said, "I came in to check on the bay. We can leave it at that. The door isn't locked."

Hollis froze. Breed made a move, the gun in his left aimed at Bishop's chest, his right aimed at his head. It was a juggling act.

Bishop stayed with Hollis. "Okay. You want to do this, tell me what it's about. How much?"

"Between me and the man what wants you bleeding."

Bishop nodded to the Breed, and Hollis said, "Not him! He's Mex and Comanche. Got no money and nothin' to say."

"Unlike you."

"Crazy, crazy mouth." Hollis let the blade settle in one hand. "Do you even get what's happening here?"

"Yes. Do you?"

The rig snapped into place and fired, blasting Breed off his feet before his next breath. Bishop had aimed low, tearing through the meat of Breed's left leg.

Breed gritted his teeth, fingers clamped on the wound, blood and flesh mushing through them, but not allowing himself a sound.

The bay bucked against its stall.

Hollis backed into a corner, slashing, the blade jabbing at nothing. Pure panic filled his eyes.

Bishop brought the rig up an inch, arm straight and locked. Smoke had cleared from the first barrel. The second was ready. "He's going to die if he doesn't get to a doctor. If you know about me, you know I can help."

Hollis slashed. "Tuck said you was too crazy to doctor no more!"

Then slashed again, with a giggle.

Bishop blocked it with the shotgun barrel. "You're a damn fool if you don't see I'm giving you and your buddy a chance."

Hollis looked to Breed coughing up blood then back to Bishop. He turned the blade, making a show. "So—what's *your* offer?"

"You keep living. Who's coming for me?"

Hollis said, "But if you ain't dead or dying, then I will be. That's what they said, and I'm stickin' to that."

"That knife's nothing. Around your feet? That's your friend's life. You're losing your chance, boy."

Hollis took a step out of the blood pool, wiping the soles of his boots on his pant leg. "But—they're payin' out a lot, and you can't match it."

"I can better it." Bishop's voice stayed low, train thunder behind it. His movements extended the rig, shifting automatically, the barrel pointing directly at Hollis's face. "You can die right now or maybe you live and they never find you. You've got ten seconds."

Hollis said, "A second ago you were a doc. Now the bastard comes out. Goes with that fancy gun."

"Who put up the bounty?"

The answer was a stammer. "A-an a-army of f-folks. Some of 'em d-dead. We've got to bring you back with your guts spilt, so they can watch you die. Or your head, make sure you're gone. I-I could've sure used that m-money." Hollis squeezed his eyes tight, waiting for the second barrel.

The bay whinnied and bucked, busting the silence, fighting its ropes. The rest happened in moments. Breed brought up a pistol, throwing back the hammer. Bishop turned, fired, the second blast spreading Breed across the floor and walls. The train whistle shrilled.

Hollis charged the side door and yanked it wide open.

Bishop shucked two shells and reloaded. He half-stepped, calling out to Hollis, who dove from the car into the darkness. His jump missed, and he rag-dolled into a tree, bone and branches snapping together—not even giving him time to scream.

The whistle yelled as Bishop hung in the open door to see Hollis's body by the tracks. Bent almost in half, his chin between his shoulder blades, the cowpoke was left behind, getting farther and farther away as the train rounded the next curves.

Hollis was gone, dead by choice.

Bishop dragged over what was left of Breed, letting him fall from the car before straining to shut the door with his one hand.

The bay kicked at its stall, splitting lumber, crying out. Bishop moved to his horse, its head thrashing. Dodging its jaw, he reached out to run his hand along its neck, gently scratching and repeating *Nahotse* over and over. The Cheyenne word had come to him out of the dark. As he said it, the bay's muscles stilled, its heart stopped pounding.

Bishop's did, too.

He stayed for a few miles before walking back to his car.

The coach was empty. A single lamp at either end cast a dim, yellow glow over the seats. Slumping next to a window, he wondered if Chisum had bought every ticket. He pulled the shade, put his feet up and hat down, and tried for some peace.

* * *

"These are yours, Doctor."

"Sure as hell, you shouldn't call me that." Bishop turned in his seat, the shotgun automatically leveled.

Farrow took a step back, grinning. Bishop lowered the rig, locked it.

Farrow said, "Whoa. My fault. That's not how you approach an armed man."

Bishop nodded at the joke as Farrow put a black leather field medical kit and a volume of Edgar Allan Poe next to him.

"I don't know what all was in that bag. Tucker probably helped himself, but you've still got a lot of instruments. Some I can't imagine what you use them for."

Bishop opened the kit with his left hand and looked inside for the first time in months. He picked up a muscle clamp and manipulated it. "I—I know."

"Hope I don't find out. I admire the gold initials."

Bishop regarded the Lt. Bishop on the side in raised gold, most of which had flaked away, fracturing him. "That was my wife's idea."

"The Poe stories belong to her?"

"Somebody else."

The red-hooded riders charged through the Laramie Mountain pass, keeping themselves ten across as they gained on the Butterfield Coach.

The coach driver cracked the reins on the six-up, and the horses broke fire on the new road, pulling ahead, legs in perfect sync, sweat pouring from their backs. Next to him, a bearded man with a scattergun turned himself around on the seat, taking count of how many red hoods were coming for them.

Driver pushed down a small grade, then brought the

horses up hard, the stagecoach swerving, but turning sure as they reached the new road. They jolted from the grade onto the road, the passengers calling out as he pushed the horses for all their speed.

Beard waited for a Rider to get close, and got off one shot before his chest and back exploded. Driver wiped blood from his eyes as Beard fell, hitting the road, coach wheels crushing his legs.

The Fire Riders bore down.

A Fire Rider ran his stallion up close to the coach team, hair rubbing hair, leaping from his horse to one of the leaders. The driver snapped his whip at him, biting nothing but red hood. Fire grabbed the lines and pulled back, slowing the team. The others caught up as the coach rumbled down, the horses winded, their mouths foaming.

Fire swung off the leader as one of his men tossed him a bayoneted Springfield rifle. He caught it and trained the barrel and knife on the driver, who'd jumped from his seat with his hands up and Beard's blood drying on his face.

Fire's voice was accent-thick, but loud enough through his hood. "This is all for you, to stand and deliver!"

Two more Riders opened the coach, hauling the sisters out first, letting them tumble with the tiniest of screams. The snoring roughneck was next, arms high, followed by the young fellow with the gun in his boot.

Colby came out last, hands raised, taking deliberate time. "I don't know about the ladies' purses"—he helped them to their feet—"but if you want real money, I'd suggest you're looking in the wrong place."

Fire pushed the bayonet against Colby's chest just enough. "Maybe I slit your stomach. Maybe you swallowed a fortune in gold when you saw us riding up."

Colby never lowered his arms, but nodded toward the young man. "You might check him. He has a new Colt in his boot, nickel-plated, possibly never been fired. He won't draw it because he was going to rob the strongbox with the help of the driver."

The young fellow tangled his feet, falling against the coach brake. "That's some dirty wash, mister! You don't know me!"

The other Riders formed a sloppy circle around the coach—demons on skeleton mounts, not uttering a word, holding repeating rifles and polished sabers.

Colby said to young fellow, "You've been perspiring and trembling since we left the way station, and had plenty of time to bring out that pistol before they stopped us."

Snoring said, "That don't prove nothing except he's a coward. Me, I ain't got no gun."

Colby acknowledged that with a nod. "But I don't hear our driver contradicting me."

Fire swung the rifle around to the driver, who said, "We better let it go, Henry."

"Why'd you open your goddamned mouth? They didn't know what the hell—"

The rifle shot blew apart young man's cheek. He fell, eyes open, hand twitching around the Colt Lightning he'd pulled. The sisters cried louder as Fire brought the bayonet flush with the bottom of the driver's jaw, the tip slicing the skin.

"How much did you take, the money?"

The driver's head was back, his eyes toward the sky. "About fifteen thousand in scrip and gold."

"Give me only ten. Count it out."

Driver said, "I don't get this."

"Do as you been instructed."

Fire pulled the bayonet away as the driver snatched the bank deposit bag he'd stashed under the boot.

Handing it over, he inched back, smearing the trace of blood from his throat. "You better figure it out. I don't want no mistakes."

The driver counted out the money. "You rob the line, we take a cut, cross territories, pay the toll. That's the new law. You savvy that much?"

Driver said, "Understood."

Fire nodded, and a rope whipped around the driver's neck, jerking him to the ground. All guns stayed on the passengers as two riders stuffed a bandana deep into the driver's mouth and lashed his hands and feet tight.

They held him down, and Fire knotted the line to one of the team, unhooked the traces, then fired a shot by the horse's ear. It bolted, dragging the driver, screams choked, across the flats.

Fire watched for a moment, turned to the passengers, and said, "Now he understands good," before smashing Colby in the jaw with the stock of the rifle, spinning him down.

"Get on a horse, nelly son of bitch! The way you're dressed, somebody pays something for you!"

Colby stayed on his knees, holding his face. "Will you allow me my luggage?"

"Get it. Maybe pay for that, too!"

Colby pulled himself to his feet, holding on to the side of the coach. He pointed to one small valise and the Navajo blanket stuffed with his arsenal.

A hooded rider grabbed them both and secured them behind a saddle. "Mother Mary's tears, this is heavier than my son! Silver or gold?"

Colby hauled himself into the stirrups, his face numbing. "Hardly."

Fire said, "I'll find out myself. Don't get no ideas. That horse does what I want only." He pointed to the young fellow in the pool of black-red soaking the sand. "He's dead. You're not. Take that to church."

The sisters held each other, and Snoring stayed on his heels as Fire swatted Colby's horse. It started a run, following the straight road. Fire took off, keeping a few steps behind, his rifle casually aimed at the back of Colby's skull.

The other Riders held, then turned out their circle and followed, pushing their "ghost horses" to gallop for the foothills.

The funeral director held his nose with two fingers as the autopsy surgeon cut away the gunnysack shroud. There'd been leakage, and the fabric had fused with the corpse's skin, which tore with the sack. A small metal tray at the dead man's feet caught the runoff.

Keeping both hands buried in his overcoat pockets, Virgil Chaney stood by the display coffins as the surgeon worked.

The surgeon threw out words. "You told me your cousin was shot."

"Indeed he was, by a special double-barreled model."

The surgeon stepped from the corpse and dipped his hands in a bowl of antiseptic. "It must have been very special, because this man was stabbed to death."

"That's not what I was given to understand."

"Hold your nose, then look for yourself. He's been rag-tagged back together, but those are stab wounds in his chest, not gunshots, and certainly nothing with a shotgun. Maybe your killer had two weapons, but your cousin met his end from a knife."

Chaney stepped from around the coffins, taking a small, black camera from one of his pockets.

The funeral director broke a grin. "That's one of those super cameras? Sub-miniature? I've heard of them, but never saw one in person a-fore."

Chaney focused the lens on the body "Then today is lucky for you, isn't it?"

The surgeon said, "I understood only Army spies were allowed those."

"I'm a new kind of spy . . . for *Harper's Weekly*." Chaney

snapped the picture, took out the small, dry negative plate, and slipped it into a protective envelope. "I understand he was seen with a young Cheyenne maiden of some temper. He met his end in a hotel room she and the shotgun-man occupied."

The surgeon laughed and poured a tumbler of gin. "Lots of people end up on this table for that reason. I don't know who did the killing or who had their pants down, but nobody used a gun. Now, what about his disposition?"

Coughing from the odor, the funeral director piped in with a voice that was two cats fighting. "Should we select a coffin and make plans for an immediate service?"

Chaney said, "That odorous bag was appropriate for my cousin. Put him back in and deposit him in the nearest well."

The surgeon said, "Up to you, but I always think people deserve a decent burial, even if they didn't have a decent life."

Chaney was already at the door. "I'll make sure to quote you."

The tall man with the lean mustached face and dark suit was in a freight wagon, checking his watch and the ammunition stores stacked behind him, when the train pulled into the Lincoln County station. He didn't get down from his seat, but waited for Farrow and Bishop to step from the single coach among the boxcars.

Farrow blinked at the New Mexico sun and the heavy smell of the stock pens. They walked to the wagon, while behind them hundreds of head of cattle were loaded onto the train from a large corral. Manure dust and shed hair thickened the air.

Farrow blew his nose. "Really stings."

Bishop said, "It's the business of your boss."

"Yours, too. That blood on your coat, from last night? That's your badge of honor."

Bishop adjusted the brim of his hat, catching the shadow. "There was no honor involved."

"Just survival. You and Lincoln County are going to fit together fine."

At the wagon, the man holding the reins said, "You Bishop? You're with me."

Bishop looked to Farrow. "So, this is where I earn my freedom?"

"Everything costs, Doc. I'll take care of your traps."

Bishop climbed aboard the wagon, keeping the shotgun flush with his side. "You're from the Chisum spread?"

"I work for him like everybody else around here. Name's Pat Garrett. Welcome to the war." He snapped the reins, and the team quickly stepped around the drive that circled the train station before leading out across miles and miles of Chisum country.

CHAPTER SEVEN
Battlefield

The range had no end. Grass-thick land washed beyond the horizon and then beyond that. Pat Garrett pointed out graves of sheep herders caught stealing water and reminded Bishop just how much influence great cattle barons like John Chisum had on the bright future of the new healed United States. "This was wild country, not safe for anybody. Mr. Chisum's changed that. Need the water? Just ask. Some grazing time? Same thing. Follow the rules, Mr. Chisum's law, you'll have no problems."

Bishop said, "That's a hell of a speech."

"And believe every word. I was a lawbreaker once. I came around."

"For money."

Garrett said, "Man decides about his future. That's why you're here, ain't it?"

Bishop adjusted the rig by his side, but couldn't get comfortable.

The wagon bucked as Garrett took it off the road and onto a trail leading to a small flat between grassy hills.

Bishop heard gunfire echo as they got closer. Shots in scattered volleys were followed by cannon-like reports.

Garrett said, "The enemy's hid. We're just trying to flush 'em out." He brought the wagon over a small rise so Bishop could take it in. The enemy position was an old adobe with a collapsing thatched roof and small corral. A sleepover for cowboys moving herds. A dead man hung on one of the corral rails, two exit wounds in his back, his hands clenching a rifle, eyes filmy and open.

The shooting had stopped for reloading. A thin layer of gun smoke lingered over the Chisum men who'd been killed in the last hour.

Garrett angled the wagon behind a flurry of blooming Yellow Bells that offered cover. The distance to the hut was about sixty yards, with no-man's-land in between.

Bishop stood, looking for movement among the dead. "You got a lot a men out here?"

Garrett said, "Maybe eight left. We know there's two, probably more, in the cabin."

"Four for each."

"How many don't count for much if they're well-heeled."

A rifle barrel parted the shutters of one of the hut's two windows, resting on the sill before letting loose. It was rapid fire, followed by more from another rifle right beside it. Never stopping. Chisum men were hit bloody and hard. Spun around by slugs, then hurled aside by their force, their bodies were torn to nothing.

Eyes were punched by bullets when men raised up from behind logs and boulders, trying to return fire. Another shooter let loose from behind the adobe. Slugs ripped the brush, the cover, ricocheting off the rims of the wagon wheels. The horses bucked, kicking the wagon back.

Garrett pulled Bishop to the ground, gave him a signal to wait. They grabbed the team's harness, held them steady.

Gun thunder from Chisum men in the tall grass powdered holes in the adobe, chewing windows and doors. The dead one by the corral was hit by strays, the impact lifting him off the fence and dropping him.

The shutters slammed shut.

Garrett kept low at the back of the wagon. "Better not of hit the horses. That's a good team." He threw open the gun and ammo boxes, looking to Bishop. "You're in it now. Hadn't you better load that thing?"

Bishop's voice flattened out. "I'm ready."

Rifles laid down fire as the Chisum men ran in from gullies and trees, bullets chasing them. One old boy rolled down a slope, came up, put two hopeful shots into the adobe, then tried for cover. "That'll burn 'em!"

A slug from the hut tore through half the old boy's rib cage, a second pushed his voice out the back of his neck.

Others made it to the Yellow Bells.

Worn and bloody, they were all cowboys laying somewhere between sixteen and sixty. Sporting old-trail faces and busted knuckles, some were using guns for the first time in years. They grabbed water and ammunition, filling canteens, cartridge belts, and Winchester repeaters.

Bishop handed a cup to one of the boys, a man in his thick-cut forties, lying on the ground, coughing blood.

Thick Cut drank, then doused his face. "Feels cool."

Bishop said, "You best forget about this fight."

"That ain't why Chisum's payin' me."

Another said, "He ain't payin' enough for this."

Garrett looked at the bunch. "Everybody in that cabin must be hit."

A cowboy spit. "Yeah? They're still shootin' us to pieces!"

Maynard, whose nose had been creased by a bull's hoof, broke through the brush, shouldering a wounded man. He carried a big-bore .76 in his free hand, dumped the unconscious cowboy by the wagon with the other.

"Damn fool tried to go around the corral where that one sum'bitch is hid out. Took a pepper ball in the leg."

Garrett's question was "What about the one who shot him?"

Maynard said, "Back inside, waitin' for me to blow his head off. And I'll oblige him."

Random shots ripped from the adobe. Maynard returned fire without a target, letting loose. "Eat that, ya pecker-licking bastards." He cracked off his rifle until it hammered empty. He dropped to one knee, still cussing.

An old cowhand said, "You sure as hell got 'em runnin' scared, Maynard."

Garrett said to Bishop, "Tell me if we're gonna have to bury this one."

Thick Cut said, "You talkin' about me, Garrett?"

Bishop checked Thick Cut's eyes, opening his lids with his left thumb, then mopped the bullet wound with a handkerchief. "Who's down there anyway?"

The echo from the last volley was still rolling as Maynard grabbed some fresh shells, cocked them into his Winchester. "Goddamn fence-cutters—"

"And all goddamn good shots," the old cowhand interrupted.

"Workin' for them wormy bastards in the red hoods!" Maynard looked to Bishop. "And he wouldn'ta been shot, except Garrett had to fetch you!"

"You got way too much mouth."

The voice was a woman's and full of Missouri. She crouched next to Thick Cut, both hands tight above the bullet wound, squeezing. Small in her denims, with auburn hair framing a round, almost pale face. Freckles across her nose, and green eyes gave her color.

Bishop said, "Good. Use all your strength," before wrapping his belt around the cowboy's leg in the exact spot where Rose had clamped it, slowing the bleeding from the blown-apart artery. She deftly switched hands from the leg to the end of the belt, pulling it tighter before looping it off.

Garrett reloaded his pistol and said to Bishop, "Guess you're the field medic, too."

The cowboy's eyes rolled back and his breathing shallowed. More gunfire came from the adobe. Bishop instinctively shielded his patient. Maynard and Garrett cracked off rounds from behind the brush, swearing to send somebody to hell. Anybody. Every bullet from Maynard's .76 was a stick of dynamite, killing the adobe. Packed mud, hay, and wood, blasted.

Two other Chisum men boiled the air with Winchesters, laying fire at targets they couldn't make out.

Everyone held up, waiting for screams. Something.

Then, return blasts came from behind the shutters through a tear in the roof and pinned them down.

Maynard spit. "Them cutters a damn army? We're gettin' it from everywhere!"

Rose said, "I spied them first, and there's three in that adobe! Only three!"

"One's dead, and we're still outgunned!"

Bishop said, "This man's dead, too, if we don't get him out of here." He and Rose gathered Thick Cut's legs, one of Chisum's men got under his shoulders, and hefted him into the wagon bed.

Chisum's man said, "Sure hope he pulls through. I like his coffee."

Rose said, "I can get him out the back road."

Bishop elevated the torn leg with an ammo box, settling his body. Thick Cut's head rested on a folded blanket, when a bullet hard-jerked him to one side. The slug tore through his right temple and blew out his left before splintering one of the wagon's wooden slats.

All guns turned.

The Fire Rider was charging from a small hill, coming in from behind the Chisum position, firing a Spencer Springfield, taking another cowboy dead off his feet.

Garrett steadied and shot twice at the Rider's horse, ripping through its neck, crashing it forward.

The horse screamed.

Rifle flying, the Rider lurched from the saddle, tumbling with the animal, then hitting the ground face-first, almost killed. The horse lay heaving, legs chopping and body twisting, a red geyser from its throat misting everything around it.

Rose stood by the wagon, took aim through the Yellow Bells, and fired her Colt .45 clean, giving the stallion peace.

The Chisum guns were dead-on the Rider as he rolled onto his back, pulling at his hood to breathe.

Garrett ordered, "Hold fire! We want him alive!"

The Fire Rider managed to get to his feet.

Garrett kept his gun trained, his voice low to Bishop. "If I have to shoot, think you can put him back together, at least so he can talk?"

"Aim for his legs." The barrels of Bishop's rig unlocked with a move of his shoulders, but they stayed angled toward the ground as he called out, "I know you're hurting, but try and come toward us!"

Garrett yelled, "Hands up, fingers spread!"

The Rider took a shaking step, then stumbled. He was more than fifty feet away from the Chisum guns, bloody and moaning into the grass.

"Don't go to him."

Bishop was halfway up. "He'll not make it."

Garrett said, "Or he's luring you out. I don't need that." He yelled to the Rider, "Show your face! Surrender, and we'll come for you, this man's a doctor!"

Garrett's words were cut by two shots pumped into the Rider's chest, blowing out his back. Shots ripped the Yellow Bells and the wagon. Sniper fire. Garrett dove under the wagon, scanning the ridge, shooting at a glint he thought was a rifle barrel.

A couple of Chisum men ran from the cover of the

brush, firing wild at the adobe hut, before diving for an old water ditch. Slugs punched their throats, sending them tumbling then landing . . . dead.

The shutters on the hut were wide open. The gunmen inside sprayed the area with rifle and pistol rounds. Maynard's warrior cry was above the sound of the guns as he bull-charged the adobe, pumping shots from his Winchester .76. His war whoop and the rifle fire were constant.

A bullet through his cheek spun Maynard off his feet. Another shot, blowing out his shoulder, dropped him.

Garrett and Rose opened up with their rifles as Bishop ran to get where Maynard was lying. Darting from side to side, then coming low around the side of the corral, Bishop had the rig at waist level, the hammers back, and the trigger line slacking.

Maynard's face was slick with blood. Bishop turned him over. Still alive. Shots ripped. Bishop whirled, his duster flaring, the rig coming up, snapping into place. A slug blew through Maynard's boot. He cried out. Bishop moved, tightening the trigger lines with his shoulders.

Ducking, he got to the adobe, the shotgun shoulder-high, barrels extended, and locked. He pressed against the wall. A rifle flamed from the window right above his head.

He sprang up, blasting the shutters apart, tearing the gunman in half.

Bishop dropped, pressed tight against the wall again, then saw Garrett throw a signal. He waited a few heart-beats, then pulled the second trigger to almost firing, straining against the trigger.

A second gunman jerked open the front door, leveling rifle and pistol. Bishop fired, blowing shot through his chest.

Bishop snapped the breech, shucked the shells, brought two down from the bandolier. An automatic motion. He swung around as a Fire Rider charged from the other side of the corral.

The Rider in red, a rifle slung across his back, leaped his horse over the rail fence, and drew a Peacemaker out of a holster. Bishop pulled both triggers, sending him flying out of his stirrups as if God's fist had punched him.

The Rider landed dead, his hood filling with blood like a water bag.

Bishop fixed on the corpse for a moment, fragments of memory bombarding him—other riders in hoods and robes; men he'd killed with the rig; a slaughter along a stretch of railroad tracks; and a grenade exploding beneath him.

For that instant, he felt the blast again.

He looked away from the dead rider, the flashes vanishing as quickly as they'd come. Around him, the rolling echoes of the guns were fading, and the natural quiet of the place was replacing them.

Victory or surrender, the silence after a battle was always the same. Bishop had heard it too many times, but there was something else.

Chisum men began coming down from their positions behind rocks and gullies, limping, shouldering each other.

Their voices, cries of the wounded, grew louder, striking Bishop's ears. He snapped the gun to his side, the rig no longer a physical and mental extension of him, but something separate. Focus came back to his eyes as he knelt by Maynard, checking his pulse.

Pat Garrett was standing beside him. "You're quite a medic . . . with one hell of a gun. How about him?"

"Steady. He's made of tough stuff. Stupid, but tough."

"That one by the corral was sniping," Garrett said. "That's why we're losing this thing. We got three of theirs, and we're burying, what? Eight? Ten?"

"You'd know better than me. They're scattered all over this battlefield."

"Battlefield." Garrett made his point. "Now you're seeing the light, Doc."

Bishop didn't respond. He just stood, not acknowledging the smoke still drifting from the double-barreled weapon at his right as Rose brought up the wagon to load the dying and the dead.

CHAPTER EIGHT
Blood Ties

The purple on the trimmed woodwork of the master's suite had dripped into a twist of color that wriggled to the floor. Mayor O'Brien carefully wiped the paint, keeping away from the wallpaper he'd just smoothed.

Sheriff Tucker reclined in the barber chair near the bed, adjusting his neck as Soiled Dove made the last, short strokes with the straight razor, lopping the stubborn hair under his chin. "I thought the whole point of that money was so you could put down the paintbrush and worry about runnin' the town."

O'Brien said, "This is running the town, Tuck. Giving a new business every advantage."

Soiled Dove wiped the razor clean on a towel. "And we appreciate it."

Tucker smiled. "I know you do, darlin'."

O'Brien dabbed a bit of purple on the baseboard. "So where are the bodies?"

Tuck said, "They were a few miles down the tracks. I just had 'em put in the old icehouse."

"Without ice."

"I know it's busted down, but they both got family that'll want 'em buried. Been kind of cool lately, so it'll be a day or two before they go ripe. Got any of that rosewater, darlin'?"

Dove took a small bottle of scent, sprinkled it on a warm towel, and wrapped Tuck's face. He settled back, giving a quiet groan.

O'Brien stood. "How do you explain what happened, Tuck?"

Tucker shrugged, the warm towel hiding his expression. "Them two both got records. Hollis never was any good, and Breed just did three years for robbery, so it ain't nobody's surprise that they turned up shot."

With Tucker unaware, O'Brien moved to the barber chair, standing right beside it. "There's quite a price on Doctor Bishop. We've got the chance to really set this town up, but we can't have any muddy water, Tuck."

Tucker smiled. "Let him out, and take 'em down."

O'Brien whipped the towel off Tucker's face and spun him around. Catching the chair with his foot, the mayor leaned into him. "Do you understand what I'm getting at?"

"Yeah, yeah. I get it."

"Then say it."

Tuck looked at Dove, whose face was a mask, then back to O'Brien. "None of this can come back on us."

The mayor nodded, reached into the toolbox beside the paint cans on the floor, and took out a stack of hundreds wrapped in a paper band.

"That's more of Farrow's new money, ain't it?"

"No, it's yours. Twenty-five hundred." He dropped the stack of bills onto Tucker's lap.

The sheriff eyed the cash, but didn't pick it up. "You've been real good about cuttin' me in, and I appreciate all of it."

Soiled Dove said, "It's not a gift."

Tuck toweled his face again. "I get it, I do, but I've

never really pulled the trigger on no one. Not to kill 'em. I talk big, but Man of Peace was my campaign slogan when I ran for sheriff, remember?"

O'Brien said, "And this is about keeping *our* peace."

Harvey was stretched out on the bunk in his cell at Paradise jail, his leg splinted with two pieces of thin pine, a lash of heavy rope keeping it straight. He took a long pull from a bottle of Don Sauza, letting it burn his mouth before swallowing. His complaints started as soon as he saw Tucker by the cell door. "You gonna kick me out again, Tuck?"

"You're fine, you're fine."

"'Cause I'll want paying."

Tucker kept his eyes to the floor. "No, Harv. You did good."

Harvey drank again. "Damn right I did." He sniffed the air. "Aunt Petunia's ass, where have you been? Don't tell me. I know. Rosewater perfume! See, I can't do them things now 'cause of this busted leg."

"You want one of the girls to come down, see you? I'll pay."

"I don't feel like doin' nothing, and that's your fault, too. I always play the fool, Tuck, but when you give me the high sign to get the whip, teach one of these birds a lesson, I'm on it."

"You've been a real help, Harv. I haven't always been a good brother-in-law. I know that. I think Esther's real lucky to have you."

Harvey regarded Tucker. "That mean you're going to get me a real doc to fix my knee?"

"We're going to take care of that."

Harvey sat up, holding the makeshift contraption that was setting his leg. "Hell, if that one-armed son of a bitch hadn't busted me up, I'd say get him!"

Tucker moved to Harvey, settled on the small stool

next to his bed. "That'd be kind of a funny deal, since the doc busted you in the first place."

"That's what I said."

"How bad are you hurting?"

Harvey got the last swallow, then smashed the bottle against the cell bars. "I need another, is what! Or something stronger. I been shot more than once, so I don't know why this pains so bad."

Tucker said, "I know it pains. I tried to make a deal with Bishop when he was suffering with the terrors, trying to give him a little relief."

"Hell, that man's crazy, and you let him out!"

"You know why."

"Yeah, cash from that Farrow that I ain't seein' none of. I sent them two after him, and they come back dead, so I don't get none of that bounty, neither."

Tucker slipped the pistol from the belt loop near his back, keeping it down as he spoke. "I know it ain't fair, Harv, but we'll get this straightened out."

Harvey said, "I'm tired of waitin' for you to do right by me, Tuck. I'm tired of gettin' beat down for ya, delivering your messages, and gettin' into fights that you don't want to mess with." He lay back on the bed. "I got nothing because you give me nothing. When my leg heals, I'll ride on. Let you tend your own patch."

"What about money . . . and Esther?"

Harvey ran his fingers through his beard, had a little snort of a laugh. "Hell, she'll be glad to see me gone. You've said it a thousand times. I figure you're smart enough to dip into your cash, keep me satisfied, till I figure out the rest. Maybe find Bishop myself, collect that bounty." Harvey grabbed his leg, rocking forward on the bunk. "Goddamn a mule, my leg's burning."

Tuck took the money stack from his shirt pocket and handed it to Harvey.

Harvey held the money with both hands, then looked at his brother-in-law.

Tuck said, "It ain't like you don't deserve it."

"There was a time when I really did try to be a good husband." Harvey's hands stayed wrapped around the stack even after the bullet from Tucker's gun took off the back of his head.

Colby's jaw was still stinging from the rifle blow, but he didn't let that distort the beauty of the Wyoming countryside stretched out before him. The grass was a lyrical wash of green and blue, one color giving way to the other as the tall blades bent with the breeze.

In the distance, a herd of buffalo grazed, some taking water at the edge of a small stream. Colby rode easy, having a deep drink of the day and his surroundings before saying to Fire riding next him, "We're always thinking of money. Makes us forget the treasures right in front of us. The great creation."

Fire scowled. "What the hell are you going on about?"

Colby angled a little closer, he and Fire only a foot or so apart, their animals snorting at each other. He slipped the Uberti 1875 from the snap-pocket inside his jacket.

His voice was clear, cheerful. "Take off your hood or I'll put a bullet in your spine in an exact spot that won't kill you, but will set you on fire. You'll be begging me to put one in your brain. And then I won't."

Fire glanced over his shoulder at the other hooded riders coming up from behind. A couple exchanged words, hands on guns, and then one shouted, "Everything all right?"

Colby said, "They can't help you. They're not good enough."

Fire called out, "Yah, it's all fine." His voice was an

Eastern European bark, spitting out his words like they were plug nickels stuffing his mouth.

Colby said, "Well done." He motioned to Fire's head. "Hood."

Fire pulled it off, revealing a shaved head.

He was older than Colby expected, and fatter, with a face that was a mush of huge, drunken leftovers— bulbous nose, veins mapping cheeks, and a thick neck. He didn't speak. Just sucked his teeth, keeping everything to himself.

Colby said, "I can barely understand you when you wear that thing, and as we're currently working for the same man, it's right to finally know your face. Let them know, too." He gestured with the pistol. "Do it."

Fire turned and waved to the men in hoods riding behind them. They shrugged. Some returned it.

Colby said, "That's good. Friendly."

"You're full of jack-sass."

"And you're not garbled anymore. They call you Hunk, correct? For Hunkie."

"Name's Bogdan."

"Your father's a coal miner. Your brothers, too."

"You threw insults about my family's honor, threatened them."

Colby said, "During the last cattle raid, you were argumentative. I actually wanted to kill you. After striking me today, well, I just want to be very clear about where we stand."

"You think I'm to take this?"

Colby went through the files in his mind. "You've had blight for two years and are about to lose your farm. Your wife, Frieda, where will she go? And your two boys? Want me to tell you their birthdays?"

Hunk said, "You don't got to prove it."

"It's my business to know as much as I can about the people I work with. It can be a little confusing when everyone's wearing a hood."

Colby gave a friendly wave to the Fire Riders while keeping the gun aimed at Hunk. None of them made a move. "The one on the speckled pony? With the little finger missing? Claims he lost it in a gunfight? His wife chopped it off when he forgot their anniversary."

Hunk said, "Okay. So you know much. Then you know they're not going to like it, me riding in like this."

"The charade worked. The coach passengers think I was abducted, and we're far enough along we can drop the pretense. You're just no longer in charge."

"Yah, I see the damn gun. Very fancy."

"And it cost me. You understand why I can't allow myself to be seen in a compromised position, led by you?"

"You don't want the big bosses to think you're sucking hind teat."

"Very good." Colby turned again in his saddle and called out to the Riders behind. "Gentlemen, do you mind if Hunk steps down, and I take charge?"

The response was mumbled through the red hoods covering their faces.

One Rider managed, "Long as money's waitin' when we get back!"

"Excellent!" Colby turned back around and said to Hunk, "You're still scout, leading us in, but I'm in command. Don't worry, you don't have to salute."

Hunk said nothing, his tall horse keeping pace along the grassy trail toward Rawlins. Colby rode alongside, holding the gun on him, enjoying the day, and whistling a beautiful tune.

CHAPTER NINE
Bleeding Soldiers

Seeing the dust from the wagons and men rising in the distance, Farrow brought two horses to the crossroads leading to the Chisum Ranch. Rose was driving the team, with Bishop in the back of the open wagon tending Maynard and several cowboys that had been rough-bandaged and were still blood-wet.

She angled through a steep turn, heeling the wagon and making the horses run close to the edge of the road. The wheels jumped. Farrow signaled for her to stop. She pulled up, the pair snorting, a dry fog of dust settling.

"What the hell, Farrow? We've got to get these men inside so Doctor Bishop can tend them!"

"Take 'em to town. Bishop's wanted in the big house."

Bishop said, "These men are . . . my patients."

"An hour ago you didn't know them. They work for Mr. Chisum. They'll see his doctor in Lincoln. You're needed elsewhere. Don't make me insist."

Bishop said to Rose, "Don't waste any more time on this. Get going." He dropped from the back.

Rose slit the air with the whip, ripping the team off at top speed.

Farrow presented the reins to Bishop's bay. "He made the trip in fine shape."

Bishop mounted up as a convoy of Chisum men approached, Garrett leading them. Some were walking-wounded and others rode, leading horses soaked in foamy sweat, dead men tethered to them. A bottle of milky tequila was passed among bloody hands.

Garrett slowed to Farrow. "Here to offer comfort, Farrow? They're all on the payroll. They deserve something."

"The worst-off are on their way to Lincoln."

Bishop said, "The worst are head down on those saddles."

"The men have chuck waiting for them by the bunkhouse."

"You're a hell of an errand boy."

Farrow looked to Garrett. "I do my job, which includes extending Mr. Chisum's hospitality to you for dinner. Doctor Bishop's accepted. Should I tell the boss of this ranch you have other plans?"

Garrett was taken aback. "No, I'm obliged. Let me make sure this bunch is taken care of."

Bishop said. "I can help."

Farrow said, "Mr. Chisum wants you now, Doctor. Garrett's perfectly capable. He'll join us later."

Garrett said, "It's all right, Doc. You earned a good meal."

Bishop looked back toward the men. "There's a lot of dead and injured." He brought the shotgun across his lap. "Mr. Chisum and I are going to have some real words over this . . . dinner."

Farrow said, "Fine with me. I eat in the kitchen."

* * *

The washbasin was a new model with a built-in pump and porcelain catch-bowl. Bishop leaned against it, pulling his shirt off over the shotgun rig.

Claude Ray knocked, then opened the water closet door just as Bishop freed his sleeve. Balancing himself on one leg and a willow peg, he held a clean shirt in one hand and a shot of Suits Kentucky Bourbon in the other. He was just over the hump of twenty, and didn't look like he shaved his blond fuzz more than once a month. "Mr. Chisum's compliments."

Bishop took the drink. "Unhook me in back? That buckle?"

Claude Ray loosened the straps as Bishop pulled the double barrels away from his half-arm, the skin around the elbow joint raw and bloody from the shotgun's kick.

"If you don't mind my saying, that's quite a contraption."

"It has its uses." Bishop rinsed the raw joint, then dabbed the arm with a towel while noting Claude Ray's leg. "Right above the knee. How'd you lose it?"

Claude Ray opened the rig's side breech and examined the back straps. "Dustup down by the Pecos, but Mr. Chisum didn't toss me out after they cut me down. Let me rest up here and paid for the surgery."

Bishop reached for the clean shirt. "Your boss sounds like a hell of a man."

Claude Ray put the rig beside the washbasin. "That's his starched button-down you're putting on, and that was his whiskey."

John Simpson Chisum stood formally by the tall-backed chair made from dark wood, one hand in his pocket, nodding as Bishop entered the large dining room with the domed ceiling.

Bishop paused to take in the man he'd heard so much about—surprisingly slight of build, a thin face, set jaw, and weary eyes. Bishop knew the look. Wars won, battles lost. Years had left deep marks on the cattle baron who sported precisely cut clothes, a mustache, and iron behind his eyes.

Chisum welcomed his guest, the Tennessee in his voice intact. "Doctor Bishop, I can't tell you how pleased I am that you're joining me in more ways than one."

Bishop, in Chisum's collared shirt with the empty right sleeve pinned back, held the shotgun rig in his left. "Mr. Chisum, there were a few minutes today when I thought I'd never be sitting down for a meal again."

"I offer congratulations on your victory. Also, apologies."

"Taking down those men isn't what I expected my first afternoon."

"Why don't you lay your weapon over there?" Chisum gestured to a dry sink against the farthest wall. A beautiful piece, it was in keeping with the rest of the room and the perfect place to display an array of imported liquors, custom cigars, and other vanities of a Big Auger.

Bishop was caught by the large oil painting immediately above the sink deft in its detail of the Tennessee Twin Rivers campaign. The surviving soldiers wore red-soaked rags, their uniforms unrecognizable, standing among a litter of dead comrades from both armies. An engraved plate on the gold-leaf frame identified the battle.

Chisum said, "The artist captured the horrors, didn't he?"

Bishop's stare was fixed on the dead. "From what I recall, and what I saw today. Thanks to you."

"This isn't how I wanted us to start. Again, your specialty gun can rest right there."

Bishop put down the rig. "Were you at Twin Rivers?"

"I wasn't, but I'm Tennessee-born. Lost family and friends. I was making sure our boys had plenty to eat and praying the conflict would end."

"I'm sure you did all right."

Chisum's correction was measured. "Trading Confederate scrip for cattle, trying to get rid of that money before the surrender? I would've done better to feed the cash to the herd."

"That bad?"

"End of the war, family gone, debts I couldn't pay and no way to settle. No animals and no kin. Dead broke like everybody else and their grandpa."

"Everybody else doesn't own half of New Mexico."

"We both know that's not true. I got new beef contracts only when the army was whole again. Lots of struggle till then, trying to build something." Chisum nodded toward another art piece. "The painting near the window? Now, that's a fine piece of work."

Bishop moved to the beautiful depiction of branding time during a New Mexican winter, all shaded blues and white.

"Even got the jingle-bob of the ears. Every piece around this room is like a different part of my life, from the war till now," Chisum said, looking over to Pat Garrett standing in the entranceway, waiting to be formally brought to the table.

Garrett had brushed his suit, kept his hat in his hands. "It's a real tribute to Mr. Chisum."

"Call them records of what we've accomplished so far. All are the work of American artists. I don't need a European to show me my own country. Patrick, please sit at the place next to me."

Bishop said, "There's a lot of room on these walls."

Garrett took his seat as two maids and Claude Ray set out calabacitas, beans, and fruit.

"Room for what happens next, Doctor. I'm hoping you'll be there to see it. Please sit."

Bishop's place was on the other side of Chisum, opposite Garrett. The maids, all high cheekbones and beautifully proud, poured wine. The younger topped

Bishop's glass, casting a glance with fierce eyes. He met them.

There was a lightning strike of White Fox . . . battling her enemies.

Chisum's voice pierced Bishop's memory. "That skirmish wasn't the best way to be introduced to life here in Lincoln."

"Excuse me, Mr. Chisum, but . . . bullcrap. You got me to see your war up close, believing I'd throw in with you if I survived."

Garrett drank his wine, silently proud that Bishop was using his words. Claude Ray set out the rack of roasted pork.

Chisum started carving. "You've got the wrong idea of me, Doctor. I'm not that calculating. I don't play with anyone's life. My men or yours."

Bishop said, "That's good to know. And I survived."

"We want to find a way to stop these raids, get back to business. No more blood. I've been in this fight before."

Claude Ray limped back to the kitchen, balancing on his one leg, almost losing the dish, and then catching it.

Garrett said, "He got pecosed."

"I don't appreciate that, Patrick," Chisum said, then offered corunda to Bishop. "The frontline of the last cattle war was the Pecos River. That's where Claude Ray got ambushed. Anybody got shot, the boys called it 'getting pecosed.' If you'd been with us, maybe he'd still have his leg."

"Mr. Chisum, these last forty-eight hours have been all kinds of hell. You paid a lot for me to be at this table. It's time to speak plainly."

Chisum regarded Bishop. "I'm losing men and stock every week, and frankly, I can't afford either. We're down to bones and scraps, and the damnable Fire Riders are the reason."

Bishop said, "Your scraps are enviable."

Chisum was settled against his high-back chair. "I

intend to hold on to what I've got left. The Fire Riders aren't taking any more from me."

Bishop said, "Farrow claimed we shared a common enemy."

"You disagree?"

Bishop chose his words. "I have . . . suffered . . . at their hands."

"And did real damage back. I know about your injuries, even the ones we can't see. How much of your battle in Paradise do you remember?"

"Not as much as you'd like."

Chisum took a drink. "I have a plan, and I want you to be a part of it. That's very important to me. Patrick, you're going to be leading this."

Bishop said, "My own wars haven't gone as well as yours."

Garrett said, "You're a sure man with that double barrel, and you saved some lives today."

"I had help from a young lady who earned more than her share of your gratitude. All the men did. They bled for it."

Chisum said. "My men are treated well."

"The ones that live?"

Garrett said, "All of 'em. And Rose is taken care of. No worries."

Chisum said, "Doctor, you're making your points, but I need your medical expertise and that special rig. You're a hell of a combination."

Bishop regarded Chisum. "You said I might have a choice."

"I already gave it to you, and you chose dinner instead of a noose. Good, sound thinking."

Garrett snorted a laugh as Chisum continued. "You're here, and I'm offering the opportunity to finish what you started. You won't be going it alone."

Bishop said, "I'd have your private army backing me?"

"Just my men. Think of them any way you want. I want the Fire Riders, so do you. Why not throw in? Help win this war against the red hoods, wipe out the scourge. You'll be riding out rich and with peace of mind. What's all that worth to you?"

"I have a lot of blood on me. So do you."

Chisum didn't push back. "When the time comes, I'll have to settle with my Maker. I know that. As for your death sentence, the good people of Paradise are a forgiving lot. You're no killer to them now. You're an infamous character who spent time in their jail."

Garrett said, "Stroll back into that town, they'd buy you drinks all night."

Chisum said, "You can win us this fight, Doctor Bishop."

"I'm just one man, Mr. Chisum, and not a whole one, but what's left isn't for sale."

Chisum said, "You haven't taken any money from me. In fact, you're the only one who hasn't."

"My soul's intact, even if the rest of me isn't—"

"A man who underestimates himself makes a terrible mistake. As far as I'm concerned, you're the most important person for a thousand miles."

"Because we want death for the same people?"

Chisum said, "Let's say we both have unfinished business. Partnerships have started on a lot less."

"No." Bishop looked toward the shotgun rig just feet away, the barrels pointed at him. "I told Farrow I wasn't a hired gun."

John Chisum said, "Not a hired gun. An ally."

The little blond girl pushed the feet of the hanging corpse, giggling as it swayed. It had been on the turret for days, birds pecking at the head and hands, pulling his shirt, pants, and flesh to pieces. His shoes were gone, and his feet were coal-black from the blood gathered in his soles, the toes curled back into nothing.

The girl's hair was stiff as old wheat, and she maneuvered it away from her eyes, snorting through a pug nose that took up too much of her face. She said to the dead man, "See, this is what happens when you don't play by the rules," then gave the body another push.

The rope holding it groaned, and the knot slipped, dropping it a foot. She jumped back just as she heard her father's voice.

Albert Tomlinson, a bookkeeping ledger in one hand and a small lantern in the other, called out to his daughter. "May Flowers! Leave that dead one alone, and send these boys out with a song!"

May Flowers defiantly nudged the body one more time before singing. Her angelic voice carried delicately across the open yard where riders in red were mounting up. Two of them checked the repeaters in their saddle slings, shouldered them, and listened.

"Yes, we'll gather at the river, the beautiful, the beautiful river; gather with the saints at the river, that flows by the throne of God."

A rider with few teeth pulled his hood down, adjusting its fit, before grabbing a torch from an oil barrel and lighting it. He fell in with the two who'd checked their rifles, and they looked back at the perfect voice with the bulbous eyes and snout nose.

She was still singing: *"On the margin of the river, washing up its silver spray; We will talk and worship ever, all the happy golden day."*

The three rode out the gates, the smoking yellow torch cutting the midnight dark.

"Gather with the saints at the river, that flows by the throne of God."

Albert moved behind his daughter, easing her away from the dead man hanging, letting May Flowers's voice follow the riders as the torch became a lightning bug, dancing for a moment, then gone.

Colby's horse stayed true, following the slight curve of the trail. It was a forgotten stretch across the Wyoming flat, and he envied the animal's night vision, keeping around gopher holes, and just enough ahead of the riders behind them, so he could have a good shot at each.

Just in case, he figured the order, as he always did to stay sharp. He didn't have to turn around to know who was where. He could feel it. Hunk was out front, with the others following two across. They all had their hands casual on their guns, and one had a bowie knife in his belt for show.

Hunk came up alongside Colby. "You ain't losing me."

"Just getting the lay of the land. You'd say so if I was riding in the wrong direction, correct?"

Hunk kept his head down. "Got nothing to say about nothing."

Colby saw the ball of fire in the distance, moving toward them at a full gallop. "Gentlemen, hold up."

The men heeled, standing in their saddles to see the three Fire Riders charging out of the dark, becoming more distinct. They moved from blurs of motion, to shapes of red, to men in hoods and flowing tunics. The one holding the torch rode point, those with the repeating rifles flanking him. They came up too fast, heeling their horses to one side, avoiding collision.

The Rider with few teeth and the torch barked, "Where the Sam Hill is his blindfold?"

Hunk looked up, but Colby answered. "There's been a change in command, so no blindfold needed."

Torch nodded to the rifles on either side. "There's a right way to bring a man in, and this ain't it."

The Uberti pistol was in Colby's hand, leveled between

the eyes of Torch's red hood. "Before you try anything, understand I'll put two in those with the rifles before your gun's raised. Your horse is skittish, so he'll bolt, and then I'll put one between your shoulders before finishing with the headshot. I thought you should know the sequence of events,"

Torch said, "Snap my fingers, and these rifles—"

"You'll have a bullet through your eye before your thumb hits your forefinger. We take money from the same man. That doesn't put us at the same skill level."

"You're all the chin music, ain't ya?"

Colby said, "Think of this. Bring me in as a corpse, you'll have a great deal to answer for. I do the same for you, I don't think I'll have too big a problem. Now, how do you want to proceed?"

Torch's horse pawed at the ground as he knuckled the reins, looking at the men behind Colby to see their move. Nothing.

Colby said, "They just want to get paid. The fact is, Hunk knows the way in, so we don't need an escort. Just your light."

Torch back-stepped his horse. "I know how to follow orders!"

"Good. You can say I used guile to trick Hunk. And you."

"Guile? What the hell's that?"

Colby said, "You'll all be properly educated, I promise."

Torch angled his pinto around, quick-spurring it into a run. The flame was kept high, orange sparks spitting, leaving a trail behind. Colby and his band followed. Those with the rifles broke to either side.

Colby nodded to each. "Don't worry, Hunk. If anyone's reprimanded, it'll be me. You won't lose your status."

Hunk finally raised his head. "Think I don't know, but I do. Think you're too smart, but you're not. *Te voi ucide—o zi.*"

"*Nu ai nici un secret.*"

Hunk nodded, appreciating that Colby had spoken to him in his own language, assuring him they had no secrets between them. Colby sped his horse slightly ahead, and began to whistle.

The porch was wide, running the length of Chisum's house. He stood at the freshly painted railing, drawing on a briar pipe, keeping watch on John Bishop and Pat Garrett walking to a bunkhouse. Bishop carried his shotgun rig, and Garrett an unopened bottle of Chisum's best bourbon. Garrett had a hand on Bishop's shoulder, exchanging low tones.

Farrow stood with Chisum without a sound or a glance, eyeing the conversation neither of them could hear. "Garrett sealing the deal?"

"I doubt anything Patrick or I say has much impact on Dr. Bishop. He's a man of his own mind."

"Yeah, what he remembers."

"He's always to be treated with respect."

"I've spent my time with him." Farrow took a glass from a small table, checked it for spots before pouring water from a flowered pitcher. "He's the key to these raids. If he rides out and gets captured or killed, your men won't be responsible."

"You mean my hands will be clean?" Chisum checked the pipe bowl, tamped the tobacco. "Never happen. Not now, not anymore. Good or ill, my brand's on everything."

"Do you want me to take the next step or not? Your choice."

Chisum relit the pipe. "Damn right it is."

"There was a strategy. That's what I've been following. You want to change up?"

"Meeting Dr. Bishop has given me pause, that's all. It's called having a conscience."

Farrow wetted his throat before saying, "Mr. Chisum,

you want to head off defeat, offer your enemy something they'll never get otherwise. Don't you? You're risking everything you've got."

"Speaking to me like I'm a fool is a serious mistake." Chisum watched the smoke rise and vanish as the night settled on the miles he owned. A zone-tailed hawk screamed, its voice carrying over the flats. "That's a victory cry; he's got his prey."

Farrow said, "I've done my job, said my piece, earned my pay."

"No, you haven't."

The towers of the prison were falling-down silhouettes to Colby; ruined, sloping giants against a night sky. Torch signaled approach, someone inside the prison responded, firing a shot.

The front gates parted.

Colby's horse threw back its head, sidestepping as a gunman with a shaved head sprung from a hidey-hole by the stallion's legs, like a striking rattler. Colby brought the chestnut around, holding it tight. The animal bit at the air, but didn't buck. Didn't panic.

Shaved Head threw aside the Shoshone blanket that had hidden him under the sand and climbed on behind the last Fire Rider passing, the rifle anchored on his hip.

Colby said to him, "Welcome aboard."

The prison gates were fully opened. Heavy canvas, painted to look like stone, hung over one door, trapping the light of the cook fires and oil lamps inside.

Torch charged through, followed by the convoy of Colby, Hunk, and the rest. Shaved Head dropped off the back of the horse, helped close the gates, and threw the huge bolt.

Colby took his horse to the middle of the old prison yard. The others went to a stable hidden behind another canvas painted like ruins from a fire. Just to the side of the camouflage were a short-barreled Bulldog Gatling gun, tripod, and ammo.

Colby slipped the Uberti back into his jacket, taking in the place and its mask. The surrounding walls were ten men high, laced with a mile of rusty-tooth barbed wire. Sections of the wall had been blown apart by massive explosions, leaving twisted iron supports and mounds of shattered concrete behind.

The ruptures were filled with crates of bullet brass and slab lead, the rubble hiding a new forge for making ammunition. A bullet maker was working, pumping air for the furnace, melting lead, and pouring ten slugs at a time into molds.

He gave Colby a toothless grin. "Aye, a friendly cuss. Can't shoot worth a grandma's turd, but loves making bullets." Reg Smythe extended a giant hand in greeting. "Mr. Colby, I presume."

"You presume correctly." Colby noted everything about Smythe seemed overgrown—thick red hair, thick English tongue, gin-blossomed face on a head cut from granite.

Smythe said, "You're the one what changed up the rules on us. I *was* Sergeant Smythe, now just Reg." Smythe's squeeze numbed Colby's fingers before he got his hand back, worked the blood back into it.

Colby asked, "So, Bogdan made his report?"

"That damn name's too hard to spit! He don't work that fast. Besides, he can't write. Hunkie told me you took over. Not a problem here, mate."

Colby said, "I won't abide second-rate treatment."

A stable hand took Colby's horse and walked it to a newly built structure with a tented exercise paddock on one side of the yard.

Colby said, "Quite a place."

Smythe looked up. "Been here more than twenty-five years . . . as a sergeant of the guard, not behind the bars."

Colby judged the man to be well over six feet tall, but

he was almost doubled over, his legs dangling useless as he leaned on two heavy crutches. Dead weight.

"And not always a cripple."

"Where did you take the bullet?"

Smythe balanced himself on the crutches topped with stuffed leather. He moved forward with his arms and then pulled himself to them, like a dog dragging broken legs. Colby stayed alongside.

"Run-in with an old prisoner. Now, he's not walking the earth, and I am. Almost. But I never question the Lord's providence. Build an empire, you pay the price. Am I right Mr. Colby?"

"Indeed, Mr. Smythe." Colby noted an area bordered off as a target range, men challenging each other with long-staffs. They were crude skull crushers, but learning. More canvas, shredded into strips with brush and branches sewn on, hung from wire stretched between posts, hiding the training from the outside. "Breeden's Rangers?"

Smythe drew his crutches up, smiled. "You're good. The only unit to make proper use of camouflage in the conflicts, but that's not my thinking. I sold Dev Bishop an old trick of Blackbeard's—take a shipwreck, outfit it with the newest guns and men ready for attack. Lying on its side, no one suspects nothing . . . until it's too late."

"How long have you wanted to try that?"

"Since I was a lad about ten when me dad told me the tale."

"I thought I heard the sea coast in your voice. This prison's quite the shipwreck."

Smythe's laugh was burned into the back of his throat. "Biggest ever. Everything's got to be protected. These men are going to be a true army. Not yet, but soon."

Cases of cavalry rifles were stacked open, gun sections wrapped and tied. A couple Fire Riders assembled the weapons, set them on wooden racks next to the firing range. Perfect assembly line.

Colby said, "Ah, the new carbines. Devlin took my suggestion."

"Lifting them from a troop train was hell's own job, but your thoughts do not fall on deaf ears, here, boy-o. Now, if we can learn that idjit to make the ammunition for 'em, we'd be rolling in clover." Smythe took himself a few feet closer to the entrance of the cells. Like the rest, the stone building was smoke-scarred, with shattered windows and a hole in the roof. But it was all paint and lumber fooling the eye.

He made a sweeping motion with a crutch. "More than a hundred stationed here, most taking the old cells, but they want for nothing. We've got med wagons, good horses, good food, decent whiskey. Better than anything else they've known."

Colby saw the crazy quilt of Riders' faces.

Smythe said, "Ex-slaves, coolies from the railroads, Swedes from the mining camps, Dagos and Jews run out of the waterfronts."

"Different without their hoods, yes?"

"Nope, the same. They all thought they were going to get a chance out West, and got cheated out of it. That's how Dev rounded them up." Smythe's grin broke his face in half. "We've got the men spoiling for a fight, an arsenal of over five hundred weapons, including a Gatling, mines, and grenades. That's something to brag on."

"All perfectly camouflaged. From the outside, just a place for coyotes to hump." Colby said, "You could take an entire town."

"Or a bloody state. Dev Bishop'll lay it out for you."

Colby nodded toward the hanging corpse.

Smythe said, "A renegade who didn't share our vision. He's past ripe and should probably come down, but still a good reminder."

Colby said, "What about him? Indispensable, too?" He nodded toward Hunk, who was taking a glass of store-bought rye at a mess table, watching a couple kids wash the white skeleton paint from the horses, scrubbing them down.

Smythe looked to him, then back to Colby and shrugged. "He turned in his cash like he was supposed to, and you're here. Does his job okay."

"But not with a standard of excellence."

Colby slipped a blade from his blanket of weapons, fitting it in his palm perfectly as he moved across the yard. He brought it down fast, slicing Hunk's ear cleanly from his head.

The ear dropped to the ground, and Hunk followed it, screaming. "*Fiul dacă o căţea!*"

Colby walked easily back to Smythe, wiping the blade clean, folding the ear into his monogrammed handkerchief.

Smythe said, "Now, that's a Cheshire grin," then barked, "Get him taken care of!"

Colby said, "He struck me, which was a mistake, but he can still hear to take orders. I was precise."

Fire Riders pulled Hunk away, dragging him to the med tent in the corner of the yard. Hunk tossed them aside like rats in the well bucket, but more tackled him. Brought him down. One Rider calmed him with two whacks of an axe handle. The doc had a drink then started sewing him up.

Smythe slapped Colby on the back. "Right. You've had your treat for the evening."

"My head's clearer. When do I see your Mr. Bishop, the one with both his arms?"

Smythe spit a laugh, dragged to the cells. "Tomorrow. We're waiting for a word from a man inside."

Hunk's voice was blasting from the med tent, "*Am de gând să te omoare, banditule!*"

Colby said, "Never been called a bastard in Romanian

before. I was afraid my language skills were getting rusty, but Hunk's given me some good practice."

"Get some sleep, mate."

"Oh, like a baby."

The room was at the end of a narrow passage that laced the top tier of the prison's main structure. Colby followed it to the last door, marked FILE ROOM, and went in, shouldering his Navajo-wrapped arsenal.

He put the arsenal at the foot of the small bed that still had some spring and didn't seem ticky. Wooden cabinets, labeled PRISONER DEATHS, and ATTEMPTED ESCAPES had been pushed to the walls, making room for a small table with a pitcher, bowl, and towel.

Colby daubed the last few hours out of his eyes with the moist towel, before opening the file folder that had been left resting on his pillow. The first page was a wedding photo of John and Amaryllis Bishop, each one smiling wider than the other. The sepia had begun to turn and was spotting the image with brown, like dried blood sprayed across the bride's dress.

Colby daubed his eyes again, thinking aloud. "The good doctor with two arms."

Rose loosened the wrappings over Maynard's wounds, the blood on the sterilized cotton having dried in a starry pattern and stuck to the gauze bandage around it. Bishop moved the cotton several inches, centering it on the wounds. "Keep the pressure on the bleeding point, there."

Maynard looked up at Bishop, sniffed agreement. "I've had it worse. Think they hit slugs that were already inside me." He let his eyes drift before snoring.

Chisum's other men lay stretched out on their bunks, bandages around arms and chests. Legs elevated, a head completely wrapped. The ones who were awake got a few shots as Garrett went from bed to bed, pouring Chisum's bourbon.

Rose said, "This feel like an infirmary to you, Doc?"

Bishop straightened. "One of the better ones. Chisum's doctor did a good job."

"He said the same thing about you."

"Make sure they tend to their dressings, but that's good stitching. He layered the wounds." He said to the room, "You're all going to heal up just fine." He looked back at Rose. "And you're a good nurse."

Still in her denims and bloodstained shirt, she bobbed her thanks, then laughed. "I didn't have much choice."

Garrett said, "What about your supper?"

One of Chisum's older men grabbed coffee from the stove, poured her a cup. "She ain't had time to eat, been too busy helpin' us! Garrett, you sit at the big table now, tell me how many we're gonna bury before this mess is done. I served the Union, came on to Chisum's to cowpunch, that's it."

"Hell if I know," Garrett passed the cup to Rose. "That's why Doctor Bishop's with us. Help with the peace."

The old fellow said, "Can't come too soon for me. I don't like getting shot."

Bishop moved to the bed where the shotgun rig, a blanket, and some necessaries had been put. "Still not sure what I'm supposed to do."

"That don't sound like much of a promise."

Garrett said, "He's with us."

Bishop held back his answer for a beat.

Rose stepped in, "Let the man get some rest. Hell, we could all use it."

The old fella said, "I just need me some more Chisum bourbon."

Rose smiled. "That, too."

Bishop started for the back door, all eyes on him. Garrett almost made a move, but poured shots instead, holding the bottle to the light before tipping it, a holdover from his bartending days. He saved the heel of the bottle for himself and drank, watching Rose follow Bishop into the dark, dutifully carrying his medical bag.

"Hurricane's Mr. Chisum's top horse." Linus brought the chestnut out from the end stall. She was more than twelve hands high, with perfect ears and a white diamond between her eyes.

Farrow pointed to a scrolled saddle hanging in the tack room.

Linus tied Hurricane. "He never said nothing about his best horse or one of his best saddles."

Farrow crowned his felt hat with the side of his hand. "I'm on a special mission for Mr. Chisum. It'll be just fine."

Linus laid a clean blanket across Hurricane's back. "It ain't that I don't trust what you're saying, Mr. Farrow, but lots of smiths tried for this job."

Farrow slid fifty neatly folded dollars into the pocket of Linus's leather apron. "I've got a ways to go tonight."

Linus smiled. "And you're just now out of the barn."

Farrow took out a silver money clip straining with bills and held it out.

Linus glanced. "You can travel without cash?"

"There's something waiting for me on the other end." Farrow's hand didn't move.

Linus secured the saddle straps on Hurricane and grabbed the clip without another word.

Bishop found a place beyond the light-throw from the bunkhouses, and laid out his blanket. He set the shotgun rig in some grass and settled.

Rose put the med bag next to him. "They think you're heading for the barn. Don't get up." She sat, tucking her knees against her chest. "Just so you know, if you did take off, I wouldn't blame you."

"That doesn't go for the others. Especially Garrett."

"He's working his way up. Mr. Chisum found him. He was a stick man behind a bar. Now he's eating at the big table, with you. You didn't work your way up around here. You didn't have to."

Bishop said, "Chisum bought me out of a jail cell."

"We know all about it. You're all they could talk about for the last week."

"You know why?"

Rose looked at him. "Because you're the shotgun man. The avenger. You're in the papers. They think that'll scare off folks who want to raid our cattle."

"I'd never think of myself that way, and Chisum knows it."

"Mr. Chisum has a way of turning things in his direction."

"That what happened with you?"

Rose picked up a piece of grass, chewed before voicing her thoughts. "I've been around since the Pecos. Things happen, you stick to what you're good at. I know horses and cattle, and can shoot all right."

"That doesn't mean you're caught up in someone else's land war."

"Actually, it does." Rose watched Bishop untangle the straps of the rig, lay them straight on the blanket, then said, "Today gives us some history, so I'm going to be a little forward."

Bishop folded his sleeve around his half-arm. "I think I was, a little, so be my guest."

"I know something's going to bring you into this fight all the way. I ain't sure what it is, but you've got skin in this game."

"That might not be the right way to put it."

Rose laughed. "All right. See, you wouldn't guess from the way I present myself, but my woman's intuition is pretty good."

"You present yourself just fine."

Rose whistled through the blade of grass then tossed it. "Really? Don't want to bunk inside? That wind over the flats can bite."

"I've had a lot of inside lately. This'll suit me."

Rose stood, dusting her britches. "You know what's best for you."

Bishop stood too, offering his hand. They turned as the man in the tall hat rode full-out for the main gate. They watched Farrow and Hurricane for a few moments, fast-moving shapes outlined by moonlight, then Rose walked toward the collection of barns and service houses. Bishop lay back on the blanket, finally getting some peace behind his eyes.

CHAPTER TEN
Plans for Dying

The skull shattered with John Bishop's hard landing, teeth erupting from its jaw, falling back on him like rain as he hit the bottom of the pit. He rolled to one side, feeling the mountain of bone and shreds of hardened flesh powder under his weight, shifting like a sinkhole of sand, giving way. Swallowing.

His wife and son were beside him on the pile, just brittle remains—tufts of hair, eyeless sockets, faces locked in silent screams.

He heard the sound of pistols cocking, and instinctively tried to protect his family, cradling them as bullets ripped him from above. Slugs tore his back and neck, a geyser of blood spraying Amaryllis's dried skin.

He brought the shotgun rig, slick with his own blood, up from his side and fired both barrels at the figure dressed in a flame-crimson robe. Looking down at him from the edge of the pit, he held a smoking gun in each hand. The shotgun blasts hit the figure in the chest, but didn't kill. Somehow, he stood. Strong. Ignoring the massive wound, taking a step closer to the edge.

Letting Bishop see his face.

See himself . . . John Bishop . . . dressed as a Fire Rider.

He curtained his eyes with his palm, denying what he'd just seen, and sat up. Taking two shells from the bandolier, he slid them into the rig as his stronger self stood above him. With two good arms and two good hands, the image looked down into the death pit, defying one-armed Dr. Bishop to do something.

A blast from the shotgun was meaningless.

Bishop wrist-snapped the rig closed and lurched forward, trying to aim over the piles of bones to blow away the man with his face.

Just destroy the face.

Bishop's mirror image steadied his pistols and said, "You're where you should be, Johnny. Dead. With your family. Actually, you're obliged to me."

Bishop made the move to pull both triggers.

The barrel flames and the roar of the pistols came first, slug-punching Bishop backwards, deeper into the pit, more bullets hitting him as he fell.

Falling, he managed to pull the triggers, firing into the darkness. Into nothing.

Still falling.

"They killed 'em all!"

The voice barely made it through. Vibrations from the gravel wagon kicked Bishop in the head, waking him, bolting him to his feet. He cleared his eyes of the dream as the driver ran the horse team hard toward the gravel turnaround in front of Chisum's house.

He yelled again. The alarm bell rang.

Men and riders broke from the bunkhouses, pulling on jackets and boots, shouting to each other to meet the wagon. A few had torches, streaking the sky before the sun broke.

Bishop called out, "Garrett!"

Pat Garrett slowed his horse and tossed him a canteen.

"Get the sleep out of your throat. Chisum will want you to see this."

"What's going on?"

Garrett threw away the word: "Massacre."

Rose ran from the small hut behind the barn, Claude Ray limping beside her, trying to hold her back. He grabbed for her arms, a piece of her blouse. She twisted off, leaping onto the back of the wagon as it jack-tailed to a stop.

Garrett and Bishop rode up just as Rose yanked back the canvas covering the bodies, twisted on top of each other. She pushed an old man's corpse aside to find what was left of the towheaded kid who knew how to ride and rope.

Bishop was down from Garrett's horse when Rose screamed.

It came from someplace deep inside as she tumbled to the ground, spitting up air and coffee. She jumped on the first empty horse she could grab and broke it into a run toward the hills.

John Chisum stepped onto the porch, buttoning his shirt as the other men crowded about the heap of bodies in the wagon. Above it all, the younger maid watched from Chisum's bedroom window, the curtains breezing around her as she brushed her hair. And listened.

Chisum demanded, "Where'd you find them?"

The wagon driver already had a flask in his hands. "One of the Arkansas fingers, scattered on the riverbank. Animals got to a few, but I knew 'em by their clothes. Didn't look to me that none even got to draw a weapon."

Bishop turned the bodies over. Half-faces were frozen in surprise, with a bullet hole just above or below an eye socket. The backs of their heads were nothing but hair matted over gaping exit wounds.

Garrett said, "Army sniper. I'd lay money. That's not chicken shooting."

Chisum said, "We captured one of the Fire Riders,

and they killed their own rather than have him talk. Just a boy."

Claude Ray hung on the side of the gravel wagon, looking down at what'd been left of Rose's nephew. "Rose kept hoping he'd make it back, maybe stay on. She prayed for it. Really prayed."

Chisum said, "These are the kind we're dealing with, Dr. Bishop."

Bishop was thinking of his son. "I know."

"Get them buried, and place a marker so Rose can find him when she comes back."

Claude Ray said, "She's not safe out there alone."

Bishop said, "Let her ride it out."

"Sound advice." Chisum moved to the railing, leaning forward. "I want every man—"

"You ask some of these men to mount a horse, their wounds will open, they'll be dead in an hour," Bishop interrupted. "They shouldn't even be out of bed."

Leaning on a rifle butt, Maynard said, "I got business to finish with these bastards, and I'm gonna finish it!"

Chisum said, "Only the able-bodied will have a part in our response, so get yourselves ready. Maynard, I wouldn't try to stop you. What about you, Doctor? Are you included in this?"

Bishop looked back at his bedroll, with shotgun rig and medical bag beside it, then to the bodies. "I am."

The young maid watched the men scramble before turning from the open window, and picking up her dress from the floor beside Chisum's bed. She stepped into it, ready to serve breakfast.

The blood on Colby's handkerchief was darker than before, and there was more of it. He seized again, gulping air, then spit tar-red across his own monogram when someone pounded on his door.

He didn't have a chance to answer before a little girl,

strings of black hair over a mean face, pushed the door open with her foot. Her head was too large, and one shoulder was weighted by an oversized carpet purse. She lurched into the room, wobbling a tray with one glass of buttermilk and a single piece of dry toast. "This is your'n. My arm's going."

Colby took the tray, and April Showers moved to the bed where his Navajo cache was unrolled, and all the weapons laid out. He put his breakfast on top of one of the cabinets, watching her.

She seemed to sniff at the blanket before touching the leather-pocketed corners that held sets of custom-made knives. She played their edges with her fingertips then looked up at him. "That's all you want for break-fast?"

Colby wiped a string of blood from the corner of his mouth, drank the stomach-soothing buttermilk. "It's more than sufficient."

"I don't know what that means. I swept this room out three times 'cause Mr. Bishop said it weren't clean enough for you."

"You did a fine job. Thank you."

The little girl examined the rest of the armory—the barrels of the rifles and pistols wrapped and cushioned, the ammunition, telescopic sights, special attachments beside them. She picked up a Colt short with a cus-tomized Beretta barrel. "You use all these guns?"

Colby unwrapped April from the pistol. "Not all at once."

"You don't have to talk at me like I don't know noth-ing. My dad's Tomlinson. You're the special killer."

Colby froze his smile and didn't answer. "I saw a little blond girl last night. Your sister?"

"Yeah. Not even a year older, so we got to do our birthdays on the same day. That's a cheat."

"She can sing."

"Like a dying frog. I'm better. Much."

"You'll have to favor me with a concert sometime."

April Showers squinted at Colby, trying to figure. "You got all them special guns and knives, but you talk like an old lady. Don't make sense."

Colby finished the buttermilk. "Your father, where is he this morning?"

"I ain't supposed to take you there. You're to see Mr. Bishop. Your eyes is yellow like my cat's, right before she died."

They'd moved into the hallway. Holding his new target file, Colby pulled the door behind him. "No key for the lock, but I'm positive everyone here is trustworthy."

"There's that lady talk again."

April Showers was already down the small, stone access way that led from the old prison offices to the cells, the too-big purse swaying from her shoulder. She slipped the knife she'd stolen from Colby's cache into a pocket. "You got something else besides them guns? Money? Or maybe pretty earrings you took off somebody's grandma?"

"You ask interesting questions."

"And you special-kill people."

Colby let the echo of their voices drop off against the stone, but didn't respond.

She said, "Everyone here's a thief, and they all shot somebody, or done some stabbing. Not as much as you, but they got their own business, so don't pay no attention to me. That's how come I know everything about this place."

"I think not paying attention to you is a vital mistake."

"I do what I want, except when I got the heavy lungs. See this here?" April opened the purse, took out a celluloid breathing mask attached to a small, leathered box by a length of rubber tubing. She held it over her face. "Keep it filled with ice. Makes me take air when I can't."

"I've never seen anything like it."

She took the mask off, wrinkled her snout. "Crazy

doctor with one arm made it, and give it to me. He didn't even know me, but that's what he did. I'll always recall that."

Colby said, "Sounds like a grown-up worth knowing."

"I heard you. Ought to get him to make you one."

The access way turned into an open landing where fire-damaged paintings of the previous wardens galleried the walls. Traces of black powder and soot laced the about-to-collapse ceiling.

"These here are the men what kept everybody prisoner in this hellhole."

"You know, my son doesn't use language like that."

Beyond the portraits was a heavily armored door that she hit with tiny fists. "Then he ain't in the real world." She hit the door again. "Fancy don't mean nothing. The last warden put all this up to fool everybody. It's all about foolin' people so you can pull it off behind their backs."

Colby said "How old are you, truly?"

"Don't get no ideas." April kicked the door twice and a bolt was thrown from the opposite side.

Hunk's punch was hard. He pulled back, then landed his knuckles into the shaved man's jaw again, like firing two rapid shots from a revolver.

Colby judged from the blood spray across Shaved Head's skull that he'd already taken at least three hits, maybe four. Hunk half-stepped back, lowered himself, then laid into Shaved's side, his ribs snapping beneath the skin.

April Showers squeezed Colby's arm with excitement. Shaved Head collapsed, begging for mercy as his knees folded together.

But no one could hear his voice over the cheers and hoots of the Fire Riders in the arena that was the prison's old common area. Two tiers of cells stacked like iron cages were built in a semicircle with a catwalk running their length and iron stairs joining them. Fire-twisted, but with crude repairs, they were now barracks, not jail cells.

In the center of the commons were the old wooden chow tables and a whipping post from the War. The Riders stood on the tables, rifle and grenade crates, surrounding Hunk and Shaved Head, thundering with each punch. Laying bets on the survivor.

Smythe crutched himself through the crowd, his voice topping everything. "All right, ladies, you're missing the point! This is training. It's not Saturday night at the bloody Palladium!"

Hunk was about to make another move, but Smythe put up his hand. "In the cells! Drag-ass down here for a lesson!"

Colby looked up to the second tier of the block and watched Riders peel out of the bunks in their cells, putting down guitars and letters, wandering down from the catwalks and old guard stations. They'd afforded themselves some creature comforts, all stolen, making each cell their own. One watched from his rocking chair, enjoying a pipe.

April Showers pushed around Colby, perching on top of the whipping post as Smythe shouted, "A man what steals from his own brigade is no man! Not under my command!"

The crowd circle tightened.

Hunk wrapped one hand with a thin, metal cord used to secure ship's canvas to decking, then looked to Smythe, who gave the nod. Two Riders lifted Shaved Head by the shoulders, and Hunk held up his chin, before pulverizing his jaw with the wrapped fist.

Hunk looked directly at Colby when he hammered the blow, then another, pulping Shaved Head's face to nothing.

Smythe said, "All right, a little too far, but you'll remember this—when you steal, it's for the brigade! Kill? For the brigade! Got it, boy-o?"

Shaved Head rolled over onto his back, eyes blistered shut, teeth tearing through his lower lip, grabbing that last gulp of air, and then—done.

April shrieked, the crowd cheered again, a few singing Romania's anthem "*Hora Unirii.*" Hunk grabbed a towel to dry himself off, careful around his missing ear.

April tried to sing along, but couldn't. "I don't know them words."

Hunk never broke his look at Colby.

"You really do keep yourself in check. I'd heard that."

Colby turned to see Devlin Bishop standing behind him, sporting a pressed shirt, pants, and manner.

Dev took Colby's hand to shake it, guiding him away from the crowd, as Shaved Head was dragged off, leaving a wide smear of blood across the floor. Others got out of the way of the corpse and settled their bets.

Smythe barked, "School's out, ladies! Time to pay up!"

Dev said, "Little reminders like this are important for the men. Keeps them on their toes."

"He rode in with us, seemed like a decent enough sentry. How much did he appropriate?"

"Does it matter?"

Colby said, "I get it. It's the act, not the amount."

Dev smiled. "I'm going to recall that."

Hunk threw his towel, and April Showers caught it, the smell stinging her eyes. She pulled the mask from her purse, covered her mouth and nose, and turned the crank on the small device, letting the cool, new oxygen fill her, while fixing her eyes on Colby and Dev Bishop.

Colby held up the target file. "This made for interesting reading."

Dev said, "As long as you can do something about it. Watch yourself."

Colby quickstepped to one side as a trapdoor lifted from a section of stone floor in front of him. Dev grabbed hold of an iron ring attached to the door and hefted it back. The telegraph operator scrambled the last of the steps from the solitary cells below.

Dev held out his hand. "The information?"

The operator held out a length of yellow telegraph tape, eyes blinking in the morning light. "Yes, sir, with date and time, just like you said."

Colby asked, "Good news from the belly of the beast?"

Dev Bishop regarded him. "It's why you're here."

April Showers watched as Colby and Bishop vanished behind an always-locked door on the far side of the old cellblock, with Smythe hauling himself after. She touched the stolen knife in her pocket and smiled under her oxygen mask.

John Bishop ran his hand down the bay's neck, stroking its length as he walked him from a stall. The horse was rested, well-tended.

Outside the corral, Bishop threw a leg over his back and pulled himself up with his left arm. Chisum men lined up by the ammo shed next to the stables, getting new stores of ammunition and extra guns.

Maynard stood unsteadily at the end of the line, his wounds wetting his bandages, but loosing a war whoop when Chisum and Garrett rode up.

Chisum said, "Men, I'm damn proud of each of you. You don't have to worry about your families or your pay. I'm doubling it."

A cowhand said, "My salary goes to my wife and kids. That's why I'm doing this."

The crowd agreed and Maynard broke through. "Hell, I'm doing this to get another crack at those red-hoods!"

Chisum said, "I guarantee you'll get both! Dr. Bishop, would you take a ride? Let me show you what we're fighting for, and how we'll win."

Bishop angled over to Chisum, who led his men away from the ranch.

The grassland was an open stretch, protected on all sides by sloping hills creating a small valley. Four hundred head of Angus cattle were scattered between the hills, either grazing easy on sweetgrass or settled by the small bent of a running stream. Cowboys with rifles poised rode the loose edge of the herd.

With Garrett and Bishop beside him, Chisum heeled his horse to a crest above the valley. The horse stepped too close to some brush hiding a flock of prairie chickens, and the birds broke wild, cawing loudly as they flew away.

Two cowboys heard the noise, looked up from their position at the far end of the grazing basin, saw the three men on the hilltop, and went rifle-to-shoulder before Chisum signaled them with a wave of his hat.

Chisum said, "Right now they'd take a shot at anybody riding up."

Garrett said, "They're better than that, sir, but they're damn nervous."

Chisum lit his briar pipe. "With good reason. That's prime stock, birthed, raised and nurtured here. My stock, my sea of grass."

Bishop said, "It's a beautiful picture."

Blue smoke drifted from Chisum's mouth as he spoke. "Except for some scrub herds, about all I have left. Patrick, you've a map in your saddlebag."

Garrett unfolded the map onto his lap. It detailed the Goodnight-Loving cattle trails from Texas to Montana, and had eleven red slashes scattered over three states.

Chisum said, "Each mark means men and stock lost to the Fire Riders. Men buried, cattle stolen."

Bishop leaned from his horse to look. "How much has it cost you?"

"Well over a million dollars, Doctor. But my men?" Chisum pointed to the cowboys, "Just working for wages, but I know the name of everyone that died and take care of their families."

Bishop said, "They can't fight a trained army."

"I won't dignify those terrorists by calling them an army, but you're dead right. Cowhands don't stand a chance."

Garrett said, "Before we move out, Mr. Chisum, why not request a cavalry escort? You've got the contract for the government beef. When the Riders attack, the soldiers can mow 'em down. Job's done."

Chisum said, "Fire Riders have spies, Patrick. One word leaves this ranch, and they'll know what we're doing before we do. See a patrol, and the Riders'll never come close until the soldiers move on. Then they'll wipe us out. We've got to go it alone." He nodded to Bishop. "That's how the good doctor took them on."

Bishop said, "You keep saying that. I barely got through it alive."

"But you did, and left a pile of their dead behind." Chisum put another match to his pipe. "We're forcing the enemy's hand by moving those four hundred up the northern trail to a cow town set off the main. Called Myrtle."

Garrett said, "Beg pardon, sir, but why're we headed to Myrtle? It's little more than a hole for a dog to pee in. Why not push into Colorado?"

"Because it is just a hole, and it'll lure the bastards in. They'll think we're just stopping over."

Bishop said, "You're sure the Riders will try?"

Chisum took the briar from his mouth and tamped the bowl. "I trust history. They've been targeting my smaller herds with less men. They leave no survivors and take every animal."

Garrett said, "And they've always come in at night."

Chisum said, "It's two days on the trail, but you've got

to reach Myrtle by sunrise to give yourselves a full day to set up for a raid. Let them think we're drinking, whoring, and sleeping. Anything but ready."

Garrett half-agreed with him, "They'll get a surprise . . . I hope."

"Patrick, it's your reconnaissance, your decisions on who goes where. You've got the pen, a barn, and hotel for cover."

"There are a couple new men, supposed to be pretty handy, taking the place of the ones we lost."

Chisum said, "Mr. Tunstall's volunteered a few guns as well. " He turned to Bishop. "They're going to hit us hard, and anything you can tell Patrick will help bring our victory. Defeat's not an option."

Bishop said, "My old captain used to say the same thing before every battle, and he lost a few. I know you've got a lot at stake, but so do we all."

Chisum's eyes were back on the spread before them. "We've got to make this a safe country again."

Bishop's half-arm jerked in its sleeve. "You're welcome to anything I can remember, as long as we all agree I'm here on my own business."

"You're riding out with us, Doctor. That's all that matters." Chisum turned his horse and started down the slope to the herd.

Garrett watched the cattleman break toward his animals before sidling to Bishop. "You were on the fence last night. What changed?"

"You put any stock in dreams, Garrett?"

"You mean what the Navvies and Cheyenne preach?"

Bishop gave it a moment, then nodded. "Something like that."

"Can't speak for anyone else"—Garrett turned his horse—"but I'm not a damn fool."

* * *

Devlin Bishop sat at the warden's high desk. A large chart behind him showed the Fire Rider raids across three states, each one marked in red. Smythe got himself into a chair, pulling his legs out of the way for Colby.

Dev opened the target file. "Mr. Colby, everything's here that you need?"

"More. I'd seen most of the newspaper stuff before. Your brother's a rather famous man."

Smythe snorted. "That's the damned wrong thing to say, boy-o."

Dev said, "You're not wrong, Mr. Colby. John's gained some infamy, that's for true."

"You tried to have him killed and failed. His revenge quest has captured a certain, shall we say, public spirit? The man with the .12-gauge arm, perfect for the penny dreadfuls."

"If you're going for some kind of laugh here, I'm not getting it."

Colby said, "I just want you to understand that special circumstances like your brother require special compensation."

Dev was smiling. "Hell, I knew that before you did."

A quiet tapping on the door brought Tomlinson in, his steps not making a sound. He placed a sheaf of papers on the desk, straightened them, then inched away, folding his hands together.

Dev nodded. "You know Mr. Tomlinson."

Colby extended a hand to shake with a flourish. "Indeed I do. Still favor the Marlin Standard? I've also had the distinct experience of meeting your young daughters."

Smythe killed the laugh up from his belly.

Dev tapped the folder. "Mr. Tomlinson calls this your retainer. There might be a lot of work coming up, and I don't want to have to chase you down."

"I've always made myself available when I can."

"Always with a new price. Instead, you're going to be regular pay, maybe not as high as you'd like, but steady."

Dev stood, revealing a bullet hole in the center of the chair. He poked it with his index finger. "You know it's the only time I've ever purposely taken a life? Slug passed right through Warden Hog. He didn't even blink. I knew, if I was going to sit here, I'd have to claim it as my own."

Colby said, "A coup?"

Smythe said, "You ain't far off, boy-o."

Dev sat on the edge of the desk, arms folded, looking down at Colby. "I was in solitary for four years with a man who knew history. My schooling's spotty, but I can listen. He taught me what the ones he called 'Empire Builders' did. In Rome, Greece, places like that. When he wasn't fever-crazy, he made a lot of sense."

Smythe said, "In the Indian Nation, all the way to California, there's almost no law. There aren't enough men to back it up."

Dev looked at the map. "The law will come with the people, but if we're there first, they'll have to pay to be safe, to not be robbed. To stay alive."

Smythe said, "Oh, and they will."

Colby said, "That's a fine, old business practice. You learned a lot from your cellmate. I'd say you're well on your way."

"Right now's the time to figure out if you're going to be a part of it."

Tomlinson added a meek, "It does offer security, Mr. Colby."

Colby picked up the contract. "I haven't said no, but I do have a condition. Payments aren't to be made to me, but put in a trust account for my son. When that's arranged, we'll visit this again."

Dev looked to Tomlinson. "Get it done." To Colby he asked, "Well?"

"You have a time and place?"

"My brother will be riding with a herd of Chisum cattle up the northern trail to a small depot. Mr. Chisum's been a great source of income for us."

Smythe said, "Aye, but you can only hit a man so many times, then you ruin him for the future."

Colby said, "Protecting future investments. That's wise."

"Chisum and I came to terms."

"He turns your brother over, and you allow him to get back to his cattle business?"

Dev retook the warden's chair. "Forget turn over. My brother's got my blood in his eye. He needs putting down."

Smythe said, "Aye, the mad-dog kill."

Dev handed the target file back to Colby, who flipped to the last pages, stopping at a fading, glued-together photograph of the Bishop brothers. John, about ten, his brother a few years older, standing together, with hair and collars slicked, and grinning wide. Dev's hand was on John's shoulder, which is where the photograph had been cut in half.

"My father had that done, figuring it would please our mother. She's the one who cut it, but Pa sent me that piece during my last stretch."

"When you were condemned to death?"

Dev frowned. "I changed them plans."

"And so you did. In the next days, we'll right the family wrongs. Are the descriptions of the special shotgun accurate?"

Smythe said, "That came from me. I saw it up close and lived to tell the tale."

"It'll make a fine addition to my collection."

The buffalo hide had just enough give for the shears to cut through. It was an older piece, curling at the edges, but Linus worked through them, cutting it into a triangle, then fastening it to a pony-sized bridle strap.

He looked up from his craft at John Bishop, who was leaning against the workbench, affixing springs to either side of the shotgun support pieces.

Linus said, "I did the best I could to curl that wire tight. You sure those are small enough?"

Bishop screwed the springs down between the metal sections that bent at his elbow and supported the gun barrels along the arm extension, making a shock absorber. He gave the left side one last turn. "Fine job."

"That should take up some of that kick."

"And kick it does, like a blind Missouri mule."

Linus laughed, holding up the buffalo hide. "This'll go around your elbow so you can brace it without plowing backwards whenever you shoot."

"You're good at what you do, Linus."

"I don't get to work on things like this. Usually, I'm just shoeing the horses, the few we got left anyway. I'm not bellyaching"—Linus held up the completed elbow brace—"but this was a hill to climb. I like to test what I can do."

"You did right well."

"A fix up isn't the same as starting from scratch. The man who made this rig knew what he was about."

Bishop gave it a moment, then said, "Yes, he knew about weapons." He steadied himself as the blacksmith secured the shotgun rig's straps across his shoulders. Bishop adjusted the gun's soft-lined arm-cup around his right elbow joint, finding comfort, as Linus threaded the chain from the triggers to the small silver ring that anchored it to his left side.

Linus said, "Give it some slack."

Bishop held out his arm as if being fitted for a Sunday suit, and Linus cut two links from the chain, then used pliers to twist it back together. Bishop lowered his arm, the trigger line pulling exactly as it was supposed to.

Linus slipped the elbow pad onto Bishop's arm, then fastened the small strap. "Between this pad and those springs, that mule kick should be a kiss in the dark."

Bishop stepped away from the table, cocking his arm, the shotgun snapping into place.

Linus stood back to admire the whole apparatus. "That's quite a rig, and now it's Mr. Chisum's."

Bishop shook his head. "No matter what happens on this drive, what I'm doing isn't for sale."

"Glad to hear it. He's a good man, but he owns everything. I'd like to breathe somebody's else's air for a while, but I know I probably never will."

Bishop slipped on his shirt.

Linus helped with the buttons. "You do need two hands, Doc."

Bishop studied Linus's face. "Who's the Apache, your mother or your father?"

Linus handed Bishop his beaver pelt bandolier. "My mother is Jicarilla. Chisum lets her have her own place two miles down the road. Most take me for Mex."

Bishop took the bandolier lace in his teeth, tied it off like a bandage with his left, before filling it with shells. "Reach my medical bag."

From the bag on the workbench, Linus took out a folded sheet of paper laying on top of the instruments.

Bishop slipped the last shotgun shells into the bandolier sleeve, nodded at the paper. "Can you make that? I figured it out this morning, but my writing's pure chicken scratch."

Linus laid the paper flat and smiled. "No worries. I'm schooled to read." He studied the drawing and the dimensions on the page. "Uh-huh. I can do this, and it'll be a good job, too."

"No doubt."

Linus regarded the plans. "Doc, that gun, that was your idea? Like this here?"

"It was in my mind, and I got the right man to build it. He had two hands."

"Funny. We're rigging you with this double-barrel, then you give me this to build. You're really two different kinds, ain't you?"

Bishop said, "Like being half Apache?"

Linus didn't disagree.

Bishop brought his shoulders together. He felt the chain working in concert with the straps, become taut, and set to pull the triggers. All in one motion.

Linus inched the medical bag toward him. "Doc, looks like you're all set."

Colby had a bolt-action rifle in his hand when the fire erupted again in the back of his throat, choking him. He grabbed hold of the foot of the bed, spit bloody strings into the washbasin, gulped water from a pitcher, then spit again.

"Try this here." April Showers held out her breathing mask.

Colby took it, placing it on his face as he'd seen her do. She cranked the small handle on the device, circulating cool, oxygenated air through the rubber tubing to the mask, easing the coughing. He lay the rifle on the bed and sat at its foot, holding the mask over his mouth and nose as the little girl continued working the machine.

"Helps a lot, don't it? You don't have to say nothing, because you can't. I know."

A moment later, Colby wiped the corners of his mouth with his stained handkerchief, gulping his words. "You came just in time. You're right. That's a marvelous thing."

"Yeah, works good for me. I wanted to see what kind of gun you was going to take."

Colby stood. "Child, the less you know, the better." He splashed water on his face.

"You people always say things like that, like I ain't old enough. I saw the beating. And didn't I just save your hide?"

"Not exactly."

Colby dried his face, the spell over. He was tall and intimidating as he regarded the little girl with the disastrous face. "You're not the type I normally do business with, but I'll trade you. Five minutes on your machine, for the knife you took this morning."

April squinted, wrinkled her snout. "Won't tell nobody I got it?"

"If you don't reveal that I needed that mask."

April shrugged. "Not sure what that means, but I'll keep your secret, if I get to keep the blade."

Colby said, "Just use it with discretion."

Linus turned the iron plating in the coal scuttle with a pair of long tongs, heating the tip of the iron, then pounding the end to a thin, flat point. He cooled it in a metal wash kettle full of water.

Steam rose as Chisum rode into the stable and got down from his horse. "Did you see Dr. Bishop?"

Linus put the thin, iron plate back in the scuttle, heating the tip to refine its shape, then took the horse's reins. "Yes, sir. The doctor's ready for the drive."

"Good." Chisum glanced into the largest stall. "Where's Hurricane?"

Linus relieved the horse of its saddle. "Mr. Farrow's still got him."

"Let me know when they return. That's a fine horse, though. Fine ride."

"He's one of yours."

Chisum stepped out of the stable's back door, walking to the house, where the young maid waited for him by the kitchen. He didn't say a word, but placed his hand on her belly before going inside.

* * *

Blinded again by tears, Rose pushed through her rage, keeping her horse running full-out. The animal broke hard through the tall grass, finding the road to the Lincoln train station, and followed it by instinct.

They came in fast, and she twisted the reins, pulling the mare back. Her eyes were soaking, but she hadn't intended to end up there. Rose wanted someplace else. A clearing. The edge of a brook. But it is where the horse had brought her. Stopping short. Snorting.

"It's all right," she said, patting his neck. She rode along the trail from the road to the loading platform, before pulling up. Two men from the ranch loaded a coffin from a wagon to a boxcar. A name was written on the coffin lid in chalk, and she recognized it as one of those killed in the massacre the day before.

Rose turned the horse toward a stretch of grass on the other side of the street, swung off the mare without hitching it, and settled on a park bench that had been dedicated to John Chisum by the town council. Arms tight across herself, Rose rocked back and forth, saying something only she could hear.

Hurricane nickered, and Rose looked up. Chisum's best mount was tethered to the only rail across the street. She stood and walked to the horse.

Farrow watched through the window of the small café directly opposite the train station. Rose ran her hands across Hurricane's back, finding the Chisum brand before kissing him on the nose. His lips curled back, and she fed him an apple core she had in her shirt pocket.

Virgil Chaney was at the small table, too, as were a sarsaparilla, still foaming, a short whiskey, and three boxes of Havana cigars. He examined the contents of an envelope, counting the money inside. Satisfied with the total, he looked at Farrow, who was still staring into the street.

"Something's truly captured your attention."

Farrow said without turning his head, "Just a minor annoyance outside."

"Worth a picture?"

"Hardly."

Chaney held the envelope just out of reach. "You're guaranteeing that Bishop's riding out with Chisum's men?"

Farrow faced him. "I've been working to make this happen for months. He's going. All the directions, everything I gave you, are accurate."

Chaney handed over the cash, smoothed his lapels. "You do very well for yourself, Mr. Farrow."

Farrow slipped it in his jacket without looking inside. "You know, I actually like Dr. Bishop, but his death has presented a number of opportunities."

While tapping the camera case on the chair next to him, Chaney said, "I don't want to kill him per se, but it's imperative that I witness it."

Farrow looked back into the street to see that Rose had ridden off then turned to Chaney. "And you will. Just don't forget to give proper attention to the entire event. The massacre will be newsworthy."

"Sir, above all else, I am a journalist."

CHAPTER ELEVEN
Riding Hurt

"That thing won't go off, will it?"

Bishop was on the edge of a low-slung cot, the shotgun locked by his side, as he checked Maynard's dressing. "Not if I don't want it to. One of you put some antiseptic on this cotton, will you?"

A cowhand with a bandage swathing half his face dripped pine tar syrup onto the cotton ball Bishop was holding. He wiped the dried blood from Maynard's stitching and the swelling around it. "Wrap it again, but tighter this time. He needs the pressure."

Maynard bent forward, pain gut-punching him as the cowhand relaced the bandage. Bishop put his supplies back into the med kit and tossed a roll of gauze to an injured drover on a far bed, who caught it.

Maynard winced. "You say I can't go on this drive, that Chisum won't allow it. But that'd be a damn fool thing to do. I been in on this war since the start."

"Oh, going to see it through?"

"I don't know what your stake is"—Maynard shifted,

pain from the gun wound slicing him—"but I don't leave no fight unfinished."

Bishop snapped the med kit shut. "What if I said you weren't in any condition to finish it?"

"Then I'd kill ya."

A cowboy said, "Hell, Maynard, you wouldn't even be here except the doctor dragged your worthless ass out of that field!"

Maynard said to the cowboys in the bunkhouse, "I know he done a good thing, but now he's got to do another by not gettin' in my way!"

Bishop stood, the rest of the house watching from beds and corners, waiting for the shotgun to snap upward, taking a firing stance. It stayed locked. "A lot of these men need time to heal, but I can't truly stop anybody."

Maynard grinned. "Especially me?"

"I wouldn't even try. You're strong as an ox, twice as stupid. A few hours on a horse, and those stitches start coming apart? You might be in for a surprise."

"If I'm on that horse, I'll take care of the rest."

Rose's kiss was brief, just brushing Claude Ray's cheek, before she opened the corral gate and brought out her brown and white stallion. He supported himself on the fence, watching her tie down her bedroll and a Winchester scabbard.

She had washed and changed clothes, but seemed more exhausted than before, her eyes and mouth permanently down.

Claude Ray said, "Honey, this is all going to be taken care of, but you've been real lucky, so far. Those fence-cutters? You could have gotten really hurt."

Rose checked her mount's new shoes, and Claude Ray tried again. "We owe Mr. Chisum, but this ain't like it was before. How many did we lose yesterday? You won't have a third of the men we had at the Pecos."

He took a step on his peg, grabbing hold of a fence post. "I don't want you to end up like me . . . or worse. That'd kill us both. Mr. Chisum's a good man. He'll understand."

Two cowboys jumped the rail fence, slipped ropes over their horses, and brought them out of the corral.

One of them said, "Claude, I wish I was stayin' here with you, keepin' the frying pan hot!"

Claude Ray let it go. He said to Rose, "We'll figure another way to pay Mr. Chisum for his kindness."

Rose pulled herself into the saddle and looked down at Claude Ray looking up at her.

He said, "I know you're hurting."

She put a hand on his cheek before falling in with the other riders.

"Paradise, you know it?"

Dev Bishop and Tomlinson were in the prison yard as the Fire Riders packed gear and horses, putting on tunics and sheathing blades to their belts. Dev checked an army carbine and handed it off while Tomlinson referred to his notebook, looking up his PARADISE entry.

"I've not been to that part of Colorado, but we've transferred over fifty thousand dollars to their bank. I'm unclear as to the nature of this investment."

"You're meeting a woman who calls herself Widow Kate. Can't miss her. Round as a fat mule's ass, lives in a wheelchair. She's behind this deal."

Tomlinson said, "I'll put her, and it, under a magnifying glass."

"Check her plans, verify the money she's kicking in. If it's real, the whole town could be ours. When you're back, the drive'll be over. We'll have a fine herd to add to the stores and maybe Paradise, too."

Tomlinson said, "And the question of your brother will have been answered."

Dev looked to Tomlinson. "You've a way of saying things without saying them, bookkeeper." He started across to the camouflaged ammo cache. "It edges me."

Hunk was beside the break in the outer wall where the hand bombs and dynamite were stored behind a painted canvas. He hefted a ten-count crate of Adams grenades onto the back of a pack mule and lashed it secure.

Dev said, "Don't be blowing holes in that cattle. It's supposed to be fine breed stock."

"These are for the Chisum men. I know what to do."

"I know. You're commanding this, Hunk."

Hunk cocked his hat to one side, away from his missing ear and the stitches that had sewed his wound together. "So, maybe I'm worth more than my fists?"

Dev nodded. "More . . . or you wouldn't be riding for me."

"Then what about the dandy man?"

"He bushwhacked you."

"Never again."

"He's on his own special business. Let him do his work. You take care of Chisum's men and the herd."

Hunk knotted the line tying the crate. "Oh yes. The easy part."

Dev said, "Spill the right blood, show everyone they'd be damn fools to go against us, and you'll never have to worry about anything. Ever."

Hunk took Dev's hands, smothering them with his own. "No blood on these"—he dropped them—"but I have family, and they need taking care of."

Dev took a cigar from his shirt pocket, cut and lit it. "Bogdan, that's why I want you for this. You're a man who knows how to make a right choice."

It was the first time Dev had called Hunk by his proper name.

Hunk extended one of his paws. "I have gratitude. *Sunt recunoscător.*"

At the Chisum ranch, John Bishop put gun oil, a clean rag, and two boxes of .12-gauge shells into his medical kit before tucking it into his saddlebag. He got onto the bay, his long coat draping, hat pulled down, double-barreled rig in place.

Claude Ray limped to him, peg leg dragging, waving an arm. "Dr. Bishop, this is your business. My wife's not right-headed. She shouldn't be going, but grief won't let her stay."

Bishop said, "I'll try to turn her around." He gathered the reins in his left hand. "You should see Linus."

Claude Ray glanced at the blacksmith shop, turned back to say something else to Bishop, but he was gone.

In the prison yard, the Fire Riders brought their horses to the center, tightening saddles and cinches.

By the weapons stores, Colby worked with Toothless, finishing the prep of his special ammunition. Toothless fit a lead slug into a casing held in the bullet vise before Colby pressed the side of a Chinese dragon dagger into the soft lead, then quickly pulled it back, the pattern of the knife's tail perfectly dividing the tip of the bullet into small sections.

Toothless cackled like hell and brought out more slugs he'd poured from a mold, fitting them into the brass he'd laid out.

Dev watched the procedure. "Doesn't the slug flatten when it hits the chest?"

Colby patterned another slug. "On the contrary. These are high-velocity rounds, so the tip splits apart after it enters the target, then moves through the insides, stirring them." He made a circular motion with his hands. "Like a cook with a good stew. Much better than shrapnel."

"Whatever you say"—Dev examined a completed bullet—"as long as you've got what you need for the job."

Colby took a piece of ice from a small bowl. "I'm very satisfied." He put it in his mouth like a chaw of tobacco, cooling his throat.

GOOD FRIEND CHISUM I HAVE SENT
ALONG SOME OF MY BEST MEN TO ASSIST
IN YOUR MISSION. IT IS UNFORTUNATE
THAT WE FIND OURSELVES HAVING TO
RECLAIM OUR LANDS AND BUSINESSES
FROM THESE MARAUDERS BUT IT MUST
BE DONE AND I HAVE EVERY FAITH IN MR
GARRETT TO ACCOMPLISH THIS. I AM
GUILTY WITH REGRET THAT AGE PREVENTS
ME FROM RIDING ALONGSIDE BUT I
WOULD ONLY BE A HINDRANCE.
I WISH YOU ALL GODSPEED. KNOW THAT
ALL I HAVE IS AT YOUR DISPOSAL.
SINCERELY HENRY TUNSTALL.

Chisum was on the crest, reading the wire a final time, then pocketing it, and watching the drovers start the herd out of the valley toward the northern trail. The cattle were obedient, with a few stragglers easily shooed back into line.

He loved to watch the movement from the back of the herd to the front—the wave of motion and muscles under hair as the animals followed each other to the next place for water and the place for camp after that.

Chisum missed the sound, the dust, the coffee. Missed being a part of it.

Pat Garrett rode up. "Those jingle-bobs will fetch a great price!"

"That's not what they're supposed to fetch."

Garrett dropped his voice. "I know that, Mr. Chisum. And the men know it, too."

"Who's riding"

Garrett pointed out the crew. "I picked our fellas who're best with a rifle to put them around the town. Maynard's still bandaged up, but he can fight. Rose insisted, and she's a better shot than most. And him." He nodded to a young man in a sombrero, taking a wide turn around the back of the herd, getting between a couple strays and the stream. "Name's McCarty. He's one of Mr. Tunstall's. They say he's too quick to shoot, but that might be a good thing."

"Remember the time when only the trail boss needed to carry a gun? Man put a rifle on his saddle if he wanted something special for chuck. Now, we have to ride out with enough guns to face a band of Commancheros."

Garrett said, "These are violent times."

Chisum stayed on his men and cattle. "Patrick, this drive's to end the war, so we can get back to business."

"It's what we all want, sir."

"Back to business, Patrick." Chisum let his words settle, then added, "Just don't be foolhardy."

"I'll do what's best, sir."

Chisum looked back to Garrett, who tipped his hat and rode down to the moving herd. Something weighing him down, the cattleman climbed onto his horse slowly as Bishop brought the bay to the vantage point and stopped.

Bishop said, "Well, Farrow told me you always get what you pay for."

Chisum eyed the bandolier, the leather-gloved left hand, and the shotgun, steady in the special sling hanging from Bishop's saddle so it would rest parallel to his leg. "As much a warrior as any I've seen coming across the flats."

Bishop said, "Still a one-armed man, Mr. Chisum."

"You're facing down our enemies, Doctor." Chisum wasn't looking at Bishop when he said, "I wish you all the luck."

"I never had much of that. Just strange chances."

Smythe had put on his best double-breasted jacket and had polished his shoes even though his dead legs would drag them through the slop of the prison yard. He crutched his way down the stairs from the gallery of wardens to where his men had brought their horses into formation.

He pulled himself to the weapons rack as Riders took the last of the carbines without chatter, only purpose. They nodded and pulled on their red hoods. The horses stirred and there was the rattle of tack as the men took their mounts, but no other sound.

No jokes, no passing of whiskey.

Dev Bishop faced the yard and Riders from the gates, standing on several blocks of stacked granite like it was a pulpit. He acknowledged Smythe, then raised a hand.

Tomlinson, flanked by his snouted daughters, leaned between them. "Sing."

"Rolling home, rolling home; rolling home across the sea, rolling home to dear ol' England, rolling home, fair land to thee."

Smythe watched Dev drop his hand, signaling the Riders to move out. In his fire-red tunic, Hunk rode point, holding his right hand to the temple just above his missing ear in the European style of salute. He sliced the air as he rode past Dev. Colby followed two horses back, his select arsenal secured behind his saddle.

The other riders, horses freshly painted as skeletal demons, all rode with formality, respecting their mission training. Rifles, specially made battle axes, and long swords hung from belts and saddle sheaths.

In perfect union with the movements of the troop, the girls' voices lifted the sea shanty Smythe had chosen. A troop. That's how he saw them. He straightened himself on the crutches to stand tall, beyond his useless legs. The nerves were dead, but he wasn't. His troop was ready for battle, and if he couldn't feel anything below his hips, he could feel pride.

Tethered to the last rider and weighted with grenades, the pack mule was the last to clear the gates, just as the girls sang their final note. April Showers threw a quick punch at her yellow-haired sister. Tomlinson yanked them apart.

Smythe called out, "Girls, you did me proud!"

Dev moved across the yard as other men stowed horses, stolen rifles, and supplies.

Smythe nodded a greeting. "You stood inspection. Did everyone pass muster?"

"They're not ragtag anymore. Your doing, Sergeant."

Smythe crutched himself along as Dev walked. "If Chisum delivers your brother, then you've broken him. Every cattleman in the territory will be running scared when they read about it. That's one hell of a thing, boy-o."

"When you'd come down to the tombs and beat me so I couldn't eat for a week, ever think it would end up like this?"

"Things can change." Smythe stopped, slashing a line in the dirt with the tip of his crutch. "That's the way I used to think. You crossed a line I wouldn't, which is how come you were a prisoner and I was the sergeant of the guards." He dragged himself across the line, his feet erasing it.

Dev said, "And now you've crossed it?"

"It never truly existed. We were always of the same stripe. We just wore different clothes," Smythe said.

"Sometimes a uniform's nothing but a clean rag. It took me a while to come to that."

Dev said, "Major Beaudine told me that a man's only measure is the loyalty he inspires."

"See, you didn't leave me on that mountain with a bullet in my back. That's why I'm still here." Smythe put his crutches forward, pulled himself along. "I'm glad that lunatic died screaming, but he wasn't wrong."

The kneecap was plated tin that Linus had hammered around a section of fence post, rounding it out in Chisum's stable. He'd cut according to Bishop's plans, hinging it, then fastening iron struts on either side that curved to an ankle as a leg would. The base was a thin piece of iron Linus had forged to a length matching Claude Ray's foot.

"The doc wanted you to have something better than that damn peg you're always dragging." Linus held out the artificial limb, but Claude Ray made no move, staying by the stable entrance.

"Linus, that's really something. Probably too good for me, but I'll wait till my wife comes back before trying it."

"You don't want to surprise her?"

Claude Ray said, "Rose was there when they outfitted me with this piece of pine. I want her here for this, too."

Linus worked the knee's smooth motion. "You could take her dancing."

Bishop stayed back, trailing the Angus herd as they spread out across acres of scrubbed grassland. Pat Garrett peeled to the side, giving signals to the outriders who were threading their way around, keeping the cattle moving toward a cut in the hills that led to the northern Colorado trail.

Bishop watched Maynard struggle in his saddle, shifting his pain, while the new kid in the sombrero rode the length of the herd, back and forth, whistling and yee-hawing the cattle's pace.

Rose rode drag behind them all, the animals kicking up a moving curtain of dust and hair to ride through. She pulled her kerchief up to her nose as Bishop moved up beside. The bay stayed perfectly in step with Rose's stallion, keeping Bishop close enough to hear over the sounds of the drive.

"Break now, you'll be back at the ranch in time for lunch."

Rose leaned from her saddle, swatted a straggling cow behind the shoulders to get it to catch up with the others. "That sounds like Claude Ray talking."

"I told him I'd try."

"I figured you'd understand my doing this better than anyone."

Bishop said, "You're not facing one man. This is a tactic to bring down an attack."

Rose didn't look at Bishop, but the animals and cowboys in front of her. "I know what I'm riding into. I've done it before."

"Brave as anyone I've ever seen, Rose, but you've got a husband. I'm alone. That's the difference."

Rose pulled her kerchief. "It wasn't my nephew they killed. It was my baby boy . . . from before Claude Ray. They killed my son. I never—" She broke from Bishop, then rode to catch up with the herd.

CHAPTER TWELVE
Assassins

"Sure tastes like Colorado, don't it?"

A Fire Rider, hood bunched up, licked coffee from his thick mustache then poured himself a little more from the fire by the chuck wagon. The other riders were scattered about the orchard. Another small campfire burning at the far end showed rows of apple trees and inky silhouettes of the horses nibbling at them. The moon was large and low, with a light spring snow dancing in front of it.

Mustache drank again, melting the snowflakes that had been caught below his nose. He turned to Colby. "Don't know what you're missing. This is damn good coffee."

Colby was sitting by a small kerosene lamp, making notes in the Bishop shotgun file. There were scribbled surmises about the rig's black powder grain, figuring something heavier given the amount of buckshot dug from the Riders already killed. He made a column of numbers of possible extra shells Bishop carried, figuring how fast he'd run out of ammo, and the rig's original make, in case he'd faced it before.

He made another notation, then finally said, "I'm glad you're enjoying it." His finger pressed the bullet wound on his neck, the quick sting of pain keeping him focused as he wrote.

"You know we got orders not to talk to you, to leave you to your own patch?"

Colby glanced up at the figure that was blocking his light. "And you're disobeying those instructions. Why?"

"Find out what makes you so special. Maybe I'd like to improve myself."

"I doubt that, and I doubt this."

Mustache backed on his heels as Colby stood and walked toward the chuck. He called out to Colby's back, "Walking away? That's a grievous insult."

Colby took a closer look at the last piece of peach pie and checked the night's bean pot that was hanging over a flame. "You're trying to start something, but I can't imagine why. You're not insulted. You're finding an excuse. We all have our work, so let's leave it at that."

Mustache said, "How much you getting paid for yours?"

Colby stayed by the chuck wagon and called out to the riders who were just beyond the firelight, their red tunics browning in the shadows. "Bogdan! You're supposed to be in command here. Are you going to take control of this?"

Hunk stood, backed by a line of Riders. Two had drawn pistols, the others were waiting, fingers tapping guns and knives hanging from their belts.

Hunk said, "These men are my command. Mr. Bishop said you were on your own."

Mustache's face was suddenly close to Colby. "You ain't part of this raid."

Colby was steady. "I don't owe an explanation, but I'll

say I have a special mission. My own raid, if it makes you feel better."

"Special? With them rifles?"

Colby said, "Bogdan, you should stop this man."

"He said you was on your own. You said it, too." Mustache kept pressing forward, chest out, his chin a locked challenge. "This 'special mission' sounds kind of piddling. Hell, I'd bet real money I could do your work better than you, make that 'special' pay. I don't think Mr. Bishop cares who pulls the triggers tomorrow, ain't that so, Hunk?"

Hunk stayed put. "He just wants the job done. What we trained for."

"Your training seems to ebb and flow. I was very impressed with our exit this morning, but not so much by your actions now. You seem determined to challenge me." Colby had moved to the back of the chuck wagon, sorting through the salt, ground pepper, and tins of spices. He palmed a small can, popping the lid with his thumb. He kept his back to Mustache, feeling him advance.

Mustache said, "Well, that clears the road, don't it?"

The powdered mustard flew from Colby's hand as he turned, a splash of yellow directly into Mustache's eyes. He yelled, tumbled back, and Colby shot him in the chest three times with a small-caliber Smith & Wesson he had in his belt.

It happened so fast, the echo of Mustache's voice and the roar of the gunshots faded against the distant hills at the same time. Mixing there, then dying in the rocks.

The light spring snow dusted Mustache's face on top of the mustard, slopping it into a yellow mask. The coffee cup never left his hand. Colby tucked the pistol behind his back again and took a few steps away from the corpse as the other Riders came in for a closer look.

One said, "damn fool," and another laughed in the back of his throat.

Colby said, "Gentlemen, I apologize. We have our separate missions and upbringing, but this should never have happened."

The Rider who'd choked out a laugh said, "Hell, this raid don't depend on that jackass."

"What say you, Hunk? Was this some sort of last-minute test before the battle?" Colby pulled his watch chain from the small pocket on his vest and displayed Hunk's ear that he'd threaded onto it. It had started to shrivel, but kept its shape. He gave it a little twirl, saying, *"Eşti un măgar."*

Standing in front of a fire now, Hunk didn't answer the insult, just watched as Colby put his trophy back in his pocket. Finally he barked to the others, "We all got much work to do! Someone check the horses, make sure none have bolted."

Colby stepped over the body, settled by his lamp, opened the Bishop file again, and continued his notes.

John Bishop held the *Police Gazette* at an angle, catching a bit of light from the Chisum chuck fire to see the pen and ink rendering. The double barrels were blasting at the same time, tearing through the guts of two finely dressed men, while two more lay on the bank floor in pools of black blood. His teeth were a wide grimace, his one hand locked in an angry fist. Just behind him, what looked like a widow woman was on her knees, praying.

"Too many teeth, and I think they've got me a little short." On a blanket, resting against his saddle, the rig off his arm and beside him, he flipped through the penny dreadful with his left hand, not giving further reaction to what he saw.

McCarty shifted from one leg to the other, formally holding his sombrero, but not concealing his excitement.

"Kept that magazine for better than a year. Always wanted to see the rig in person, see if it was true."

"Am I robbing the bank or protecting it?"

"It don't matter, does it? They wrote it up."

Bishop said, "They surely did."

"Well, can I? Look at the rig?" McCarty's words were breathless, and Bishop gave him permission with a look.

McCarty picked up the shotgun, handling it as if it were made of spun glass and antique gold. His smile split his face as he opened the side-breech, looked down the barrels, and checked the tightness of the triggers. He whistled. "How fast are you with this thing?"

"I've learned."

McCarty used both hands to lower the gun back onto the blanket, careful not to tangle the shoulder straps and trigger lines. "I'm good with a Colt, feels natural in my hand; most folks can't see it leave my holster. But that double barrel, well, the way it's rigged, it's really a part of you."

After consideration, Bishop said, "It is. Now."

McCarty's voice dropped. "How's that feel? To be . . . the same as the gun?"

"Not like this." Bishop tapped the page, then handed back the *Police Gazette*, its cover screaming *SHOTGUN—THE TERROR OF THE WEST!* by Virgil Everett Chaney.

Pat Garrett came down from the edge of the pine woods where the herd was tucked for the night. He was riding a hammerhead roan a good two hands taller than anyone else's so he could look down on his men, even if they were saddling a good horse. He eyed McCarty from his saddle. "This one bothering you, Doctor?"

Bishop said, "No, we've been having an interesting talk."

McCarty frowned. "You don't have to be on me, Garrett. We all know why I'm here."

Garrett said, "And you're gonna have a chance to

prove your reputation real soon. Need you thinking clear. Get some rest."

McCarty threw Garrett a defiant salute and a quick laugh, then reached to shake Bishop's empty right sleeve. He quickly switched to his left and said, "A lefty. It was nice to meet you, sir. Honor to be riding with you." He got on his horse and rode to where a few drovers were catching sleep or coffee.

Garrett dropped, pulling a bottle of bourbon from his saddle with him. In one motion, it was open and being poured into a shot glass with initials PJG engraved across it. He handed it to Bishop. "Gave it to myself for my birthday. A little something fine."

Bishop listened to the herd, watched the hired guns roll dice by the fire or practice their technique. They were flickers in the night, drawn in streaks of orange from the flames. One was spinning a Winchester from his hip then firing on an empty chamber. McCarty was laughing, showing off his lightning-quick draw.

Bishop handed Garrett the empty glass. "They can't wait."

"Hired guns always want to show off."

"Like shavetail troopers."

"They're getting extra pay, and know this isn't just about moving the cattle."

Bishop nodded toward Maynard a hundred yards away, slumped in his saddle, snoring loudly. His horse stood eating at some tall, wet grass.

Garrett said, "He's earning his wages for sure."

"Those bandages are filthy. Damn fool won't let me clean him up."

"Nobody ever accused Maynard of having any sense." Garrett poured a shot for himself. "So tell me, Doctor, how'd you take on so many of the Fire Riders?"

Bishop talked to the sky, trying to put things in order. "I didn't know they existed until I was in the middle of a fight. I was tracking the men who killed my son, and they came down on us."

"The red demons, right?"

"That's what they looked like that first time."

"How many did you put down?"

Bishop frowned. "I-I don't recall."

"Then the train?"

"Later, but yes, then the train."

"That's what impressed the crap out of Chisum."

"I try to remember. It's still broken pieces, but you're right when you called it war with them. Attack, pull back, attack again in a new way. Battle skills."

Garrett drank his own shot. "Like the cavalry or Crazy Horse?"

"Either."

"You didn't let go of any of this with Chisum."

"He's not riding into anything."

Garrett studied the empty shot glass. "That's why he's got us."

"I recall they used dynamite on the tracks. And a Gatling on the troopers. Those sounds stayed with me."

"The Riders used grenades, too?"

Bishop looked to Garrett. "So they tell me. That, I don't remember so clearly. Maybe I still have half a one in my skull."

Garrett laughed. "Not a surprise."

"Now let me ask you a question. What am I doing here? Why did Chisum go to all this trouble, instead of letting me hang?"

"You saying you're sorry you didn't?"

"I'm saying I don't know what I bring to this fight"—Bishop lifted the rig—"other than this, and I doubt that's worth all the money he's paid out."

Garrett said, "Chisum was having you ride in, come hell or high water."

"That much was always clear. Are you supposed to keep me alive?"

Garrett corked the bottle and stood. "Doc, I'm worried about keeping myself alive."

"Get back to Chisum's big table?"

"My intention is to be a regular guest."

Bishop said, "You're an honest man, Patrick. I appreciate that."

"I've got a few moves figured for us, but if this fight busts open, you might be on your own."

"That suits me to the ground."

Garrett took the reins of his horse, ready to lead it away. "I know you got some thoughts on Rose. Frankly, I don't need a dead woman on my hands."

Rose's voice carried from the edge of the woods. "You want to know about Rose, why don't you ask Rose?"

Garrett brought the hammerhead around as she walked from the pines, hitching her belt.

"The Doc's got nothing to say. This is on me. And no matter what's ailing me"—she made a jerking motion with her whole body toward the boys by the fire—"I'm still as good a shot as any of these you got." Rose looked to Bishop. "Well?"

John Bishop stayed lying against his saddle, his only hand on the shotgun rig, and said to Garrett, "We're both here on personal business. Rose is looking out for herself, and I don't doubt her marksmanship."

Garrett said, "As long as she does what I need her to when this thing starts."

Rose said, "I'm standing here, right?"

Pat Garrett rode off.

Rose cast a look down at Bishop, who had pulled the shotgun closer to him and tilted his hat down. His voice came from under its shadow. "See how you feel in the morning. Give yourself that much judgment."

* * *

It was the mandibles that Farrow saw first—the large jaws, ghostly white, with the fanged canine teeth, moving in and out of the tree line. Then breaking. Running.

Farrow's horse twisted against the reins, the skeletons roaring out of the dark, surrounding him. The painted ribs, spines, and legs of the horses glowed in the moonlight.

He drew a Colt as the Fire Riders closed their circle around him. "I've never seen you done up like this. Must scare the hell out of the farmers and rubes."

"It does good with everyone." Hunk broke the circle, bringing his skulled stallion next to Farrow's own. Hunk's face was uncovered. He handed Farrow a small parcel.

Farrow said, "So, you're the deliveryman?"

"I command. They do what I order."

Farrow threw looks around him as the Riders brought their horses two steps closer. Dead-eyed stares came at him from their hoods. He could see shouldered rifles and blades.

One Rider bled the air with a Prussian saber before turning its polished edge toward Farrow's throat and holding it there.

Farrow said, "Well, by fire or the sword, eh?"

Hunk said, "What's your meaning by that? Answer quick!"

Farrow watched the saber. "Just the motto of another group I work for."

Hunk put his words into pieces. "You . . . double . . . the . . . deals?"

Farrow said, "That's why I'm paid."

Hunk's large hand almost covered the Smith & Wesson it held, the barrel seeming like an extra finger.

The parcel went into Farrow's jacket, his hand glancing at the pistol he had holstered, but he judged the situation, and simply raised his arms in surrender. Farrow never lost his tight-lipped smile of advantage.

Hunk chuckled. "You look a damn fool."

Aimed directly at Farrow were guns of all type and blades that were less than a foot away. He said, "Absolutely no offense intended. I'm here to take you into Myrtle."

"What time the Chisum men coming?"

"That's been worked out. I won't tell you wrong."

Hunk eased the gun back to his belt, which signaled the others to raise their weapons. The saber remained.

"What time?" he asked again.

"We figure around noon."

The saber went back into its sheath. No one said another word.

Farrow brought down his arms.

The evening dusting had picked up, and Farrow turned his collar against the snow as he started out of the camp. The hooded Riders on painted-fleshless horses followed.

CHAPTER THIRTEEN
The Bleeding Ground

The storm came through a jagged break between two Rocky peaks, a natural wind tunnel turning raindrops into skin-slicing needles. It was a half hour past sunrise, but the rolling clouds darkened the sky like midnight.

Bishop stayed the trail with the bay, duster buttoned to his throat, the rig slinged. Sharp rain soaked him, but he felt good. Ready. He'd slept with no nightmares, no slashes of memory.

The others, sporting rubber slicks and pulled-up bandanas, kept the cattle moving with the storm beating their backs. McCarty, sombrero tilted back, not caring, waved to Bishop, locking his arm at the elbow imitating the double-barrel. He hooted a laugh before running his horse along the trail's edge to the front of the herd.

Maynard followed, struggling to keep pace, fighting his wounds. His bald-faced mare drifted close to a bull that knocked them both away. He lurched in the saddle.

Garrett charged up from behind, swatting the bull with a coil of rope, water spitting off its hide. "You said you were up to this! Getting these to town isn't even half of what we're supposed to do!"

Maynard was pale, sweating in the cold. "Don't doubt I got some fight in me!"

Garrett said, "I'd bust your jaw in half if I didn't need every man."

The rain was coming in buckets as Garrett angled off on his tall horse, not letting Maynard throw another excuse.

Bishop stood in his stirrups and called to Maynard over the storm, "Let me check you out!"

Maynard didn't turn around, just fought to stay mounted.

Rose rode up on her brown and white from half a mile back, having kept her distance for the night. Beside Bishop, her eyes were fixed on the cattle and hired guns, water pouring from the brim of her hat. She said about Maynard, "I guess some folks just can't accept help."

"Garrett thinks we'll hit Myrtle in an hour."

"Good, that's good."

They rode for a bit, then she said, "Look, I don't want to hear nothing about my time to turn back."

Bishop said, "Some folks just can't accept help."

"You're on a vendetta for your family, just like I am for mine!"

"Don't make comparisons."

Rose finally looked at him. "When somebody you love is killed, why does it seem that another killing is the only thing makes you feel better?"

"Fact is, it doesn't."

"Then what are you riding for?"

Bishop let the rain answer.

Colby organized his ammunition in neat rows within easy reach, along with two pistols, and a polished stiletto. When he was satisfied with the arrangement, he opened a hinged cedar box and admired the new Fiedler telescopic sight resting in its velvet lining.

He secured the scope to a Winchester 1875 Single Shot with a jeweler's screwdriver from a set in his vest. Hunk's ear dangled on a gold chain from the vest pocket like a watch fob. He slipped bundled sheets under his knees for comfort, then brought the rifle to his shoulder. Setting his elbow on the windowsill, he adjusted the precision eyepiece on a twenty-cent coin lying in the muddy street below until it came into sharp focus.

Bishop, Garrett, McCarty, and Rose had all taken up the side of the trail to ride ahead of the cattle, their horses deep in the slop. With Myrtle less than half a mile away, Garrett raised his hand to slow the herd.

Garrett said to Rose, "You and McCarty are at the back."

Thunder tidal-waved over the hills, with another jag of lighting. The cattle felt the sound in their spines, smelled the lightning burning the wet air.

McCarty threw a look at the herd. Stirring. Uneasy. Batting each other, locking horns. He said, "I don't blame 'em. Scares the hell out of me, too, when God gets angry."

"They're ready to run."

Garrett said to Rose, "Keep them back. I'll tell you when."

McCarty poured out the water trapped in his sombrero, then tied it under his chin. "That sounded like an order, Mr. Garrett. And you know what? I'm gonna do her!"

McCarty galloped off. Rose's eyes, frustrated and dark, locked on Bishop, and she was about to say something, but whipped her horse around, riding after the sombrero.

Maynard cut between some broad-shouldered albinos,

almost colliding with Rose. He was gripping his chest. "I'm ridin' in the cow crap. You pushin' me off this fight?"

From his higher position, Garrett looked down on him when he said, "The Doc and I take stock of the situation—"

"Take stock?"

"That's right. Then you'll obey orders like everybody else. Might just keep you alive."

"Keep favoring that one-armed son of a bitch, and you're the one's dyin'!" Maynard struggled his horse around, before taking it through a small break in the storm-bent trees leading away from the trail.

"Good riddance." Garrett lit a short-rolled cigarette, then said to Bishop, "So how many times have you ridden into hell on purpose?"

Bishop drew the rig. "I think you've been reading the penny dreadfuls, Garrett. It's not like that." He moved his shoulders, taking up the slack of the trigger lines that ran up his sleeve to the rig's brace.

"You son of a bitch." Garrett laughed under the thunder as the two rode the last minutes toward Myrtle.

The side of Hunk's head still bled when he crooked his neck the wrong way. He was in the corner shadows, cramped against a mildewed hay bale, holding balled linen to the wound. The riders with him kept their horses and voices down.

One whispered, "Hunk, can you lend me an ear?"

Some nervous laughs spewed from the others.

Hunk daubed drying black blood from the stitches where his ear used to be, thinking of stabbing the *tâmpit* with the big mouth. "You've had your joking. Be ready to attack."

One of the men was holding a sword. "You're a foreigner. I carried this when I was with Bloody Bill Anderson. I know how to send a message."

Hunk said, "You're not the one in charge here. Just be ready to follow."

The rider kept the blade poised, making a short, chopping motion like he was cutting off a head.

The heavy rain curtained the wood and iron junk piled at the foot of what was Myrtle's main street. The roof of an old caboose and a blasted-apart potbelly stove were stacked along with empty flour barrels and railroad trash, giving perfect cover.

Bishop and Garrett brought their horses in close. Garrett leaned out of his saddle, taking in the town. "Same old hellhole."

Bishop thought Garrett wrong. Myrtle wasn't a hellhole, it was a T-shaped corpse, silent and rotting. Just a few buildings stood around an old cattle pen attached to a twisted rail spur where a dilapidated freight car, front wheels missing, had been left for dead years before. Lean-tos and shredded army tents, roughly patched together for prosties, took up the rest of the street that ended in a small crossway.

A ragged and empty two-story dry goods emporium stood at its center. A shattered window on the second floor was being beaten by the storm, its curtains blowing out from the inside.

Bishop took the bay a few steps from the junk pile for a better view. Nobody walked into the street for a look-see of the strangers bringing in a herd. The only sound was the rain overflowing gutters and water troughs.

Not even a dog barked.

"We've got targets on our backs."

Garrett said, "Hell, yes."

The air had the taste of ashes and felt hot in the storm.

Bishop snapped the rig into a firing position from his hip, throwing beads of water off the barrels. "I'd just gotten my medic stripes, and we'd crossed into North Carolina, an open field, corn stacked in huge piles across it. We couldn't see the enemy, but we knew. They sent us in anyway."

"How many were killed?"

"More than half the company."

Garrett shook his head. "That, you remember."

"In pieces."

"We sure as hell don't have a company backing us."

On Garrett's last word, glass dropped from the broken window on the second floor of the dry goods emporium at the end of Myrtle's main street.

There was the silhouette of a rifle.

The water blowing around the window frame hazed Colby's aim. He wiped the telescopic sight and his eyes, then tried fixing on his target again. He sensed Bishop and Garrett behind their cover, knew if he had even half-an-inch break right or left, he could put a bullet in a skull, reload, and finish before the first target hit the ground. Making two shots count was a test of reflexes that Colby enjoyed, and there was great satisfaction when it worked.

He also wanted to see the travel pattern of the special bullets he'd fashioned and the impact of the slugs creased with the knife blade. All things a professional considered.

But there was no clean shot through the rain. Yet.

Rose and McCarty were behind the last of the herd, a couple leather bags with wagging tongues. Another low roar of thunder scattered a pair of shorthorn bulls, and Rose watched as hired guns threw lassos, stopping the running cattle and pulling them in.

They looked at Myrtle just ahead of them, but were handling the animals easy, like they were told.

She called out to the gunman who was shoving the

bulls back into the herd. "You're riding too close! They're already spooked!"

"Chisum claimed a special job! There ain't nothing special about this crap!"

Rose had her revolver in hand, under her rain slicker. "I'm working, same as you."

"Except I know what to do proper with a Colt Six." The hired gun rode off.

McCarty said to Rose, "Forget that cow pie. Garrett told you what's what?"

"You've got his fool orders. I'll follow mine."

Chaney stood in the doorway of the emporium's second-floor room where Colby was positioned at the broken window with his rifle. "They're showing caution about coming in," the reporter said, then checked the exposure on his small camera. "A picture before the slaughter of Chisum's men and then one after, to shock and amaze."

Colby quick-aimed a Derringer Four-shot Pepperbox at Chaney's face.

"I have an arrangement with Mr. Farrow."

Colby remained silent.

"Your employer wants the world to know how dangerous his group is. I'll tell the tale, and you do what you do, Mr. Colby."

Colby leaned forward, bringing the Derringer closer.

Chaney nodded. "I look forward to photographing John Bishop's corpse." He bowed slightly, giving it a flourish before shutting the door behind him.

A cough ripping him, Colby dropped the Pepperbox, then cupped his hands, caught some cold rain blowing in, and splashed his face. He spit blood into a handkerchief before aiming the Winchester at the rotting pile of wood and railroad iron at the end of the street . . . focusing on a target he couldn't yet see.

* * *

The bay and hammerhead were moving antsy, but Bishop and Garrett kept them reined tight, using the junk pile as a shield against the storm. Staying hidden.

Garrett said, "Break, and we'll be slaughtered faster than pigs at Easter."

"Lay some cover. I can get behind those old tents, work my way up, take care of the sniper in the window."

"Got that feeling like in Carolina?"

Bishop agreed with a look, and Garrett continued. "We don't know how many Fire Riders are lying in there. Chisum sure as hell waltzed us into it."

"It's what we signed on for." Bishop leaned forward in the saddle, ready to try. "I'm still on my own business. If I go in, they'll come right for me. I'll do what damage I can, but it'll give you all a fighting chance, maybe close in on them from the back."

Garrett said, "You're no use as a dead legend, Doc. Who do you distrust more? The Fire Riders or Mr. Chisum?"

Bishop's shoulders were rolling, tightening the shotgun lines, the weapon aimed from his hip. "It's an even split."

"How do I fare?" Garrett brought up his fine Colt with the scrolled barrel and fired three shots into the storm. The sky reacted with a hot spiderweb of lightning that lit up everything for miles.

That was Colby's cue.

He fired just to the left of the Colt's barrel flame, estimating the location of his target's head behind the junk pile. The slug tore into the old caboose roof first, the lead splitting into threes as it was meant to, then out the other side, creasing Garrett's hat.

Garrett swung the hammerhead around as Colby's

second shot sparked off a busted coupling hitch inches from Bishop's temple.

Slivers from the ricochet sliced Bishop's face. He smeared the blood with his fingers, and Garrett grabbed the shotgun, holding him back. The bay twisted, pawing at the ground. Garrett nodded down the trail, water sloshing over the brim of his hat.

Bishop looked.

The herd was stampeding through the rain, legs pounding full-out, bulls and cows spread out across the trail, moving like hell.

Roaring toward Myrtle.

Hunk took the shooting as the signal. The battle cry *"Luați-le în iad!"* erupted from him as he leaped his horse from the old freight car. Fire Riders jumped alongside him, clearing the doors, and onto Myrtle's main street. Red tunics flapped like demon wings, their painted horses rain-smeared white, making them ghosts.

They hit the deep mud running, guns and sabers drawn. The storm exploded, blowing a hole in the sky above them.

Thunder roared.

On the trail, Rose and McCarty ran the herd from behind, shooting over them, whistling and screaming. The cattle charged faster. Heads down, horns slicing wet hair and rawhide, and eyes bloody-wide as they stampeded Main Street, ripping through the corral on one side, tents and outbuildings on the other.

Charging the Fire Riders.

Wild, the cattle plowed into men and horses, sharp horns piercing flesh, stallions screaming and bucking, throwing their riders. The red hoods scrambled, mud and soaked tunics weighing them down, as they shot at the herd before being trampled. Arms snapped and ribs powdered. Broken hands held on to destroyed rifles and bent-in-half swords.

Horses cut the air with ghost-painted legs, flailing wild, before falling back, bellies gored by longhorns, crushing riders tangled in their stirrups.

Lightning crashed.

A pair of Riders took their horses behind a rail fence, firing at two Chisum men riding alongside the cattle. They hit them both, sending them spinning off their saddles before being crushed under the stampede.

Quick screams sounded, then blood erupted.

From behind the junk pile, Garrett shot one Fire Rider in the head, and Bishop blasted a hole in the other's chest. The cattle busted down the corral fence, running in panic and dragging the corpses with them.

Hunk jumped his horse over the bodies of his fallen men, making it to the barn near the rail spur. The walls of the barn shook as the cattle smashed them from outside, the planks buckling. Hunk ran to a back stall and untied the mule with the case of grenades on its back.

In the street, a Chisum gun rode in fast, staying wide of the cattle as they trampled the last of the corral, splintering it. He pulled a repeater from a scabbard, lever-cocking it in one motion, not seeing what was behind him.

Bishop spied the outline of the Winchester taking aim from the emporium. He swung the bay around, firing a warning blast. The Chisum gun didn't heed and the sniper's bullet blew out his throat.

Bishop watched him fall. He snapped the rig to his shoulder and pulled the reins on the bay as the gunman hit the ground.

Bishop broke from his cover.

In the window, Colby slammed home another shell, aimed, and found Bishop galloping for the stampede.

He wanted a clean head shot, but Bishop threw himself to one side of his saddle, keeping the rig low, circling around the running cattle, using them for cover.

Colby swallowed the blood backing into his mouth and fired anyway, the slug hitting another Chisum man square in the chest, picking him up, and dumping him on the street.

Decent kill.

He loaded again as Bishop rode out of his sighting.

Thunder roared again.

Rose and McCarty kept the cattle running, pushing them from behind to keep pulverizing Myrtle.

McCarty said, "You're doin' fine, miss! Just keep one hand on your gun." He saluted Rose, then ran his horse behind the junk pile where Garrett was positioned with a rifle. McCarty dropped from his horse and stayed down, waiting for the enemy charge, grinning as he checked his pistols. He howled a laugh. "You didn't think you were gonna keep me with the cow asses, did ya?"

He popped shots from behind the old potbellied stove, shooting the Fire Riders who rode around the boxcar to the rail spur, trying to escape the stampede. Hard targets.

"That's nine." He looked at Garrett. "That's the ninth son of a bitch I ever killed!"

Garrett's words were flat. "It's good you're keeping count."

McCarty fired again, wounding the Rider. "Hell, Garrett, ain't this why I'm here?"

Bullets from the Riders splayed around them, and McCarty and Garrett dropped back from the junk heap, letting the Riders come around the side of the destroyed corral. Garrett shot two, sending one heaving into the slop, the other opening up with a pair of pistols, angry at being hit, and swearing like hell.

McCarty killed him between the eyes, the red hood splitting with the slug, revealing the Rider's surprise.

McCarty whistled at his own shot. "Ten. Ten men. Who can lay claim to that?"

Garrett kept up the rifle fire. "Just give cover!"

Bishop charged into the battle, coming up on the other side of the running herd, the shotgun braced against his shoulder infantry-style, ready to drop and shoot.

Suddenly, the ground shook.

The first Adams grenade landed in front of two Chisum men, blowing them sideways off their horses, animals landing on top of them. The rain turned the yellow heat of the explosion white, bloody mud bursting with it.

Panicked blind by the blast, the cattle were running in all directions, trampling the dead, tearing into men and the last standing buildings.

Bishop's horse veered at the grenade's impact, almost losing footing in the rainy slop. He kept the reins sure, and the bay responded. Leaning forward, close to the horse, Bishop plowed through the deep mud.

No slowing down. Almost there.

The next grenade hit a Chisum rider from behind, the force tumbling his horse forward at a full gallop, neck twisting into the ground. The rider landed hard, his arm snapping. He tried standing. A sniper's shot put him down, landing him next to his thrashing horse. Pat Garrett fired the shot that mercy-killed the animal.

In the window, Colby reloaded, seeing Bishop dodging the stampede, then tearing through the blowing smoke from the grenades.

Lightning struck. With cattle scattering around him, Bishop leaped the bay to the small trail running parallel to the main street. Hidden by the old tents and lean-tos, it was the walkway for hookers and railroad men to get in and out, and too narrow for a horse and rider.

Taking cover, he rolled from the saddle and forced the bay down to the ground between the tents in a single motion. Coming up with the rig snapping out directly before him, barrels aimed, he shot at the Fire Riders riding against the Chisum men.

He caught one in the chest, turned, and fired again, tearing another off his horse at the knees.

Bishop's head pounded, a wash of blood filling his eyes from inside, casting everything he saw with a red shimmer. He was "seeing blind," reflexes faster than before, senses sharper. No hesitations. Instant.

Beyond instinct, beyond the adrenaline of combat, he'd transformed into something else, Bishop was finally the weapon.

Colby watched the Fire Riders go down, admiring Bishop's speed and deadly aim—nothing random, no counting on the spread of the buckshot. He calculated Bishop's position from the tilted direction of the last blast and fired from the window.

The slug danced an inch from Bishop's head as he dove. Springing the rig's breech, he reloaded then snapped it shut. Automatic. Bishop let fire go, spreading another Fire Rider with buckshot, dropping him into the stampede. The cattle were still running. Onto the side streets they ran, pulverizing storefronts and men, their cries and the thunderstorm the same.

Dodging to a new cover position, Bishop loosed first one barrel and the next, blasting rider after rider. Dead off the saddle, the bodies fell as he shot another before the first hit the ground. He grabbed the second box of shells from his saddle, filled the bandolier and both barrels.

The Rider with the Bloody Bill sword dove from his horse into the tent canvas, and came up firing, pistol in one hand, saber in the other. Bishop blew his arm off at the elbow, the sword spinning away, then finished him with the second barrel.

He breached, reloaded, and aimed for his next targets, trigger lines set across his shoulders. He fired again before running the length of the street, using the cattle for cover. He dropped to the ground opposite Hunk's position in the barn door.

Hunk pulled the strap on another Adams grenade and hurled it, the blast tearing open the junk pile, ripping jags of iron and wood shrapnel through the storm.

McCarty and Garrett were foxholed behind the junk pile, debris slicing above them. The explosion sent their horses running. Garrett came up and opened fire on the hotel room window, cracking off a series of shots.

Colby ducked against the window frame, Garrett's slugs punching the walls around him. Another spasm choked his throat. His hands were shaking as he grabbed a handful of shells, loaded, and fired at a distant Chisum rider. He watched him drop and felt better. Spitting the acid from his mouth, he loaded and scanned for Bishop.

Colby said to no one, "You are mine."

Hidden by the far corner of the emporium, Bishop was facing the barn and out of Colby's sight. The last of the cattle were slamming each other, still crying, but slowing.

The thunder was rolling off.

At the end of the trail, the last of the cattle were running into Myrtle while the storm travelled back toward the mountains. Their horses throwing mud, two Fire Riders rode down hard from a cross street and trapped Rose along the edge of the main trail. Their horses blocked her as she tried bringing her brown and white stallion around. They jammed her ribs and then her back with rifles as she turned. For a moment, a rifle barrel brushed the edge of her jaw, and she felt the sight.

One Rider, blood streaming from the edge of his mouth onto his hood and tunic, managed, "Chisum let you do this? Get yourself killed for this flapdoodle?"

Rose said, "What about you? Earning your pay?"

The Rider pulled off his soaking-wet hood and ran one hand across his bleeding sandpaper face. "Sorry, lady, but you work for Chisum. I got to show something for today other than some missing teeth."

At the barn door, Hunk yanked the strap, setting the fuse on the next grenade. He leaned out, reeling his arm back to throw toward the junk heap where Garrett and McCarty were laying rifle-fire cover.

Bishop triggered, tearing open Hunk's knee, folding him. The grenade rolled from his hand, the fuse sizzling inside its iron globe.

Bishop saw a break between the cattle and ran from his spot. Slipping. Dodging.

Colby fired, hitting a shorthorn cutting in front of Bishop, colliding against other cattle and bringing one down. Howling screams and bloody chaos continued.

Colby shucked the spent cartridge.

Slammed by the animal, Bishop rolled toward the barn, scrambled to his feet, and grabbed the Adams from a deep hoofprint. He hurled it with his left hand toward the second-floor window.

Colby reloaded.

Hunk yelled a warning.

The grenade spun in the air, leaving a tail of smoke and coming into focus as Colby pressed his eye against the telescopic sight.

Rose didn't move as the Rider raised the rifle to point at her heart. She eyed the rifle but stayed even in her tone. No panic. "Did you ever ride with a young boy? Great with a rope? You should know, since you killed him so he wouldn't talk about your raids."

"I don't know what the hell you're talking about."

Near the emporium the grenade exploded, hammering their horses. They reared, Rose and the Rider fighting to stay on.

Rose's pistol blew apart her rain slicker, catching the Rider in the chest. She turned, and fired again, clipping the second one's shoulder. Red sprayed from his side as he whipped his horse toward the small cut off the trail.

Rose stayed fast behind him, even as the first Rider was lying on the trail, counting his heartbeats and feeling the cold wet of the ground where he knew he'd be buried. His eyes were locked open to the light fall of rain.

The injured Rider pushed his horse, cutting through the trees, the water in the branches above drenching him. One arm blood-coated and useless, he jerked his horse too far to one side, slamming himself into a branch.

Almost on top of him, Rose pulled the stallion back, bringing up her pistol, when he used his good arm to hurl his Winchester, the weapon spinning. She ducked, the rifle breaking against a knotted trunk behind her. He lurched his animal down the rest of the cut, pushing to the open clearing on the other side of the trees.

Rose and the stallion stayed tight around the tall pines, leaping a large tangle of roots. Finally breaking from the woods, they came out onto a field of tall grass that had been flattened by the storm. Cattle that had found their way to the spot were calm and grazing. A few nudged each other, and some were lying down in the cool wet grass, tending to their own.

The injured Rider was there, catching air, his hood off. He was about thirty, his anonymous face softer than his partner's. His mouth sagged open with pain as if he were silently screaming. He looked up as Rose came to him, the pistol protruding through the blast hole in her rain slicker. "How many times you gonna shoot me?"

"Did you know a boy who rode with you?"

Not hearing the question, the Rider continued. "Look, you all beat us down good, looks like. I don't know how many are alive, but you can tell that to Chisum."

Rose stopped her horse less than ten feet from the Rider and looked beyond him to see Maynard sprawled in the field; a bullet in his face had taken off his nose and part of his cheek. She pointed at Maynard. "I rode with him."

The rider looked, then tried to get on the good side of the conversation. "I'm truly sorry. I didn't kill him, but I know how that is, loyalty and such."

"He was a jackass."

"I'm sorry about that, too."

"You work with somebody, it counts. That's how come I can tell you knew my nephew—a boy with sunny hair, better with a rope than anybody's business. Tell me about the raids you did together."

The rider's bloody arm was drooping, but his words were coming faster. "I heard you ask a-fore, I don't know nothing either. I don't. There's a lot of us he could've been with."

"All you getting rich, stealing cattle? Robbing banks? That's why you killed him, so he couldn't tell the law it was you?"

"I swear on Mary's virgin eyes, I never killed no one. Never robbed no bank. I did okay with cattle, but if you don't shoot, I'll take myself home and never stray again."

Rose said, "That money, that's what my nephew dreamed over. All he could make rustling. Like you. You knew him, I know you did. You filled his head with those bad notions, got him killed."

The Fire Rider was wishing he had a gun, anything, when he said, "I—I'm married."

Rose ignored it. "Just a boy. Got himself killed riding with you damnable red hoods."

Before he could beg, Rose sensed something behind her. She kept her gun trained, but turned in her saddle and saw a man on Hurricane crossing the field at a quick trot.

She was about to call out when Farrow shot her.

CHAPTER FOURTEEN
Wounded

The ammo in the bandolier was spent.

Bishop dug into his pockets. Nothing. He breached the rig, pulling the dead shell from the right barrel, then checked the live round on the left. He shut the shotgun as quietly as possible, muffling its locking with his palm, and setting its position straight from the waist . . . to gut-shoot.

He had one heavy-grain shell, and no idea who or how many he'd be facing when he reached the top of the stairs that led to the emporium's second floor.

Blood still washed across his eyes, turning his vision hellish. He was on the top step when his strength erupted again, kicking open the door to the room in the corner, tearing it off its hinges. He stepped inside.

The window had been blown apart by the Adams grenade.

Scorched by the blast, the frame and wall plaster were lying in the middle of the floor. Colby's special ammunition was scattered. One bullet had been driven into the door like an arrow by the Adams's force, splitting the wood.

The only signs of Colby were the spatter on the wall about the height of his shoulder—if he was in his sniping position when the grenade blew—and one of his monogrammed handkerchiefs, also bloodstained, dangling from a jag of broken glass.

The last of the storm was soaking the room.

Bishop backed out, turned into the hallway, triggerlines drawn tight from his elbow, when the white-hot flash blinded him.

Minutes before, Chaney had mounted the Stockwell camera on a small tripod of his own making and positioned it at the end of the second-floor hallway. His ears were still ringing from the grenade, and he kept shaking his head to clear them. He poured the mix of magnesium powder onto the flash tray, then pressed himself against a wall, squatting on his haunches out of sight.

He'd seen Bishop in the street below, and tried for a picture of him walking toward the emporium, shotgun raised, with Hunk lying a few feet away, screaming over his bleeding leg, but the rain was still falling. Focusing his spy camera through the old windows was difficult. The image could have been mushed into a gray fog so he'd switched to the Stockwell, sure it would give him what he wanted.

His index finger was on the flash powder igniter, thumb on a cable to the camera's shutter release as Bishop was a blur of motion, kicking open the door to Colby's room, charging in.

Chaney held his breath. "God, to damn that—" He never finished.

The magnesium flash filled the hallway with hot light, and the barrel flame from the shotgun exploded at the same time, blowing apart the camera, lens, and bellows. Buckshot ripped the wall and sent the tripod spinning as Chaney ducked, still feeling the heat from the flash pan. Screaming out in pain, he clamped his hands over his blood-wet face.

Pat Garrett's boots sunk ankle-deep as he moved around the litter of corpses on Myrtle's main street, checking faces for his own men. Every step was a chore as the mud tried trapping him, holding him in place as he bent over each body for identification. He used his rifle as a crutch to pull his long legs free of the slop and get to the next.

He kept his collar turned against the easy rain that was washing the blood from the dead men and animals before forming rivulets that snaked down the street, emptying into deep puddles of reddish brown.

With a whistle, McCarty leaped over a puddle, then helped Garrett turn a body that had been pressed deep into the street by the weight of a fallen horse.

Garrett wiped away inches-thick mess from the face. "This is one of the guns who came with you."

"Jim something. Good man, decent with a carbine, but slow."

"He took it between the shoulders."

McCarty said, "Mr. Tunstall thought highly of him, but I got more of those red hoods than he did."

Garrett straightened up. "I wonder if the sniper's keeping count, too."

"Then he knows he lost, don't he?"

Garrett freed himself and found a solid patch next to another sprawled corpse clutching a Colt long barrel. It was a Fire Rider, his side opened by a shotgun blast. There were more, at least twenty, lying among the remains of the cattle-smashed storefronts and fences. Some were recognizable, others weren't.

Garrett took the Colt from the dead Rider, checking its action and saying to McCarty, "You shoot well under any circumstance."

McCarty was standing by a horse that was nudging the twisted body of its dead Fire Rider with its nose. "Hell, I wasn't the one who got those down by the barn and all them coming from that railcar." He stroked the horse neck to withers, its demonic disguise smearing off on his fingers. "The doc doesn't like being a legend, but after this crazy fight? I don't think he's got any choice. This'll be another fancy cover."

Garrett used the rifle butt to pry the body of a fat Fire Rider from the wet. "Maybe you'll get lucky and they'll write about you, too."

McCarty couldn't help his grin. "Here's to hoping."

Garrett turned the fat rider over and pulled off his hood—an outlaw. His nose was beaten flat, giving him a pig's snout. "I know this one, even shot him once, raiding cattle. Did you get him this time or was it me?"

"I shot that hog at least once!" The voice was one of Garrett's men, riding in from behind the shorn tents and wreckage.

Flanked by a few others, all were torn, tired, and bloody, but they'd made it through the skirmish. The battle relief played on their faces as one lit a cigarette then passed it along.

The first rider said, "Thank ol' Jesus there's more of us standing then there is them. We earned our pay, but it was that shotgun made the difference."

Chaney was sloppy deadweight, making no effort to walk, as Bishop hauled him down the back steps of the emporium, half carrying him on his shoulder like a bulging flour sack.

They reached the bottom of the stairs, with Chaney muttering, "You slaughtered me," over and over, the dried blood on his face cracking as he spoke.

Bishop hefted his one good arm, adjusting Chaney's

weight, and kept moving, not saying a word or looking at him.

A heavy piece of the windowsill, blown apart by the grenade, crashed to the ground, just missing them, as Bishop carried Chaney around the side of the emporium to the front of the barn, then let him crumple into the mud.

Chaney said, "I'm the one making you famous, and you slaughtered me . . ."

Not yet was Bishop's thought, but his mouth stayed clenched, taking in the litter of corpses that began at the barn and stretched the length of Main Street. Fire Riders, clutching guns and sabers, were nothing but sacks of flesh wrapped in red shrouds that had once been their robes and hoods. Useless.

And John Bishop was the reason why.

Any empathy he'd felt once was gone. He wasn't allowing himself that reflective moment over fallen enemies anymore. It was pointless. They were dead. He wasn't.

Metal scuttled at Bishop's feet.

He turned, bringing his boot down hard, pinning Hunk's hand to the barn floor, his fingers clenched around another Adams grenade. Hunk hadn't pulled the primer pin strap, and Bishop pressed with his heel, cracking a bone.

Hunk grabbed his blown-apart knee, spitting out, "*O să te omor, fiu de căţea!*"

Deaf to Hunk's and Chaney's crying, Bishop picked up the Adams, judging its weight in his palm and how the iron globe helped balance the double barrels that were his right side. He held the grenade out before him. The weapon felt natural, the way a scalpel had felt the first time he held one as a medical student. Different times, and now, a different place in his mind.

There was movement in the distance.

Bishop looked past the end of Main Street at the

horse galloping up-trail toward him. Perfect movement with head down, but no rider. Still shimmering red and running fast.

Rose's stallion broke past the junk heap, leaping over a bomb crater, and landing in the center of the street. The horse was slowing stride on its own as McCarty took a jump to grab hold of the bridle, then eased it to a stop by the corral's shattered fence.

The brown and white stood among the dead, Rose's saddle tilted to one side, a stirrup broken, and blood smeared across the horn and seat.

The wet smell of the sheep's wool broadened Colby's nose as he lay in the tangle of barbed wire. A few ewes nuzzled him as he struggled to sit up, metal jags digging at him through his clothes.

The impact of the grenade had propelled a piece of wood into his shoulder, but he'd managed to keep his rifle, and to stumble down the back stairs of the emporium, through the smoky fire of the explosion.

He didn't remember finding his horse or riding away from Myrtle along a back trail with the shotgun blasts and the screams of the Fire Riders echoing behind him. Finally losing consciousness, he'd fallen from his saddle.

He'd never ridden away from an assigned target before. Those thoughts were cut in half by a hot jolt as his eyes rolled back, catching a flash of his own rifle pointed directly at his face, before he lost consciousness for the second time.

She came into his view, and the wash of blood that John Bishop saw through started breaking apart like water beading against polished leather. He angled the bay from the cut in the trees to the slope of grass where Rose was lying.

Gunshot and bleeding.

She was on her side about twenty feet from Maynard's body, and quite still. With every step closer, Bishop's vision cleared, the pounding between his temples vanishing, allowing the sounds around him to enter.

He pulled up his horse, closed his eyes tight, then opened them. The sky had lost the last tint of his blood to become the blue-gray after a storm. Streaks of sunlight showed Chisum's cattle grazing along a high ridge.

Bishop could feel each breath completely filling his lungs as he dropped from the bay and pulled his field medical kit from a saddlebag. Running to her, he jangled it open with his left hand, his voice with him again as he called out, "Rose."

He repeated her name louder and louder, but she didn't stir.

Other riders were coming in. McCarty was on the brown and white, with Garrett the last to clear the tree line on his tall hammerhead. Chaney and Hunk shared a Fire Rider horse tethered to Garrett's saddle, both of them with hands tied and fresh wounds.

Chaney mumbled to anyone and the ground, "Slaughter of the innocents . . ."

Garrett said, "Write it down, Chaney."

Bishop was kneeling, the shotgun locked straight at his side. He had two fingers beneath Rose's jaw, checking her pulse.

McCarty said, "I think I know what you're doing, but never seen it done that way before." He got down from his horse.

"Don't tell me she's dead, Doc."

"I can't, because she isn't. Get a bedroll."

McCarty took a blanket from behind his saddle and spread it on the wet grass while Bishop laid out bandages, antiseptic, and the wooden case for his surgical equipment. He flipped the latch, thumb-popped the lid, revealing the polished knives and instruments in their velvet-lined casket. He chose the proper scalpels with instant precision. Bishop's moves with his med kit were as instinct-sure as breaching and firing the double barrel.

His instructions were clear. "Rose first, then the Rider, then Chaney's mouth. Garrett, get that slick off her. McCarty, take the bottle of carbolic, that one in the middle, and soak some linen."

Garrett pulled the rain slicker over her head, the rubber sticking to her bullet wound. He freed it carefully, then tossed it aside, as Bishop cleaned the wound with antiseptic.

"Turn her."

McCarty and Garrett put Rose on her back as Bishop cut around her shirt, pulling away the bloody cloth to see if the bullet had torn deeper, done any worse damage. A medium-caliber slug had entered clean on her left side, just below the rib cage.

Bishop angled her to examine the exit wound. There wasn't any. A slash of flesh bubbled in the center of a black and purple bruise that spread along Rose's hip, exactly where the bullet had lodged itself.

McCarty said, "You're really gonna operate on her now?"

Bishop turned to the instrument case, taking a "bleeder" scalpel, opening the razor-styled blade from its wooden handle with quick motion. "I'm going to patch her, so you can get her to a proper doctor."

Garrett held her in position, halfway on her side. "Chisum's doc is probably the best for two states, but Rose thinks it's you."

"Right now, she doesn't have much choice," Bishop said as he swirled the bleeder in carbolic before slicing across the purple bruising. The blade glanced the edge of the embedded slug. "Just skidded under the surface." With blood erupting around the scalpel, he peeled back the skin.

McCarty sopped the blood with linen.

Bishop dropped the bleeder and grabbed bullet-extracting forceps. "Ever think about medicine?"

McCarty was wincing, looking away. "I'm smart enough to know I ain't got the brains for it."

Garrett said, "You've seen a hell of a lot worse than this."

McCarty still wouldn't look. "Yeah, but not with women."

Bishop used the small porcelain scoop on the end of the instrument, pressing it against a plane of raw muscle under the slug before gently rolling the lead out of the wound crater. "She's lucky. It didn't break apart."

Chaney called from his horse, "Is that what you do, Doctor? Shoot them, then sew them up? Create your own patients?"

Bishop laid the extractor aside. "Maybe you should write it that way."

Garrett held a curved suturing needle that Bishop threaded with carbolic catgut. He took the needle, saying, "Except, I didn't shoot her."

Hunk yelled, "No, me you shot! *Bastard nebun!*"

Bishop said, "You're next," while lacing Rose's wound, bringing the tissues together as Garrett cleaned around it, following the perfect stitching. One-handed, Bishop took the sutures through the sides of the wound, pulling it closed with just enough strength, before tying it off and cutting it. It wasn't the work of a field butcher, but fine surgery.

Garrett said, "And you say you can't remember a damn thing."

Bishop rubbed his eyes, his vision still clear. "She'll need something clean."

McCarty got some new denim from his saddlebag as Garrett and Bishop finished her bandaging. "So, what do you tell Chisum?" Bishop asked.

"That we fought the battle, lost some good men and a quarter of the herd, but wiped out some Fire Riders." Garrett slipped one of Rose's arms through McCarty's clean shirt. "And Rose is still alive."

Bishop said, "Get her to a doctor before sunset."

McCarty finished the buttoning. "Mr. Tunstall said something about Chisum paying out a victory bonus." He turned, waving his sombrero toward the Chisum men who were rounding up the herd and gathering them along the far hillside. "Hell, if anybody ever earned any victory money, we're it. Miss Rose, too."

Hunk let a word drop. "Wrong."

Garrett stood. "You said something, Hunkie?"

Hunk met Garrett's stare. "You're wrong. About the victory. Wrong."

McCarty said, "Hey, I counted the dead, ya gut-eater! We both did. There's a hell of a lot more of yours than ours lying back there."

"You don't know what has happened today. It was *afacere*—a deal. Worked out." Hunk bent forward, holding his knee with bloody fingers. "We're all fools."

Garrett took a step, but Bishop moved beyond him instantly, pulling Hunk off the saddle and dumping him on the field—like tossing a rag doll. The huge man landed hard, before Bishop planted a foot on his chest, pinning him down.

"Are you talking about the massacre? That?"

"I won't be killed by you—!"

"What was worked out? What did you mean?"

"*Dumnezeu*—!"

Bishop smashed the edge of the double barrel against Hunk's knee. He screamed. Bishop's one hand went around the thick throat, squeezing Hunk's voice to whispered curses. *"Prostii!"*

"I can help that knee"—Bishop kept his left hand on Hunk and raised the rig again—"or crush it. Use the bone saw from my kit or put it back together. Understand?

Hunk nodded.

"Choose."

Hunk spoke after Bishop released his throat. "Don't . . . don't take my legs. Doctor."

"Tell me what you meant. What deal?"

Hunk connected with Bishop's eyes, saw something red-shadowed and dark filling them. "It was set for us. We knew when you would be there. That's why we were waiting."

Garrett said, "To steal Chisum's cattle, but we beat you down with them, instead."

Hunk bent his head back, sucking in moist air. "Not just the cattle! I was told to leave you hanging, like butchered. Let this Chaney take pictures to show everyone to fear us, so they'll pay up."

McCarty spit. "Didn't work out that way, did it?"

Hunk said, "You were more clever as fighters than we thought. But, you were to lie down when we attacked. Not fight so hard, and let us have the doctor."

Bishop took Hunk's windpipe again. "Why? Why did you think that?"

Straining to tears, Hunk swung one of his giant hands and gripped Bishop's shoulder, trying to break him off. Bishop squeezed harder with his left. Muscles steeled, he raised the shotgun like a club.

Hunk finally let go, and his words poured out as Bishop allowed him air again. "Farrow. He told us. He led us into the town, gave all the information."

Garrett said, "There's an honest-to-God son of a bitch."

Bishop said, "Farrow always works for somebody. Who wanted me? Chisum?"

"You are dead now, what do you care?"

"You're right. I am dead." Bishop jammed a knee into Hunk's chest, pressing his entire weight against him, pressure-choking. "Who wanted me!?"

"*Neică*—brother. Your brother. He did all this."

* * *

Colby felt the barbed wire biting as he was coming to, swimming back from a deep, painful sleep. The jags were in different places now, not that accidental tangle when he was caught in the fence, but at his wrists. Coils across his chest bound him to a sheep-shearing chair.

The boy with patchy beard and worn overalls checked the ties holding Colby in place, daubing his fresh blood as if he was catching random drips from a freshly painted fence. Satisfied, he took a step back, watching Colby's eyes struggle open.

He drew a cup of water from a rain barrel and threw it into Colby's face, then filled it again and held it to let him drink. The water cooled the acid in Colby's throat. Lambs in a side pen bleated, poking their snouts through wooden slats as if trying for a better look.

The boy said, "My father always splashed his face as he was coming back from a bout. From that barrel, in fact. You seemed to be in need."

"I'm definitely not drunk."

The boy stood in front of Colby as if he were on sentry duty, speaking as if afraid of mispronunciation. "I found you tangled in our fence, and you didn't move. You hadn't died, so, it must be drink. I know a thing about drink. I found all your guns, so I know you came for me, mean my family harm."

Colby pulled on his wrists bound by the barbed wire to the chair's sloping back, designed to keep the sheep comfortable and in place while being shorn. With each pull, the wire cut deeper, bringing him sharper focus. He said, "No, I didn't. What's your thinking, son?"

The boy held up the watch chain with Hunk's ear dangling. "This isn't what a Christian man of no harm wears. You are an assassin, working for the cattlemen.

We got sheep, so you are to kill us. That's easier to figure on than *a-b-c*."

Damp lamb's wool was the air, and Colby could see two-blade shears hanging on the wall, large tubs for boiling, and bales of fleece stacked around the barn. Ten sheep stalls, open on one side, allowed the stock to wander as they pleased.

That didn't escape Colby's sense of humor. "It pleases me that the lambs have their freedom." He twisted on the rotating seat of the shearing chair, loosening the wire holding him there. Back and forth. The razor barbs sliced cloth and skin, almost to muscle, but started to give. "You treat them better than you're treating me."

The boy said, "They can be trusted. My father had another regulator tied to that shearing chair for three days. When he was awake, he spoke of his work. I know your reasons for being on our ranch."

Colby settled. "You're wrong as you can be, son, about why I'm here."

The boy moved to Colby's weapons. "That's not what I see."

"I understand, son. I do." Colby worked his wrists and ankles. "May I have some more water? Wouldn't it be soul-proper to give me some?"

The boy took the cup and filled it. He was skinny, with a long reach, and kept as much distance as he could as he put it to Colby's lips.

Colby drank, his body turned slightly in the shearing chair, his arms stretched behind him, bent at the elbows. "Thank you, son. I'm sure you're a fine provider."

The boy lowered the cup. "I have learned from my father—"

Colby head butted the boy, then smashed him with a raised knee, catching his chin as he fell onto him. He scissored both legs, bound at the ankle, on either side of the boy's neck, clamping him tight.

It had taken seconds. As the boy struggled, his arms waving, Colby called out, "I know you're there. You can come out. It's all right. Don't be afraid."

Lambs cried as the dumpling worked his way over the edge of their stall, tumbling to the floor. His eyes were as big as his four year-old face, and he wiped his tears on the sleeve of a nightshirt.

The boy got out, "Jacob, run for the house!"

Colby asked the child, "Your brother? Do you want to help him? Bring me those shears."

Jacob stood frozen, tears running down his cheeks.

Colby growled out, "Jacob, if you want the bad dream to be over, bring me the shears right behind you. Can you reach?"

Rose slumped unconscious in the saddle as McCarty swung onto the brown and white. Wrapping his arms around her waist to sit her straight and steady, he laced the reins through his right hand.

Garrett placed her feet in the stirrups, adjusting them sure, before pulling a small sack from the inside pocket of his long coat. There was the rattle of gold coins as he tossed it to McCarty, who caught it with his left.

"Your victory pay. From Mr. Chisum."

"You could've kept it hid. I'm obliged to you, Garrett." McCarty called out to Hunk, "I told you, gut-eater!"

Hunk snorted as Bishop turned the handle on a brass Petit's tourniquet.

Drawing the strap slightly tighter above Hunk's freshly bandaged knee, Bishop said, "Hold it."

Hunk took the handle.

Bishop slipped a finger between the strap and the side of Hunk's leg. "It's slacking. This is a field piece. We need something to hold the pressure more exactly. I don't want you to lose that leg."

Hunk smirked. "Oh, yes, I'm sure of that."

"Just hold it."

As Bishop started packing his field kit, Hunk said, "So what to do? I save my own leg, while you ride me to an execution? Do it here. Easier."

Bishop shook his head. "Not here."

Garrett placed a hand on Bishop's shoulder, then held up the victory pay. Bishop glanced, but didn't move for the money, just put the rest of his instruments in the kit.

Garrett said, "You surely earned it, Doc."

"Chisum's got nothing to do with me anymore."

"Hell, we all know that. You didn't take a dime, but he wanted you to have something to help after, if you made it out alive. Maybe for your next war."

Chaney was adjusting the wrap of gauze across his cheek. "That's more compensation than I'll ever see for my pain."

Garrett said, "Mr. Chaney, I've known fellas cut themselves shaving who were in worse shape."

Bishop took the sack, slapped two gold pieces into Chaney's hand. "For your camera."

Chaney was defiant. "I have another."

"I know." Bishop turned to Garrett to return the gold, but he was walking for his horse.

Without turning around, he said, "You made the right choice, Doc. Take the money. Help yourself. God knows the men calling the shots have plenty."

Bishop stored the money and medical kit in his saddlebags, before throwing a leg up and saying to Garrett, "You've got my patient. Get her home."

"We'll do it. Hope you get home, too."

Hunk yelled from the back of the horse he was sharing with Chaney, "Garrett! I'm your prisoner, you need to take me to a doctor, then to Chisum!"

Garrett was on his horse. "Not my prisoner, and you've already got a doctor."

"But this one tried to kill me!"

McCarty brought the brown and white around, keeping Rose secure with his arm, cradling her. "If the doc wanted you dead, you'd already be buried."

Chaney held his hand against his bandaged face as if he was going to break into pieces. "I intend to quote you, Mr. McCarty."

McCarty howled, "Get my name right!"

The outriders started moving the cattle herd from the far hills, heading them back toward the trail slow and easy.

McCarty, holding Rose, broke the pace. He could feel her struggled breathing against him and urged the brown and white. The horse moved steady and fast, getting ahead of the herd, and following the trail to the next town.

In a moment, they were through the trees. Bishop approved. Rose's chances were good.

Pat Garrett tipped his hat, which Bishop returned, before locking the rig from his waist, and looping the tether line from Chaney and Hunk's horse to his own saddle.

Chaney said, "I won't be buried next to this immigrant."

Hunk said, "I wonder how you're looking with a grenade in your mouth."

Bishop looked to Hunk. "Just keep pressure on that leg."

The shears were too big for Jacob's hands as he tried closing the blades through the barbed wire, only to have them slip sideways or clatter to the barn floor.

Colby kept Jacob's brother trapped, his knees locked around his neck, ready to snap it with a single twist of his body. His voice was soft. "Try again, son. This is magic. If you set me free, your brother goes free. Just cut the little wire, that's all."

Jacob wedged the blade around the wire knot, trying to get a grip, the shears slipping away from his stubby fingers. Finally, the edge of the blades cut one of the wire ties, pulling the barbs back from Colby's wrist.

"Look at that. Your brother's almost free. Just like magic. Try again."

Jacob jammed the shears under the wire for the last time, catching a piece of wire between the blades, then squeezing it with all his tiny strength. Wires popped apart, and Jacob fell backwards against a sheep stall.

He was sobbing as Colby brought his arms from around the shearing chair, sitting up and releasing his brother. The older boy sagged to the floor, his brother throwing himself around his neck.

Cutting and pulling, Colby unwrapped the coil from around his chest. "Boys, I'm going to need some help for the next few days. You have to take me in."

Jacob held on tight, as his brother said, "You can't be in the house. Father won't allow it. Best ride on, sir."

"You're a strong boy." Colby freed his ankles. "I would say your father is gone, or—"

"He'll be back in the winter," the older boy said, cutting Colby off. "He'll be back before Christmas."

Colby stood, his clothes soaking from the barbed punctures across his body, and the large tear in his shoulder. He managed a step, steadying himself on the edge of the sheep stall. "I'll be gone long before then. Help me inside."

Bishop stood among the bodies of three Fire Riders, the dried mud plastering their red tunics with spatters of gray, hoods pulled away from buried faces. He was holding the Bloody Bill saber, broken off and jagged just above the haft. The shotgun rig was poised on his right side.

Chaney was in front of the ruins of the emporium, adjusting the lens on his miniature camera as far as he could. The short glass near-rounded the image, taking in Bishop, the dead men, and beside them, Hunk, with his hands tied and leg bandaged.

Chaney held the camera steady. What he was seeing was distorted, but true. Bishop kept still until Chaney said, "All right. You wanted to send a message, Doctor. This will surely be it."

Bishop said, "You're the one who sends the messages. I'm sure you'll give the story a lot of special touches when you write it."

"I'll invent very little this time."

"You can probably take the bandage off in a week, but keep your face clean. Avoid infection."

"Doctor, you still haven't made reference to who I am or my family's history with you, which is rather colorful."

Bishop said, "I've known who you are since Paradise. Somebody told me your cousin's name is on the list of men I've killed."

"It's quite a lot of names."

"My burden. He was the gambler?"

"A poor one."

Bishop nodded. "He certainly used poor judgment. Are you looking to settle?"

Chaney flourished. "Not now. There's too much reporting about you I have to do. That's my priority above personal concerns. And . . . I choose not to be shot by you twice in one day."

Bishop turned to Hunk, who was still mounted, and slipped the broken saber under the tourniquet strap, turning the handle halfway. "That should work. Give your hand a rest."

The handle steadied the pressure, allowing the proper amount of blood flow to the damaged knee.

Hunk nodded. "It's . . . it's better. Feels better."

Bishop knelt by one of the dead Riders, a shotgun poking out from beneath his blood-sticky tunic. He wrenched the weapon away, opened it, and took out two unfired .12-gauge shells, then found half a dozen more in a side pocket. He slipped six in his bandolier, loaded the rig, then hung a small canvas sack containing the last of the Adams grenades off his saddle horn.

Hunk said, "That Chaney's taking another picture."

"I hope he gets a good one."

"They won't like you taking ammunition from their dead."

Bishop climbed onto the bay, the newly loaded rig angled at Hunk. "Seems appropriate to me."

Hunk said, "So, I'm the prisoner. Now what?"

"Death, probably. But Hell first."

Chaney fitted the last small negative plate into the camera and steadied himself on a piece of the emporium balcony laying in the street. The battle hadn't gone the way he was told, but what had happened he could sell all over the world.

He waited, thinking how sure he'd been that Bishop would go for the killing shot and finish him off, but had doctored his face instead. Then, insisted that he take photographs.

Bishop was bringing his horse around, and Chaney had the miniature camera solid in both hands, his thumb holding the shutter open long enough to balance the muted daylight, long enough for the tiny negative to capture a battleground littered with enemy dead and Bishop riding away from it, a Fire Rider prisoner tethered behind him.

The shutter clicked.

CHAPTER FIFTEEN
Resurrections

Sheriff Tucker rested the Henry rifle on top of the cremation urn and sighted. He was close, maybe ten feet away, but wanted to see the bullet enter, enjoy its exit, and the aftermath. That thought made him smile.

He kept the rifle aimed at the oversized, green-lacquered coffin, a gold-inlaid dragon coiling around it twice before the head and tail met on the highly polished lid. The dragon's eyes were red jewels that shone in the broken bits of light coming in from the shuttered windows of the workshop.

The voice seemed to come from the dragon. "Just how damn stupid are you, runt?"

Half-hidden by the huge coffin, sitting up like a corpse reacting to a formaldehyde gas bubble in its stomach, a man rose. Dead-thin, with crude stitches joining his forehead and hairline, a souvenir of a scalping, the outlaw looked to have been killed years before.

But there he was, lighting a cigar and paying little attention to Sheriff Tucker or his threats.

Scalped Outlaw said, "Wave that Henry around all

you want, but I'm not doing a goddamned thing until I see the boss man."

Albert Tomlinson leaned against the ticket agent's window of the Paradise train depot, reaching for a stack of telegraph messages that he could see had his name across the top as RECEIVER.

"That's the way to ruin your suit!" Junior heaved his words as he shuffled in through the back door from the stables, dragging a canvas mail sack behind him. He got himself to a stool and held on. "That's wet paint on the window. Put on not ten minutes ago. I'm surprised at you, Mr. Tomlinson."

Tomlinson instantly yanked back his arm, then pulled his glasses down his nose, peering through the bottom lens of the bifocals, examining his jacket for stains. He brushed at his tweeds, picking off a bit of tacky paint. "You have a number of urgent communications for me."

Junior's wooden teeth got in the way of his words. "I was going to send a boy. Any problem getting anythin' from me since you been here?"

Tomlinson spotted another smear of blue. "No, your work has been satisfactory, so far."

"You bet it has. The mail should interest you."

"The package to my daughters?"

Junior said, "Already sent." He fished into the sack and handed Tomlinson a rolled newspaper before moving to the telegraph desk and sorting through the messages with shaking arthritic hands. His habit was to lick his thumb, separating each telegram at its edge, then pulling it from the pile. Tomlinson had three.

Junior handed over the telegrams. "Sorry about your jacket, but we're getting a fancy do-over, too."

Tomlinson put the telegrams in his side pocket without reading them. He stayed with the newspaper, turning its pages.

Junior pointed to an article. "My good friend wrote that piece. Know what happened in our jail, don't you? Right across the way? That Shotgun Bishop was here. Now he's killin' like it's open season."

Tomlinson didn't answer. He walked from the ticket window, around the side of the station, following the newly built planked sidewalk. He didn't look away from the article, purposely shutting out the activity and rising noise around him.

Up and down the street, crews were painting storefronts, replacing windows and doors, hauling away piles of flood debris in flat wagons. Even the graveyard next to the jail had been mowed and its fence whitewashed.

Music leaked from a couple joints, the sound of the morning pianos scraping each other before mixing with the work voices in the street—shouted greetings and orders and the constant sounds of hammers and saws.

What wasn't being built was reopened. Paradise was full of railroad men, cowboys, and laborers staying over for a night or a week, but all for sure leaving their pay behind.

Tomlinson quickly avoided two workmen hauling a chuck-a-luck table into an unfinished saloon. Some old boys hung out by the front door, waiting for it to be set up.

One of the workmen stumbled, catching Tomlinson's attention. "That table's worth more than your house. I'll be back to check installation. These . . . gentlemen . . . are anxious to play."

One old boy belched out, "The Sheriff'll lose more cash than all of us put together! That dumb son of a bitch couldn't find luck if it bit him sittin' down!"

There was more hacking laughter until Tucker busted the jaw of the laugher with the butt of the Henry rifle, swung around, and slammed another in the gut, dropping him to the sidewalk.

It had happened so fast, Tomlinson didn't even have time to turn around. The gamblers were sprawled around his feet, yelling and cursing. The laugher spit a tooth and some pink.

"Those are potential customers, Sheriff."

Tucker casually wiped his glasses on his sleeve. "This little lesson in respect won't stop them from betting their pockets. Your problem's across the street."

They waited for a liquor-heavy wagon to pass before crossing to the coffin maker's.

"How long was John Bishop in your jailhouse?"

"At least a month, till Chisum bailed him out. You know all this . . . or you ought."

"It was a missed opportunity. You should have killed him when you had the chance."

"I just do what the money tells me."

They were standing beneath a sign that read YOUR VESSELS TO HEAVEN—$19.95

Tucker said, "You're in charge. Have at it."

Tomlinson entered the front room of the coffin maker's shop where the finished models were set out. A few were made of rosewood, metal handles at the feet and head, but most were painted pasteboard, with a place for a name on the lid, and Paradise scrolled alongside so the insects would know where you ended, broke.

Tomlinson had Tucker cock the rifle deliberately for the sound, but made him follow behind two steps as he strode into the workshop. Months before, that would have been unthinkable, but the bookkeeper's mild nature had been replaced by a sense of authority over the men whose salaries he was controlling. The curved posture was gone, his words carrying quiet force. He told the dark of the room, "I'm paying you. This stoppage is unacceptable."

A ring of smoke drifted from behind the opulent green-lacquered coffin, before the scalped outlaw sat up. He glanced at the smoke and said, "You're sounding like a yard boss I had, or an overseer. I never paid neither of them no never mind. Get ready to open your pockets, boss man."

Scalped Outlaw grabbed a sledgehammer and rolled away from the coffin. The barrel of Tucker's rifle followed him as he went to the back of the workshop and swung the hammer from his shoulder, smashing a corner wall. Three heavy swings broke through the planking, revealing an open tunnel behind. Scalped Outlaw pounded with the sledge and kicked the pieces away until a man could pass through.

Tomlinson said, "We know about the tunnel."

"That's an access way to the old gold mine, vein lasted all of a month. I worked it, with an outhouse-crazy Sioux who gave me this haircut." Scalped Outlaw jutted his head toward Tomlinson and Tucker, who had the rifle pointed directly at his skull.

Tucker provided some information. "That's when this place was actually supposed to be a paradise. You can't tell me nothing."

"Yes, the very reason I hired you and gave you plans as to what was needed. There's no secret here. I hired you." Tomlinson emphasized the word to remind Scalped Outlaw of his position.

"If there ain't no secret, why's the runt pointing that Henry at me?"

Tucker said, "Try *runt* one more time."

Tomlinson put a hand on Tucker's shoulder. "The sheriff's here because there's a disruptive employee making threats."

Scalped Outlaw held the sledge with both hands, ready to swing as Tomlinson moved to the smashed wall and peered into the tunnel.

It was thick with spiderwebs and the dust of rot. Globed oil lamps, smashed and hanging loose, had once been attached to wooden crossbeams supporting the tunnel's opening, but a little deeper, the timbers were piled together with rubble from the falling-in sides and an unsupported roof.

Tomlinson said, "Follow the plans."

"Want me to crawl in, shore that up, and build another entrance? I'll need extra men. Drag in some of the teamsters who're spending time in the pleasure houses, double my pay, and give me a taste. You might get what you want."

"A taste of what?"

"The gold you're pulling out of there. Half of every dollar sounds about fair. And that, I want in writing."

Tucker said, "Like you can read."

"Good enough. That tells me you're serious about this."

Tomlinson wanted to see how far it would go. "Or?"

Scalped Outlaw said, "These things collapse all the time. Would probably take a lot of your new street with it." He leaned back next to the casket, taking a deep drag on his cigar. "Keep the runt away from me or I'll hump him dead with that rifle."

Tomlinson watched Tucker for a beat, the purple tinge around his ears spreading with his anger. "Get him ready for work." He walked back out into the sunlight and traffic.

Tucker smashed the outlaw quickly in the neck with the rifle barrel, choking the smoke in his throat. Scalped Outlaw heaved onto the floor.

Tucker shouted, "Suck on it! Like your mama and the field hands. C'mon!"

Scalped Outlaw opened his lips, but not his teeth.

Tucker smashed again, parting his jaws, and shoving the barrel of the Henry into the side of his mouth. "This is what a runt does. You're going to get in there and start building, while they work out the details of your contract. Do it, or I'll blow a hole in your cheek, or take it a step further than your Sioux friend. Ever seen a tongue split? How you think you'll talk after that?" He took a deep breath. "Ready for work?"

Scalped Outlaw nodded, the gun barrel knocking into his teeth.

Tucker pulled back the Henry. "Only one rule in Paradise—respect the man with the badge."

The girl held up large, udder-shaped breasts, so Widow Kate could see the two symbols tattooed just beneath them.

Kate was trying to lean forward, eyes squinted, her own stomach blocking her, but read, "*Feng kuang.* That means *crazy.*" She brought her wheelchair back a few turns, letting the girl tuck herself back into the bodice that was barely holding her together, her pale-white curves fighting any restraint.

Soiled Dove, in a finely appointed purple dress and dangling earrings, kept an arm around the girl, gently stroking her shoulder and lifting her chin so her eyes would meet Kate's when she spoke.

Kate said, "You worked in San Francisco. Got that mark for killing a customer."

"Yes, ma'am." The girl looked to Dove, then said, "He couldn't be pleased, and I'd tried for sure. He broke some of my personal things. A turtle comb and a hand mirror. I used one of the pieces to protect myself."

"It's good you told me."

The girl lowered her chin again as Kate wheeled behind a massive desk that had once belonged to the captain of the Pacific ship Siberia. She didn't look up, waiting for Kate's verdict. Dove's touch never left her shoulder.

Kate ran her hands across the plush fabric of dragons carved into the chair's armrests and drummed her fingers as her Chinese cook silently set out a luncheon tray.

The cook retreated on bound feet, and Kate still

hadn't said a word. She shifted her massive weight in the wheelchair, its upholstered back automatically adjusting for her comfort with a quick clicking of small gears. It was an elaborate mechanism, but elegant and imposing. Perfect for her.

Soiled Dove said, "I was thinking of the new house."

With swollen fingers, Kate picked up a ceramic spoon shaped like a duck and dipped it into a bowl of bird's nest soup. Holding the spoon was a chore. Bringing it to her mouth, even more of an effort. She swallowed. "You won't be working here in this house. I have a new house just down the street, and I need one like you there. I've had difficult johnnies in the past, but there'll be nothing like them in my places, so forget about that tattoo."

The girl glanced up with her eyes. "Yes, ma'am."

"Dove will tell you what I expect in your behavior."

Dove whispered in the girl's ear, "No worries," before opening the office door and letting her out.

Tomlinson was standing in the hallway. She shut the door on him, turning to Kate. "You'll want me here for this, won't you?"

"Why?"

"This is about our future . . . business."

"Tell Mr. Tomlinson to wait a few minutes, then he may knock."

Soiled Dove seemed frozen in her spot, unblinking, as Kate sipped some more soup and read the newspaper that had been laid out neatly next to her luncheon tray.

Dove said, "I've another ten girls coming in this week. Do you want to see each? Or I can find them spots."

Kate adjusted the light of the ornate jade lamp on her desk to look closer at the photographs of John Bishop standing among a mountain of dead Fire Riders. "Do what I ask."

Soiled Dove stepped out of the office, shutting the door behind her.

Kate gave herself a moment, fixed on Bishop. "Oh,

Goddamn you, Doctor," she said with a shake of the head that was disbelief and admiration together.

She was counting the bodies, her finger making a dent in the newspaper as she spotted each one, when Tomlinson's knock came three times. She took another spoonful of soup before allowing him entrance. He wasn't fully in the room when she said, "So what happens now?"

"I'm not understanding the question."

Kate rolled quickly to where he was standing, his hands in his pockets in near-rude defiance. "Your new demeanor doesn't suit you . . . or me."

"I just solved a labor problem."

"It's an insult to imagine I'm not completely aware of everything that happens in Paradise. I'm not worried about the backs needed for work. I'm talking about money."

Tomlinson's shoulders were curving inward. "Well, ask again. Just be specific."

Kate said, "John Bishop killed a cadre of your riders, and not for the first time—"

"I've seen the photographs, read the exaggerations."

"He's a hero in these papers that show him with one of yours as a prisoner, which means he'll take the war right to you."

Tomlinson said, "I don't disagree with a thing said."

Kate pushed herself a few feet closer to Tomlinson, making him take a stumbled step back as she stubbed a short finger into his chest. "I want to know about the money. Are the deposits going to be there? You've had a setback, but I'm making Paradise new again."

Tomlinson said, "I know what we invested in. I approved it."

"You can do that from a shallow grave?"

Tomlinson's voice dropped, his confidence draining out in front of Kate. "I'd ask that you control your famous temper."

Kate's eyes narrowed in the round folds of her face, making them almost disappear: "I know Dr. John Bishop . . . well. He's done me a good turn before, and I repaid in kind."

"Me as well."

"Would you like to see my scars?"

Tomlinson said, "Bishop truly helped my youngest daughter. He was kind."

"Think that makes a difference? You work for his brother, and he'll put down anyone who stands between him and that killing. It's what tears him apart, what drives him. I *know* this man."

"But, we have an army."

"Nothing but targets."

"That's foolish thinking. We have an organization spread across the Southwest to control all outlawry."

Kate snorted. "That's a hell of a term."

"That's why you came to us. To build our town."

"My town."

"Correction. Our investment."

Kate said, "Partial, and maybe your best one. You'd do well to remember who set this all in motion."

"You and your fleshpots are to be admired, ma'am." Tomlinson held out the three telegrams. "Devlin Bishop is authorizing another hundred thousand dollars. He believes in your *City of Paid-for Sin,* and these . . . family issues . . . won't stop business. I won't allow it."

Kate said, "I doubt it will make any difference. Paradise is my dream, and I expect to die here, even have a coffin built just for me."

"Yes, I believe I've seen it. Stylish."

"I expect to have one death. John Bishop's had a dozen. So far."

Tomlinson said, "You're taking that trash too seriously."

"You won't stop him, sir. If I had the Texas Rangers, the army, and John Bishop coming for me, I'd worry about Bishop." Kate rolled back to her desk and took a small opium pipe from an ivory box, which also held the penny dreadful with Bishop on the cover. "What the hell. If anything does happen to your Fire Riders, I can't swing a dead cat without hitting someone who wants in on this."

She dropped a small bead into the bowl as Tomlinson said, "You won't need anyone else. If I drank, I'd say we should toast to a . . . secure partnership."

Kate lit the pipe and drew it in deep, then stabbed a finger at the photograph of all the dead Riders and said, "I can't do that, because you, sir, are not secured."

The creek was rain-swollen, water running fast and just reaching the belly of Bishop's horse. He glanced over to see Hunk, feet dangling in the current about an inch, his wrists loosely bound, but the rigged tourniquet holding.

They reached the other shore, which was the edge of a carpet of sweetgrass that stretched open for miles toward the Rockies, the creek weaving alongside. Bishop swung off his saddle, keeping the rig against his shoulder and letting the bay drink as he freed the knot that tethered Hunk's horse to his own.

Hunk, who hadn't said a word for more than twenty miles, managed to say, "Set the horse free, because now you're to kill me?"

"Get down off there. I want to check that knee."

Hunk sat up straight, bringing his one good leg around, and balling his massive fists in case Bishop pulled him from the saddle again.

"You need help." Bishop offered a shoulder and Hunk took it.

Bishop attended to the knee, cleaning and adding another stitch. Hunk jolted back when Bishop touched some swelling on the outer side of the leg. He gave

Hunk a piece of leather to bite on as he tweezed a last fragment of buckshot from the edge of the tissue.

"When you get shot, often it's not loss of blood that kills. It's the germs on the bullet. The infection does it."

Hunk spit out the leather. "Still, your gun."

"You're damn lucky to be alive anyway, with that ear."

"We don't have a good doctor."

"Where?"

"Nowhere." Hunk shook his head. "He's what they called a field butcher. You know what that is?"

"It means he's done a lot of amputations. So have I."

"But not this time."

Bishop said, "You have information I need. I don't even know if a one-armed man can perform an amputation. I mean, do it clean. That's a funny problem, isn't it?"

Hunk chose his words carefully. "Yes. Funny."

Bishop daubed the stitches before rewrapping the leg. "I might have to do you, the way they did me. Do you know what happened to my arm?"

Hunk was holding the handle of the saber with the two inches of broken blade. "They would read about you at the fort. Everything."

Bishop took the saber, twisted the blade through the tourniquet strap, and turned it, keeping it taut.

Hunk said, "I don't understand you. Are you going to kill me or not?"

"Gangrene might still do it for me. If I lose patience or think you're used up, I might." He started for the creek. "Or maybe I'll get you back to your wife and kids."

Hunk said, "That won't happen."

Bishop dropped on the bank, splashed water into his eyes with his one palm. He kept it there, feeling the cool of the water, but the double barrels were swivel-aimed from his hip, always on Hunk. "When you die is up to you. Twenty years from now . . . or twenty minutes."

Hunk's face was locked.

Bishop said, "My brother. You're taking me to him. You said the 'fort.'"

"You still don't even know everyone that you're fighting . . . or what."

"You'll show me or that leg will pain you till you're begging me to take it off."

"There are two men in you. Fighting all the time, I think."

Bishop said, "Then you have good reason to be afraid."

Linus pumped the bellows of the smith's furnace, heating the coals, before edging in the new horseshoe. He drew the air for extra heat, then turned the shoe, the iron-black giving way to molten yellow. He had the iron on the anvil, hammering it around the horn, forcing a turn, when Claude Ray came to the open door, watching him work to the center of the shoe, hot sparks flailing.

Claude Ray stepped into the stable. "New ones for Hurricane?"

"I imagine Mr. Chisum will want all new after we get her washed down."

Claude Ray hung on the side of the workbench, the artificial leg Bishop had designed for him, right where it had always been since Linus built it. Linus turned the hot iron, heating the other quarter as Claude picked up the prosthetic, working the knee back and forth.

Linus said, "You ready for that now?"

"You did real good, fine work."

Linus punched the shoe's nail holes, sweat washing his face and arms. "Chisum showed us Garrett's message. Rose has been to the doc and is coming back to you to heal herself up." He dropped the shoe in the cooling bucket. "She really went through the storm, so maybe it'd be nice if there was a different man waiting for her at home."

* * *

Coming up the Chisum road, the brown and white stallion walked easy, protecting Rose and her injury as she sat up straight in the saddle on her own. Garrett was alongside on his hammerhead, keeping in step, keeping an eye.

Behind them, McCarty and the outriders broke off, riding across the open stretch beyond the stables and corral. McCarty whistled before galloping toward the pasture where the remaining herd was being gathered.

John Chisum was on the porch, the maids and staff milling around him. There was excited chatter, but he stood alone by the railing, waiting for Rose and Garrett to get to his lawn before taking the front steps and meeting them with an outstretched hand.

Garrett got off his horse before Linus and a stable boy led it off. Chisum eyed the animal, patted its neck, and then said to Garrett, "Where's Farrow?"

"He's gone, Mr. Chisum, along with your prize horse. That's after he tried to get us all killed and shot Rose. But we're here . . . and most of your men and most of the herd."

"Don't misunderstand me, Patrick." Chisum took hold of Rose's horse and helped her down. "You don't know how glad I am that you're back safe."

Rose said, "Me too, sir. I got some back. I did that."

"So I heard." Chisum helped Rose into the arms of the youngest maid, her belly swollen by weeks. The maid shouldered Rose toward the main house, the other maids coming up to briefly hug her.

Garrett said, "This shouldn't be a victory dance, Mr. Chisum. There's a lot dead left in Myrtle. We beat the Fire Riders, but we're told that wasn't the plan, that Farrow had something else in mind."

Chisum said, "I don't know a damn thing about that, but there was a . . . negotiation."

Garrett's laugh was ironic and someplace deep. "There always is."

The Chisum cowboys brought their horses in, got handshakes and slaps on the back.

Chisum tipped his hat to them, shook a few hands, then said to Garrett, "They wanted Dr. Bishop. You knew that straightaway."

"Uh-huh. So did he, but couldn't figure why."

Somebody handed Garrett a glass of whiskey. "But, they got him all right."

Chisum coughed. "Dead?"

"Hardly."

"Where is he now?"

"Tending to his own business. He brought down the most of the red hoods, and I gave him his money." Garrett finished the glass. "Mr. Chisum, I'm saying it out loud—they were waiting. We were set up not to win this, but we did. Maybe it's about time you declared yourself."

Chisum said, "You're on the side of right. You have no worries on that score. What about Tunstall's guns?"

"McCarty made a good show of himself."

"John will be glad to hear it."

Garrett said, "You spent a hell of a lot on Bishop, maybe to give him up. But most of us are here because of what he did. His fight. As I see it, this battle makes all debts to you paid in full." There was a threat under Garrett's words and his forward leaning stance with his gun.

Chisum let them both pass. "I'm damn proud of you, Patrick. You're an asset to this ranch, and I hope to see you tonight at dinner. In the chair next to mine."

Garrett held out his glass. It was refilled.

The youngest maid helped Rose almost to the porch steps before they stopped. Rose whispered something to herself as she saw Claude Ray by the corral gate. In a new pressed suit, he was standing on two legs. He was holding a small gathering of violets in one hand, hanging on to a fence rail with the other.

Words didn't happen as he let go of the fence and started toward his wife. Taking an unsteady step, the prosthetic snapped into place. Stiff. Trying, he waved to Rose then took another step. Better each time, but he fought for balance.

Rose went to Claude, almost catching him, her own wounds burning. They got hold of each other with both arms and wrapped tightly. The flowers dropped from his hand, scattering at their feet.

Claude Ray didn't break and held Rose tighter. "Not dancing, but close."

Bishop pushed the bay fast along the field of tall grass, Hunk's horse keeping the tether between them straining. A nye of pheasants broke from the grass, splitting in two directions, darting away. Bishop aimed from the saddle and fired both barrels, bringing down three birds. He slowed the bay, then cut into the grass to pick up the kill and hang them from his saddle.

They were good shots, and the pheasants weren't buckshot-chewed.

Hunk said, "Good to see that thing can kill something other than men."

Bishop was actually smiling. "Enemies."

Hurricane reared back, legs kicking wild as a rope went around Farrow's chest and another went around his neck before he was hurled from the saddle. His chin hit the ground, head snapping back as two Fire Riders lashed his ankles tight. Farrow rolled to one side, squirming against his bonds, his Sears Roebuck vest and jacket caked with mud, dust, and someone else's blood.

A Rider pulled a rag from the water trough and stuffed it into Farrow's mouth, killing his screams.

Smythe was at the prison gates, jabbing at Farrow with the end of one of his crutches. "That was supposed to be our victory, mate. Splashed all over, to scare anyone who might come up against us. You said you had it worked out, but you didn't, did you? If you'd done it right, you wouldn't be in the spot you're in now, right? Aren't I right?"

The rope was tossed over a butcher's gallows and Farrow was pulled into the air by his ankles. He swung back and forth.

Smythe pulled the rag from his mouth, sloppy water following. "Am I right? You corked it up."

Farrow's eyes were closed tight. "This is making me sick! I can't be upside down!"

"You won't be for long."

"I got Chisum's trust and did what I was supposed to do!"

"Saying it don't make it so, mate."

"How could I know Chisum's men would fight like that? Or the Shotgun would take you all on? You wanted a massacre!"

Smythe said, "Yes, we did."

"I did my damn part!"

Smythe stopped the swinging with his crutch as hooded Riders gathered around, breaking from the mess table and passing a bottle hand-to-hand. Some had torches. All had guns and blades. Farrow cried out over all their murmurs and accusations.

Newspaper pages blew across the yard—Bishop and the Fire Riders scattered everywhere.

Dev Bishop broke through the crowd of his own men to look Farrow in the eye as he hung like a hog for butchering. He put a hand on Farrow's chest, holding him steady. "You let that photographer take pictures of my men. And my brother. And their bodies. Even after the fight, you could have stopped that. The photographer was your man, but you ran off. It looked like Gettysburg—my men dead and everybody seeing."

Smythe said, "Oh, big mistake, mate."

Farrow coughed out, "But everyone's still afraid of you, your raids."

Dev said, "Not as long as they see my brother defeating us." He looked to one of the Riders, who was holding a machete.

Smythe said, "Opening that throat will tell a story."

Farrow's eyes were wide with panic. Dev squeezed his arm, reassuring him, "This is a failure from a man who's a coward, not a traitor. Different kind of punishment."

Bubbles frothed from Farrow's nose, the tears rolling back into his eyes. "That's right! I'm no traitor. That's why I came back here. To show you. I work for you."

Dev threw a look, and Smythe shoved the rag back into Farrow's mouth, tickling his throat to choking.

Dev turned and walked away as the first shots hit Farrow's body, followed by a volley of others emptying their pistols into the hanging target. The rag erupted from Farrow's mouth, his body spinning in place with every bullet strike. The last ones hit the ropes, and Farrow dropped to the ground, shredded.

Smythe looked to Dev, then said to the men, "He gets buried proper."

Dev was holding Hurricane by the bridle. "This is a damn fine animal. One of the best I've ever seen."

Smythe said, "Then it wasn't a total loss. That's one of Chisum's best, and you took it from him."

Dev didn't have a word back. Just pulled himself onto Hurricane.

Smythe stood before him, leaning on his crutches. "We're not letting this defeat stand, Dev. We've still got Colby and all these fightin' men. I don't think your brother's crazy or fool enough to take us all on. That's bloody suicide."

Dev snapped the reins, and Smythe twisted out of the way of the horse. Hurricane cleared the prison gates, moving fast and perfect into the Wyoming night.

Smythe gestured with his crutch toward Farrow's still-tied body. "I don't want that stinking rat here! Burn him!"

Bishop said, "The fort, which direction?"

"It's dark. How can I say which way? Or anything. I am confused by America." Hunk turned the pheasant on its skewer and took another bite. His hands were still tied, but he managed.

Bishop sat nearby, his meal finished, his eyes fixed on the open dark around them. "You're running out of time with me."

"You can't remember nothing?"

"Tell me what I want to know."

Hunk said, "You sound like a town policeman. Police or sheriff, that's the only thing in this country that's the same. Since I got here, everywhere I go, someone talks a different talk, different language. No wonder you can't understand each other. I'm from two countries, so worse for me."

Bishop was sitting up, his attention somewhere else. "How can it be two?"

"Born in Bucharest, but joined Russian Navy. *Docher*—stevedore. You know this? My term ended and I had choice of Rumania or here. My wife and I went to Virginia, and I dug coal."

Bishop was listening to something far off drifting toward him. He set the gun hammers. "Why didn't you stay?"

"Private mine, did well. Workers all Rumanian, some Poles. Fire Riders kept raiding the shipments. They were taking our money anyway, so I joined. Lots of trash, the others. Like me, they came from other places, trying to find money to stay here."

Bishop stepped toward Hunk, drawing his knife. "Is that why the loyalty?"

Hunk followed the blade with his eyes. "I don't have nothing better than them, and now, I'm prisoner. So, everything's much worse than ever."

Bishop was hearing something in the dark, whispers he couldn't make out. No animal calls or low whistles. Words. He hooked the edge of the knife between Hunk's wrists. "Think they would rescue you?"

"Your brother said I was a leader."

Bishop yanked the knife upwards, cutting the bonds. "So, you think you're worth something to him."

"Now I run, and you can shoot me?" Hunk's words were still hanging, when the Fire Rider charged out of the dark, billowing red and laying pistol fire.

It was all of one motion, Bishop and Hunk diving out of the way of slugs tearing around them, punching a canteen and ricocheting. The Rider turned close on his horse and charged back, ready to empty another six.

Bishop dropped to a knee, and shot upwards, the blast slamming the Rider sideways, his body hanging in the saddle, the horse still running into the dark.

The second Rider leaped from the shadows on the other side of the fire, slashing Hunk with a cavalry saber, a revolver in his other hand, shooting wild.

The bay and Hunk's horse tore away from the shots. Bishop turned, fired a barrel with his shoulders, sending the Rider falling forward, the legs of his tall horse buckling. Horse and Rider slammed to the ground, the Rider diving away. He sprang up, bringing up his gun and opening fire.

Bishop hit him with the second barrel, blowing out his chest. The horse scrambled, and ran. Bishop brought down two more shells from the bandolier, loaded and closed the breech. The barrels swung around from his hip, locking into place as he turned.

Hunk was on his feet, turning in one spot and holding a knife in front of him. His eyes darted from one side to the other, looking for movement. This was the Fire raiding pattern he knew and had used himself. Attack, pull back, and attack. Keep the target guessing.

Bishop was by the low fire, searching, the rig set.

Hunk faced the dark just beyond the light. He knew a third rider was going to come in from behind. Could feel it in the silence. No whispering. No signal.

Instantly there, the Rider came running in fast, using a Winchester repeater, slugs tearing. Hunk leaped forward, grabbing the animal around the neck, his feet dragging as the horse ran, the Rider pounding at him with the butt of the rifle.

Hunk's massive hands locked around the horse just behind his head. His arms coming together, he pulled it down, slowing its run until it folded to the ground.

The Rider jumped from his saddle, kicking away from the horse and grabbing his rifle. On his feet, he cocked it, firing one shot.

Bishop opened both barrels on the Rider's chest, rocketing him backwards, the repeater firing into the sky.

The campfire was done, the last bits of orange dying. In darkness—not even stars—Bishop and Hunk took to the ground. The Rider's horse bolted to its feet, ran toward a black void, and was gone.

Bishops whispered, "How many do you think they sent for you?"

Hunk was catching his breath. "I don't know. The one with the sword, that was my friend, also from Bucharest."

Bishop said, "Call out."

"What?"

"Maybe some more of your friends are around."

Hunk tried to see Bishop's face, but the dark was total. He was a shape against miles of blackness.

Bishop's disconnected voice was flat. "I'm still giving you a choice. They won't."

Hunk finally spoke. *"Acest lucru este Bogdan! Cine este acolo?"*

An Ozark voice yelled back. "Hunk, you know I don't understand that loco crap of your'n!"

Bishop asked, "Who is it talking?"

"It's Ellis." Hunk called out, "Grudge Ellis! Everybody dead?"

"Yes, they all are. What about the shotgun man?"

Hunk felt Bishop's hand on his arm and said, "Shot and crawling away to die."

Ellis called back, "What about you?"

"I'm hurt."

Ellis said, "I'm coming in and I'd appreciate you not trying nothing." He lit a torch, let it flame, and held it before him as he crossed the field to the small flat where Hunk and Bishop had made their cook fire. He carried a Navy and kicked at the body of one of the Fire Riders with a hole blown through him.

Hunk was down, leaning on his good knee, still holding the knife, when Ellis pointed the pistol at him. "I'm real sorry about this, Hunk. We been trailing you since Myrtle, thought we'd get more of Chisum's men, but, you know, we didn't want no other fight right away. So we rested up."

Hunk said, "Until tonight."

"Well, we got our work to do. And you know you can't come back with us. Mr. Bishop and that Tomlinson don't allow that."

Hunk stood. "Yes, when you're gone, you are gone."

"That's right. You should've been dead already, but I guess you got some cat in you. Turn around? Make it easier on both of us, probably."

Hunk stepped away from the torch, his arms folded

across his chest. But he didn't lower his head or close his eyes. He just stood, waiting for the shot.

Finally, there was a sound. A gurgling.

Hunk turned to see Ellis drop to his knees, the cavalry saber protruding from his chest. The torch rolled out of his hands, and the weight of the pistol took his other arm to the ground, followed by his chin. Ellis's eyes were wide and wondering. They stayed open.

Bishop was standing behind Ellis, the rig down at his side, his hand slick and red with the blood from Ellis's back. He looked down at the body, the blade run through it, then to Hunk, who was holding the torch above him, throwing out a full circle of orange light.

Bishop said, "Are you going to tell me what I want to know? Show me?"

Hunk peered at Bishop. "Your eyes—"

"You're a Fire Rider, You want to be with them, be with all the others?"

"You save me, then kill me."

Bishop said, "I warned you." He moved his shoulder, and the shotgun sprang from the elbow, settling at his right hip, trigger lines ready. His expression was a mask as he favored his left side for a moment, shifting his body so the shotgun compensated, rising half an inch for a perfect kill shot.

"Time is now up. You decided. You're of no use."

CHAPTER SIXTEEN
Séotä'e

From "The Angel of Death Strikes Without Mercy—
Again!" by Virgil Demetrius Chaney:

> Neither prayers nor bullets will ever stop
> him! Doctor John Bishop, who lost his
> family at the hands of filthy curs, now
> brandishes a double-barreled shotgun made
> of God's steel, meting out bloody justice to
> all those who wrongly cross his path.
> The latest scene of slaughter and
> justice was a small cattle town of the
> peaceful kind, where families live and
> grow in a Christian manner. That peace
> was shattered by the arrival of the demonic
> force known throughout the Southwest
> as Fire Riders, who invaded the town for
> their own evil purposes, only to be
> thwarted by Doctor Bishop, also known
> as "Shotgun" or "The Angel of Death."

Acting alone, Shotgun brought his own style of justice to over one hundred demons, sending them to their maker by way of a fiery hell, spit from the end of his two-barreled arm extension. I was there, witnessing it all and taking the photographs before you, at great and distressing risk to my own life and safety.

Try as I might, I could never turn away from the sordid, bloody end of these devils, much as I wanted to. They are a prime example to all lawbreakers as to what to expect when you draw yourselves against Shotgun.

But we, as citizens, must always ask the ultimate question—is this man a true spirit of justice, meting out bloody ends to those that deserve it, or a wanton, dangerous, criminal who belongs dancing at the end of a strong rope? We, the citizens of this great land, deserve to sleep peacefully and secure.

Retired Army Captain DuPont Creed of Del Norte, Colorado has called Dr. Bishop "a mad dog, who needs to be put down with all force."

Hero or insane killer who slaughters at will? Those questions and more will be answered in future issues.

The man with three chins said, "You really ain't got nothin' here I want. On the counter, I mean."

White Fox turned the newspaper over to see the photographs as the man examined the buffalo hides.

He ran his fingers through the short hair, laying out and checking the thickened skin on the planked door between two salt barrels. He was making a show of his expertise even though his eyes were rolling from Fox's shoulders to her ankles, then back again.

She had her hair tied back, revealing the perfect planes of her face, but not allowing any kind of vanity. Her leathers were loose and absent of any Cheyenne markings, and she kept a black duster draped around her shoulders. She was almost lost in it, with the collar up past her ears and the right sleeve pinned to the side.

"They're calling you *Séotä'e* because you're coming and going like a ghost. Nobody never sees you no more." The man with three chins waddled around the trading post, one hip grinding as he knocked at some hanging beaver pelts and pottery with a cane that was actually an old wagon wheel spoke. "Now, don't start that *nomáht-sé'héó'o* stuff with me. I savvy, know it means *thief,* but I can't give you no real money. This is trade. I'll allow two dollars apiece for them buffalo, and that's a fair bargain. And don't put on no high manners to make me think different."

Fox looked up, her fierce eyes peering over the clothes. "No, you cheat."

"I'd put myself against any post this side of Red River. I don't give short weight or hold back blankets when the snows come. I don't live big on your backs." Three Chins hoped for a reaction, but she gave him nothing. "Fine. Be a damn statue, but there ain't no more buffalo need, so I ain't giving you more credit than two dollars. You used to be kinder to me, would smile."

White Fox folded the newspaper, the photographs seeming to hurt her, and put it neatly in the outer pocket of the duster. All very deliberate and with purpose.

Three Chins watched. "I got that for you. Like I done all them magazines and everythin' else about that Shotgun. You want to know so much about him, it's like he was kin." He looked away before asking, "Is he kin to you?"

She said, "No."

"That's good." He moved closer, brushed the edge of the duster with the wagon spoke "You got yourself so wrapped up, I can hardly see nothing of you anymore. You shouldn't hide like that."

"Not hiding." She put her hand on top of his and guided it to the counter. "Three dollars, trade."

All three chins worked his smile. "You got yourself five hides. Now that's only fifteen." He strained behind the counter, retrieving a small boxed cavalry medical kit from behind the barrels then wiping dust off it with his elbow. "This is all you wanted last time, too. You doctoring?"

Fox looked at him. "We have the need."

"You get your medicine when the army says so. They find out I've been trading out these kits, they'd have me in stocks for ten years. That's a hell of risk, but I'd take it . . . for my wife."

She kept her hand on top of his, moving it gently. "You have one in town."

The old woman with the long knife rocked in her chair by the front of the trading post, watching White Fox put the Cheyenne war club back in her belt as she moved to her horse, put the medical kit in a deerskin sack that she slung across her back, then unhitched her painted mare.

The old woman smiled all gums and never stopped her chair or whittling.

Three Chins stood by the door, holding his swollen hand. He shouted, "That's the second time you've busted my knuckles. There won't be no third. You ain't welcome here no more. Tell Dull Knife and the rest it's your fault they can't do no business!"

Fox turned to Three Chins. "You have a cooler. Put your hand there."

"I don't need no words from you. Here!" Three Chins hurled a stack of penny dreadfuls, newspaper clips, and flyers out the door, a strong Montana wind carrying them. "Them's all about Shotgun! That one by your feet? Somebody's even put up ten thousand dollars for his killing!"

Fox picked up the bounty notice as Chins said, "You savvy that? Ten thousand dollars! I'd like to see you go after that money. Get yourself shot in half!"

Three Chins looked to the old woman who'd carved the snout of a timber wolf out of sugar maple. "Grandma, you got nothing to do with this." He slammed the door, throwing the wooden bolt from inside.

The old woman kept carving. "He never was worth nothing, honey."

White Fox thanked her with a look, mounted the painted pony, and rode for the North Moccasin foothills, the Shotgun leaflets still scattering.

Hunk's hands were free and his knee felt better. He adjusted the blood flow from the tourniquet as Bishop had showed him. He manipulated the saber handle, looked up, and saw the barrels of the shotgun rig leveled on him, even as Bishop was turned, talking to the man standing by the gated fence.

They were on the first part of the Del Norte Toll Road, leading into the mining town, then the Blue Mountains. Bishop paid for their passing and was asking some questions of the toll taker, who answered with waving hands and pointing.

Hunk watched, still captive, but not a prisoner . . . because prisoners were worth something. He thought about the men he'd been chosen to lead—or at least, friends he'd ridden with—and how they all wanted him dead. Because of what they thought he knew.

That bit made Hunk laugh to himself as he regarded his massive, powerful hands. His only true worth. He'd torn off his red tunic and wore a dead friend's coat with a large, bloodstained rip made by a cavalry sword. That made him laugh, too.

The toll taker was excited to see "that shotgun" in person and opened the gate. Bishop nodded his thanks and brought his horse around. He and Hunk rode through at the same time, the shotgun aimed at Hunk. Bishop's eyes were fixed on the road leading to the distant town ahead. He was keeping his own pace, his own thoughts, not having said a word since they'd fought the Fire Riders at their campsite the night before.

The horses were fed and watered, the afternoon bright, and for Hunk, the Colorado sky as open as he could want. Everything around them, the road and the miles of yellow-green to the mountains, was hopeful.

The rig stayed steadily on him. Bishop could take him out with the slightest gesture of his body. If Hunk broke his horse into a run, he wouldn't make it.

He said, "I told you where your brother was."

"You did. Finally."

"The prison in Rawlins."

Bishop adjusted his shoulders, moving the rig with both barrels directly at Hunk's face. "Nothing decent there. You said you didn't even know how many men were there."

"I said it changes."

"And you didn't know where my brother does his business."

"They never let me up there. They wanted me out riding."

Bishop said, "They led you to slaughter."

Hunk said, "I know they want me dead, so I'll take you to the fortress, but we're going deeper into Colorado now."

"Other business first."

"Where we are going, is it to kill someone? Of course. What else?"

Bishop turned to Hunk. His eyes had cleared the

blood wash from the night before, but his face was still a mask. "It's to see someone who wants to kill me."

Colby held the Smith & Wesson Rimfire by its small wooden handle, thinking of the first time he'd ever used such a weapon.

The boy who had bound him to the sheep shearing chair was standing not five feet away. He was several years younger than Colby's youngest kill, and the thought of targeting a boy so close in age to his own son gave him pause. He didn't like to think himself capable of that, even as a moneyed assignment.

The thought shattered as quickly as it had come to him. "Simon, take this."

Colby gently positioned Simon's fingers around the Rimfire's handle, then lowered the boy's arm, letting the gun hang. "Feel the weight first, get used to that against your wrist, yes? That's what you have to get used to, and then bring it up."

Simon lifted the weapon. "It's not that heavy. I thought a pistol would be more difficult to handle."

Colby said, "It's still too big for your brother."

Simon wasn't sure if he should smile at the remark. He looked at Jacob, who was sitting by one of the fence posts, giggling. His nose wrinkled as a lamb flopped onto its belly in front of him, wiggling for attention.

Simon was trying to imagine his body and manner stiff. "Any gun is too big for his hands. I hope that always will be."

"Is that what your father would want?"

Simon cracked off a shot, not hitting a well bucket on a tree stump. The lamb bleated and ran away at the noise. Colby helped Simon steady his hand, before a harsh cough turned him away. He covered his mouth with a monogrammed handkerchief, spotting it with blood.

"Mr. Colby?"

"I'm fine. You're the one who must do the work." He mopped moisture from around his eyes, caught a breath. "It takes time to know how to shoot properly."

"I would never touch a handgun if there was drink available. Never. It is important to me that you know that."

Colby put a hand on Simon's shoulder, patting his starched shirt. "You're a responsible young man. I'm leaving this pistol and some cartridges with you. I want you to practice, though."

Simon lowered the gun again, then raised it to position. "Mr. Colby, this is not how I assumed things would go between us."

"If a stranger came onto my property, and I doubted him, and had that chair? I'd do the same. Very creative. But I only fell into your fence."

"Yes, sir. I understand that now."

"And I never was here to do you any harm."

"Yes, sir. I understand that, as well."

Colby shucked the one round fire and loaded the pistol's revolving cylinder. "I've slept, am healed well enough, bandaged up, and had some decent stew. Making sure you can defend your home seemed like an appropriate way to pay back your hospitality before riding on."

"It's appreciated."

He handed Simon the gun. "But if I was here for the wrong reasons, you need to know how to handle a proper weapon."

"Did you teach all of this to your son?"

Colby dabbed his bloody mouth. "No, his life doesn't require it."

"My father would say he was fortunate. It's not easy to be here, to protect this place."

"Now, that's a steady hand. Good. Your father's going to be very proud when he returns."

Simon turned again to his brother. "Jacob, check the stalls. See about the water."

The four-year-old wobbled for the barn, a few lambs tagging behind him. He slipped in the wet grass, came up laughing. Simon waited for his brother to reach the open side of the barn and start crawling through the slat fence before turning to Colby. "My father is gone. Not coming back. Jacob doesn't know."

"Run off by the cattlemen?"

"No sir. He drowned in the Little Colorado. He was helping build the ferry down by the river crossing and was caught under the boat. I asked if it might have been drink, and the ferryman wouldn't say, but I feel sure."

Colby turned Simon to him, looking directly into his wide eyes. "Son, I have to cross the river, to find the bad man I've been tracking."

"Yes, sir, I know. We found some of your papers over by the fence you knocked down. Do you recall that?"

Colby allowed a smile. "I do, indeed."

Simon held up the pistol. "We never had a near crossing before. My father would have to ride a full day out of his way to find a shallow. This crossing would be his gift to you for helping my brother and myself."

"This will be a fine help, son."

"He's an outlaw, the one you're after?"

Colby said, "The man obeys only his own laws. So, I'd say that qualifies."

"You considered your answer carefully, like a teacher. And he only has one arm, yes?"

Simon straightened his white shirt, checked his collar button as if centering himself before raising the pistol to the position Colby had shown him. He fired three shots. One of them sent the bucket spinning away.

CHAPTER SEVENTEEN
The Blind Dead

He claimed everyone called him Old Chaw. His legs had been amputated at the waist. He'd strapped wooden blocks to his hands with oil-stained belt leather and planted them on the floor in front of him, leapfrogging forward using his arms and shoulders. His Union tunic was worn to tatters, the coattails ragged to nothing after dragging behind him for years, but the gold sergeant's stripes on his sleeves shone like they'd just been stitched on with new thread.

Chaw said, "The crazy bastard's out back." He moved faster than most men walked, half-rolling around corners, then jumping three steps ahead.

Bishop followed him into the rooming house, and Hunk walked stiff kneed beside him.

Set off from Del Norte's central street and flanked by stock pens and loading platforms, the house had been a day lodge for teamsters. As Del Norte grew, businesses pushed in other directions, forgetting that side of town and the men living there. Now it was a place for soldiers who'd run out their pensions and their road.

Everything about it, even under a clear sky, had surrendered.

Chaw stopped at the kitchen door barely on its hinges and looked up at Bishop. "Where'd you lose your arm? My legs are somewhere at Chickamauga."

"Mine was after the war."

"After? It's still goin' on, ain't it?"

As Bishop held open the kitchen door with the rig, Chaw said, "You didn't lose nothing. You traded up!"

They moved inside, a pot of sour coffee boiling over on a rusting two-burner. In the rest of the kitchen were pots with week-old beans, stale bread by the sink pump, and a sack of grits crawling with bugs.

Chaw pulled a wrinkled tie from his pocket and held it out to Hunk. "Captain Creed puts a high regard on respect and dressing proper."

Hunk said, "Bishop knows this man. I don't."

"He tell you he was blinded? But he'd still value that tie."

Hunk tied the tie as Chaw forwarded himself to the back door on his arms. "Where the hell you hail from, anyway?"

The steps leading from the kitchen porch to the small yard next to the alleyway were missing the bottom two. Old Chaw made the jump, landing on the soft grass next to the pile of dirt from the open grave.

"I asked for all things, that I might enjoy life; I was given life, that I might enjoy all things." It was a young voice, but commanding, and continued as Bishop and Hunk stepped into the yard. "I got nothing that I asked for, but everything I hoped for."

They took a place next to four old men in army uniforms, standing around an open hole dug near the side fence. A body, wrapped in a moldy blanket and pieces of a battle standard, had been dumped there like so much old washing.

The old men used rosewater to cover the smell of bottom-turned whiskey and their dirty uniforms, but the sweet just made it worse. The four mourners were of different ranks—one sported a Confederate long coat—but all looked spiritually caved in.

Hector Hayward paused his reading, looking up from the prayer book as the Reb set Old Chaw on an apple crate, to make him the same height as everyone else.

Hector saw the shotgun and his eyes went to the rig first, then to Bishop and Hunk. He tried not to react, but failed, losing his place on the page. Finding it, he continued. "Almost despite myself, my unspoken prayers were answered. I am among all men most richly blessed." He closed the book, regarded the military men hanging on to each other, knowing what should come next.

Old Chaw said, "It ain't right if we don't fire no salute. Owner don't allow no firearms, says we're too old to handle 'em."

The Reb took a cap and ball from his long coat and held it up with whiskey-shot hands. Chaw grabbed the pistol and looked to Bishop.

Bishop said, "I didn't come here for this."

"Then why the hell are you here?"

Hector said, "Doctor, would it really put you out to do something for a dead man?"

Bishop cocked the shotgun rig and stepped back. Extending his arm, he fired the first barrel into the sky, then the second.

A murder of crows broke from a tree, and there were shouts from someplace across the back alley. The mourners began filling in the hole with flat spades.

Chaw said to Bishop, "Ain't none of this legal. You better git before the constable comes around. Tussling with you would be the biggest thing he ever done."

Hector was already up the steps, the kitchen door clack-slamming behind him. He stood by the attic doorway, pressing close to the raw-brick wall, bracing a Union service revolver with both hands, and aiming for a head shot to the next person in.

The door was an old rug nailed to the top of the frame. Hector watched it move as it was pushed aside. There was a shadow. Closing his eyes, he locked the hammer with his thumb before the gun was knocked clean across the room by the shotgun barrel.

The pistol landed without going off.

"Nice weapon." Bishop stepped in, followed by Hunk, who angled himself sideways, ducking the ceiling beams and dragging his injured leg.

Hector shrugged. "It was Captain Creed's. The one he lost in the river. I fished it out for him a year ago."

Bishop picked up the gun. "Hector, why'd you think you needed this?"

"I got pretty scared when I saw you, sir. You weren't . . . expected."

"I wasn't expecting the captain to be dead, but you sure as hell made me feel welcome."

"It's just . . . your reputation now. It's quite something."

"So now you're afraid of me?"

Bishop tossed the pistol onto one of two small beds in a windowless corner. "You never were before."

Around the beds were scattered copies of the *Police Gazette,* some old newspapers, a portable field telegraph with wires dangling from it. Patched trousers and two shirts hung on a line. All of which Hector was packing.

Bishop picked up a beat-to-hell saddlebag and handed it off. "Don't let me stop you, son."

Hector's hair was darker and he was three inches taller than the last time Bishop had seen him but he still moved like a schoolboy unsure at the blackboard.

Hector reached for one of the clean shirts as if he'd be shot in the back.

Hunk tore it from the line. "You had a gun on us, boy. Act like it."

Bishop said to Hunk, "You wouldn't know from the greeting, but this young man saved my life."

Hector put the shirt in the bag. "When we found you by the tracks, that was more blood than I could stand. I was sure you'd be dead by morning."

"The doc told me it was you who took me in."

"I figured I owed it." Hector moved about the room, never turning his back, snatching up his belongings. "That Miss White Fox, she got me out of those woods, and the Captain, well, he didn't want to see you die from the Fire Riders, not after they put us out."

"You helped me so Creed could come back and kill me himself?"

"That was in his mind, yes sir."

Hunk laughed. "Boy, you were with the Riders?"

Hector's eyes locked on the bloody bandages around Hunk's arm and chest, the corrupted leg outstretched. Hunk seemed monstrous to the boy as he dropped himself onto a bench, examining an empty vodka bottle that had rolled across the floor. "Why, yes sir. I surely was there with them. In that prison and everything."

Hunk pulled the cork.

"A mule skinner gave that to the captain in trade for his army sheath. We traded off almost everything he had."

Bishop kicked the stack of papers and digest magazines. "I'd think after you talked to the newspapers, you wouldn't need money."

"Well, they don't pay much. When they'd write about you, the captain had me read it out loud and figure something else to say. I'd telegraph it in. I learned to use that key pretty good." He put the portable telegraph kit next to his other belongings. "Is that why you're here? What we said in the papers?"

"It's how I found you." Bishop adjusted the rig to lay against his shoulder. "I'm here to settle accounts."

Hector stopped bundling his clothes and bit his lower lip. "Sir?"

"I'm going to Rawlins. You've been inside."

"Yes, sir?"

Bishop said, "I told you, I'm settling accounts. With my brother. I need someone who knows that prison."

Hector's stammer returned. "Y-yes, I've been inside. A-a-and so have you. You visited your brother. H-he told the story . . . often . . . many times."

Hunk said, "Your talk is worse than mine, boy."

Bishop said, "You saw me when I was near dead."

Hector's words were barely there. "I can't never forget it."

"That's my problem. I have forgotten. That grenade took a lot from me, son. Some things I just don't remember. I've got to know what I'm walking into."

Hector swallowed hard. "What about this gentleman? You've got the boots, that red stripe. You're a Fire Rider, sir?"

Hunk raised the empty bottle in a mock toast as Bishop said, "He came after you did, doesn't know all the secrets of that place. You crawled all through it. Said so in one of the Penny Dreadfuls."

"Yes, sir. I—I said those words. That story paid us the most." Hector put a hand into his saddlebag, finding a small cotton pouch. "Doctor, I owed the captain. He took care of me, and I promised I'd see him buried. It wasn't the best, but it was with his friends. I did it."

He pulled a pair of blue-paper sunglasses from the pouch and held them out. "He hated you so bad for needing these, being blind. He figured a way to kill you and get your brother to take us in."

Bishop said, "You have reason to help me."

Hector drew himself in, finally standing straight. "I listened to revenge talk for years. I don't want to hear nothing like that no more."

"I'm not saying it's right. It just is."

Hector gathered up the things from the bed and filled the rest of the bags. "You remember Mr. Fuller? He's in Oregon with his family, offered me a job working timber. Or maybe I'll go Virginia way. Find a good school. Everybody I'm around, since before I was a shaver, is shot and broken. I'm sick of it. There's a lot more going on in this country than folks killing each other."

Hunk said, "That boy, going to try for president?"

Hector looked to Bishop. "Don't you just want to be a doctor, again?"

Bishop took a step toward Hector, the rig still in place, his words measured, even and quiet. "I'm settling accounts."

"You figure on me riding in, so you can get killed? And me with you?"

Hector pulled down the washing line. "No, sir." He looked to the pistol lying on the bed, then to Bishop. "If you're going to kill me, let's get it done."

"Hector, all I want from you is some information. I'm on my own business, and you're not part of it."

"They're having a town meeting just down the street in an hour. Forming a vigilante group to protect us against any more Fire Rider raids. If they knew who I'd been with, they'd hang me. This gentleman, too."

"You claimed to know secrets."

Hector buckled the saddlebags. "There's explosives buried all along the outside walls and in some old tunnels. If Mr. Bishop hasn't used it, it's still there."

Hunk said, "I never heard of nothing like that."

"There's tunnels all through the prison. Some your brother had built, others been there forever."

"These tunnels, he hid money there?"

Hector said, "Maybe. The captain, he gave me a book on mapmaking so I could study up. I figure I can draw it out for you."

Bishop said, "Do it. Please."

Hector sat at the small table, tearing the back page from the prayer book, and using a flat-lead pencil to sketch a diagram of the prison fortress. His lines were precise.

Hunk watched, then approved with a belch. "The yard has one side that's nothing but guns."

"That's different from before." Hector made the adjustment. "You're not riding with them anymore, sir?"

"Not no more."

Hector indicated the locations of a tunnel running the circumference of the main cell block and a series of false walls on the upper floors—places where he used to hide. "I don't know about now, but one day I found some guns, and cases of ammunition in a couple old closets. They said the guards would sell them out of the back to the Indians, but I don't know what's left, if anything."

He handed the map to Bishop. "When you get inside, Doctor . . . well, I wish you both luck. Honest and true."

They walked outside to a stable. With canvas topping nailed down to one side, it was barely a shed.

Hector took a saddle with hand-tooled scrolling and Creed's insignia and cinched it to a solid, well-built mare. "When we sold the captain's horse, I think that's when he started dying. But I'd never let him lose the saddle."

Bishop said, "I was always sorry about his eyes."

"Now I know it was his own fault, for not taking care. But I couldn't never tell him."

"Hector, I wanted to settle accounts with you and the captain. No matter why, you didn't leave me for dead." Bishop handed him the sack of Chisum gold. "It'll help you get where you're going."

Hector took the sack, almost dropping it because of the weight. He didn't look inside, putting it directly into his saddlebag. "I'm thanking you, Doctor. Feels like quite a bit."

"I thought you and the captain deserved something."

"Maybe I should stay and get the captain reburied proper, not planted like a potato the way his buddies did it."

Bishop shook his head. "You said you were leaving. That's best."

Hector pulled himself onto the horse, then slipped on Captain Creed's sunglasses and looked to Bishop. His eyes were blue-masked discs. "The captain would have hated that I read from the *Confederate Prayer Book*, but I couldn't find our Union one."

"You did fine, son."

"I meant it when I said good luck."

Bishop watched the young man take his horse with Captain Creed's saddle down the alley and around the stock pens. He let him ride out of sight before stepping from the stables to where Hunk was waiting with their mounts.

Hunk said, "Think I'd be running out?"

Bishop got on the bay. "No, now you've got your own reasons for going back."

"That's a truth. Besides, I don't get far with this knee. Rawlins, now? We could do it in two days."

"Not without weapons." Bishop angled himself, and the rig adjusted with barrels down close to his knee, then locked for the long ride. He brought the bay around to one of the side streets.

The ferryman cranked on the rope that secured the flatboat to the other shore, pulling it closer to the other side of the river, a calm offshoot of the Colorado that split into smaller rushes of water along a wooded bank.

Colby stood by the ferry railing, his horse tied and his arsenal blanket-wrapped behind the saddle. He watched a kingfisher dive, miss, and fly off. "Those boys told me their father helped you with the building of the dock."

"I'm just the ferryman."

Colby was watching a bird arcing toward the trees. "And a fine one, too. You know everyone on the other side of the river? A little beyond the trees? Ever heard of a crazy white man, lives by himself making guns and bombs? Kills the Indians, then dances with the corpses?"

The line was taut, the ferryman cranking it through, taking them to the shore half a foot at a time and giving no heed to a word Colby was saying.

Colby pressed. "That's quite a legend, if it's true. Is it?"

"I'm just the ferryman, mister."

The kingfisher dove again, snapping up a minnow just under the surface.

"That's one of the largest of the species I've ever encountered. I envy you, my friend. You see and hear all kinds."

The ferryman stepped to open the bow railing, pulling it aside for Colby and his horse to get onto the bank. "How much money you got?"

The Fire Riders were two over the saddle, one of them shot in the face and the other with two bullets in the chest. Their horses were tied together and being led by a Rider with a wild gray beard, who'd been shot in the shoulder.

Hurricane was at the water trough, April Showers brushing him down, gently singing "The Little Old Cabin in the Lane."

Dev Bishop stood by, arms folded, smiling. "He likes you, girl." He turned at the screams in the yard.

Smythe crutched his way toward Gray Beard dropping from his red-spattered horse.

"They wouldn't buckle. None of 'em." Gray Beard said, shaking off his tunic. "I never been shot before."

Smythe said, "You did better than them, boy-o. What happened?"

Dev patted the little girl's shoulder before making his way to the middle of the yard as other Riders gathered round.

Gray Beard said, "We stopped a freight wagon on the old coach road, told them to give up part of their load to cross through, and they opened up on us." He swung his arm in circles, trying to find some comfort. "Sweet Mary's backside, this hurts."

Dev said, "Did you get anything out of them?"

"Just these two dead. And Phil, he owed me five dollars."

Smythe said, "Get to the medic. Take care of yourself."

Gray Beard started walking to the medical tent beyond the gunsmith. "This ain't supposed to happen. Folks are too afraid to go against us. These boys weren't afraid of jack."

Dev frowned. "We can't have this."

Smythe said, "Paradise is almost done. Just the way we want it, and run right. That'll be more money than any of the bloody hijackings."

Dev said, "Not if people think nothing happens if they don't pay." He raised a hand, catching the eye of an eager Rider, a kid with a Winchester.

Three shots were cracked off as one, and Gray Beard was done. Hurricane stirred at the sound, but May kept brushing, kept singing.

Smythe said to Dev as Riders picked up the body,

"These men aren't the problem, right? Jesus, we're killing off more of our own than anyone!"

"He failed. There's been too much of that." Dev went to Hurricane, took a brush, and ran it over the horse's back and sides.

May was still humming and smiling.

Smythe said, "It's your brother, boy-o. They're making everyone defiant, taking their cue from him. 'The dead man who came back to life.' To wipe us out!"

Dev kept combing. "Are you quoting?"

Smythe nodded. "The *Police Gazette*. He's got the cover again."

CHAPTER EIGHTEEN
Three Talons

The woods along the slope were dense, the thickest pine branches overlapping each other from tree to tree, forming a dark green barricade. Moisture in the air mixed with that bit of cool drifting from the running creek a few yards away. All that should have let Bishop sit back in his saddle and take it in.

It was a natural calming place.

But Bishop lurched forward, keeping the bay very deliberately along the small cleared trail. He stopped once without speaking, then continued on. Hunk was nearly alongside. If he slowed, Bishop did as well, keeping the shotgun rig ever present within Hunk's eyesight.

Hunk said, "You're riding like we're going into the worst battle. I don't see it."

The trap sprung, the first pine crashed across the trail in front of them. Blocked, the horses chopped back. Bishop and Hunk tried for a run, but a trip wire snapped, propelling large pine branches from either side of the cut into their chests with cannonball force. Both men were knocked from their saddles.

Hunk crashed onto his jaw, then his knee, the pain bolting him. Bishop landed on his back, a huge boot pinning both barrels of the shotgun against the ground. A hand clamped instantly around his throat. The fingers were slippery with blood.

"Let's go, dead man."

Bishop knew the voice and brought up his knee, pounding into some bulging kidneys and forcing the bloody fingers to let go. He rolled away and sprang to his feet, slamming the shotgun up under the bearded chin of Noah Crawford.

Crawford yowled. "Jesus, Doc, if I had any teeth, you woulda knocked 'em all out!"

Bishop said, "Show me where you're cut."

Crawford pulled back the deer hide to run his hand along the rolling folds of his scarred belly, trying to find the knife wound. Blood had already soaked through his Union suit, but the injury was invisible to him.

"It was along in here. Mealy bastard used one of my own against me."

Bishop said, "Move your stomach."

Crawford used both knotty hands to hold up the flesh. "Knife I was making for years, recognized the handle. Goes in real smooth, fine edge. Whoever you stick don't know he's dead till he drops. Sold a lot of those."

Bishop traced small red streaks to a deep slice in Crawford's abdomen, the skin folding in on itself. "That's a good incision. Might as well have had you in an operating theater."

Crawford took the knife from a pocket, his blood drying on the long blade. "Told ya it was a good edge. He knows what he's doing, and he's got the deadeye for both of ya."

Bishop said to Hunk, "Get my kit."

Crawford stopped Hunk from the horses with a

bloody hand as large as a grizzly's paw. "I'll take care of myself."

Bishop was settled by a rusting steel grave marker, the last in a small row among four others in the clearing of the pine woods just down the trail from Crawford's dugout. The wet grass around the Dr. John Bishop marker was tall, curling against the name.

Crawford said to him, "Sorry you ain't down there for real?"

"Yeah, most days I am." Bishop stood, his left hand on his marker, the shotgun rig automatically shifting into place with his movement.

Crawford nodded to the rig. "Still workin' fine. I hear the tales, take pride in that gun. It was a good job I done."

Hunk, bandaged fists clenched, stood into Crawford, thinking of a move. "Why you attack us?"

The mountain man was actually larger than Hunk, and looked down at him. Swathed in animal hides stitched together like an insane quilt, he wore a dead man's boots with blades cobbled to the toes and bearskin half-gloves on hands that were also clenched into fists.

Bishop answered the question. "If you'd reached my place, he'd have popped you off like turkeys in a run."

Crawford's beard was a thick tangle, crusted around the eyes, and didn't move when he spoke. "I don't know who you are, friend"—he shoved Hunk back—"but getting me riled is a big mistake."

Bishop said, "He's with me, Noah. That's enough."

"For now." Crawford dropped his paw. "That Colby wanted to know when you'd be along, then stuck me to see what I'd give up. Clamped my mouth. He said didn't matter; you'd be here sometime. Was real cocky about that, too. Left the blade in, said something about 'preparing.' Didn't care if I knew his name, thought I crawled away to die."

Bishop said, "You see a sniper's rifle?"

"Hell, he's got an arsenal with him." The voice burst through the hair again, pointing to an oak that had been split by lightning. "There's four bottles of bug juice Crows left to appease me. Bring one."

Bishop said, "So, you're still called *Vóhpóóhe*?"

"I'll always be White Claw. Among other things."

Hunk knelt by the split tree, finding the bottles and some leatherwork and necklaces of hanging bear's teeth all tucked into the trunk's scorched openings. He took a bottle, pocketed a necklace. "The Indians, they set all this out for you?

"So I'll leave 'em alone." Crawford grabbed the bottle and splashed some white whiskey on the wound. He took a deep breath at the searing pain. "That'll wake up your guts for sure!"

Bishop said, "Where was the claw when you got stuck?"

"On the kitchen table next to my coffee. A jackass mistake. He got me from behind while I was feeding the horses. Took a good Colt Lightning off me, too. I'm gettin' that gun back. How much ammo you got on you?"

"The bandolier's it. I was counting on you." Bishop went to the one grave set off from the rest. A wooden cross with a name long weathered away marked it, but its dirt was freshly turned. "I recall reading about a coffin full of weapons."

"What the hell you talking about, *recall*?"

Bishop said, "He could have a Gatling gun down there, and I know you got traps and gun stashes everywhere."

"Better take a drink 'cause you're damn out of luck. Business been draggin' for a year. There's nothing in that grave but an empty box."

Hunk stiff-walked to the bay and took the canvas sack with the Adams grenades from the saddle. "We have these two."

Crawford said, "You allowed them damn things to clank around like that? Could've lost a good horse."

Bishop said, "That's what we've got."

Crawford said, "I watched him set up in the trees behind the corral. Wait till the sun drops, and we'll Crow-pounce. Close in, hang his insides like the warriors do it."

"If he said he was prepared, he means it." Bishop's words were quiet. "He wants to face me down. You don't have to get between that."

Crawford took one of his giant steps to the graves, stepping to the other side of the markers. "Doc, we've got history, and both hate this bastard. Being stabbed don't bother me, but don't be actin' high-toned about it. Supper'll taste a lot better knowin' he's bled out." He turned to Hunk. "I take it you're in on this, since you're riding together."

"I'm Shotgun's prisoner."

Crawford snorted. "I'll be a fiddler's bitch!"

"I want this Colby guy, too." Hunk touched the stitching on the side of his head where his ear used to be.

"He did that? There ain't a whole man between the three of us!"

Bishop was sitting next to his own marker, taking a small pull from the bottle. "Awful stuff. I've been spending a lot of time around graves lately."

With a chuckle, Crawford grabbed the liquor back. "Yeah, what's that tell you?"

The sun had just vanished behind the treetops, down to the horizon, when Bishop walked toward the dugout from the small side trail cutting the edge of the woods. The night birds were starting their song and the horses in the corral, stolen from a pony express depot, stirred along the high fence, nudging each other.

The weapon lines were tight across his shoulders, the

anchor chain biting his skin and drawing on the triggers as he moved a few steps closer to the whitewashed dugout wall decorated with Cheyenne symbols and a large painting of five metal talons dripping red letters that formed the word *Vóhpóóhe*. He stopped, the mechanics of the rig clicking into place and bringing it to elbow height.

There were footsteps. A leg dragging.

Bishop got clear, moving to the corral, then stopping at a pool of Crawford's blood by the fence.

Hunk took position by a corner of the building. They didn't exchange looks as he threw the Adams grenade toward the woods. Spinning, the interior fuse burned down.

The pine trees blew apart at the middle, tops falling forward, crashing into more trees as pulverized wood spread into the air. The first gunshots came from beside the explosion as if the shooting was from the burst of heat.

Bishop fired into the pines, blasting through the brown fog of wood and smoke at a target he could only guess was there. More shots rang out. He turned, bringing the rig up from his waist, holding it straight out to follow movement through the trees. A shadow. Something.

He fired the second barrel, and ran low for the dugout, breached, and reloaded, the echo of the grenade explosion still coughing through the woods. He waited until it faded. Silence. Then he heard a sound like bones breaking before two blasted-in-half trees crashed into each other, hitting the ground.

Shots tore from the far side of the woods at that moment, random gun flames in the dark.

Bishop shot at the position, then held, watching as Crawford sprang up from behind the corral's water trough, pulling the ribbon on the last grenade, and hurling it with all his force.

Fire burst with the second Adams, eating the tops of the pines, twisting them into the air upon detonation. Straight gunfire pumped from a corner of the woods at the same time, the slugs tearing into the corral fence. The horses charged out. They broke the rails, leaped, and ran as Bishop reloaded. He moved to the edge of the woods, dodging the horses and hunting for the target.

The rig adjusted itself, coming up to a middle-firing position as instinct made Bishop turn, pulling back on the trigger lines. Still turning, he saw Colby step from the shadows aside the house.

With two pistols raised, he fired the Remington Double Derringer first, then the Schofield. The slugs pounded Bishop's chest, knocking him down. Colby kept with the Schofield, every shot an explosion of force from the pistol.

The last horse jumped the corral fence, running from the sound, smoke, and fire.

Bishop lay on his back, duster torn by bullets, his left arm still twitching.

Colby moved to him, both pistols still aimed. "You were a hard kill, sir. I know your history well, but I confess I regret not knowing *you*, because I have a thousand questions—"

The first barrel blew through Colby's chest, sending him spiraling backwards as Bishop sat up and fired again, throwing him against a fence post before he dropped to the ground.

Bishop made it to his feet as Hunk moved to Colby and knelt by him. Colby's eyes were wide, fearful. Both pistols were still tangled in his fingers. Hunk gently took the guns, then clamped one massive hand over Colby's mouth and nose while looking down at the watch chain with his ear dangling.

Crawford whistled, then threw the long-bladed knife,

which Hunk caught with his free hand. He tucked the blade behind Colby's ear and started to cut.

Colby's eyes were even wider as he recognized Hunk, and the realization of his last moment dawned. Then he went slack.

Hunk looked down at him like he was about to spit. "That's what I wanted, so he'd know it was me taking his last breath."

Crawford said, "You going to finish the job? Looks like he had a piece of you for a souvenir."

"Not important now."

"Doc?"

Bishop nodded, opening his duster and revealing a slab of thick buffalo hide across his chest. Slugs from the two guns were splattered flat against it. He pulled off the hide with his left hand and let the steel grave marker he was wearing behind it fall to the ground.

The dark was the dark, even after the bag was pulled from Chaney's head, and the bandages unwrapped from his eyes. He could feel someone pulling on the dressing of his facial wounds. "That's me, damn it! I'm already deeply scarred."

Chaney sat with his back against a cold stone wall, wanting his sight to adjust to the room and the shadows moving in front of him. Red tunics, ghosts of color, as they hovered in the two pitch-black doorways on the other side of the subcellar.

Chaney could see a bit more, taste the damp as he spoke. "Would one of you untie my hands? You're obviously in total control. Where would I run to?"

Startling him, Dev Bishop's voice came from behind Chaney. He stepped in front of him, holding a bellows camera. "Nowhere, so you'd best settle in."

"Settle in for how long, Mr. Bishop?"

Dev liked the recognition. "As long as it takes for you to write ten of those stories."

"I had no idea you appreciated my work."

"I don't. You're not telling things right."

"Oh, you want me to extol the virtues of your Fire Riders, rather than condemn? Not an easy task, sir, considering."

Dev had moved closer. "Smart aleck. I don't need help recruiting. They're lined up out the door. This is about you showing the world more than a stack of bodies and making a false hero out of the man with the shotgun."

"Not my choice."

Dev slapped Chaney's bandages. "Did we do that to your face?"

Chaney jerked his head back. "Your brother, Mr. Bishop, shot me. And killed one of my family."

Dev was considering his words under a laugh. "I see. So you're a coward, and that's why you write what you do."

"My editors claim that our readers admire your brother for, what they see as, standing up."

"Against?"

"Well . . . against your supposed aggression." Chaney quickly added, "Their words, not mine."

Even closer, Chaney felt Dev's words against his face. "Then you'll knock him down. Make your people understand that the worst thing they can do is favor him. You'll write about that and about tyrants like Chisum, who think they can own anything they lay eyes on. You do that?"

Chaney said, "Oh, yes. Yes, I can."

"The territory I control is open. Anybody can do anything they want as long as we're in for a piece."

"Just a tax."

"That's right, and we're a hell of a lot more fair than

the Washington pettifoggers. No blood has to be spilled. Just follow the rules."

"That goes for myself, as well?"

Dev hauled Chaney to his feet, then handed him the camera as the hooded riders stepped from the deepest shadows, all with battle knives. "More for you, amigo, than anybody."

CHAPTER NINETEEN
Warriors

The ladle had been shoved into the coals under the soup pot, heating the handle to bending before Crawford slapped the hot metal against his knife wound, searing the flesh closed. He held it, belly hair burning back, skin sizzling until Bishop yanked it from his hands.

Tossing it aside, Bishop said, "It smells like that, it's cauterized."

Crawford roared, "That's how we doctor around here!"

Bishop snapped the shotgun rig from his elbow. "And I'm the one's crazy as a suck-egg mule?"

Crawford smeared the wound with a mound of bear grease then buttoned his long flannels. "You're the one wants to take on a whole goddamned army, not me."

"How're your ribs?"

"Two, maybe a third, broken."

"Bastard wasn't kiddin' with that Schofield. I know you saved me, Noah."

"But that ain't gonna be all, is it?"

"No."

Hunk said, "You got Apache here?" On the other side

of the dugout, he was sitting on the edge of a rope bed covered in finely tanned hides, admiring the razored edge of a War Hawk Club.

Crawford said, "That's Comanche. Born to the fight, every one of 'em. A Commanch come at ya? You're pissin' and prayin' at the same time." He picked up the five-talon iron claw from the kitchen table and fit it over his right hand. "I was good with this, and that Commanch was the one pissin'!"

"How many you killed?" Hunk swiped the air with the blade.

"Raiding party come in here, grab some horses, and try for my damn head!" Crawford said. "His brothers took off, chasing my best stock, left him on his own to kill me."

Bishop said, "Always a mistake."

Crawford nodded. "That Commanch damn near got me. That war club was sticking out of my neck . . . but damn near don't count, do it? I laid his guts out so he could watch himself die. That's what scares 'em into the afterlife."

Hunk said, "Where is he, this Comanche?"

"I left him strung up for a while, to keep White Claw's legend going, then buried him down creek way someplace." Crawford moved to Hunk and opened his arms, showing the spears, shields, and axes hanging on the surrounding walls.

Hunk said, "These are all from men you killed?"

"Every damn one of 'em has blood on it, and not just mine."

Hunk looked up at a mural that covered the curved ceiling above the bed. Tribal warriors charged across the sky with shields and lances, their horses breaking through the clouds to Heaven. The flicker of the one candle by the bed gave the mural life, its shadows making the horses run, the braves cry out.

"All of those warriors riding there, you fought them?"

"Fought 'em all, and killed about half. My daughter painted it, to remind me that Indians ride to Heaven and I ain't going to be so lucky."

"Okay, White Claw." Bishop opened Hector's plans of the prison, laid them out on the kitchen table made from a tree stump. "Look at this. See what we need."

Crawford said, "That paper's for your ass. I was the first to sell army horses to them Riders. Gutted two who tried to short me, then they was good customers, bought regular."

Bishop said, "But you've never been in the fortress."

"It don't matter. See, they ain't gonna come at you one at a time, like that cocky bastard."

Hunk said, "There's more than a hundred at the prison."

"So how you gonna kill who you want to kill?" Crawford turned, punching at nothing with the steel talons. "You got that gun rig, but you need something that'll really bring blood to the claw."

Bishop regarded Crawford, then said, "The wagon by the shed."

It looked to have been an old dairy wagon, with a full-sized cooler that was painted dark red and yellow. Its sides were fringed in gold and purple, and large tassels dangled from the front and back. The door to the cooler had been replaced with stable half-doors for someone to lean out of, smiling. Light blue, it was secured with a heavy throw-bolt. The only other openings were circular air vents on either side of the cooler, repainted to look like a woman's mouth blowing kisses.

The driver's bench had been divided into two seats, with a special gun turret coming up between the legs of anyone riding shotgun.

Crawford said, "Pullin' a gun or pullin' your pecker, this is the wagon for ya." He held an oil lamp high, throwing dim yellow around them.

Bishop unbolted the split doors and peered inside to

find a bed frame, mold-eaten mattress, dirty sheets, and pieces of a broken chamber pot.

Crawford said, "Fella who owned it, called it Rolling Temptations. Only had his wife working, but he did okay, until he got himself killed, and she retired."

Hunk swung himself into the turret seat. "We can shoot from here, maybe five minutes before we're dead."

Bishop said, "That's not where I'm going to be." He checked the screwed hinges on the split door before climbing into the cooler. His foot plunged through the flimsy wooden floor, the rotten planks splitting in half, revealing a false bottom underneath.

A raccoon scrambled out.

Crawford said, "He smuggled a lot of guns, some whiskey. If the laws stuck their nose in, he had his wife shoot 'em from the bed when they opened the back. Or he let 'em get their pants off, then shot 'em. Good customer, though."

Bishop shook his foot loose. "How're you fixed for powder, Noah?"

Crawford lowered the lamp, eyes narrowing. "Well-fixed, as usual."

Bishop dropped from the back. "We'll make some cuts from the inside, pull the bolts holding the cooler, then pack the floor with powder."

"Lotta work. How long you been figurin' on this?"

Bishop snapped the breech on the rig and pulled the spent shells. "And I'm going to need some ammo."

With Bishop and Crawford pushing, Hunk pulled the wagon, backing it from the side of the dugout and over to the overhang where Crawford did his gun and smith work. He dropped the wagon's falling tongue and stepped into the work area, taking in the rows of calibrated barrel extensions, specially cut shoulder stocks, and pistol grips. Trigger and safety mechanisms were precisely laid out on two large workbenches, with fine tools beside them.

Crawford allowed himself a laugh. "Not what you figured from White Claw, huh?"

Hunk admired the pieces of a Winchester Repeater that were being refitted.

Crawford said, "Everyone claims the '73, but they ain't seen what I've done. They'll drop from heart attacks soon as they hear the cock."

"A clock maker in my village, his shop was looking like this."

"The doc's rig is the best thing I ever done."

Bishop came around the wagon, unhooking the trigger lines from the shotgun rig, letting them slacken, then bringing up his arm so that the double-barrel was in front of Crawford. "Now you've got to do better."

Crawford spit heavily and released the harness, pulling the rig from the amputated arm. The cup had rubbed the skin raw. He placed the rig on the workbench next to a box of .12-gauge brass casings.

Bishop turned to Hunk. "Pull out the floor from the back. Save the scraps."

Crawford put a can of black powder on the bench next to the casings. "Okay, Doc. We'll draw some blood, then show 'em some fire."

Hunk yanked out the flooring, tossing out the bed and the sheets as Bishop worked one-handed, knocking the bolts from the inside of the cooler with a hammer, then loosely setting them again. He took the screws from the door hinges, replacing them with wooden pegs as Hunk piled more trash from the back of the wagon.

Bishop said, "Add to the scrap pile all the metal bits you can find, then bundle it all in the old sheets."

Hunk said, "I was in a cave-in once. Most men I ever seen die. My boss got his head knocked in two, which was okay. You work this out, set off these bombs, we'll have a cave-in there, too."

Crawford packed old, reinforced ammo boxes with four scoops of black powder from a barrel, tamping, then closing and sealing each tight for pressure. Filling the false bottom, he laid the boxes side by side with a fuse connecting them, and then covered it all with a rolled canvas. He picked up several clay jugs of kerosene, putting them atop the canvassed boxes, along with the bundles of scrap wood, old gun parts, and metal shavings.

His face and beard crusting, Crawford smiled. "Blood on the claw."

Bishop set the kerosene and bundles into the wagon, tucking them into corners of the floor or nestled between the walls and ceiling. Small nails held the bundles in place, and the jugs were tied in place.

Hunk worked underneath, hammering a wedge between the iron plates, giving just enough room to pull the fuse to the black powder out from inside, then tie it off. He wiped grit from his eyes. "You got some more powder? One box, packed tight."

Crawford handed him the box. "What was that word you called me?"

Hunk tied the box under the driver's bench and secured it on either side with scraps of wood. "*Nemernic.* It means to you are the ass of a mule."

Crawford worked on the shotgun rig, adjusting the trigger tension. "I'll have to recall that one."

Hunk stood up, looked to Bishop. "We're taking a lot of Riders with us. Maybe all."

"That's the point. Don't forget Colby."

Crawford said, "Hell, I'm letting the wolves have that high-toned prick. Be disrespected like that? That'd really boil his shirt."

Bishop flattened his words. "We need him. He rides in back."

"You're the doctor. I'm just a goddamned gunsmith."

"Who has everything." Bishop held up a glass bowl of magnesium chips. "This stuff almost blinded me. You know how to finish this. I'm going to round up the horses."

Crawford poured out a powder mixture through a small funnel into the brass shell casings and said to Hunk, "He's going to get his war."

"When we fought, I saw his eyes, bloodred, and he killed everything. Then he was doctor again, fixed my leg. This time, I think he fights until he dies."

Crawford sealed the shells and loaded the rig. "So the doc's finally a warrior."

Hunk said, "I just hope your daughter's right about them getting to Heaven, for my own sake."

"Too late to worry about that, but I ain't gonna be denied my pleasures in the here and now."

Crawford pulled the claw over his right hand and marched to the corral, with Hunk following. He jammed the five talons into the back of Colby's body, deep between his shoulders. Hefting him up, he dragged him to the wagon. "Wish he could feel this, but does me some good."

Hunk gathered Colby's feet and lifted, dumping him into the back of the cooler. He settled, dead weight, on top of the tarped explosives.

Crawford bolted the half-doors. "That necklace from the tree, keep it."

"I took for my wife. I want to send her something before . . . before we do this."

Crawford shook the metal talons clean. "It's Cheyenne. She'll like it."

* * *

The rusting steel grave marker settled into the soft ground quickly with Bishop leaning on it, pressing down. He backed up a step, seeing his crooked marker between White Fox and her mother. His name had been destroyed by Colby's bullet strikes, but that felt appropriate to him.

The sun was rising off the near Colorado peaks. The morning felt fresh, the clearing better than it had the night before. The bay and the stolen horses were in sight, drinking from the small stream that followed the woods.

"It was your reputation brought that bastard here. Told me he'd read every word printed about you, even something in French. Cocky bastard."

Bishop didn't turn at Crawford's voice, just stood in front of his own empty grave.

Crawford said, "I put up them markers so folks would think you dead, get you a little peace. But you wouldn't have it, would you?"

"I tried."

"Crazier than a suck-egg mule!"

"The bloodier the legend, the more fear in the heart of my enemies. Isn't that what you told me?"

Crawford got down from his horse, carrying the shotgun rig and bandolier. "Sounds about right."

"I never said a word to those papers. They came up with everything. I'd never put your daughter into it."

"You took care of her, Doc. That's how come I helped you this time. That prisoner says you got the blood eyes. I know what that is, 'cause it happened to me."

"A blood vessel breaks under pressure."

Crawford said, "That's a doc's way of figuring things 'cause then you don't have to think about becoming something else."

Bishop was someplace else. "It's not that."

Crawford crouched by the marker with ARCHISHA— MOTHER AND WIFE—SHE LIVES ALWAYS scrolled across it and pulled away some new weeds around it. "She couldn't take it. Hung herself instead of living with a wild killer. That ain't gonna happen to my daughter, not ending up here beside her mother."

Bishop said, "You got no worries, Noah."

"Hell, she'd never do herself in, but you might get her killed."

"White Fox has got nothing to do with me anymore."

"All right then."

Crawford held out the shotgun and the bandolier with the new shells. "Dragon's Breath. Anybody tries for you, that's the taste of hell."

Bishop took the rig and ammunition, tucking the gun under his left arm "'Taste of hell.' They can use that in the *Gazette*."

"Your idea," Crawford said. "However this ends up, it's going to make history some way."

"Maybe you can sell the marker for a few dollars."

"A *few* dollars never interested me, Doc." Crawford kicked at several bent and twisted Colt pistols stacked behind the grave markers. Scorched pieces of twine were attached to the triggers, dangling loose about a foot. "What's all this?"

"Found them when I was rounding the horses. Colby tied pistols to the trees, cocked them to fire with the force of the grenade blast, give him some cover. He knew what we'd be using."

"But we still got the best of the little bastard. He wasn't no warrior." Crawford spit long. "You leave me all his fancy guns?"

CHAPTER TWENTY
Burning Down

The gold tassels hanging from the Temptation Wagon jiggled back and forth as Hunk braked on the side of a small road that gave them a clear view of the prison in the distance.

It was a squat outline against blue mountains, with the blasted-apart towers and falling-down walls giving the impression of ruins, just as intended. There were no riders approaching it, no stray horses running.

Hunk said, "Like nobody's there."

Bishop was tying his bay to the back of the wagon. "Which means they're all there."

"Yah, probably. And getting ready for a big operation. Lots of money, lots of promises."

Bishop took the shotgun rig and the bandolier with the Dragon's Breath shells from his saddlebag and handed them up to Hunk on the driver's bench.

"You captured me and my arsenal. That should restore your standing with the Riders."

"My what?"

Bishop said, "When they haul me out of the back, just

make sure you go along, carrying the rig. We've got to get inside the main building, then follow the tunnels."

"Maybe I find gold, and you find your brother."

"Lock me up."

Bishop moved to the back of the wagon, throwing open the half-doors and climbing inside. He got around Colby's body, which was wrapped and tied, and made it to a corner. The explosives, kerosene, and shrapnel were all in their places around him and properly covered.

Hunk was at the door. "So now you're my prisoner."

"Just get us inside. And when the battle starts, don't be near this thing."

"How we get to be comrades?"

Bishop, decapitated by the deep shadows, said, "A common enemy. Something Mr. Chisum believed in."

"So does your brother, believe me."

"What's your name?"

"Bogdan."

"Hope I see you again."

Hunk snorted, shut the doors, and bolted them, leaving Bishop in total darkness.

The string of fresh horses came first, followed by a howitzer, and then two flat wagons of cavalry rifles. Red-hooded riders flanked the stolen weapons, riding in a showy circle around the prison yard as Chaney fixed his camera to a tripod.

He was focusing on ten Fire Riders standing with guns shouldered and sabers drawn, the horses and cannon passing behind them. He was experimenting. Trying to catch motion as an energetic blur, offsetting the posed Riders in the foreground.

Chaney had told the prison telegraph boy, "I'd like to leave one image behind with my name on it. It'll be worth more than the price of a tacky newspaper. Hell's rings, they're going to kill me anyway, so why not try?"

He opened the lens exposure, and extended the bellows to its full length, before changing the position of the flash pans to throw optimum light. Chaney thought for a moment, eyed the Riders, then moved the pans again.

Dev Bishop watched the yard from the small, barred window in the old warden's office, with Tomlinson beside him, his two daughters wrapped tightly around their father's legs. "This will be on every front page."

Tomlinson said, "The howitzer's a good addition and very effective for certain assaults, but you have an entire town to think about. That's your income stream."

Dev glanced back at the open ledger on his desk surrounded by a pile of notes and summaries. "Your world's on the desk. The howitzer, maybe that's my world."

Both girls pulled on Tomlinson's knees for attention, and his hands went gently to them. "Begging your pardon, Mr. Bishop, but you're not seeing what change is coming."

Dev was looking down into the prison yard again, past the horses and men to connect with Smythe. "I do, accountant. You do not. Not the way it matters."

Smythe gave Dev a wave from where he was by the open front gates, leaning on his crutches. He was watching the road that led to the entrance, seeing something fast approaching, and had to grin. "I'll be a cockeyed son of a bitch." Then he yelled, "Pickets! Make a line!"

Hunk steered the Temptation Wagon into the prison yard. Even seeing all the familiar faces pointing rifles and pistols, he didn't snap the team into a run. He slowed. The bay, still hitched to the back, slowed too, snorting.

His wounded leg was throbbing, and he felt moisture around the stitching where his ear used to be, but Hunk ignored those nerve stabbings, and brought the wagon to a stop beside the target range. He tossed a hand to the red hoods aiming at him.

He listened for a sound from Bishop inside the wagon, but there was nothing, just the gold tassels rapping against the purple sides. Guns followed Hunk climbing off the driver's seat, landing stiff-legged, just as Smythe dragged himself over from behind the Gatling gun, taking a small-caliber Colt from his belt as he moved.

Smythe said, "Well, this is like seeing a Highland ghost."

"Because you send those *câini* to kill me?"

"I know some of your talk, boy-o. Those were your brother Riders, supposed to bring you in, but you didn't give them much chance."

Smythe leaned by the horse team, the pistol casual in his hand. The other guns were moving in closer to Hunk, a foot at a time. One kid pulled off his hood, wiped the sweat from his eyes, but never dropped aim of his rifle and bayonet. Hunk disregarded all and walked to the back of the wagon.

Smythe said, "You're travelling in interesting style, boy-o."

Chaney turned his camera around, focusing on Hunk and all the weapons pointed at the same target as if aimed at a giant rattlers' nest.

Hunk brushed a Rider aside with a massive hand, stood beside the bay, and said to Smythe, "You know this fine horse?"

He threw over the bolt, opening the doors, then took Colby's body by the ankles, pulling it out, and letting it sag to the ground at Smythe's feet. It was a tangled bundle, with Colby's head exposed, face slack, and eyes filmed over.

"The fancy talker. You give him special job to get the man what belongs this horse. And look." Hunk pushed on Colby's sagging body with the toe of his boot. "Look how he failed."

Smythe said, "Killing Mr. Colby, now that's a bold move."

"Yah, and this." Into the back of the wagon, Hunk barked, "Get out of there. Now."

Dev was leaning into his office window, palms flat against the wall, watching the yard as his brother climbed from the wagon.

John Bishop's only hand was in the air, surrendering to his brother's men.

Dev's breath caught somewhere deep inside him.

By the wagon, Hunk said, "See. I'm the one didn't fail."

John Bishop finally lowered his left arm and looked to Hunk when the first rope wrapped around his neck, pulling him off his feet. He clawed, the rope being pulled tighter by one Rider, choking, while another lashed his ankles tight.

Dev shouted the order through his barred window. "The Tomb!"

Some Fire Riders heard him.

Excited and laughing, Chaney captured it all, switching out negative plates as Bishop was dragged across the yard, twisting in the dust, Riders running alongside.

Victory shots popped the air while the old bullet maker tossed empty brass like it was confetti bouncing off Bishop's chest. Smythe said to Hunk, "Very well done, boy-o. I'd give you full marks."

Hunk watched John Bishop for a moment—a roped prisoner struggling before he was hauled into the old cell block—then reached under the driver's seat, taking out the double-barreled rig and the ammunition bandolier. He said to Smythe, "Everything, all from this Shotgun."

"Devlin will be most appreciative. I'll see to it."

With the Colt aimed at Hunk's gut, Smythe pulled the rig away from Hunk. "How many of my men did you get killed in Myrtle? You had a case of grenades, and still lost everyone. Didn't even bring back Chisum's herd."

Hunk felt a bayonet's jab at the base of his spine.

Smythe split the breech of the rig and examined the shells. "How many of my men, boy-o?"

Fire Riders took the horse team bridle, and led the wagon to the other side of the yard.

Hunk watched his prize capture rolling off and said to Smythe, "He wanted the brother more than anything. I figured that would be enough to make me all right. Take me inside so I can show my prisoner."

Smythe shook his head in wonder. "Aye, you've got as much brains as a mountain of slag."

The giant's moves were unexpectedly fast. Hunk turned, grabbing the rifle and bayonet from the Rider behind him. Wrenching it upward, he nearly bent the barrel. The Rider fired, shooting wild. Hunk pounded him down with the butt of the gun, spun, and buried the blade deep into the chest of another Rider attacking.

Hunk's voice was a roar, jerking the speared Rider off the ground, then pitchforking him across the yard. His dead weight smashed into the red hoods by the rifle targets.

The moment of silent shock offered only breath and heartbeats. as Hunk swiped his stiff leg into Smythe, taking him off his crutches. He freed the bay, swung on, and charged.

The Riders opened fire. Gunshots flew and orders were shouted. Smythe rolled onto his hip, shoving his dead legs aside with both hands, then leveling the Colt, shooting twice. A slug blew Hunk's shoulder, spraying red, knocking him sideways. He stayed on the horse, leaping over the howitzer, and running beyond the prison gates.

Across the yard, Chaney clicked the shutter release on the bellows camera and threw his head back, shouting, "Yes, yes, indeed!" He looked up to the warden's office window, and Dev Bishop was gone.

The broken-stone floor sliced John Bishop as he was pulled through the corridors and down the steps to the main cell block, the rope tightening around his throat. His eyes rolled and pain in his head erupted as they let him lie, a crowd of Fire Riders moving in around him.

He saw the little girl with the breathing device over her mouth, watching.

The device he'd made.

April Showers waved, saying something into her mask as the trap door opened. Bishop was picked up by the shoulders and ankles and hurled to the cells below.

She could hear his falling as she drew again through the tube attached to the oxygen box.

Beside April Showers, Dev also watched his brother. Holding a Navy Six, he said, "That's not the man to favor, little girl. Not to help your papa."

"He helped me." She looked up at Dev and kept inhaling deep.

The Fire Rider with the German accent kept his right arm extended, aiming the rifle as he brought his horse closer to Hunk. The two flanking him rode up, then fell into step beside the German, waiting for orders. They had all sprung from the hidey-holes outside the gates, and had trailed Hunk to this point.

The German was straining, but had his aim. "That was a good shot, a good one the English made, but not for killing."

One of the Riders, the scalps of Union troopers hanging from his belt, nodded toward Hunk, who was now barely on the bay, bloody arms dangling, eyes closed, his chin pressed against his chest.

The German said, "That's not all his blood."

The Rider said, "He's bled out deader than Honest Abe, which is the only honest thing he ever did."

Hunk blew a hole in the Rider's chest before he could turn and share the laugh with his buddies. The other Rider flanking the German was surprised, never even getting his gun above the leather before Hunk shot him perfectly between the eyes.

Both fell from their horses, leaving the German pointing the rifle at Hunk, who, in turn, had one of White Claw's specialty .45s pointed at the German. The recut grip fit perfectly in Hunk's large hand, and the new trigger guard accommodated his fingers.

The barrel of the pistol seemed inescapable, and Hunk said, "You're not shooting, Karl."

"I can, still."

"You'd have already. You see how they turned on me. They can do the same for you."

The German kept the rifle up. "Ride out, Bogdan."

"Ride with me. Let me show you something. You'll have the rifle." Hunk urged the bay to a run, and the German followed, holding the Winchester out to his side, aimed at Hunk's bleeding shoulders. The two men rode for a time, circling back toward the prison, then taking their horses down a series of grassed hills to a small road that led to the oldest part of the structure.

Like the rest of Rawlins Penitentiary, the stone wall was fire damaged, with large sections taken down by the cellar explosion from years before. Rock and corroded steel were piled up, forming their own new wall.

Hunk got off his horse, taking a few steps to where a trench had been dug along the foundation.

The German asked, "What are you showing me?"

"Money, Karl. All Bishop's money, buried in the tunnels here."

"A fairy tale I've heard before."

"A kid was here. He told me. Explosives also buried here, like we used in the mines."

Hunk knelt, grabbing at large sections of muddy earth inside the trench and digging it out with his fingers, revealing the edge of a dynamite case. "See? He's right about the bombs. He said there could be gold, too. Help me find, and I'll give you share."

Karl had the rifle aimed downward from his saddle. "They promised a reward for you."

"Dev Bishop or the English with no legs, they ever pay extra? For anyone? Or given us fairly for what we stole? No, but they shot me quick enough. There's a crawling tunnel there. That's how they get out. Leave us to hang."

Karl quietly housed a shell, cocking the repeater.

Hunk moved to him, the end of the rifle barrel almost flush with his chest as he looked up at his friend.

The German said, "I only know what they tell me to do."

"If you're not joining, I need another gun." Hunk grabbed the rifle, jamming it inward, then yanking it hard, snapping the German's arm at the elbow.

He screamed as Hunk took the weapon, checked it.

"I didn't shoot, Karl. Gave you a chance. Get more men if you want, but I'd go home to my wife. Now." Hunk swatted the German's horse, watched them dart back up the hill, and away. Then, he pried open a case of dynamite.

The young woman and the boy were smeared with blood.

"*—as beautiful as the day I married you . . .*" John Bishop's voice was a drifting whisper in his mind. His mouth parted, thinking he was speaking, but words were a dried nothing. Pain streaked behind his eyelids as he turned his head, reaching out for the photograph of his wife and son, curled into a loving embrace. It was his favorite.

But wife and son were soaked through red, and their image, their faces, crumbled in Bishop's hand as he tried to hold them, the pieces sticking to his fingers.

"You're nearly dead . . . and closer to them now than you've been in years, brother. You should thank me." Dev Bishop was halfway down the iron steps leading from the main cells to the condemned underground where prisoners sat in darkness, waiting for their turn with the hangman. It was called the Tomb because it got them used to being buried. He had the Navy Six and was gesturing toward an old cell, the door twisted apart. "That's where I was the day you came. That last one, remember?"

"Killed—"

"What?"

John Bishop tried speaking again, but nothing came out. He crooked his neck, taking in the empty cells from where he was lying. Bent metal bars became skeletons and the stone walls, stained by blood and fire and stretching upward into nothing but black, gave the feeling of a deep pit. A stench of rotting, something sweet and dead, stung Bishop as he slowly eased himself up, resting his only forearm on the bundle next to him.

It was Colby, still wrapped and bound, with the ripe setting in. His "John Bishop Target File" was littered across him, those family papers and photographs sticky with his blood.

Dev said, "Surrounded by death, but you're a doc. Used to it. That's one of my men, a real professional gentleman, and you killed him. How many dead is it, brother? One story I read declared over forty. I'd double that. I think it's right—you and one of mine that you shot apart—buried in the same pit."

In the tunnel behind the Tomb, Hunk had stopped crawling, wedging himself against a boarded and bricked access way sealed over with mud. His shoulders touched either side of the tunnel walls, and there was no room for him to raise his head as he slipped a quarter stick of dynamite up through his jacket with the tips of his fingers until he could grab it with his teeth and drop it in front of him.

He heard Dev Bishop on the other side of the wall. "Only one life have I personally ended, and I'm the outlaw. You're the hero. Funny world, ain't it?"

John Bishop, surrounded by the cells, could see his brother standing, holding the gun.

"We're . . . supposed to . . . blood."

"Going to try about being brothers? Hell, the day you was born, I was finished." Dev got louder. "Now that's a fact. You got it all, so I made my own way, run territories, command these men."

"Mae . . . maniacs."

"Yeah, a few locos, but mostly soldiers nobody needed anymore, and raw-backs looking for work, half of those not talking American. Hell, I couldn't read or write till a year ago. Not bad."

Bishop was sitting up. He slapped his right hand in a puddle of rainwater, brought it to his face, drinking what he could. Aware of movement—something in the dark beyond him, he said, "I did . . . nothing to you."

Dev had raised the pistol a bit, but stayed his place. "Nothing to me, or for me. Dumbest thing, you comin' here to visit. Getting yourself set up. A leader can't have no family ties. That's one way he gets brought down." He took a step down with his right leg, bracing himself on the landing to absorb the kick of the Navy Six. "You had your fine time, and fine life. I had this."

Bishop's words cut against his vocal chords as he moved his left hand beneath Colby's wrapped body. "Kill . . . killed my family."

"You've caused me a hell of a lot of trouble, and all because I couldn't put a bullet in you my own self."

Bishop pulled Colby to him as Dev fired the first shot, punching the corpse in the back and legs, thudding dead tissue and bone.

The gun flames lit the Tomb, the sound bouncing off the stone walls a thousand times, colliding every moment.

In the first jail cell, the access panel from the tunnel split open, pushed out by Hunk's knees and elbows.

Dev fired again, the slug biting Bishop's leg as it tore into the cloth wrapping Colby's body. Bishop reached in to free the gun he'd put in the dead man's hand.

Red hoods charged from the back cells, shooting wild. Bullet strikes ripped the floor and Colby's body. John Bishop still shielded himself, trying for the gun.

Hunk tossed the quarter dynamite, the explosion blowing apart the wall, sending pieces of the cell, section of the door, flying. A hood turned, as a bent iron bar spun into him, piercing his chest and knocking him dead off his feet.

Hunk jammed the Winchester through the access way and opened up, taking down two Riders who were trying to stand after the force of the blast.

Outside rang the clanging of a general alarm.

Dev stumbled on the stairs. Holding Colby's body, Bishop couldn't free the pistol, so he squeezed the trigger with Colby's stiff fingers. The shots blasted through the corpse bag, cutting Dev at the hip.

Hunk tore through the access way into the Tomb, shooting a Rider charging from behind the iron stairs. Bishop brought Colby's arm up and shot the last Rider in the chest.

It was over in seconds, Hunk's and Bishop's ears were ringing like church bells as they made it to the iron stairs. Spots of Dev's blood led to the trapdoor, which was closed and barred tight.

Bishop crawled back to Colby's body, pushing aside

the torn bits and pieces of the target file until he found
one of his wedding pictures with only its edges stained.
He slipped the picture into his shirt. Hunk gave him
White Claw's pistol before clearing the wood and brick
from the tunnel access.

Hunk went in first, scraping his way against the earth
walls. Bishop took himself along on his one arm, the slug
from Dev's gun working deeper into his leg.

The alarm was constant, but dulled by the tunnel.

They hauled forward, rats running across their shoulders, then down their arms. They kept moving. Faster.
Bishop's amputated right arm shook the rats off, his left
propelling him to the tunnel's end.

The crawl dumped them into an open area, part of
the original prison's root cellar. Hunk twisted himself
onto the floor. Bishop rolled out, rats scattering after.

The room's damp was years thick, and what light
there was snuck in around the old trap for the slide that
had been the vegetable scuttle.

Bishop said, "We can't have them using that."

Hunk lit a full stick of dynamite and threw it into the
crawl.

CHAPTER TWENTY-ONE
Detonations

Minutes before, Smythe had adjusted his crutches, bringing himself a foot closer to the Temptation Wagon parked on the yard near the bullet maker's.

Chaney was checking the image on his wet-plate camera, directing four Riders behind Smythe to hold their rifles, "in that Geronimo pose." He said to Smythe, "Hoist your victory. Be proud, now."

Flash pans were aimed directly at the subjects, and all had eyes strained open with expressions frozen—serious. Smythe smoothed his suit lapel and held the shotgun rig high.

The pans burst white-yellow, exactly as the first dynamite explosion from the tunnels rumbled the ground.

A kid asked, "Are—are we being attacked, sir?"

Smythe ordered, "Sound the general, and all Riders to defense positions! Battle ready! Now, ladies! NOW!"

The kid rang the alarm bell standing in the corner of the yard.

Riders snatched guns from the racks, ran to stations along the walls, and climbed ladders to sniping perches, hoisting extra ammo cases by rope and tackle. Tarps were lowered, disguising potential targets as the bullet maker slapped pistols into the hands of Riders running for the corral, saddling horses, bringing them out.

The howitzer was rolled into place, aimed through a port in the front gate, facing the oncoming enemy. It was loaded and primed.

Smythe raised himself on his crutches, pleased, before taking himself to the main building, the rig hanging from his shoulder. Riders dashed around him, taking up weapons and throwing salutes that Smythe returned with pride. He got himself to the top of the main cell block, looking down as Dev slammed the trapdoor to the Tomb shut, then bolted it.

Pain threw Dev off balance, blood from his hip painting his right leg. He recovered. "Call off the alarm!"

"You need doctorin'."

Dev went up the main steps, favoring his leg and cocking a glance. "I know you gave the order so take the men off the wall, Smythe. I'm in command."

"I know, but I ain't ignoring that blast or who shot you. The men are at the ready and damned fast."

Dev wiped his blood onto his hand. "They're still not like the Apache. That's what we need for raids. How you need to train them."

Smythe chose his words. "The men are ready for *this fight*, son." He held up the shotgun rig.

Dev dismissed it as if talking about his brother. "He's in the Tomb, dying. Means nothing now." Before Dev reached the metal landing, Hunk's second dynamite charge exploded in the crawl tunnels.

Bishop and Hunk came up from the cellar by the old service stairs and moved into the main corridor, Hunk with the Winchester, Bishop with the specialty pistol. Both took a few steps then held, listening for movement in the maze of narrow halls and accesses. Bishop wagged his arm, getting used to shooting lefty. Thumbing the hammer, Hunk turning quickly from the waist, firing two slugs into the throat of the Rider at the end of the corridor.

The Rider was collapsing to the floor as Bishop fired down the hallway, laying out two more running up from the opposite side. Clean head shots to both. Coming around, he killed a third, brandishing a saber.

Again, it was over in seconds. Hearts stopping before the last of the gunshot echo faded off.

Bishop left most of the third red hood on the wall, quickstepped around Hunk, and walked deliberately down a far length that turned into the open hallway of the second floor. He stopped, suddenly looking down at the black-haired little girl holding the breathing mask to her face. They were feet from the door to the warden's office, Tomlinson standing behind April Showers, with May Flowers' arms wrapped around his waist.

He carried a small satchel, and they were all in their travelling clothes. April Showers' device-breathing was as loud as the alarm. "Are you coming with us?"

"Later."

Bishop nodded toward the door. "My brother?"

Tomlinson said, "Smythe went in with your gun. That's all that I saw. I'm taking care of my family."

Bishop scooped April Showers under his left arm and carried her to a small alcove away from the office. May Flowers ran after her sister, with Tomlinson beside.

He looked to Bishop, then called out, "Smythe! I need to get in the office!"

Smythe said from behind the door, "I told you to scoot you and your girls out of here!"

Bishop and Hunk took places on either side of the door, weapons raised. Bishop, coiled, eyes washing red, signaled Tomlinson to try again.

"Is anyone there with you? Devlin, is he there?"

Gunshots ripped the door and frame and into the corridor, hitting the walls. Tomlinson pulled his girls to the floor, covered them both as Bishop shot the large hinges apart, the iron sparking.

Hunk sledgehammered the wood, splitting it in half, and they plowed into the office. Bishop fired over Hunk's shoulder, hitting Smythe at the warden's desk.

Smythe got off two more shots, one slug skidding against one of Hunk's ribs, the other missing. With Bishop and Hunk before him, he let the pistol sag in his hand. The office was wrecked, their guns casually aimed.

Everyone was wounded.

"You aimed high, Doctor. Hit my shoulder. That was on purpose, I'm sure." Smythe, his face pulped, looked to the safe in the corner, door wide, and money gone. "Aye, you're too late."

The shotgun rig and bandolier were laid out on the desk as trophies, and Smythe pushed them toward Bishop, his movement opening his jacket, revealing the wound in his stomach, blood spreading wide and dark. He slumped back in the leather chair with the bullet hole. "Your brother didn't shoot high. You really set him off. You're the one man he can't seem to kill. He beat me with your rig, then shot me for good measure. After cleaning us out, of course." Smythe actually laughed at this last.

Bishop said, "You've got a chance to survive your wounds, if we get you out."

"Can't help being a doc?" Smythe pounded on his unfeeling legs. "I'd not be looking forward to more of this. Struggled along, goin' home a rich man. Maybe buy me-self a new pair of legs, or at least a sweet strumpet for a bride."

Smythe raised the pistol.

Hunk pulled up the Winchester, cocking it.

"You're taking it all down, are you? Everything we built?"

Bishop said, "This place should be ashes."

"And then his little town?"

"If that's where he's hiding."

Smythe said, "When I was chief guard, I called this the Abyss, from Dante's *Inferno*, running the last circle of hell. Then your brother started talkin', and I helped him take over. I was conjuring something great and followin' a man what couldn't read or write. My old dad's laughin' from his grave at a fool son."

Bishop fit the rig over his half-arm and bloody shirt, settling into the amputee cup.

Smith said, "These fellas trained well and are finally gettin' it. It won't be no easy battle, even for you, Doc."

"I never wanted it to be," Bishop said, slipping his left arm through the shotgun brace, bringing the trigger lines tight.

Hunk opened a box of cigars on the desk, and grabbed a fistful, saying, "But we will be inflicting pain."

Smythe had the pistol angled to his temple and said to Hunk, "Of that, I have no doubt. Never seen anyone stronger than you, boy-o, or more tilted than the doctor. Accountant, you're keeping your girls in the hallway, yes?"

Tomlinson gathered the girls to him, but April Showers twisted away, trying to see, as Smythe fired the shot.

"You've protected my girls so far. I just want to get them to safety."

Bishop said, "And the satchel of money."

"There'll be more men coming."

Bishop was tying off the bandolier as they made their way down the corridor, Tomlinson and his girls leading.

Hunk said "The kid, he showed us where there could be treasure. Made a map."

April Showers ran ahead and around the corner to the open landing that brought all the lead ways to the old and new prisons together. She stood in front of one of the fire-scorched portraits in the gallery of previous wardens. "I also told that lady-talkin' man about this place. Go ahead, you're the scary giant."

Hunk took hold of the painting and lifted, removing it and an attached section of the wall, wood painted as stone, that hid the way to the old execution chamber.

Tomlinson said, "Warden's escape."

Bishop's head was down, pain increasing with his heart beat, eyes flooding red. "The stores?"

Hunk kept the cigar in his teeth. "And treasure."

Tomlinson said, "You'll find what you need."

April Showers tightened the ties around Bishop's arm "Sometimes, thinking about you gives me nightmares. Other times, okay."

Tomlinson took the hands of his daughters and quickstepped them away. The sisters turned, wrinkled their noses, then ran with their father.

Out of sight, May Flowers started to sing, the beautiful sound drifting back.

Bishop and Hunk went through the false wall and onto a dirt slope that had been graded by the wheels of carts weighted by stolen weapons. They made it halfway.

Standing guard, a Rider with two revolvers stepped out from behind a stone arch. He tried to say something cocky as he shot.

The flash of the Rider's guns and the magnesium-fire explosion of Dragon's Breath from the shotgun collided in midair. The flame swallowed the Rider, then the black powder and buckshot blast tore his chest and threw him backwards off his feet, his body open and red tunic on fire.

He rolled off the slope to the chamber floor.

Bishop pulled the shell and reloaded from the bandolier. "Blood on the claw."

* * *

In the prison yard, Riders separated themselves into patrol units, charging the main building, following the gunfire. They broke on either side to close in when ordered.

His daughters on either side of him on the driver's bench, Tomlinson braked his prairie schooner with the wildly colored canopy at the main gate. Two Riders standing with the howitzer blocked the way out.

"We have business to conduct for Mr. Bishop. Open the gates," Tomlinson ordered.

One of the Fire Riders stepped forward. "Yeah, and where the hell in creation is he?"

Sweaty and with his hood pulled back, the other one said, "Somebody's giving us what for!" He pulled the cannon aside.

Tomlinson pushed his glasses up on his nose and gave the reins a quick jostle. The wagon lurched forward. Chaney ran up from behind and crawled in. Rolling back, he tucked his legs under his knees, camera and negatives cradled in his arms like newborns.

Tomlinson had the team out of the prison gates, his snout-nosed daughters singing, "*Yes, we will gather at the river; the beautiful, the beautiful, river—*"

Tomlinson patted the valise next to him. "That's good, dears. Give them one last chance to hear it."

In the old execution chamber, rotting nooses hung above a gallows platform. Empty grenade casings and cannonballs were stacked on its thirteen steps.

Hunk said to Bishop, "Stretch the neck. Your brother, he'd threaten that some days."

They managed around the crates labeled PROPERTY OF U.S. CAVALRY, THE ARMY OF THE CONFEDERACY, THE UNION NAVY, THE NAVY OF THE CONFEDERATE STATES, VIRGINIA VOLUNTEERS, SMITH & WESSON GUN WORKS. Hoods and tunics were in a large pile next to Apache spears, next to machetes, next to clubs, next to battleship shells, and next to mines.

"Your brother thinks he's a conqueror. I just wanted money."

Bishop said, "This . . . place can't be his monument." He tore open a box of .12-gauge shells and filled his pockets. "I'll get the front gates, take the cannon. You set off this lot and bring down the cells."

"Doctor, maybe a better way. Your bay's on the other side. Get it. Find your brother. I'll do this." Hunk's wounds spattered the top of his boots. He wiped them on his trouser legs. "I'm not going nowhere." His words weren't reaching Bishop.

The doctor loaded a regular shell in one barrel of the rig, Dragon's Breath in the other. "I can give us two minutes. Cross the yard then get the wagon."

Hunk watched him reach with his left arm and put two fighting knives into the right side of his belt. "This is what you always wanted, I think. I see what you are now. *Răzbunare este pace.* Revenge is peace."

Moving as they did when raiding houses with Quantrill, shooting innocents, Fire Riders with rifles ran the hall to the warden's office, then held by the smashed doorway, ready to shoot to pieces the first thing that moved, or made a sound. For that moment, everything was still.

One Rider gave a nod, and they peeled into the office, stepping over the wreckage. They found Smythe, a bullet hole in his temple and all the money gone.

The same Rider said, "In on this attack, took the easy way, knowing we'd hog-hang him and cut his throat."

* * *

Hunk crouched by some barrels, leveling the Winchester, covering Bishop from behind. The rifle felt heavier to him, his hands and eyes wet from strain.

Bishop looked over his shoulder and touched the brim of his hat before stepping through the blown-apart section of the old wall. He threw aside the disguising canvas and walked into the day, the rig leveled from his hip, White Claw's pistol held confidently in his left hand.

It took seconds for him to take in the positions of the Riders around the yard, the closeness to the horses, the howitzer, and his final target, the Temptation Wagon. He'd work around the base of the high wall, taking out any men there, reload, keep moving toward the wagon to get underneath.

Bishop hadn't taken his next step when a Rider scaling the back wall shouted, alerting the yard, then opened up with a revolver. Bishop shot once, cutting him through the eye.

Hunk cracked off cover fire.

Red hoods charged from behind the med tent as Bishop moved, firing the first .12-gauge barrel to the chest of one, turning and then shooting the Dragon's Breath.

Fire erupted from the barrel, slamming a second Rider backwards, his hood on fire. The buckshot tore through him, then burning and wounding a third.

Tunics were in flames as Riders dragged away the dying and dead. Screams and confused orders. Hunk didn't let up, pumping shots into two more. Bishop fired precisely with the pistol, dead-hitting four Riders running for horses. They spun to the ground.

Bishop made it to the old barricades. He reloaded the pistol and the rig. Slipping a Dragon shell from the bandolier, the oil from the beaver skin pelt sliding the brass into the double-barrel, then making a single movement snapping it shut.

The blood washed through his eyes, completely staining his vision. Riders' red tunics were gray moving targets. Gray uniforms. He waded in, not waiting for the first shot or giving surrender any chances. Attacking and advancing on the enemy.

Moving from the cover of old stones, Bishop fired a Dragon shell at a stack of ammo cases, blowing them apart and igniting them. Moving again, he leveled another Rider with a .12-gauge blast from the second barrel.

Brass shucked, he reloaded one-handed, but faster than a rifle shot.

Bishop tore into Riders coming from all corners of the prison, trying to surround him. It was turn and fire—shotgun, pistol, then shotgun again—hoods hitting the ground, dead before weapons could even be aimed.

Quick-moving to the wall, Bishop got closer to the Temptation Wagon. Reloading on the way.

The ammo boxes were burning, brass casings heating.

Gunfire burst from the top of the walls, along the barbed wire. Hunk emptied the Winchester, punching a sniper with shots to the chest. Body jerking forward then back, the sniper fell screaming.

Bishop kept to the ground, sighting his target, then, moved for the wagon.

At the same moment the sniper slammed to the ground, the ammo cases exploded.

From the chamber, Hunk fired off the last cover round from the Winchester, grabbed a box of ammunition from a shelf, then stopped. His eyes fixed on what was behind the boxes, and he gave a shake of disbelief at what he was seeing.

Silver, light beading from it, neatly stacked in rows.

Hunk moved to the shelf, holding his hand against the bullet wound in his belly, ignoring his knee, and picked up one bar. ALFRED NOBEL COMPANY was pressed into the silver foil.

Hunk's smile straightened. Breaking the silver wrapping with his thumb, he revealed the caked white gelignite underneath. He ran a finger along the edge of the explosive, then had to laugh to himself. "The silver he found."

He took the Cheyenne necklace from his pocket, saying quietly, "*So ţia mea.*"

Exploding ammunition from the yard filled the chamber with smoke and the shrill of bullets as they bounced off empty iron shells of rockets and grenades.

Hunk ducked the ricochets, the necklace back in his pocket against his heart. Blood stuck his shirt to his body, and he had to grab hold of an old Confederate standard pole to steady himself.

Hunk stiff-walked to the gallows where the stolen percussion mines were placed side by side on the fifth step.

Ammunition rain covered Bishop as he ran around the side of the wall. A slug pierced his shoulder, tearing him sideways, but not slowing him down. He was behind the hay bale targets, the Temptation Wagon directly across the yard from his position.

His rested his right half-arm on a hay bale, the barrel of the rig searing hot. The hay started to smoke. He angled the rig straight from the shoulder and a little downward at the fuse protruding through the iron plates under the wagon.

Behind Bishop, a Rider ran in fast on a new pony, drawing down with a Colt to shoot him in the skull.

Bishop cocked around, swinging the rig up and sending buckshot through the Rider's gut. His body sloped from the saddle, the horse breaking across the yard as guns along the walls opened up, slicing the air with a barrage of rifle fire.

Blood ran down his arm, soaking the rig, but not affecting Bishop's aim. The double-barrel was directed, the thin chains from the trigger tight across his back, and through the harness to his left hand. A slug ripped next to his face, but he didn't flinch.

He couldn't.

Bishop pulled the line, the Dragon's fire exploding from the rig like a spear. Flames lit the fuse, the buckshot ripping the wagon's purple wood and iron.

He pulled himself around the targets, the rifles pinning him down. He loaded two .12-gauge shells, dove from behind the targets, and shotgunned the top of the wall, pushing the riders back from their positions, away from the wire.

The fuse burned to its end.

Smoke burst from the bottom of the wagon, the burning powder sprouting into black wings before the first explosions hurled the wagon into the air, the sides blasting apart in large, razored pieces.

Red hoods were beaten by the shrapnel, the flying wheels cutting them off their horses, an axle pinning another to the ground. The force blew through the prison wall, collapsing one side, throwing Riders from their sniping perches, burying them beneath rock and metal.

The second blast was the fireball, the kerosene jugs igniting in burst after burst. Flames ate the air, spitting shards in all directions. The fire ignited the bullet maker's tent. More powder blowing it apart. The medical tent burst into flames that snake-jumped to the training area.

Guns, staffs, and bows, all devoured.

Riders were still shooting, trying for Bishop through smoke and panic. They broke from the side buildings, not running fast enough, the charges around the walls exploding inward. The ground erupting.

The howitzer keeled over, the cannonball pulverizing

the gates as the horses crashed the corral, leaping through the burning ruins to the open road.

Surrounded by the last of the running horses, Bishop pulled himself onto a stallion and raced out as more fiery debris fell, spiking the ground like volcanic ash.

In the chamber, Hunk stood over a flat percussion mine that he'd placed on top of silver gelignite bars he'd stacked on the gallows. Holding himself by the thirteen steps, damaged and bleeding, with the last bit of strength in his massive body, he thought of family, life in the mines, and treasure.

Riders burst in from the upper halls and came down the dirt ramp. With rifles shouldered, they dropped to their knees as a firing squad. One of them shouted, "Betrayer!"

Hunk regarded them with, "*Răzbunareaestepace*," before using his last strength to bring down the butt of the Winchester on the mine's trigger.

The trigger clicked. And there was a flash.

CHAPTER TWENTY-TWO
The Trail

A thick fog had rolled in from the mountains in the afternoon, but split away as the sun went down and a steady snow began falling.

Widow Kate bunched her fur collar around her chins, one hand on the pistol in her lap. Mayor O'Brien pushed her wheelchair to the edge of the front porch of the House of Pleasures, giving her a wide view of Paradise's main street.

The freshly painted saloons and hotels threw out some light and a little music, but that's all. There were no fights or raised voices. Just some random sounds. Seemed most were waiting.

O'Brien touched a match to the bowl of the opium pipe Kate was holding.

"The cold comes on, and I feel everything ten times worse." She drew on the smoke. "I've got to be taking care of that. This year. Get some of my health back."

O'Brien said, "We've got a lot to tend to."

Kate nodded, watching John Bishop ride his bay from the opposite end of the street, pausing at the corral by the train depot, then bringing his horse to the hitch post directly in front of her. He didn't climb down.

"God have mercy," Kate said. "Look at you. Face all scarred. That gun and those are your damned eyes? You're the image of death, Doctor. Just the image of it."

"His horse is in the corral."

"The beauty he took from John Chisum? Likes to brag on that. Too much."

O'Brien said, "Your brother's here, and he isn't. It's his town, but the man could be anywhere."

Bishop said, "Mister, you're taking a real chance I won't shoot."

Kate drew the last on her pipe. "We heard about Rawlins. There being nothing left but a hole in the ground. Devlin didn't know if you were killed or not. I bet against it. He was taking care of business until less than an hour ago, then he lit out."

"Kate, you knew me once as a patient man. Don't count on that now."

"You settling family business, that's good for me, but then it's settled. You're not to come back here, stepping into my affairs."

"I'm not a lawman."

O'Brien said, "There's one waiting. If that goes bad, well, Tucker knew the risks."

Bishop said, "Where?"

Kate smiled, drew out the pistol from her lap, and pointed it toward the coffin maker's place.

The double doors to the coffin maker's were open, breathing just a bit on their hinges with the night snow. Rig poised, Bishop stepped into the dark of the front showroom. The rows of pasteboard caskets seemed like the shadowed shapes of gunmen standing in the corners, against the walls, or playing possum laid out on a table.

The first drops of blood he saw were gathered in a

pool, the imprint of a boot drying along the edges. Fine repeated drops went farther into the showroom, making a pattern around the rows of coffins.

Bishop said to the dark, "My brother. That's all I want." He took a step, following the blood, when Scalped Outlaw leaped from a far corner, tackling him from behind, slashing with a long blade.

Bishop was halfway around, smashing Outlaw down with the side of the shotgun, sending him to the floor.

Scalped Outlaw crawled to his feet again, his jaw wobbling free and yowling, "You're the most famous man I ever kilt!" He charged, waving the blade, and then the knife from Bishop's belt was in his chest, buried to the hilt, a move so fast, Outlaw didn't even see it. He touched the knife's handle, trying to believe what happened, then dropped his own weapon before stumbling backwards into a paste coffin, legs dangling over.

Bishop said, "Tucker! Your man's done!"

No response. Only faint music from the street.

Bishop kept the rig up, his eyes back to the floor and the droplets leading into the workshop. He stayed with the blood, rig locked from his hip, and called the sheriff's name again. Even more than in the showroom, there were places to hide—rows of leaning caskets, large sections of lumber piled against the walls, coffin lids propped with them.

The blood continued but was smeared as if the wounded had fallen to one knee, then crawled through it. Bishop followed the direction toward the back where he could see the edges of a handprint against a wall.

Jags of memory cut through him—*gun against his temple, the whip across his face*. "It's not your jail now, Tucker. You got paid for tonight. Don't try anything. Maybe live to spend it."

He took another step and saw the reflected movement in the polished surface of Widow Kate's green-lacquered casket. The lid of a coffin by the doorway moved just enough for a pistol to emerge. Chromed, the barrel caught the light.

Bishop fired, tearing the coffin and Sheriff Tucker in half, scattering them on the floor. He cleared the shells from the rig and reloaded with buckshot and his last Dragon's Breath before going to the back wall.

More than a single handprint showed above the opening that had been broken through and then shored up, leading into a small shaft from the played-out gold mine. Someone had lingered at the break, supporting themselves as they gave orders or prepped a trap for anyone following.

The shaft was dim yellow, lit by small, fluted oil lamps that had been mounted on the rebuilt walls. The blood was harder to see, drying and mixing with the color of the earth.

Stepping in, Bishop drew the rig in close.

Dev using the mine for escape wasn't a surprise. The papers had written about his getting out of prison twice before by digging tunnels. Bishop had been a surgery student when he read about his brother in the same dreadfuls that now wrote about him.

On shoring lumber, he found more blood and another handprint slick and wet with the mountain damp. Or new, which meant that Dev could by lying in wait around the next turn.

Bishop turned down each lamp that he passed, making his way farther along the shaft, keeping his own pace despite the bullet in his hip towing him back. Crouched, his hat scraped the mine ceiling.

He doused another lamp so not to be a silhouette-target, followed a blast of snowy cold coming from the mine opening just ahead, and stepped into the bases of a series of small, black-rock mountains.

He wrenched the lamp from the wall before ducking beneath the last support beam and walking into the blue winter night. He stood by the mine opening, peering at the crags of the rocks, trying to sense movement.

The clear sky and mountains were still, meeting just right. The cold coming from them hit Bishop clean and felt good. Pure. That he could draw deep into his lungs.

He knew he was bleeding again and figured his chances of getting the job done before bleeding out. In a moment of instant knowing, he dove into a mountain crevice before the first shots tore at him.

He found his place under a ragged cliff, the gunfire coming from an outcropping above. He scrubbed the snow from his eyes and saw the cast of Dev's shadow before him, backed by the light of the winter moon.

Bishop watched the shadow of Dev's movements on the ledge above, his inching along the side, gun aimed downward, trying for a back shot.

Dev said, "You're trapped, John. You ain't gonna hit me with a shotgun blast from there. You can hide and freeze or come out. Hell, you've wrecked everything I built, killed my men."

Bishop was eyeing the shadowed moves, setting the aim of the rig from his elbow and angling it upward. He saw just a bit of his head, then a bit more.

He called out to his brother. "All I wanted was what I had. You could've left me alone."

"No, I couldn't." Dev laid down three shots in quick succession, rapidly firing down to the rocks, but leaning forward on the ledge. He broke his shots, waiting for Bishop to fall out dead before him. He took two deep breaths and thumbed the hammer again.

Bishop swung out from the crevice, letting fire with one barrel, catching Dev in the arm and gut. Spinning him over and off the ledge.

The winter air held the smoke of the gunfire as a thin fog that Dev fell through, hitting the rocks, ripped by jagged edges, then rolling to the base of the small hill.

Bishop walked down to him, the rig extended, and

the lamp in his left hand. Dev still had his Navy as he stood, everything about him sliced to the bone, but still reacting when he saw John Bishop's solid blood-red eyes.

"Jesus—"

Bishop said, "There was a time, I couldn't even recall your face." He cracked open the lamp and hurled the broken well at Dev, soaking him with the oil. "Now, I remember everything."

Dev almost laughed through his bloody teeth, using what he had left to bring up the pistol and shoot as the Dragon's Breath shell erupted from the shotgun rig.

The flames engulfed him, the buckshot blast blowing him back and down the rest of the mountain. A fiery heap, rolling yellow and orange, the oil leaving a burning trail of acrid smoke behind the dragon's tail.

There was a scream, and Bishop glanced to see Soiled Dove standing at the end of a small trail by the mountain base, holding Hurricane by the bridle.

She screamed something at him again, but he didn't hear as he watched the fire at the bottom of the hill burning smaller and smaller.

The apple tree was bare, but the branches had reached out in all directions since the time Amaryllis had planted it. It was her favorite thing, caring for that tree, and Bishop liked leaning against it, his back to the grave marker of his wife and son.

The bay was drinking from a trough and reacted when White Fox ran her hands across his back as she passed. She was wearing her leathers, her hair straight and tied in long braids to hold it against the wind.

Bishop looked up at her but couldn't stand.

She said, "I didn't know what I would find here."

"That letter you wrote, all in Cheyenne . . . I figured it out."

"You remembered your words."

Bishop said, "Eventually."

She bent down to him. "Everything the woman said to you, she predicted?"

Bishop gave that a moment. Without looking at her, he said, "I don't know."

White Fox put an arm under his shoulder.

Connect with

Us

Visit us online at
KensingtonBooks.com
to read more from your favorite authors, see books
by series, view reading group guides, and more.

Join us on social media

for sneak peeks, chances to win books and prize packs,
and to share your thoughts with other readers.

facebook.com/kensingtonpublishing
twitter.com/kensingtonbooks

Tell us what you think!

To share your thoughts, submit a review,
or sign up for our eNewsletters, please visit:
KensingtonBooks.com/TellUs.